Step... grown up... m...

His... had spent his youth in a wild Montana lumber camp on the edge of the frontier.

But neither of them was ready for rough-and-tumble tomboy Jessie Randall, or refined city-girl Elizabeth Caldwell, the two women who would change their lives forever.

Don't miss the fireworks when the Ferguson brothers each finally meet their match in

The Gentleman & The Hell Raiser

Relive the romance...

by Request™

Two complete novels by your favorite authors!

About the Authors

KRISTIN JAMES

Whether writing as Kristin James or under her real name, Candace Camp, this award-winning author of over forty historical and contemporary novels has long been a favorite of our readers. Although she originally earned a law degree and became a practicing attorney, she soon gave it up to become a full-time writer. Now her books have been published in twenty-two countries and fifteen different languages, and she is the recipient of a *Romantic Times* Lifetime Achievement Award for Western Romance.

DOROTHY GLENN

Dorothy Glenn is the pseudonym for a national bestselling author of over thirty-four romances, most of which are set on the American frontier. With that background, it's no wonder that Dorothy got together with longtime writing friend Kristin James and came up with the terrific idea of companion books featuring heroes who are brothers.

CONTENTS

THE GENTLEMAN

Kristin James

Prologue

1866

The young boy watched his mother hurry around the cabin, stuffing clothes into a big cloth bag with handles. There was something odd about her manner—a nervousness and haste—that made Stephen excited and fearful, all at the same time.

He gripped his wooden whistle more tightly in his fist. It was his favorite toy; his big brother, Samuel, had carved it for him with his pocket knife. Samuel was the person Stephen loved most in the world, next to Mama. He seemed to Stephen a grand and glorious person who could do all the things for which Stephen was too young. He was kind, too, letting Stephen help him, and often playing with him. And on cold winter nights, when Stephen snuggled up against Sam's back, he felt safe and protected not only from the cold, but from all the other dangers of the world, as well. Stephen was convinced that there was no one else in the world as wonderful as his big brother, no one as intelligent or brave or skillful.

This morning, Papa had taken Samuel into the woods with him to work. Stephen had wanted to go, but, as usual, he was not allowed. He was too young. He hadn't fretted about it. It was too common an occurrence to get upset about. Besides, he enjoyed the lessons he always had with Mama in the morning. He knew the alphabet and his numbers now, and he was starting on reading and doing sums.

But today there had been no lessons. Mama had hurried through the dishes, then had begun scurrying around their small cabin, packing.

Now she shut the bag and took a long, slow look around the one-room house. There was something in her eyes that made Stephen want to cry. He went to her and leaned against her leg, one hand clenching her skirts. She glanced down and summoned up a small, brittle smile to reassure Stephen. She put the bag on the floor beside the door, then sat down at the table and began to write on a piece of paper.

Stephen followed her and watched her, still leaning against her a little, his elbows planted on the table. "Whatcha doin', Mama?"

"Writing a letter to your papa."

"Why?"

"Because we won't be here when he and Samuel get back, so I'm telling him where we're going."

"Oh. Are we going to town?" His voice rose in anticipation. The closest little community was far away, and they went to it rarely.

"Yes. But farther than that, really."

Stephen's eyes, big and brown and heavily lashed, widened expressively. "Farther than town?" He couldn't imagine such a thing.

"Yes. All the way to St. Louis. Do you remember St. Louis?"

He shook his head.

"Of course not. You were just a little thing when we left. We used to live in St. Louis. We had a sweet house there, with a flower garden in the summer. And there was a big river. You loved the river. Sometimes we'd go down to visit your grandpapa at his company, and he'd take you and Samuel on one of the ships." She smiled reminiscently, her eyes misting. "We're going to see Grandpapa and Grandmama again."

"Is Sammy coming, too? And Pa?"

The brief animation that had touched Eleanor Ferguson's face died abruptly, and she shook her head. "No. They'll be staying here."

Stephen frowned, not liking the idea, but his mother forestalled any more questions or comments from him by jumping up and taking down her bonnet. She tied it under her chin, then popped Stephen's hat onto his head. "Come now, we must be going, or we won't reach the stage station at Curryville by nightfall."

She took Stephen's hand and went outside. They walked across the yard to the shed, where she led the horses out and began to hitch them to the wagon. Stephen watched her, the funny empty feeling in his stomach growing. Though he had given up the habit long ago, now his thumb popped into his mouth. His mother finished harnessing the team and came around to lift Stephen onto the seat.

Then she returned to the house and came out a moment later, carrying the bag. As she stepped out the door, Stephen heard the sound of cheerful whistling. He twisted on the wagon seat to look.

A boy came around the side of the house, smiling and whistling. When he saw them, he came to an abrupt standstill and stared, astonished. "Ma?"

Stephen waved at his brother, pleased that he had come. His mother just stood as though rooted to the ground, staring at Sammy. Then, abruptly, she turned and almost ran to the wagon. She threw the bag over the end gate. She bent and kissed Sammy, then climbed onto the wagon seat beside Stephen.

"Come on!" Stephen called to his brother, gesturing with his hand. "We're going to see Grandpa. I'm taking my whistle."

"Ma! Where are you going? Can't I go, too?" Sammy ran to the side of the wagon.

Stephen looked at his mother. Her face was as white as

paper, and there was such sadness in her eyes that it made him cold inside. "Mama?"

Tears gleamed like crystal in his mother's eyes and spilled over onto her cheeks. "Goodbye, sweetheart. I love you. Mama loves you." Her voice broke, and she turned her head toward the front. She clicked to the horses. "Giddap!"

"Ma!" Samuel's cry pierced the air.

"No!" Stephen grabbed his mother's arm, tugging at her to stop. "Sammy come! Sammy come, too!"

"He can't," his mother said brokenly, slapping the reins.

Behind them Samuel began to run, calling out to them. Stephen struggled to his knees on the seat and turned to look. "No!" Stephen cried. "No! Sammy! I want Sammy!"

"Mama, don't go!" Sammy held something aloft in his fingers, dangling it enticingly. "Don't go, Stevie! I'll take you fishing—"

Stephen cried and screamed, choking on his sobs. He stretched out his hands toward his brother, his fingers clutching uselessly in the air. "Sam—my! Sam—my!"

Eleanor shut her eyes, tears pouring down her face, and slapped the reins across the horses' backs. The animals picked up their pace, and the wagon lumbered away, leaving Samuel behind them.

Chapter One

September, 1888

Stephen Ferguson stood beside the polished walnut casket, his hat in his hand. He was a tall, slender young man with thick brown hair and chocolate-colored eyes. His features were even and handsome, and his eyes were so thickly and darkly lashed that only a very firm, even stubborn, jaw and a wide mouth saved his face from prettiness. He was dressed in a black suit, cut to perfection, with a black mourning band tied around his arm. Even in sorrow, he looked every inch the elegant gentleman.

He gazed at the coffin, covered with a magnificent spray of roses, creamy white, which his mother had loved. Tears pricked at his eyes. He had known that one day he would, in all likelihood, be standing in this place. But he had never expected it to be so soon, so sudden. His mother had been only fifty-two, too young to die. Five days ago he had been going about his normal life in New York City, managing the McClellan and Caldwell Shipping Office, learning his grandfather's business from the ground up, as he had been doing every day of his life for the past five years. Then there had come the telegram that his mother had had a brain seizure and was seriously ill. He had jumped on the first train west, arriving in St. Louis in time to see her alive. He had taken her hand and talked to her, had gazed at her familiar, beloved face, but she had not opened those fine brown eyes, so lovely and calm, and looked at him; she had not spoken. Eleanor Ferguson had died without regaining consciousness. Now he was standing, watching, as her coffin was lowered into the grave. They were all dead now—his father, his brother, his mother, even Linton Caldwell, who had been like a father to him. All of them gone from him forever.

He glanced at his grandfather beside him. The old man was holding up well. He was in his late seventies; his hair was thinning and pure white, and the hands that gripped the hat in front of him were splotched with age. But there was no fragility in that old body. His back was ramrod-straight, and his fingers didn't tremble. Stephen knew a warm, amused pride; it was foolish to think that Hiram McClellan would give way before anything, even grief.

On the other side of Hiram, his wife leaned heavily upon his arm. Though ten years younger than her husband, she was not as strong. Tears leaked from her eyes beneath the black veil, and her heavily lined face was as pale and crumpled as old parchment.

Though the iron in Hiram McClellan would not let him show it, Stephen knew that he suffered, too. Two years ago his long-time partner, Linton Caldwell, had died. And now Eleanor, his only child. Stephen knew that his grandparents would need him more now than ever. He felt the familiar bonds tightening around him, squeezing him. That thought was quickly replaced by guilt. It was wrong of him to feel that way, he knew. His grandparents had taken him and his mother in, had raised him lovingly and with the best of everything. He owed them; more than that, he loved them. Such things were more important than any restlessness he might feel now and then. If at times he daydreamed of seeing other places, doing other things, he quickly rid himself of those dreams. He was a man who understood and accepted responsibility, who had been brought up to do his duty as a gentleman should.

A soft, gloved hand slipped into the crook of his arm, interrupting his thoughts, and he turned his head to smile down fondly at his fiancée. Elizabeth Caldwell was an attractive young woman, taller than average, with cool green eyes and thick black hair. She was intelligent and refined, everything a man could ask for in a woman. Stephen didn't think that he had ever seen her with a hair out of place or heard her utter a word that wasn't proper. She was a lady through and through, the perfect wife for a man in his position. Moreover, they had been friends since they were children. Her father and Stephen's grandfather had been partners in the shipping business since before the war, and the two families had been as close as if they were related. Elizabeth and Stephen had grown up together. It seemed only natural and right—and was the wish of both their families—that they should marry.

Elizabeth gave him a sad, comforting smile. They turned and walked from the grave site, his grandparents behind them. They stepped into the black-draped funeral carriage, and the slow procession began to wind its way out of the cemetery.

Throughout the afternoon at his grandparents' house, there was a constant stream of visitors offering their condolences. It was the custom, and Stephen knew that he had to politely greet them and accept their sympathy, but he found it difficult to maintain a polite social mask. He was aching with grief inside, and he would have liked to retreat to his room, where he could be alone with his sorrow. Of course, he did not.

But he was grateful when Elizabeth laid her hand on his arm and said, "I'm feeling a trifle faint, I'm afraid. Could we walk for a few moments in the garden?"

"Of course." He had never known Elizabeth to come close to fainting in her life. She was employing a polite subterfuge to allow him to get away.

He excused himself from the small group of people to

whom he had been talking and led her out to the formal gardens at the rear of the house. He let out a long sigh, relieved to be in the tranquillity of the garden, away from the people and the social obligations. "Thank you, Elizabeth. I badly needed an excuse to slip out. How did you know?"

She smiled faintly. "I've known you long enough to spot the signs. You looked tired and...trapped."

"You were right, as always." He took a deep breath of air, and they strolled along the pathway to a bench beside a small pool. Darting bright goldfish glimmered in the water. They sat for a while, gazing at the fish. Elizabeth took his hand and squeezed it.

Stephen pulled his mind from the sad subject around which it had revolved for so many hours and tried to focus on Elizabeth. "How are *you*?" he asked. "I'm sorry. I've been so absorbed in my own problems that I haven't even inquired after you."

Elizabeth shook her head. "No need to apologize. Your problems have been much larger and more important." Tears shone in her green eyes. "Eleanor was such a dear, good person. I shall miss her terribly. I remember how I felt when my father died. It seemed like the end of the world to me."

"He was a good man."

Elizabeth nodded. "If only he were alive now..."

Stephen glanced at her, his eyes narrowing. "What's wrong, Elizabeth? Is your stepmother bothering you?"

Elizabeth's mouth thinned into a bitter line. "I can manage her. But she is...bothersome. She thinks she has the right to order my life. She—no, I shan't trouble you with petty nonsense at a time like this."

"No, go ahead. It isn't petty nonsense if it's troubling you. What is she doing?"

"She wants me to marry."

"What? You mean, she wants us to marry soon?"

"No. She wants me to marry someone else."

Stephen stared. "Someone else? But—" He stopped,

struck by a thought. "Elizabeth, do you wish to marry another man?"

She glanced up, startled. "No! Oh, no. I have no desire to marry him at all."

"Then how can she think that you will? We are engaged."

"She realizes that. But she is pressing me to break my promise to you and marry—" She gave a sigh and looked away from him. "Judge Thorpe."

"Judge Thorpe!" Stephen shot to his feet. "Is she mad? The man must be twice your age!"

"Almost. But he seems to have formed some sort of liking for me. He has asked her permission to court me, and Netta gave it. He's a very powerful man, wealthy and influential. Netta craves power."

"I had no idea. How long has this been going on?"

"For some months now. I have tried to tell her that I am engaged to you, but she refuses to listen. She keeps inviting him to teas and parties, and she drags me along on any occasion when he might be at a function."

"I'm sorry. You should have written me about this. I shall speak to her."

Elizabeth shrugged. "Unfortunately, talking to Netta doesn't do much good. She believes exactly what she wants to."

"You shouldn't have to stay with her. We should be married. I'm sorry. I've been remiss. Your year of mourning was over long ago. I've been so busy in New York that I hadn't realized how much time had passed."

Two years ago, when Linton, Elizabeth's father, lay dying, he had been filled with anxiety about what would happen to Elizabeth after he died. Linton had begged Stephen to marry Elizabeth, to take care of and provide for her, and Stephen had promised readily. He couldn't have refused Linton anything on his deathbed, and besides, he had more or less expected to marry Elizabeth all his life.

Stephen had immediately asked Elizabeth to marry him, and she had accepted. Of course, it would have been improper to have a wedding before the year of mourning was over, so they had waited. Her mourning had ended some time ago, but Stephen and Elizabeth had been content to drift along, not choosing any definite date for their wedding or making plans. Now it seemed as though Netta Caldwell would force their hand.

"We shall set a date," Stephen went on, "for as soon as possible. That should spike Mrs. Caldwell's guns."

"Oh, but I don't want you to marry me because of Netta's disagreeableness."

"I'm not marrying you just because of Netta. We are already promised to marry. We should have done so earlier." Stephen looked down at Elizabeth. He wondered what she felt for him. Did she love him? He wasn't sure. They were good friends. But was there a bright, compassionate love burning inside her for him? He couldn't quite imagine it. Elizabeth was far too sensible and proper.

He knew that he loved Elizabeth, but it was a quiet, fond sort of love. There was none of the passion that he had felt from time to time for a mistress. Nor did he sit around pining for her presence and boring everyone around him with descriptions of her eyes or hair or beautiful white shoulders, as many of his acquaintances were wont to do over whatever lady had most recently seized their fancy. Sometimes he had wondered what it would be like to experience that kind of passionate, consuming love. The affection he held for Elizabeth seemed a rather tame thing compared to that.

However, Stephen was quick to remind himself, he probably wasn't the type of chap to throw himself so wholeheartedly into love. Besides, those passionate affairs usually wound up with the friend trying to drown his sorrows in a bottle or discovering bitterly that his goddess was a mere mortal, after all. The mutual respect and friendship he and Elizabeth had for each other were a much firmer foundation on which to build a marriage.

"Then let us think about when to do it," Stephen went

on. "Surely, once we set a date, your stepmother will have to accept the fact that you are going to marry me."

"I'm not sure anything is that easy where my stepmother is concerned. But I *will* think about a date." She paused and smiled at him. "Thank you. It's kind of you to trouble yourself with my problems at a time when you are facing such grief of your own."

"Nonsense. I will always be here to help you. Whatever is wrong."

They sat for a few minutes in companionable silence before they rose and returned to the house to continue their duties. It was some time before the flow of visitors slowed to a trickle and then stopped. By then, Elizabeth had returned home with her stepmother. Stephen asked one of the servants to have his supper brought to him on a tray, and he retired to his room.

His valet, Charles, was there, as usual, waiting for him. Stephen wished he was not. He would have liked to be alone, and he started to snap at the man to get out, but he refrained. It wasn't Charles's fault, after all, that he was British and retained a British servant's rigid view of what was right and proper. Charles would have been horrified at the idea that Stephen might dress himself and even more astounded that Stephen did not think of himself as alone when only his valet was with him.

When Charles had helped him into his dressing gown and fussed over his clothes to his satisfaction, he finally left the room, and Stephen flopped onto his bed with a sigh. He lay staring at the dark green tester and thinking of his mother. Eleanor had been his only family—Eleanor and his grandparents, and he knew it would not be too long before they were gone, too. He could hardly remember his father and brother. He had been only five when Eleanor had taken him from his father's home. He had never seen Papa or Sammy again. Only a few months after they arrived in St. Louis, Eleanor had told him that both of them had died in a timber accident. At first he had thought of them often, but over the years the memories had faded, until he couldn't even clearly remember what they had looked like.

He had asked his mother questions about them, but the sadness that had come into her face at such times soon stopped him from mentioning them or the life he had known before. His grandparents had disliked his father; he had gathered that much from remarks his grandfather had made. Once Grandpapa had told him that Eleanor had left his father because Joe Ferguson was a crass, uncivilized brute. After that, Stephen had felt that Grandpapa was always watching him, afraid to see some part of that uncivilized brute come out in him. Due to the rigid social training he had received, it never had, except perhaps in the sport of boxing, which he had taken up while at college, at Princeton. Though it was a gentleman's sport, his grandfather had frowned over it. Stephen thought he would have preferred him to take up fencing or sculling.

But his mother, unlike the old gentleman, had never blamed Joseph Ferguson for anything. She had said only that she could not stand the loneliness and the vast emptiness of the land, or the freezing climate. Later, when Stephen was grown, he thought he understood why she had left. It must have been a rough, lonely life in the wilds of Montana for a woman who had grown up in this wealthy, civilized household. She had known only refinement and culture, and there had been servants to do everything for her. It must have been a hellish struggle for her out there.

Out there. He didn't exactly know where it was. No one had ever spoken of it except as "that uncivilized place," and he couldn't remember enough about it to identify it. All he could remember was looking up at immense trees all around him—and the security and warmth of lying in his bed at night, snuggled up against his brother.

Stephen sighed and sat up. Why the devil was he thinking about such things now? Was it because his mother, his last link to that shadowy life, was gone? Now there was no one who could really tell him why she had left her husband and, even more puzzling, her older child. Now there was no one who knew what his brother had looked like, or who could describe their cabin or tell him its location. He had always thought that one day he would ask his mother where they had lived, and he would travel there to see it again and to stand beside his father's and brother's graves. Now he would never do it.

This fact swelled the discontent within him. Over the course of the past few months, he had been feeling more and more wound up...burdened...trapped. Something inside him longed to break free, though he wasn't sure exactly what he wanted to break free from. There was something about having the mantle of responsibility for the business slide more and more onto his shoulders, about setting a date for the wedding, about losing his childhood with his mother's death, that made him feel as if he was being smothered.

There was a discreet tap at the door, and Harrison, the butler, stepped into the room. Stephen was surprised. Harrison was the most important in the social scale of the servants, and he rarely came upstairs on any errand.

"Sir." The butler made a faint bow with his head. "I hope this is not an inconvenient time."

"No. That's quite all right." Stephen looked curiously at the small wooden box the butler carried in his gloved hands. "What is it, Harrison?"

"I have known your mother since she was a girl," he began in his slow, careful voice. Stephen wondered where this was leading. Harrison had already offered him condolences on his mother's death. "In some ways she looked upon me as a friend, I think, despite the differences in our stations. After she was taken ill, she called me to her room and gave me this." He extended the box. "She told me that if she died, I was to give this box to you, sir. She trusted me, you see, not to pry into the contents."

"Of course. There's no one *I* would trust more." Stephen reached out and took the box from him. "Thank you."

He smoothed his hand across the mahogany top, tracing

the outline of the mother-of-pearl rose inlaid there. He hardly noticed when Harrison quietly left the room. Stephen opened the lid, and the faint scent of his mother's lavender sachet wafted out. Tears stung his eyes. He closed them, remembering when he and his mother had first moved to his grandparents' house, and he had often awakened in the night, crying. His mother had always come to him, shooing away the nanny his grandparents provided, and taken him in her arms. He remembered the soft, warm comfort of her embrace and the scent of lavender that clung to her bed robe.

Swallowing, Stephen dashed the tears from his eyes and sat down to look through the box. On top lay a pale gray envelope, which he recognized as his mother's stationery. On the front, in his mother's elegant copperplate handwriting, was his name. He took out the envelope and tore open the flap, then pulled out the sheet of paper inside and opened it. It, too, was written in his mother's hand, although the writing was shakier than he had ever seen it and filled with blotches. He began to read.

Dearest Stephen,
I am very ill, I fear. The doctor looks grave and tells me it is possible that I could have another seizure. Therefore I am writing you to tell you something that I have never had the courage to say. I have committed a great sin against you, though you must believe that I did it with a good heart, my sole concern being your happiness.

I imagine you remember that when you were very young, I took you away from your father and brother and returned to live with my family. Never think that I did not love your father, for I did. Joseph Ferguson was a good man, and I loved him dearly. But I was weak, ill and frightened, so I ran home. I took you with me because you were young enough that you needed your mother and because I could not live without at least one of my sons. But I could not bear to take everything away from Joe, his wife and both his sons. Samuel was older than you and very close to his father, and it was obvious that he already loved the same way of life that Joe did, so I left him with his father. Please believe me when I say that I did not leave him for any lack of love for him. It broke my heart to do so.

You were young enough that I expected you would quickly forget Joe and Sammy, but I had not reckoned with your devotion. Night after night you had bad dreams and woke from them crying. Daily you asked me where Sammy and Papa were and when we would go back to them. It tore my heart to see you so unhappy. Finally, I could think of nothing else to do, so I told you that they had died, hoping that this, at last, would free you from your thoughts of seeing them again and enable you to forget them and be happy once more. After a time, it seemed to work. You gradually accepted that they were gone, and you began to forget. You became happier here.

But I had lied to you. In fact, they did not die. To the best of my knowledge they still live in Montana, in the town named Nora Springs.

As the years passed, I realized what a wrong I had done to you. When you grew older, I knew that you could have met your father and brother and gotten to know them. First because of my weakness and then because of my foolish lie, I had deprived you of your rightful family.

Yet I compounded my sin by not telling you the truth then. I feared that you would hate me for the lie I had told you, for the years that I had deceived you and kept you from Joseph and Samuel. I let the time pass, putting off telling you the truth, and with each year, my deception grew worse, so that I was more and more terrified of revealing what I had done.

But I cannot die with this sin on my soul. I have to tell you now and hope that you will not hate me. No matter how foolishly or selfishly I may have acted, I love you more than I can tell you. I hope you will forgive me.

I am entrusting these letters I have written to Samuel to you. I know you will see that they reach him.

I leave you with all my love.

                                                            Mama

Stephen read the letter through, then his eyes went back to that single earth-shattering paragraph. His father and brother were alive. He sat back, the letter fluttering down to his lap. *Samuel. Papa.*

They were alive!

He returned his attention to the box in his lap. On one side of it sat a small stack of letters in envelopes, tied together with a pale blue ribbon. On the top envelope was written his brother's name. He ran a finger over the black ink, as though it were some sort of link with his brother and the life buried deep in his memory.

Next to the letters lay a small wooden whistle, crudely carved. He picked it up. It was his toy; he could remember that. He had worn it on a string around his neck, except when the nanny or his grandmother discovered it and ordered him to take the cheap thing off, for it ruined the look of his expensive little suits. Gently he rubbed it between his thumb and forefinger, recalling the times he had sat fingering it just that way when he was a child, and the momentary comfort it had given him. Sammy had made it for him. There was a moment's flash of memory of a small, rough cabin and of towering, thin trees. Evergreens of some kind, so tall they dwarfed even a grown man.

Beneath the whistle lay a set of two small, ornate silver picture frames fastened together by delicate hinges so that they closed, holding the pictures inside. Stephen opened the frames. Inside the two ovals were miniature portraits done in oil by an expert hand. In one frame was a portrait of a young boy with the same coloring as his own. The face, too, was similar to his when he was a child, though a little blunter, perhaps. The boy was smiling broadly, and the portraitist had captured the blend of boyish mischief and innocence in his young face. Stephen's heart began to pound in his chest. It was Samuel.

On the other side was a portrait of an older man; he looked to be about Stephen's age now. He stared out of the picture without a smile, but there was a certain lightness around the eyes that made one think humor lurked inside him. His face was rougher and heavier than Stephen's, but the eyes and the shape of his mouth were like his. There was no denying the family resemblance. It was his father.

Seeing their faces, memories came tumbling into his mind: the smell of his father's pipe and the feel of flannel beneath his cheek as he sat on his father's lap; sitting beside Sammy in front of the fire and watching him whittle; laughing as the man in the picture swung him up above his head and set him on his shoulders. He could remember, too, that last morning and the terrible ache in his chest, the gut-wrenching fear, as Mama rode with him out of the yard, leaving Sammy behind them.

Stephen snapped the portrait set closed and leaned his forehead against his palm, the picture frame cool and hard against his skin. They were alive. All these years he had gone his way, living his life alone, they had been there, alive. He was flooded with a thousand questions, but, more than that, he was filled with emotions that pulled and tore at him. They were his flesh and blood, his family. He had to see them.

He would leave immediately, he thought. Pack his bags and go, staying only long enough to tell Elizabeth and his grandparents where he was going. Grandpapa would no doubt be furious, but Elizabeth would be her usual calm, collected self, pointing out that with their wedding at least a year away, his being gone for a few months would hardly matter.

Stephen jumped up, shutting the box, and went to the wall to yank on the bellpull. When his valet answered a few minutes later, he set him to packing his clothes, ignoring Charles's startled, curious stare. Then he trotted down the stairs to his grandfather's study. On one wall hung a large map of the United States, including its western territories. Stephen found Montana—how far north it was!—and dragged his finger up and down across the territory until at last he found the name he was seeking. It was a little dot in the northwestern part of the state, practically all the way to Canada, in the mountains along the Flathead River: Nora Springs. That was where he was going. That was where he would find his brother and father, so long lost to him. Excitement shivered through him.

Nora Springs, Montana!

The pace of the horses began to quicken. Stephen pulled aside one corner of the window curtain and peered out, wondering why the tired horses had speeded up. He saw a small wood hut and barn ahead, with a corral beside them, and he realized that they were approaching another way station. He sighed. He had been hoping that they were at last about to reach his destination, but obviously this wasn't Nora Springs.

Stephen let the curtain fall and leaned his head back. It had been a long, tiresome journey. He had told his grandparents what he intended to do, and, as he had expected, his grandfather had been set against it. Elizabeth, of course, had been understanding. She was an independent female who didn't need her fiancé around all the time, and since the wedding was set for a year away, there wouldn't be any problem with his returning in time. She understood his amazement at learning that his father and brother were alive, and she fully agreed that he should reestablish relations with them.

He had started on the trip almost immediately, accompanied by his valet. Stephen had tried to talk Charles out of going, knowing it would be a difficult trip into a part of the country that was still rough and wild, but Charles had pleaded to come. He was mad about the West. Stephen had more than once found him reading a pulp magazine about the exploits of some Western hero or outlaw. So, in all conscience, Stephen had felt that he could hardly leave Charles behind, and he had finally agreed to let the Englishman go with him.

He had set out eagerly, excitement welling in him. He was curious and eager, not only at the thought of seeing his family again after so long, but also at the idea of traveling west, seeing new territory, stepping into a land that was unknown and still untamed. As the train had rolled north and west, he had been glued to the window, watching the familiar land change into the vast sweep of prairie and finally into the near-desolation of the flatlands of Montana. It was so empty, sparsely dotted with sagebrush, and so immense. And the sky! It seemed bluer than he had ever seen before, and somehow higher, wider, arching over the great land all the way to the horizon like a huge, inverted blue bowl.

The railroad ended in Missoula, and from there he and his valet had had to take the stage northwest to Nora Springs. They'd had to wait three days before the next stagecoach left for Nora Springs, and then, to his amazement, the stage ride had taken more time than the much longer trip by train from his hometown. They were climbing up into the mountains, and the straining horses went slowly. They had to stop frequently to change teams at the small way stations. At first Stephen had been so entranced by the magnificent scenery of the rugged mountain country that he had scarcely noticed the discomfort of the journey. But finally even the towering mountains, soaring pines and swiftly running creeks couldn't distract him from the jolting of the poorly sprung coach or the choking dust that came in through the windows. Their progress was agonizingly slow, and they had to stop at night in the small, airless way stations, where they slept on hard cots, dined on tasteless food and breathed in the perpetual smell of dust and horses.

In vain Charles brushed Stephen's suit in the morning and pulled forth a freshly starched white shirt. Within minutes he was coated with road dust again. The passengers, all male, slept and dressed in a single large dormitory-style room. Stephen noticed that the other passengers cast sideways looks of amazement at Charles as he scurried around freshening Stephen's clothes, shaving him and helping him dress. Stephen, who had spent almost his entire life being waited upon by servants and living among people similarly used to being waited upon, felt suddenly embarrassed about it. This was a hard country, and the men who lived here were hard, too. There were calluses on their hands, and their skin was dark and rough from the sun. Their daily lives were a struggle to tame nature, and he could see in their eyes a kind of stunned amusement at watching a man who had to have help to get dressed.

Stephen wasn't sure which he felt the most: embarrassment at appearing a ridiculous figure to the people around him, or astonishment at being the object of anyone's amusement. Never before in his life had anyone regarded Stephen as weak or soft. He was a man of strength in the world in which he lived, a gentleman of honor as well as a businessman of some wealth and power.

Because of this unaccustomed uneasiness around his fellow passengers, he kept to himself, conversing little with the other men. It made the journey even more tedious. On the train he had talked with several men who were glad to tell him about their part of the country and themselves. On the stagecoach, his only respite from boredom was looking at the scenery.

When they pulled into the way station, Stephen stepped out of the stagecoach with the other four passengers and walked around, working out the kinks in his muscles. He wondered how much longer it would take to reach Nora Springs. It was only midmorning. Surely they would make it there today. It would be a great relief to spend the night in a real bed in a hotel instead of on one of those miserably hard cots.

He leaned against the corral fence, watching the station worker and driver switch the horses. A slender lad in a large floppy hat joined the others and began to help them. Both men greeted him with a smile and a clap on the shoulder. He worked quickly and efficiently, his fingers nimble, though he obviously lacked the others' strength, and all the while he kept up a running conversation with the men, laughing as he talked.

When the stage was ready to pull out, the lad climbed up on top with the driver and his shotgun rider. Stephen guessed that he had begged a ride off them, paying for it with his help and lively conversation. Stephen found himself thinking about the boy as the coach started forward again. There was something about him that nagged at Stephen, but he couldn't decide what. His expressive face had been intriguing. It was a trifle small, almost effeminate, and because of that and his size Stephen guessed him to be barely in his teens. Yet his movements as he worked with the horses had been smooth and practiced, with none of the gawky awkwardness of youth. Stephen frowned, wondering why it was that the boy stayed in his mind. There was something about him…but he couldn't put his finger on it.

Finally Stephen gave up with a mental shrug and leaned against the side of the coach, trying to nap. But with the ruts and bumps in this crude road, it was difficult; every few minutes, the movement of the coach would jolt him awake, rapping his head sharply against the wall. Even with his eyes closed, Stephen could tell that they were climbing again. He hoped they would not have to stop and get out and walk to the top, as they'd had to do before at a few particularly steep inclines. Then he felt the coach begin to shift downward and pick up speed. The ground seemed to level out, yet still the horses moved at a good clip. Stephen glanced at his watch. They'd been traveling for over an hour. Could they possibly be coming to yet another way station? The horses were fresh, but still, it had been a hard haul for them uphill.

He pulled aside the window curtain and looked out. To his amazement he saw buildings ahead of them. He opened the curtain wider and glanced around. They were in a valley, with the mountains all around them, and the coach was moving along a road beside a wide strip of water. This was no mountain creek but a river. And the town... His pulse quickened. Could it be Nora Springs at last?

They reached the edge of the town. There was the marker: Nora Springs. Stephen's stomach tightened into a knot. He was close to meeting them. What would it be like? Would they be instantly family? Or remain strangers forever?

The coach pulled up to the side of a small building and stopped. A couple of men were standing on the porch. One was young and rather nondescript. The other was older, with a great deal of gray in his hair and thick beard, and he chewed incessantly. The older one spat a stream of brown juice into the street, then called, "Hey, Jess!"

"Hi, Burley. Carter." The lad climbed nimbly from the coach, jumping the last couple of feet to the ground. "What are you two lazing around for?" He glanced toward the driver. "Thanks, Harry."

"Anytime, Jess. You know that."

"Yeah," the younger man on the porch joked. "Your ma cooks too good a meal for anyone to refuse you a ride."

"That's the truth, sure enough," the driver agreed genially as he, too, climbed down.

Stephen and the other passengers emerged from the stage and stood waiting in the yard. The driver went around to the rear and unfastened their luggage. Stephen took the bags from his hands, but Charles hurried forward.

"Mr. Stephen, sir! I'll take them." The valet sounded thoroughly shocked at the idea of Stephen handling his own luggage. He seized both leather bags and inspected them, shaking his head over their condition. "There. Two scratches. Those clumsy oafs. I knew they weren't paying attention to what they were doing."

Stephen smiled faintly. "Hard to travel without doing any damage to the bags. And I expect you'll have to let me carry them. There's still the trunk, and you will need help to carry that." He glanced around. No sign of a porter. Before this trip that would have surprised him, but not now.

His glance fell on the boy, now standing in front of the porch, thumbs hooked in his pockets, talking to the other men. "Here, boy!" Stephen called to him. Since the lad had needed to cadge a ride off the stage driver, he would undoubtedly be willing to earn some money. Stephen dug in his pocket for a coin. "Where's the best hotel in this town?"

The boy and the two men on the porch turned to look at him, their faces blank. Stephen flipped the coin toward the lad, and he caught it in an automatic gesture, but he still stared at Stephen uncomprehendingly.

"Help my man with the trunk and take us to the best hotel," he explained. Was the boy slow-witted? "You. Boy." What had the driver called him? "Jess."

Every line in the lad's body stiffened. He planted his hands on his hips and his feet apart, anger radiating from him. "Are you talking to me?"

"Yes, you." Whatever was the matter with him? One would think Stephen had just insulted him instead of offering him a job. "Well, do you want the money or not?"

The men on the porch guffawed, and the driver and shotgun rider joined in. One of the men pointed at the boy, hooting with laughter, saying, "Yeah, *boy*, why don't you carry the gentleman's bags?"

Jess shot a fierce look at the man who had spoken, then turned to Stephen. He reached up and swept his hat from his head. A pair of long, bright red braids fell down his back.

Stephen stared. Good God! The boy they called Jess was a girl!

Chapter Two

Jessamine Randall had never understood why it was necessary, in order to be a woman, to wear encumbering petticoats and skirts. Being a girl of independent mind, she refused to wear them and instead wore trousers and flannel shirts that she got in boys' sizes at Swenson's Mercantile, just as she did her heavy work boots. She knew her wearing them worried and horrified her mother, but after all, it was her mother who had introduced her to the practice.

Jessamine's father, a chopper in Ferguson's lumber camp, had died when Jessamine was a young girl, crushed by a tree that had fallen the wrong way. His death had left Jessamine's mother, Amanda, destitute and heartbroken. There had been men who had wanted to marry her, but she had been unable to bring herself to do that so soon after her beloved husband's death. Fortunately, Mr. Ferguson had been kind enough to give Amanda a job by which she could support herself and her child. She had cooked for the men in the lumber camp, and, raising Jessamine in that rough place, with the bitter winters of northern Montana, it had made sense to dress her daughter in boys' clothes. She was to regret it later. Jessamine, always a tomboy and the pet of most of the tough men in the logging camp, resisted any later attempt on her mother's part to dress her as a girl.

After all, it made no sense. It was much easier to do her

work in the simple boys' clothes, and they were warmer, too. Besides, she had no interest in looking like a lady. In fact, she saw very little advantage to being a woman. The men held all the interesting jobs, while women like her mother did nothing but cook and clean up after them. It was the men who had the adventure and the fun, whether it was felling trees or sawing them into lumber or tallying figures in Joe Ferguson's mill. It was men who held the power and made the money. A woman was doomed to have none of those things and could make her way only in some menial occupation or by marrying. Jessamine had no intention of doing either one.

She didn't plan on marrying and having babies like Marian Sloane, who slaved her life away for a husband and eight children and looked like she was fifty years old when she was barely thirty. Nor did she intend to cook and clean and scrape by like her mother. She wouldn't wear dresses; she wouldn't learn how to flirt with a man, or try to please him. There was no way that she would allow something like love to lead her into a life of servitude and pain like her mother's—like that of all the women she knew.

No. That wasn't the way for her. She called herself "Jessie," not "Jessamine," that long, flowery name her mother had given her. She eschewed feminine dress and actions. And she set out to learn everything she could about the business she had grown up in until finally, when she was seventeen, she had been able to prove to Joe Ferguson that she knew his operation inside and out. He had given her a real job in his mill. It wasn't femininity that had gotten her there, she knew; it was brains and determination. And the only way to get those things noticed was to make the fact that she was a woman as *un*noticeable as possible.

The result of all this effort was that the men around the mill and camp pretty much accepted her as one of them, but they did so with an indulgent, teasing air that infuriated Jessamine. They were constantly playing practical jokes on her to try to get her to react with a feminine shriek of terror or rage, or making jests about whether she was a girl or a boy. Therefore, any reference to her sex, especially mistaking her for a boy, which was one of the men's favorite games, was guaranteed to arouse her ire. So when this stranger called her a boy and demandingly tossed her a coin to carry his bags, anger surged through her.

Jessie swung around, glaring at him, ready to take him down a few pegs. But instead, when she looked at him, her jaw dropped, and she could only stare. She had never seen a man like this before. He was dressed in a suit, something few men around here wore, except for the banker and the undertaker. But his suit bore little resemblance to those of the banker or the undertaker. His was not black, as theirs were, but a pearly gray and made of a soft, obviously expensive cloth. The style was different, too, and it had been tailored to fit him exactly. He wore thin gloves that were gray, just like his suit, and on his feet were not work boots, nor even sensible, ordinary shoes, but elegant black leather shoes that followed perfectly the line of his feet and were polished to a high gloss—or had been before they met the dust of the road. Around his neck he wore a silk cravat, fastened with a discreet pearl stickpin.

She had never seen a man dressed as elegantly, as softly, as *beautifully*, as this. She'd always heard that gamblers were fancy dressers, but none of the ones who'd come through Nora Springs could hold a candle to this man. What was he that he dressed this way? He was a city slicker, that was for sure. He didn't look like he'd last a day out here; she was amazed that he'd managed to make it this far.

He was staring at her with an equal amount of amazement, obviously dumbfounded at seeing a supposed boy turn into a girl right before his eyes. It was a look Jessie had seen before. Well, let him stare. She told herself she didn't care.

"I—I'm terribly sorry," he said finally in a well-modulated, refined voice. "I didn't realize—that is—well, I beg that you will forgive my rudeness."

Jessie had never heard anyone talk quite like he did, either. Even Elias Moore, the banker, who used big words and whose grammar was the best around, didn't speak so smoothly, with that upper-crust accent.

"That's all right. It's happened before." Jessie strove for a nonchalant tone. She wasn't about to let a man, especially a...a *popinjay* like this think that he'd hurt her feelings. She shot the coin back to him, using her thumb to give it graceful, careless spin in the air. Then she turned and spat. It was a talent one of the young loggers had taught her when she was six, and her mother had whipped her hide more than once when she'd caught her doing it as a little girl. She didn't do it anymore, but this man's high-toned speech and obvious horror at seeing a woman dressed and acting as she was had gotten her back up. She'd show him. "There ain't no hotel here," she added, purposely making her voice rougher than it naturally was. "Leastways, not one fine enough for a fella like you. They sleep four to a room, and you have to walk a block to get a bath."

Stephen's eyes had flown wide open when he saw her spit, and the news of the primitive living conditions left him almost speechless. He had never imagined anything like this. "I see."

"Best you can do is a boardinghouse. My mother runs the nicest one in town, and she's got an extra room, if you want it."

Stephen hesitated for a moment. The gray-bearded man spoke up. "She's right. Ain't no place better'n Miz Randall's."

"Well, yes, all right, then. That is, if there's somewhere for Charles." He glanced at the man standing a little behind him and to one side.

Jessamine glanced at the other man. She'd scarcely noticed him hovering there, she'd been so occupied in looking at his companion. He wasn't half as nicely dressed as the one who did all the talking. "She's only got one room. 'Course, you and your friend could share."

"Heavens!" Charles exclaimed, looking so appalled that Stephen could hardly keep from smiling. "Surely there must be servants' rooms."

Jessie looked at Charles, understanding dawning on her. "Servant?" Her gaze swung to Stephen, more astonished than ever. "You travel with a servant?"

Charles drew himself up stiffly, oozing British disdain from every pore. "A gentleman always takes his valet wherever he goes."

Jessie gazed at Charles as if he were some rare form of flora or fauna. "Does he, now?"

Stephen shot Charles a look that made him subside, then turned to Jessamine. "Now, Miss…uh, Randall, I believe it is? If you could give us directions to this establishment…"

"Better than that. I'll take you myself. It's on my way."

"That's very considerate of you. I would appreciate it."

"Sure." Jessie started toward the trunk, saying over her shoulder, "Charles, if you'll grab hold of that end, I'll take this one. It's not too far to Mama's house."

Stephen moved quickly, interposing himself between her and the trunk. "Miss Randall!" His voice was shocked. "You cannot carry my trunk!"

Jessamine shot him an amused glance. "Oh, yeah? I'm strong enough."

"I couldn't possibly allow a lady to lift something like that."

"A lady?" Jessamine repeated, blinking. She couldn't remember ever being called that before.

"I will help Charles carry it," Stephen went on.

"Master Stephen!" Charles protested. Stephen knew that he would consider it an outrage for his employer to pick up something, but Stephen quelled him with a look.

"I have managed to carry a few things in my life, Charles."

"Yes, sir." Charles's thinned mouth and stiff posture conveyed his utter disapproval, despite his acquiescence.

Jessie glanced from one man to the other. They were a strange pair. She wondered if this was the way men from the city always acted. She shrugged and reached for the two bags on the floor. "Doesn't matter to me. It's your trunk. I'll take these, then."

Stephen stared. Never in his life had he seen a woman pick up her own luggage, let alone someone else's. The women he knew would stand around for hours waiting rather than do something so unfeminine. But then, this woman obviously didn't care about appearing feminine—look at the way she dressed!

His eyes followed the pull of her denim trousers across her backside as she bent to pick up the carpetbags. Damn! Obviously he hadn't been paying attention earlier when he'd assumed she was a boy. She might be slender, but curves like that couldn't belong to a boy.

"Miss Randall, please, no. I'll send Charles back for them."

The men on the porch had been watching the whole scene with interest. Stephen's courtesy immediately struck them as weakness and tickled their rough sense of humor.

"That's right, *Miss Randall*." The younger man mimicked the way Stephen addressed her, using a falsetto voice. "Them bags're too heavy for a *girl*. Oh, no, I'm wrong— for a *lady*. Ain't that right, Jess?"

Stephen glanced at the man, frowning. These were low, crude sorts of men, the kind he wouldn't ordinarily have paid any attention to. However, they had no right to address any woman—even one dressed in pants—in that sneering way. He was just about to let them know that fact in no uncertain terms, but the girl took the wind out of his sails by swinging around and addressing them first.

"Yeah!" she retorted, dropping the bags and planting her fists on her hips pugnaciously. "I reckon that's who I am, to a lead-bottom, belly-crawlin', beer-swillin' know-nothin' like you!" She turned to the older man. "I don't know what you're doing, Burley, hanging around trash like this."

The older man grinned. "Well, now, Jessie, I was just wondering the same thing."

Jessie picked up the bags and stalked off down the street.

Stephen's eyebrows rose at Jessie's retort. Looking at the man's reddened face, he decided that there was really nothing he could add to what she had said. He glanced at his valet, whose normally expressionless face was now torn between laughter and disapproval. "Come on, Charles. I think we'd better follow the lady."

"Yes, sir."

Jessamine led them away from the stage depot along the main street of Nora Springs. The town, Stephen thought, was as crude as the men they'd just encountered. Wooden buildings stood on either side of a wide dirt street, hard-packed now, but marred by deep wagon ruts and holes that gave mute evidence to what it must be like in the spring, when it rained and the street turned to mud. Very few of the wooden buildings were painted, except for the identifying lettering—often misspelled—across the doorway. There was one major street crossing this one, on which sat a few more businesses. The only buildings of any note were a rock-walled bank with bars on the windows and a large, rambling wooden structure that Stephen could not identify. Once across this street, they seemed to have passed out of the downtown area, and now they walked past houses of all sizes and quality.

As they walked, Stephen came up alongside Jessie, carefully walking between her and the occasional traffic along the street. When she crossed to the other side of the street, he moved so that he would be on the other side of her, again next to whatever vehicles might pass. Jessie wondered why. Stephen, used to being courteous, didn't even notice what he had done. Walking between a woman and the street was as natural to him as eating or sleeping—or any of the other conventional courtesies that were drummed into all well-brought-up boys' heads.

Jessie glanced at him from time to time. There was something familiar about him, though she couldn't quite put her finger on what it was. It was almost as if she recognized him, as if she had seen him before, or seen a picture of him. But she was sure she hadn't; she would have remembered anyone like him. Still, the feeling nagged at her. She wished she could figure out what it was.

She came to a stop in front of a large, pleasant house with a wide, welcoming porch. It was painted a pale blue, with clean white shutters. There was even a low picket fence around its wide yard, along with a few bushes planted along the foundation.

"This is my mother's house," Jessamine stated with pride.

"It's lovely," Stephen answered honestly. After most of what he'd just seen, this well-cared-for place looked like a palace, even though it was modest compared to his family's mansion in St. Louis.

"Yes. Mama's very proud of it." It was obvious from Jessie's face that it was the nicest place she had ever seen. Stephen wondered if she had been outside the territory, or even outside Nora Springs. "Let's go in, and I'll introduce you to Mama. Then I have to get to work."

Work. Stephen was unused to women working, too. He knew they did, of course. After all, there were the maids and the housekeeper who worked in his home. And there were the women, mostly immigrants, who worked in the factories. Obviously this woman had little money, so that, like those women, she had to work. But why didn't she work in her mother's boardinghouse? And whose house could she clean around here? Besides, she didn't look like the poor, pinched-face, pale women who worked in the factories, or the subservient maids, with their downcast eyes.

He followed her up the dirt walkway to the house and onto the porch. Jessamine swung the door open and went inside, calling her mother. Stephen and Charles followed her into the hallway and set down the trunk with relief. An older woman bustled into the room, wiping her hands dry on a spotless apron. Everything about her was spotless. Her hair, which had once been the color of her daughter's but was more faded now and showing streaks of gray, was pulled back softly and curled into a roll at the back of her head. Her skin, redhead fair, showed wrinkles around the eyes and mouth, but they were lines of laughter, smiles and kindness, and they gave her a soft, loving look. Her eyes were a paler blue than her daughter's, as if they, too, had faded over the years. She was short and a little plump, and there was a sweet, motherly look to her, but there was also something in her eyes that said she had seen many things and few of them were kind. Stephen liked her immediately.

"Hello, I'm Amanda Randall," she said a little breathlessly, her eyes sweeping down Stephen's elegant clothes and taking in Charles hovering behind him.

Stephen bent over her hand as if she were a wealthy, highborn lady. "Mrs. Randall. It's a pleasure to meet you. You have a lovely home."

"Thank you." Color rose in Amanda's cheeks, and she almost bobbed a curtsy. Jessamine might never have seen a man like this, but her mother had grown up in Baltimore, and she knew a high-class gentleman when she saw one. "Goodness, Jessie, why didn't you ask the gentleman to be seated in the parlor?"

Jessamine shrugged and rolled her eyes. The way her mother was acting you'd think a prince had walked into her house. "He just came to see about a room."

"I was told that Mrs. Randall's rooming house was the nicest to be found," Stephen explained.

Amanda beamed. Her daughter frowned. Whatever was the matter with her mother? Just because this sissified stranger bowed over her hand like he was going to kiss it and talked sweet, she acted like he was something special. Jessamine couldn't see what was so great about him. Why, he couldn't even go anywhere without dragging a servant along to take care of him, like a little boy with his mother.

"Thank you," Amanda answered him. "I can guarantee that it's the cleanest. I'm afraid we have only one room available, but if you'd like to look at it, Mr...uh...?"

"Forgive me. I haven't introduced myself." Stephen had been so startled by Jess's transformation into a girl that he hadn't even thought to tell her his name. "You must think I'm terribly rude. My name is Stephen Ferguson."

"Ferguson!" Both women exclaimed, staring at him.

"That's who you look like!" Jessamine went on. "I kept thinking and thinking you looked like somebody I knew. It's Sam. You look like Sam Ferguson—kind of."

Of course, he wasn't as muscular as Sam, and his shoulders weren't as wide, nor his arms as powerful. And he was paler. Sam's heavier, rugged features were handsomer, she thought. Samuel Ferguson had protected Jessie many times throughout her life, and he was nothing short of a hero to her. As far as she was concerned, no man could compare favorably to him. But she could see the similarity between the two men. They were almost the same height, they had the same thick black hair, and the lines of their lean-hipped bodies were much alike.

"Of course," Amanda chimed in. "Are you related to Joe and Sam?"

Stephen's throat tightened. It felt strange to say it. "I'm Joseph Ferguson's son."

Amanda's jaw dropped. "You—you're—"

"Who?" Jessamine asked impatiently. "What are you saying, Mama? Sam doesn't have a brother!"

"Yes," Amanda corrected quietly. "Yes, he does. Joe had—has another son."

Jessamine stared, first at her mother, then at Stephen, then at her mother again. "But how—who—how come I didn't know?"

"Some things are private, Jessie. Joe Ferguson doesn't go around spouting off about his life to everybody."

Jessie felt hurt. Why had Sam and Joe never told her? Joe often ate at her mother's house. She and Sam were friends. It seemed unfair that her mother knew about it and she didn't. Why, even her own mother hadn't told her.

"Well!" Amanda was saying. "This is quite a surprise. Oh, Joe is going to be so happy to see you." She turned to her daughter. "Jessie, you must take Mr. Ferguson to the mill to meet Joe. I mean, that is, to see him." She sighed and beamed at him. "This is wonderful."

"I was going there anyway," Jessie said, her voice a

trifle surly. She felt as though this man was to blame for her feeling of exclusion from her surrogate family, and though she knew that was silly, she couldn't keep from being annoyed with him. "If you want to come along, it's all right."

"Jessie! A little more courtesy to our guest, please."

Jessie grimaced.

"Thank you," Stephen told her. "I would appreciate it very much if you would take me to my father." He glanced at Amanda, and she saw an instant of vulnerability in his dark brown eyes. "If you're sure that he'd want to see me. I—I'm not quite sure of my reception."

"Don't worry about that. He'll be thrilled to see you. He's never forgotten you."

"Nor have I forgotten him."

Jessie clomped over to the front door in her heavy boots and turned. "I'm ready to go, if you're coming."

"Give the poor man a bit of time to freshen up from his journey," Amanda told her daughter, fixing her with a stern look. "Let me show you to your room first, Mr. Ferguson."

"No, that's not necessary. I'd rather go right now to see my father."

Jessamine opened the door. "Come on, then. Let's go."

They walked into the center of town and up the major cross street on which Stephen had seen the odd-looking building. Stephen realized as they continued to walk that it must be this building, with its great pile of dirt and the odd conical side building, toward which they were heading.

Neither of them said anything as they walked. Stephen realized that Jessie was miffed about something, though he couldn't imagine what. She appeared to be a rather touchy young woman. But now he asked curiously, "What is that building?"

She gave him an odd look. "The mill? Why, that's Ferguson Sawmill. Don't you know?"

"No. I'm afraid I know very little about my father. So they cut up these pines I saw on the way here?" His voice rose a little at the end in question.

"Yeah. They have a logging camp, too, where they fell the trees. Sam's up there. He runs the camp. Mr. Ferguson, Joe, takes care of the mill. That's where I work, too."

He glanced at her, surprised. "You work at a sawmill? But what could you do there?"

Jessamine's features tightened. "Just 'cause I'm a woman it doesn't mean I'm stupid or helpless."

He was taken aback yet again by her harsh words. Why was this young woman so angry about everything? "I didn't mean that you were. It's just, well, a lumber mill hardly seems like a place for a girl to work."

"I'm not a girl. I'm full grown. And there's hardly anything about the lumber business that I don't know. I could run that mill myself if I had to. I do the books for Joe, and the correspondence. I help wherever he needs me." Her chin lifted a little defiantly. "I've been with Joe Ferguson for years."

"Ah, I see. Years when I haven't been. Is that right?"

Jessie glanced at him, surprised at his perceptiveness. "Well, yeah. That's right."

"Then I'm glad he's had such a loyal helper as you."

Jessie didn't quite know how to answer that. She stuck her hands in her pockets and walked faster, pulling ahead of him. Stephen found his eyes drifting to her denim-clad legs. He'd never seen a woman's legs so revealed before, except in a house of ill repute. They were not bare, but the denim, worn to softness, outlined her shapely curves, and seeing the shape of her legs and derriere in broad daylight on a public street sparked a flicker of excitement. It was bold; it was brazen; it was titillating. Yet there was nothing about Jessie Randall that suggested a woman of easy virtue. Stephen had the feeling that if he was to make an overture toward her, she would probably hit him with a hard right hook.

He realized how he was ogling her legs and tore his eyes away. Whatever was the matter with him? He had other, more important things to think about than some graceless hoyden's legs.

When they reached the sawmill, Jessamine ran lightly up the stairs to the upper floor ahead of Stephen and reached for the door handle. He had to almost run to grab it first and open it for her. She looked at him oddly. He was beginning to think that she had never met anyone with manners.

Inside the mill, he was assaulted by a piercing, high-pitched whine that made him want to plaster his hands over his ears. The girl didn't seem to notice it. She waved toward the left, where he could see that most of the factory lay. She said something, too, but he couldn't understand it over the loud, irritating noise. She turned toward the right, leading him down a hall, where it was minimally quieter. She walked into a large room, obviously an office, and closed the door behind her, cutting out some of the noise. On the other side of the room lay a door, and Jessamine went straight to it. She knocked on it twice, loudly, and Stephen heard a gruff rumble of a voice on the other side.

Jessie opened the door. "Uncle Joe, there's somebody here to see you."

"Tarnation," Stephen heard, followed by more unintelligible words.

Jessie shook her head. "You'll have to come see him."

Moments later, a middle-aged man stuck his head out the doorway. His thick black hair was liberally sprinkled with gray, and his hard frame was beginning to blur with excess weight. He wore a plaid flannel shirt tucked into denim trousers and heavy work boots on his feet. He frowned at Stephen. His face went slack. "What the hell...?"

Joe Ferguson took a step or two, and Stephen moved the same distance closer to him. Joe stared, unable to speak. Stephen's heart was pounding, but at least he'd been prepared for this. His father hadn't. Stephen took another step forward. "I—I'm Stephen Ferguson. I—"

"Stephen! Stevie?" Ferguson glanced around, as though he would somehow find in the room an answer to his confusion. "You can't—"

"I'm your son. My mother was Eleanor McClellan Ferguson."

Joe shook his head. "I can't believe it." Tears filled his eyes even as a wide grin spread across his mouth. "Stevie!"

He came closer, wonderingly, looking into his son's face, so familiar and yet so unexpected. When he reached him, he threw out his arms and pulled Stephen to him in a fierce hug. "It *is* you! I never thought I'd see you again." He squeezed him, then stepped back to look him over once more. He shook his head. "It seems impossible. My God, you were just a little boy."

"Five. It's been twenty-two years."

"Twenty-two years." Joe shook his head. "I can't believe it. Come in, come in." He pulled Stephen into the inner office and closed the door after them.

Jessie stood, looking at the closed door. Who was this man? Why had she never heard of his existence? Joe hadn't even introduced him to her.

She made her way over to her desk and plopped down in the chair behind it. She shuffled some papers around, but she scarcely noticed them. Her mind was on Joe and the man who had appeared out of nowhere claiming to be Joe's son. Did Sam know about him? she wondered. What would Sam say? Would he be thrilled to see the stranger, too, or was he as much in the dark as she had been?

But he must know. How could Joe have a son who was clearly an Easterner? A son who was younger than Sam? It didn't make sense. Curiosity overwhelmed her feelings of exclusion and resentment, and she sat doodling on a pad of paper, her eyes staring vacantly, trying to figure out the puzzle of Stephen Ferguson.

He was different. He bothered her. He had from the first moment she saw him—even before she knew he was Sam Ferguson's brother. Somehow he disturbed her equilibrium. When he had looked at her earlier, she had been aware for the first time in years of the masculinity of her clothes. For some reason it had hurt when he had mistaken her for a

boy. She didn't know why. He was a useless sort of a
fellow; one look at him, and anybody knew he couldn't
take care of himself out here. She doubted that he'd ever
slept in the open; he wouldn't have the strength to wield
an ax in the forest, or the skill to be a sawyer in the mill.
Hell, he probably couldn't even ride or use a gun. He
wasn't anyone; she shouldn't care for a second what he
thought of her.

Yet for some reason—maybe it was his elegant clothes
or those heavily lashed eyes that gave him the handsomeness of Lucifer before the Fall—when his amazed eyes had
run down her body to her clunky boots, she had become
acutely aware of what she looked like. Suddenly her hands
and feet had seemed too big. She remembered the stains
and dirt on her pants. She thought about the awful carroty
color of her hair and the fact that it was straggling out from
her braids, as it always did. She felt clumsy and embarrassed, which she strove to hide under her usual air of uncaring defiance.

Thinking about her reaction, Jessie frowned. It was stupid to let the man upset her. It wasn't as if he was someone
about whose good opinion she cared. What did it matter if
he stared at her as if she were some strange form of wildlife
he'd never seen before? So what if he considered her unfeminine? She'd never had any desire to be feminine.

She tossed her pencil onto the pad with a loud sigh,
disgusted at the way her thoughts kept circling around Stephen Ferguson. She shoved back her chair and strode out
of the room and down the hall into the mill. She was used
to the high-pitched whine of the buzz saw and the heavy
thrum of the steam engine that powered it, as well as the
thumping and clanking of machinery and chains, and she
didn't notice the incessant din any more than she did the
fine sawdust that drifted through the air and caught on her
hair and clothes. She stood for a moment watching as the
head sawyer and his dogger maneuvered one of the long
pine logs into position for the spinning saw. The saw bit
cleanly into the wood, and chips and sawdust flew thickly.

The very air seemed to vibrate with the power of the machine. Jessie watched, enthralled, as she always did.

A hand curled around her arm, and she jumped. In the midst of all the noise, she hadn't heard the man's approach. She turned and looked up at a large man with a mane of thick, long, dark blond hair and a reddish-blond beard, stained brown around his mouth from tobacco juice. He was the only man she knew who was bigger than Sam Ferguson; his neck and shoulders were bunched with muscles so thick it seemed almost as if he had no neck at all and his head sat directly upon his shoulders. Sawdust covered his hair, beard and clothes, and even clung to his skin. His name was Frank Grissom, and he had worked in the mill practically his whole life. Once he had been the best dogger Ferguson Mill had ever had, though he had never had the supremely accurate eye to be a good head sawyer. Now he was the mill's foreman. Jessie disliked the man, but she had to admit that he was good at his job; there wasn't a man in the mill who dared disobey one of his commands, and he knew the running of the mill from the ground up.

He smiled at her, displaying a set of stained teeth from which three were missing, lost in one or another of the fights he'd had over the years to establish and maintain his dominance. He smelled like tobacco and days-old sweat, and Jessie tried to breathe through her mouth so that she wouldn't smell him. He pulled her away from her vantage point and with him into the relatively quiet hall.

"Hello, Jessie," he said, still grinning. "You looking for me?"

Jessie gave him a flat, blank stare. For some reason Grissom had taken a shine to her; it amazed her almost as much as it appalled her. She had never considered herself pretty, dismissing her fiery hair as orange, her white skin as a nuisance and her blue eyes as pale. As a result, she couldn't imagine what any man would see in her. But then, Frank Grissom didn't have much taste or gumption, as she well knew. He seemed dead set on her.

It was a decided nuisance. As long as Joe or Sam was with her, Grissom would never dare approach her, but if he caught her alone, he always managed to put his hand on her arm or shoulder and grin at her, leering, as he was doing now, and he would talk to her in what Jessie supposed he must think was a sexually stimulating way. The only thing his heavy, often vulgar comments aroused in her was disgust, and the feel of his hand anywhere on her made her skin crawl. Just as bad was seeing his mean little eyes sliding over her body as if he was trying to see right through her clothes. She had never liked Frank Grissom, thinking him a small-brained bully of a man, but in the past year, since he had started to pursue her, she had grown to despise him.

Joe and Sam would never have allowed him to bother her if they had known about it. A few months ago Sam had heard him make a suggestive remark to her, and he had given him a choice, in a low, deadly voice, between talking to Jessie like that and keeping his job. Grissom, of course, had apologized to her sullenly. Jessie knew that if she complained to Sam, he would get rid of Grissom. But that was just the problem. Grissom was a good foreman, and if he was fired, it would mean that Sam would have to come back from the lumber camp, or Joe would have to assume the extra workload. With all the other problems they were having, the last thing Jessie wanted was to add to the Fergusons' troubles.

Besides, it would gall her to hide behind Sam or Joe. She was proud of being able to take care of herself just like a man took care of himself. Sam, by whom she measured all other men, would never go running to his father or any other authority to get rid of someone who was bothering him. He would take care of it himself. And that was what Jessie was determined to do. She could handle Frank Grissom without dragging the Fergusons into it. Eventually, no matter how annoyingly persistent Grissom was or how thickheaded, he was bound to get the message that she wasn't interested in him.

She had spent the past few months avoiding being caught alone with him, and when she had been unable to avoid it, she had made it clear that she discouraged his pursuit of her. But avoiding him greatly limited her freedom of movement, particularly around the mill, and he was so thickheaded that she was beginning to wonder if he would ever realize that she didn't want to be around him.

"I been thinkin' about you all day," Grissom went on. "Thinkin' maybe we could take a little walk tonight."

"I don't think so."

"Then how about tomorrow?" He smiled and reached out to lay his hand on her shoulder.

Jessie quickly stepped back. "No."

His grin grew. "Not scared of me, are you, Jessie?"

That was a taunt sure to arouse a reaction in her. She squared her shoulders and faced him, her chin going up. "I'm not scared of you or any other man."

"Then how come you keep hidin' from me? Huh, little Jessie?"

Her eyes flamed. "Don't call me that."

"Why? You are, you know. So little my hands could go clean around your waist and then some." He started toward her, his hands reaching out to demonstrate the narrowness of her waist.

Jessie stepped to the side, knocking his hands away, and moved around him. "It looks like a person has to hit you in the head to make you understand! I am not interested in you, and I have no intention of taking a walk or doing anything else with you. Ever. Now, is that clear enough?"

His upper lip curled into a sneer. "Yeah, that's clear. Think you're too good fer a man like me, don'tcha? Who you waiting for? You think young Ferguson's goin' to go after you?" He snorted. "You're wasting your time if that's what you're hopin' fer."

Jessie flushed. "I'm not hoping for anything. I just don't plan to waste my time with you!"

She swung around and marched toward her office. Behind her, she heard Grissom's obnoxious laugh. "When

you get tired of waitin', just let me know! I can make you
forgit ol' Sam!''

Jessie shuddered. As if any woman who wanted Sam
Ferguson would even look at a man like Frank Grissom!

She slammed into the office and plopped down at her
desk. Frowning, she snapped open a ledger book and got
to work.

Chapter Three

Stephen followed his father into his office. Joe sat on the edge of his desk and motioned Stephen toward a chair in front of it. For a long moment they simply looked at each other.

For years Stephen had had only a vague memory of his father, remembering mostly his size and his voice. The miniature in the mahogany chest had brought back his face, but Stephen had studied it so often on his journey that he was no longer certain how much he remembered his father and how much of his memory was taken from the portrait. Now, looking at Joe, he knew he remembered those eyes—bright, alive, a chocolate brown so deep they looked black. The eyes hadn't changed. His hair might now be salt and pepper instead of black, and his face might have thickened and grown lined, but the eyes were still his father's, and he knew them. He knew *him*.

"It's been so long." Joe shook his head wonderingly. "I'd given up hope of seeing you again. Are you still living in St. Louis? Married? Children?" He laughed a little nervously. "It's odd. I know you, yet I don't know you at all."

Stephen smiled. "I feel the same way." This man was his father, and he felt the pull of the basic connection, yet Joe was also virtually a stranger. "I'm not married, no children. But I am engaged. I've lived in New York City the past few years, but it looks as though now I'll go back to St. Louis to live.''

"Your grandparents? Are they still alive? And—Nora? How is Eleanor?''

Joe knew the answer instantly from the pain that filled Stephen's eyes before he even said a word. "She's—she died quite recently. It was very sudden.''

"Dead?'' His father seemed to shrink, as though something had drained out of him. "No. So young?''

Stephen nodded. "We were shocked. The doctors said it was a stroke, a seizure in her brain.''

Joe shook his head slowly, staring at the floor, as though seeing something that lay only in his mind. "Such a beautiful woman, Nora was. I lost her long ago, but still...it saddens me.''

"In a way, that's why I came.''

"To bring the news to Sam and me?''

"Yes, I suppose, but more than that. You see, until after her death, I didn't know where you were, or even that you were still alive.''

"What?'' Stephen's statement startled Joe out of his reverie. "What do you mean?''

"I thought you were dead, both of you.''

"Well! I guess that explains why you never came before. I reckoned you'd just forgotten about us, or maybe didn't want to see us.''

"No. No, you mustn't think that. As soon as I learned that you were alive, I came here.''

Joe smiled. "I'm glad. But tell me, why would you think we were dead?''

"It's what Mother told me. Apparently, when we first returned to St. Louis, I was so unhappy, always wanting to come back, that she decided to tell me you were dead. So I would accept it and get over it. Later, she was afraid to tell me the truth, to admit that she had lied to me. So she let it go on.''

Joseph Ferguson sighed. "Ah, poor Nora. She never

could bear to see anyone fret, especially you. It doesn't surprise me that she'd say that. She was inclined to get rid of a problem the quickest, easiest way possible. She didn't always stop to think about what it would mean in the future. I can't say I regret her impulsiveness. She married me the same way.''

"Then you don't regret marrying her?" Stephen studied him, wondering if he still felt bitter toward the woman who had deserted him so many years ago.

"No. How could I regret it? Those were the happiest years of my life, and they brought me two sons. A lot of sweet memories.'' He shrugged. "I don't believe in letting bitterness or hurt corrode what was beautiful before the pain. You can't ever lose memories, unless you destroy them yourself.'' He smiled faintly and levered himself away from the desk, moving across the floor to look out the window. "I'm not saying I'm a saint. There were times after she left when I cursed that woman. I laid the cause of all my grief at her feet. But I knew, deep down, that she wasn't to blame any more than I was. She missed her family and the life she'd had in the city. She hated the cold and the loneliness. The life here was too hard for her. She couldn't bear to live here any more than I could bear to live anywhere else. For months I could tell how unhappy she was. I knew she loved me, and I knew I still loved her. We just weren't meant to be together all our lives.''

He turned to his son. "I wanted her to be happy. She didn't take everything from me. She left me Sammy. I knew it tore her heart out to do that. She did it only out of love for me, so that I wouldn't be left with no one.''

"You're very understanding.''

"Just realistic. You can't expect a rose to thrive in the snow. I always knew a man like me was lucky to have her for however little time I did.'' His face lightened. "And now I have both sons again.''

Stephen swallowed. He could feel tears pricking his eyelids, and he didn't know what to say. His father returned to his perch on the desk and leaned over to pat his leg.

"Ah, I can't wait for you to see Sam again. He'll be so happy. Do you remember how close you were as boys?"

Stephen nodded and reached into his coat pocket. "I remember him very well." He held out his hand toward Joe, palm up, the little wooden whistle resting in it. "He made this for me. I can remember carrying it around everywhere I went. As I recall, there was a terrible scene once because we left it behind when we went on a visit."

"Yes." Joe picked it up and turned it over in his fingers, examining it. "I remember him making it. It was one of the first things he whittled. He still does, you know, whenever he's just sitting. Makes all kinds of things."

"Where is he? Does he work here, too? When can I see him?"

"Not for a while, I'm afraid. I run the mill, and Sam's in charge of the lumber camp, out in the woods where we cut the timber. It's a good day's ride there and back. But he'll be in town in a week. Our main saw blade broke, and we had to order a new one. Right now we're using one of the old ones, not as big or as good. The new one's coming in on the train next week, and Sam's going to Missoula to pick it up, so he'll be through here. You can meet him then."

"Oh." Stephen's face fell a little. "I had hoped to meet him right away. But, of course, if I can't…" He paused, then asked, "But couldn't I ride out to the camp tomorrow and see him? I mean, surely I could rent a horse somewhere in town, and you could tell me how to get there."

His father frowned. "I don't know. Of course you could get a horse—you could have mine. But trying to find the camp by yourself wouldn't be a good idea. You aren't used to the area. You could easily get lost."

"Not if you gave me directions or drew me a map. I'm usually rather good at finding my way."

Joe looked troubled. "That's in a city. It's different here. There's no road to the camp. You have to follow landmarks, which you aren't familiar with, and then there are the trees and the mountains that cut off your view and make directions confusing. Even the distances seem different because of going up and down hills. I don't think it's a wise idea. I understand that you'd like to see Sam sooner, and I wish you could, but—'' He stopped, and his scowl eased. '''Course, I could send somebody with you. Jessie, for instance. I could spare her tomorrow.''

''Oh, no, please, that's not necessary.''

But Joe was already crossing the room to the door. ''Sure it is. It'll keep me from worrying.''

Stephen knew that Miss Randall didn't think highly of him. He'd seen the faint contempt in her eyes as they swept over his clothes, and the way she'd looked when she found out he had brought his manservant along with him. It was clear that she thought he was an overdressed, incompetent dandy. She would not be happy about having to lead him out to Sam's lumber camp.

Nor did he want her along. She was an odd creature, and he wasn't sure how to act with her. Besides, it galled him that she thought him negligible, even an irritation. From the time he had grown into manhood, he had been considered a very eligible bachelor, and he was accustomed to women trying to arouse his interest, not to a woman who was, at best, laughing at him. He was used to being pursued in a delicate, feminine way, to being flirted with and admired, to having a woman look at him with big, limpid eyes as he talked, as if hanging on to his every word. He had often found that irritating, but with Jessie Randall, he'd discovered that the reverse was even worse.

''Jessie!'' Joe called to the girl sitting a few feet away, absorbed in a ledger book. ''Come here, girl. I guess you know my son, Stephen, seeing as how you brought him to me.''

Jessie rose and came to the door at his request, but she only looked coolly at Joe as he spoke, offering no response to his words.

''Of course, now that he's found us after all this time, he wants to see Sam right away. He wants to go up to the camp. Why don't you show him the way up there tomorrow?''

Jessie's eyebrows shot up, and she stared, momentarily speechless. The condition didn't last long, however. "But, Uncle Joe, I've got work to do. There's the payroll to figure, and it's the end of the month besides. I have to—''

"And who do you think did those things before you came along, I'd like to know? I think I can manage to do the payroll. What I'm not too good at anymore is sitting in the saddle for any length of time. You know, since I rebroke that leg four years ago, it's been real hard for me to ride.''

"I know, but—" The last thing Jessie wanted to do was to play nursemaid to this fancy Easterner. And it hurt that Joe found her so easily expendable that he would take her away from her work to lead Stephen Ferguson around the woods. He couldn't have said more plainly that what she did could be done by anyone, that it wasn't important. She had spent the last few years trying to prove how well she could handle this work, how much she belonged at the sawmill even though she was a woman, and here Joe was, as much as saying that she wouldn't be missed.

However, she could hardly refuse to do it, no matter how much she hated the idea. Joe had helped her more times than she could count, and now he was asking her for *her* help. She couldn't turn him down, especially not when he reminded her of the pain it would cause him to ride. She turned her gaze toward Stephen, her anger and frustration focusing on him. "Sam'll be in town in a week! Why can't he wait till then?''

"Wait?" Joseph Ferguson repeated. "You're asking the man to wait after he's already waited over twenty years?"

"Well, if he's been content that long," Jessie asked bluntly, "why in tarnation can't he hang on a few more days?''

Ferguson grimaced. "Sam's his brother. It's only natural.''

Jessie's mouth tightened. She couldn't very well tell Joe

that she thought his son was a selfish, spoiled rich boy who was used to having people do everything for him. It was obvious that if he wanted anything, he expected everyone else to drop whatever they were doing and get it for him. But if Joe couldn't see that for himself, she wouldn't hurt Joe's feelings by telling him.

"Please, no," Stephen spoke up, rising from his chair. It couldn't be any plainer how much she disliked him. If Joe forced her to take him to the camp, her dislike would only get worse. "I shan't need Miss Randall's help. Honestly, Father." The name slipped out, surprising him. "I can find my way perfectly well by myself. All I'll need is a map."

"A tenderfoot always thinks that," Jessie retorted. She didn't want to take him, but his almost haughty assurance irritated her. He was the kind who thought he knew everything. No doubt he thought that they were just country bumpkins. "But there aren't any street signs here."

"I am well aware of that, Miss Randall." Stephen's voice turned icy, his annoyance unconsciously heightening his upper-crust manner of speech. "However, I have managed to find my way around quite a few places in the world that were no more familiar to me than this one. Whatever you may think, I'm not entirely helpless."

"Now, Stephen, we didn't mean that," Joe began placatingly.

But Jessie interrupted him. Crossing her arms, she fixed Stephen with a flat stare. "It's different out here. Sometimes a map doesn't help. It can be dangerous."

"Dangerous?" Stephen's voice was filled with disbelief.

"Wild animals—wolves, bears, that kind of thing. Not to mention the fact that sometimes there are human animals who would as soon kill you as look at you."

"You sound like one of those preposterous magazines Charles is always reading."

"No, she's right about that," Joe agreed. "It's not a safe or easy country. A smart man carries a gun when he rides into the timber—and he makes sure he knows how to use it.''

Stephen stiffened. "And that's why you want her to lead me there? To keep me safe? You want me to take a girl along for protection?''

"Now, don't get in a taking about this. I don't mean anything bad, son.''

"Nothing bad! You mean, other than thinking I'm too stupid to find the lumber camp and such a weakling and a coward that I need to hide behind a woman's petticoats? No, forgive me, this woman doesn't wear such things, does she?'' He shot a glare at Jessie. "No doubt skirts would impede your wrestling a bear or firing a gun.''

"No more than lack of brains keeps some people from talking,'' she retorted.

"All right, now, you two. I don't want a full-scale war here in my office.''

Jessie set her jaw mutinously, but with an effort Stephen reined in his temper and gave his father a nod and a thin smile. "Of course. I apologize. My words were quite un-called for.'' He sketched a bow in Jessie's direction. "Miss Randall, I hope you will accept my apology. I was rude. Father, I appreciate your concern. However, I fear that you and Miss Randall have underestimated me. I've taken care of myself for some years now. I am able to ride, and I have a good sense of direction and have never gotten lost, even in the old section of Paris. If, in fact, the woods are that dangerous, then I shall ask you to lend me a firearm with which to protect myself. But I intend to ride out to see Samuel tomorrow, and I shall do so alone.''

For a moment there was silence, during which the two men looked at each other expressionlessly. Then a grin cracked Joe's face. "No denying you're Sam's brother,'' he said. "I thought you looked like a reasonable man, but it's apparent that you're just as bullheaded as he is. All right.'' He shrugged. "I can see I can't stop you. I'll draw you a map tonight. You can borrow my horse and gun.''

"Thank you.'' Stephen returned his smile. "Now, if you

will excuse me, I should return to Mrs. Randall's and get settled.''

"Sure. I understand." Joe paused. "You're welcome, you know, to stay with me. I'd like to have your company. The only thing is, I recently rented out our house and moved into a room here at the office. It didn't make much sense having all that space with Sam living at the camp and me spending most of my time here.''

"All right." It seemed odd to him that his father would be renting out his house and living in a single room at the mill office. He wondered if it was an indication that Ferguson Mill was having financial difficulties. There wasn't any tactful way to ask. He would have to watch for signs of it in the next few days, and if it did look as if the mill was struggling, he would be able to help his father and brother out of the problem.

"Then I'll see you at supper," Joe went on calmly. "I take most of my meals at Amanda's. Best food in town. Ain't it, Jessie?''

"Of course." Jessie watched Joe, puzzled. She'd never known him to capitulate so easily on anything.

Stephen left the office, brushing past Jessie with a nod. Jessie watched him go, then turned to Joe as soon as the door shut behind Stephen. "Joe, you aren't serious, are you? You aren't going to let him ride out tomorrow!''

"What else can I do? He may be my son, but he's a grown man. I can hardly keep him from it.''

Jessie shifted nervously. She felt guilty for being reluctant to take Stephen to the camp. That had probably gotten his back up. Then she'd had to go and point out how dangerous it was, something that would insure any man's being determined to do it just to prove he wasn't afraid. She had practically pushed Stephen into going alone tomorrow. If he got lost or was jumped by a mountain lion or encountered one of the hundred other deadly things the mountains had to offer, it would be her fault. Joe would never forgive her.

"But, Joe, think of what might happen to him. Remember that fellow from Massachusetts who came out here two summers ago? He fell off the side of the mountain, and they had to send him home with both legs broken.''

"I remember. But I have no authority over Stephen. He hardly even knows me.''

"You can't just give up and let him do what he wants. I don't want to waste a day leading him around, but I don't want you to lose a son, either!''

Joe smiled. "Then perhaps you'll do me a favor.''

"What?'' Jessie eyed him warily. He obviously had a scheme in mind, and he had just as obviously maneuvered her into a position where she had to agree to do it.

"Follow him. Don't let him know it. Just stay close enough to get him out of trouble if he needs it. If nothing happens and he manages to find his way to the camp, then he'll never have to know. But if he loses his way or gets on the wrong side of a bear, you can rescue him.''

It wasn't a task Jessie relished. She didn't like the idea of sneaking along behind anybody, spying. And it still would be a waste of the entire day. But she knew that if she didn't do it, Joe would, and his damaged leg would ache terribly. Besides, her guilt wouldn't let her refuse, nor would the knowledge of all the good and kind things the Fergusons had done for her and her mother over the years. "You know I will, if that's what you want.''

"It's the best solution I can see.'' Ferguson smiled and patted her cheek. "I knew you'd be a sweet girl about it.''

Jessie grinned. "I'm always wax in your hands, Uncle Joe.''

He rolled his eyes. "Well, if only you'd told me that years ago, I might have been able to keep you on the straight and narrow.''

"I doubt it.''

"You're right.''

Jessie turned and started toward her desk. She paused and looked at Ferguson, her expression serious again. "I noticed you didn't tell your son why you've taken to sleeping in the room under the office.''

He shrugged. "No use dumping my load of troubles on the boy the minute he appears. He's got a whole different life to lead in St. Louis. I doubt he'll be here long. I don't want to take up what little time I've got with him talking about whatever bastard damaged our saw blade. Besides, what good would it do to tell him?"

"I guess you're right," she admitted. Stephen Ferguson didn't look like he'd be any help in finding and stopping whoever had broken into the mill a few weeks ago and broken the main saw blade. "But I wish you'd tell somebody. I don't like the idea of your staying here alone. What if he tries something else? You could get hurt."

Joe assumed a wounded expression. "It's nice to know that you think I couldn't handle the sneakin' coward by myself."

Jessie sighed. They'd been through this argument before, from the moment she and Joe looked at the blade and realized that it hadn't just broken but had been deliberately ruined. Joe had been staying at the mill ever since, hoping to catch the man in the act of committing another crime. But he refused to hire anyone to help him. He refused to even tell Sam about it, saying he didn't want his son leaving the camp to come help him in town.

"All right," Jessie said, raising her hands in surrender. "I know it's useless to argue with you."

She walked to her desk and sat, pulling the ledgers to her. But her mind wandered from the numbers to the more intriguing topic of the identity of the person who had damaged the blade. Who could it be? There weren't any rival timber businesses around that might want to grab Joe's share of the profit. And she could see no reason anyone else would want to hurt the mill; it could only damage the economy of the whole town, dependent as it was on the timber business. Joe suspected it was someone with a grudge against him or Sam. Jessie was inclined to agree, since it made little sense otherwise. Still, she couldn't imagine anyone holding that heavy a grudge against the Fergusons.

Shrugging, she pushed the thought out of her mind and tackled the ledgers once again. If she was going to waste the whole day tomorrow, she'd better put in some extra work now.

Jessie pushed the swinging door open with her back and turned into the dining room, balancing a heavy bowl in each hand. The men who ate at her mother's table were all large and hard-working; they had hearty appetites, so supper each evening was a large meal, consisting of several platters and dishes of food, which Jessie usually helped Amanda to carry in.

Most of the men were already seated at the long table when she entered the room that evening. One man, however, stood to the side, hands clasped behind his back, as if he was waiting for something. It was Stephen Ferguson.

It was all Jessie could do to keep from gasping when she saw him. He had changed out of the clothes he had worn this afternoon. That fact alone was amazing—how many times a day did this man change clothes?—but what nearly caused her to lose her composure was the way that he looked in them. Jessie had never before met a man whose physical appearance could be so...well, dazzling, almost. Stephen had obviously washed away the dust of the road. His hair was its true deep black, glossy and thick, and his features seemed sharper and more distinct. The suit he wore was black, and though Jessie had thought there could be nothing more elegant than the gray suit he had worn earlier, this one was. Instead of a jacket and waistcoat, he wore a short frock coat, fitted close to his body. A snow-white shirtfront gleamed between the lapels of his jacket, and around his neck was a white cravat, fastened with a costly gold stickpin. Matching gold cuff links glittered at his wrists.

There was nothing ostentatious about him. The cravat pin and cuff links were his only jewelry. Jessie had seen other men, usually gamblers, who wore more than one gold ring, as well as huge jeweled tiepins, jeweled cuff links, and gold watches and chains with ornate little fobs dangling from them. No, Stephen Ferguson's manner of dress was quiet, even reserved, but only a fool would not have seen that years of gentility and wealth lay in what he wore.

It was a style that suited him. He was heartbreakingly handsome, and the expensive simplicity of his clothes provided a perfect frame for his good looks. Jessie thought wryly that Stephen Ferguson probably had no lack of ladies competing for his favors in his slick, rich world. She thought of her denim trousers and flannel shirt. They were much washed and faded, the pants almost white at the knees and the shirt with a pocket that had torn away at the corner. Jessie could imagine what a plain country bumpkin she must look to Stephen, and she could feel the heat of embarrassment rising in her face, even as she told herself that she didn't care what a man like that thought.

"Miss Randall," he said to her, nodding slightly.

"Mr. Ferguson." She kept her voice cool and hoped that her face looked uncaring. She walked past him to set down the bowl and reached toward her chair to pull it back.

Much to her surprise, Stephen pulled the chair out for her. She stared at him for a moment, then glanced at the chair. Somewhat cautiously, she sat down and started to pull it up to the table, but she found that he was pushing the chair in, too. She had lifted her bottom partway off the seat to pull the chair, and when he pushed it in, the chair hit the back of her legs and she plopped down ungracefully. Color flooded her face, and she kept her eyes turned down.

He walked away, and she followed him out of the corner of her eye. Her mother had entered the dining room and set her dish down, and now Stephen was jumping to pull out her chair, too. Jessie was chagrined to notice that her mother accomplished being seated with grace and ease, smiling a thank-you at the young man. Jessie began to eat quickly and silently, glowering at her plate. She felt embarrassed, which irritated her, and she disliked Stephen Ferguson for being the cause of both feelings.

Most of the men fell to their food with concentration,

just as Jessie did, but her mother, Joe and Stephen kept up a lively conversation as they ate. Jessie noticed that several of the men kept shooting curious glances at Stephen, though none of them showed open amusement or contempt, as she had half-expected they would. J.D. Bowden, the little bank clerk, practically fawned over him. That was to be expected. Though he couldn't aspire to Stephen's modish attire, he was the sort who would be impressed by it. He, too, never worked with his hands, spending his days counting up Elias Moore's money, and no matter what the weather, he dressed always in the same outfit of conservative black suit and white shirt with celluloid cuffs and a collar so stiff and tight he looked as if he was about to choke. Jessie suspected that he had already assessed Stephen's wardrobe and added up its total expense; the cost in itself would be enough to make Bowden admire him.

It was the fact that the three other men treated Stephen with deference that surprised—even annoyed—Jessie. They were laboring men, and Jessie couldn't understand why they didn't think Stephen Ferguson was a useless decoration of a man. There were just some people, she supposed, who must be awed by the trappings of wealth.

Amanda and the Ferguson men made a few attempts to draw Jessie into their conversation, but her brief replies soon made it clear that she had no interest in being included, and after that their conversation flowed onward with never a glance or remark in her direction. Even though she realized that she was being silly, the fact that they left her out made her even more disgruntled.

After supper Jessie helped her mother clear the table and clean the dishes. "Well," Amanda said without preamble once all the men were out of earshot, "you certainly weren't friendly to our new guest."

"I didn't see any reason to butter him up," Jessie replied coolly.

Amanda stopped, one hand on her hip, and gave her daughter a long look. "You think that's what I was doing?"

Jessie shrugged, unwilling to meet her mother's eyes. She knew Amanda had not been buttering him up. Her mother didn't believe in it. That was what made it even worse; Amanda must actually like the man. "Well, I don't know anything else to call it."

"He's a charming young man."

"You like all those airs and graces he puts on? I think it's silly. Like putting you and me in our chairs—as if I wasn't capable of sitting down by myself!"

"He was being polite."

"Polite! Polite's a man tipping his hat to you or saying please and thank you and excuse me."

"Or a man opening a door for you, or letting you walk through first—or pulling out your chair for you."

"Well, I never said I liked those things, either."

"That's because very few men do them for you. The men out here are rough. Most of them don't have much polish or sophistication. But they'd treat you with more courtesy if you didn't always act as if you were a boy. Why, you've worked at it so hard, everyone practically thinks you *are* one!"

"Well, I don't need all those polite folderols. What good do they do?"

"They make you feel special. Feminine. Surely you wouldn't mind it if men treated you like a woman?"

"I don't want to be treated like a woman. I want to be treated like an equal."

"Wearing trousers and clumping around in boots doesn't make you an equal." Amanda, who had started picking up the utensils from the table as they talked, paused to point a fork at Jessie for emphasis. "It makes them not respect you."

"That's not true!" Jessie retorted, stung.

"You know what you look like when you dress that way? A *boy*, not a man. And not a grown woman, either. Just a child. You know what I think? I think you wear those clothes because you're scared."

"Scared!" Jessie let out a short, indignant laugh.

"Yes, scared."

"I ain't scared of nobody."

"You're scared of yourself. Or men, or something. You're scared to act like a woman, to admit that you are one."

Jessie stared. She and Amanda had argued most of her life about the clothes Jessie wore, but she had never before heard her mother speak so harshly or bluntly about it. "Mama!"

Amanda sighed. "I'm sorry, honey. It's just that when I see a nice young gentleman like that Stephen Ferguson come into town, so handsome and charming, I always wish that you would—"

"Stephen Ferguson! Mama, you can't be serious! You think that I would have any interest in a man like that? A dandy? A greenhorn? Why, he's so ignorant he doesn't even know that he doesn't know anything. He looks like somebody just took him out of a bandbox, all clean and starched and pressed."

"Jessamine Randall! I'm ashamed of you. Judging a man by the clothes he wears or where he comes from. It's what's inside a man that counts, not how he dresses."

"I'm not! I mean, well, this is different. It's not just the clothes he wears—it's everything about him. Why, he even carts a servant around with him everywhere he goes. Can't he dress himself? I bet Stephen Ferguson can't do a single thing that's useful, and even if he could, he wouldn't, because it might dirty his jacket, or maybe even his hands." She made an expression of mock horror.

"You certainly think you know a lot about the man for a girl who's hardly spoken to him."

"I saw him. I heard him. I've seen how he acts."

"I know." Amanda pulled a long face. "So polite, so charming—terrible of him, isn't it?"

Jessie rolled her eyes. "Mama, you might as well give up. I'm not interested in any man, and most especially not in Stephen Ferguson. How could I feel anything for a man I can't even respect?"

"I don't know, Jessie," Amanda said, shaking her head. "I just wish you could find a man you could respect. But I don't know how that's going to happen if you don't stop comparing every man you meet to Sam."

Jessie smiled fondly. "But Sam's the best. There's no one like Sam."

Amanda sighed. "I know. I know. But he's not the man to pin your hopes on."

"I know Sam would never marry me!" Jessie would never admit that she had entertained that daydream more than once. She had always declared that she never intended to marry, but she knew deep in her heart that if Sam were to ask her, she wouldn't hesitate for a second. She had practically worshipped him ever since she could remember. As far as she was concerned, Sam Ferguson could do no wrong, and it made her want to burst with pride and joy whenever he smiled at her or said that she'd done a job well. "I'm not stupid. I'm not the kind of woman he'd marry. Besides, he thinks I'm still a baby."

Jessie knew Sam would never feel love or desire for her. He treated her like a younger sister—or, really, more like a younger brother! Even to think of marrying Sam was like crying for the moon. She'd never get it, and she wouldn't waste her time thinking about it.

"It's not that you aren't good enough for him," her mother went on reassuringly. "Any man would be lucky to marry you. But Sam is a lot older than you, and he's known you since you were knee high to a grasshopper. He cares for you, but..."

Jessie shrugged, unwilling to let her mother see that she cared how Sam felt about her. "I know, Mama. And I know it's not the way a man cares for a woman he's going to marry. It doesn't matter. I don't want to get married. I'm happy as I am."

Amanda's look was a little skeptical, but she didn't say anything. Arguing with Jessie only turned her stubborn as a government mule. They finished cleaning the table in silence.

Jessie went upstairs to her room, where she undressed and washed up quickly, then pulled on her modest white cotton gown. She turned down her bed; she was used to going to sleep early and rising early. But tonight she felt unaccountably restless, and she didn't lie down immediately. Instead she wandered to the window and stood looking out. Beyond the town stood the dark bulk of the mountains; a full yellowish moon hung suspended at the top of one peak, as though it had been speared by the dark thrusting point. She leaned against the window frame and gazed at it, dreamily lost in contemplation.

A scraping noise brought her out of her moonstruck trance, and she glanced into the yard below. A man stood in the side yard, clearly illuminated by the full moon. He was smoking a cigar; now and then it glowed red as he drew on it. He was turned away from her, so that she could not see his face, but she knew who he was. It was Stephen Ferguson, stepping outside for a last cigar. Polite, of course—he wouldn't dream of stinking up her mother's house with a cigar.

Jessie watched him. He, too, was gazing at the moon hanging over the mountains. She wondered what he thought as he looked at the sight. She couldn't imagine anyone from the city really understanding that wild, stark beauty, feeling it to the depths of his soul, as she did. Yet he stared, as intent and motionless as she had been.

He'd do better to come upstairs and go to his bed, she thought with a touch of acerbity. If he didn't get up early tomorrow morning, he'd be hard pressed to make it to the camp and back in one day. She grimaced. Stephen Ferguson probably wouldn't even roll out of bed until eight or nine o'clock. He was a gentleman of leisure, after all.

Jessie sighed. She didn't want to wait that long on him. Heck, she didn't want to have to follow him at all. But she'd promised Joe, and she would never go back on her word. She'd trail him until he got lost, then take him by the hand and lead him to the camp. It promised to be a long, boring day.

Below her Stephen turned, dropping his cigar and stubbing it out. Jessie jumped to the side of the window so that he wouldn't see her if he happened to glance up. She watched him as he walked into the house. In the moonlight his face was pale and handsome. She supposed that most women would find him attractive; they probably swooned all over him. But not her. Not her.

before the wedding, dropping his pipe and almost...
...boy it out, let us turned to the side of the window to that...
...he wouldn't see her... he happened to glance the slow...
...arched hand to be dashed into the house. In the moonlight...
...he face was pale and frowning. Jess supposed that most...
...woman would find him attractive, they probably swooned...
...at his charming smile... she...

Chapter Four

Much to Jessie's surprise, Stephen Ferguson came down to breakfast the next morning at six o'clock, when Amanda first started serving. Jessie was sitting at the table, sipping a cup of coffee and wondering how she was going to pass the time until he got up, when he walked through the door.

Her eyebrows rose in surprise, not only because of the early hour, but because of his dress. She had expected him to wear another one of those fancy suits. He was as immaculate as ever, not a hair out of place or a wrinkle in his clothes, but he wore simple denim trousers and a dark blue flannel shirt, with a sleeveless leather vest over it, just like any man around here might wear. He even had on riding boots, though they were of a smooth, glossy brown leather so polished that one could see one's face in them.

He smiled at her expression. "I thought casual clothing might be in order today. I went to Millburn's General Store yesterday afternoon and purchased these. What do you think? Do I look like less of a tenderfoot now?"

His tone was gently mocking. Jessie shrugged sourly. "Don't matter how you look. It's what's inside that counts."

He chuckled. "Can't get the better of you, can I, Miss Randall?"

"Don't feel bad," she told him cockily, lifting her chin. "I don't know any man who can."

His eyes were bright with amusement. "I imagine that's true."

"So, are you getting an early start?"

He nodded, dishing up eggs, bacon and biscuits from the sideboard. "Yes. I thought that was wisest. My father indicated that the way was rather rough and slow-going."

"Do you ever talk like a regular man?"

"Pardon?" He glanced at her in surprise.

"I said, don't you ever talk just like people?"

He paused, as though turning her statement over in his mind, then said, "Yes. Just like *some* people. But apparently I don't speak as the people around here do. Is that right?"

She made a brief grunt of amusement. "That's right."

"Is that why you don't like me?" he asked calmly. "Because I'm different?"

"I didn't say I didn't like you."

"Perhaps not. But somehow I've received that impression."

"I can't help what you think."

"Then you do like me?"

"I didn't say that, either."

"Then what are you saying?"

"I'm saying I don't know you, and I don't think about you one way or the other."

"I see. Well, that certainly puts me in my place."

Jessie set down her cup and pushed her chair from the table. Talking to Stephen Ferguson made her feel slightly uneasy. Besides, she had planned to saddle up before he left and wait for him outside town, but to do that now she would have to hurry.

"Well, it's been real nice chatting with you, Mr. Ferguson."

"The feeling's mutual."

"I'll see you around."

"Off to work so early? I hope I haven't chased you away."

Jessie stiffened. "Nobody chases me away. I have things I have to do, is all."

He nodded. "Of course. Goodbye, Miss Randall."

"Yeah." She turned and walked through the kitchen door, very aware of his eyes following her.

Thirty minutes later, Jessie was seated cross-legged on a boulder, hidden from the road by a thick stand of trees and elderberry shrubs, waiting for Stephen to ride by. Her horse was nearby, tied to one of the low branches of the elderberry.

At last her patience was rewarded by the sound of a horse's hooves thudding against the packed dirt of the road. Jessie scrambled off the rock and over to her horse. She laid a hand over the mare's muzzle to keep her quiet and watched the road through the branches of the bushes. In a moment Stephen passed by on the horse Joe had lent him. He was moving at a canter, glancing all around him curiously. Jessie stifled a sigh. With the way he was gazing at the scenery, he was bound to miss the cutoff he was supposed to take, as well as the identifying landmarks. His mind obviously wasn't on what he was supposed to be doing.

She untied the horse as she let Stephen get well ahead of her. Then she led the mare to road and mounted her from a fallen log. She started down the road after Stephen Ferguson. She didn't worry about losing him; she had the imprint of his horse's hooves in the damp soil to follow, and she knew of two or three places along the way where she would have a high, panoramic view of the area through which he was traveling.

To her surprise, Stephen did not miss the road that cut off to the lumber camp. Road—they all called it that, but in reality it was little more than a track, just wide enough to allow the supply wagons up to the camp. Here, the ground was covered with a soft cushion of pine needles, and it was difficult to follow the trail. So when she came to the edge of a clearing, Jessie stopped and shinnied up a tree to look for him. She managed to catch sight of Stephen disappearing into the trees at the opposite end of the long, narrow clearing. He was still on the right path.

Jessie climbed down, gave him a few moments to get into the trees, then crossed the clearing herself. So far, he was exceeding her expectations. It was another forty-five minutes before he lost his way.

It was the stream that did him in. Stephen had followed the map for some time, feeling a little smug at finding the proper path. But when he had come upon a tumbling, narrow creek he had been so delighted that he had dismounted and cupped a handful of the icy water. As his horse drank, Stephen squatted and examined the pebbled bed of the stream. It was covered with rocks ranging from small to tiny, so smooth and flat they looked almost as if they had been laid, like a road. The rocks were colored in shades of rose, blue, green and yellowish tan, as well as flat black and charcoal gray. He found when he picked up a few and held them in his hand that they dried to a dustier, duller shade, but under the water they glistened brightly, giving the clear stream almost jewel-like tones.

Unconsciously, he moved slightly downstream, leading his horse, as he gazed at the rocks, bending now and then to pick one up. So when he finally crossed the stream, he came out further southeast than he had intended, and as he turned north to correct his mistake, he passed several yards away from the yellowish rock that was the next landmark on the map. It didn't take him long to realize that he must have missed the rock, and he retraced his steps, to no avail. He began to roam, searching for it, and soon found himself in a stand of lodgepole pine, thoroughly confused.

Stephen took a deep breath and struck out through the woods. He had to find his way out and get on the path. He couldn't get lost, not after the way he'd shrugged off Joe's warnings. That strange girl who worked for his father would have a good laugh at his expense. His lips tightened at the thought of her laughing in his face, and he pushed on through the trees. Eventually he came out of the stand of tall, narrow pines and into a small alpine meadow. He sighed with relief.

He had been climbing ever since he had left town this morning, and now he was quite high up. All around him was a soaring, magnificent view of the mountains and valleys, so grand it took his breath away. Stephen thought that he had never seen a land so wild and untamed in its beauty.

But it wasn't long before unease encroached upon his wonder. He still didn't know where he was. Had he come out of the trees above, below or to the side of where he had gone in? Now able to see the sun again, he could move northward, but if he was starting off from the wrong place, his northward movement could take him far to one side of the camp. He understood now why his father had been so concerned about him going alone, how difficult it would be to find something as small as a camp of men in an area as vast as this and how easy it was to miss or mistake a landmark. It had been foolhardy of him to try to ride to the camp without a guide.

Damn! Why had he been so stubborn? Why hadn't he listened to the wiser counsel of his father, who knew this part of the country? Why had he had to get his back up at the amusement on Jessie Randall's face, so that he'd insisted on doing this alone? Idiotic male pride, that was all it had been. He had hated to think he had to be led by a mere slip of a girl. He had hated for Jessie to think so, too.

With a curse, Stephen swung down from his horse and began to walk across the clearing, thinking. It did no good to bewail his stupidity. What he needed to do was get out of this situation.

As he paced, deep in thought, he heard a sound and turned. At the far edge of the clearing sat a person on horseback. Stephen straightened, a smile beginning on his face. Thank God, someone had happened along. Now he could get directions to the lumber camp. He mounted quickly and trotted across the meadow. Across from him the stranger also started forward.

As they drew nearer, Stephen could make out the person's features, and he realized it wasn't a stranger. He reined up short. It was Jessie Randall.

Blood rushed into Stephen's face. Of all the people to come across him! Why did it have to be her? Everything she had thought about him would be confirmed.

Then he realized that she couldn't have just happened by; that was far too coincidental. She must have come after him. His father had sent her to make sure he didn't get lost. His humiliation was complete.

He waited for her stiffly, his face a blank mask to hide the embarrassment and frustration burning within him. It had taken years of rigid social and business training to acquire that polite, expressionless veneer, which allowed others no glimpse of his weaknesses.

However, to Jessie, riding across the meadow toward him, the frozen expression on his face merely looked like arrogance. It irritated her. Imagine that! Here he was lost, exposed to danger from wild animals, starvation, thirst and the chill of the nights. And here she was, coming to save him. But all he could do was sit on his horse, looking haughty, as if she were a servant who had showed up late for her job. Jessie gritted her teeth and pulled to a stop a few feet away from him.

"Mr. Ferguson," she said, with a brief nod.

Stephen read the clear contempt in her eyes, and he had seen the little smile on her lips as she rode toward him. His feeling of humiliation deepened. It was obvious that she thought of him as something less than a man. He didn't stop to analyze why her opinion of him should matter. He just reacted to his inner writhing by setting his spine straighter and his eyes harder. "Miss Randall."

Jessie glanced around the meadow and raised a mocking eyebrow. "Stopping for a rest?"

Stephen clamped his teeth together so hard that a muscle along his jaw jumped. His embarrassment sizzled into an-

ger. She hadn't a drop of womanly gentleness, prodding at
his sorest spot like that. "Hardly," he ground out, his eyes
cold and hard as marbles. "As I'm sure you are well aware,
I have lost my way."

"Oh, really? I couldn't tell it from your face."

"I'm sorry." His tone indicated that he was anything but
sorry. "Didn't I grovel enough for you? Was I lacking in
the proper amount of humble gratitude?"

Jessie's cheeks flamed at his sarcastic tone. "I didn't say
that!"

"But it's what you meant, isn't it? I was aware that you
had no interest in being a woman, looking and acting the
way you do, but I didn't realize until now that you don't
want a man to act like a man, either. What suits you? You
play the man while he whimpers and crouches at your
feet?"

"Act like a man!" She whipped off her hat, and the sun
glinted off the red-gold of her hair, plaited into a single
braid as thick as her wrist.

Strangely, a tendril of lust curled through Stephen's abdomen. She looked wild and fierce and untamable, a challenge to his maleness, and he knew a sudden, aching need
to conquer her in the most basic way. It was so swift and
piercing a desire that it almost took his breath away. He
knew that he wanted to curl his hand around that thick red
braid and pull her to him. He wanted to kiss her as hard
and as deep as he could, until she softened and trembled.
The idea left him so stunned and thrumming with lust that
he could not speak, could only sit and stare at her as she
railed at him.

"What do you know about acting like a man?" Jessie
continued hotly. "I never met anybody who acted less like
one! You're more a tailor's dummy than a man. It's obvious that you don't know how to do anything, that you have
to take a servant along with you to do the hard work, that
you're a—a—"

"A what?" he snapped, as irritated with himself and his
bizarre, lustful reaction to her as he was irritated at Jessie

herself. "A greenhorn? A tenderfoot? I believe that's what you called me before. I'm not a Westerner, so I'm not a man? Isn't that what you're saying? This may surprise you, Miss Randall, but there's a lot more to this world than this one little spot in the Montana Territory. In most places, being able to cut down a tree or blaze a trail through the wilderness or spit tobacco and hit a bug at ten feet is not the measure of a man. In a great deal of the world, culture, courtesy, a good mind, a strong character, a sense of honor and duty—these are what make up a man. Not thick muscles or a sure aim with a gun."

"Fancy words!" Jessie scoffed, unable to come up with any adequate retort.

"No doubt that makes them valueless to you," he responded dryly.

"You're twisting what I said. I never said that a bull neck or a bullhead was what made a man."

"No? Then what is your beau ideal?"

"My what?"

"Your perfect man?"

"He's—he's someone you can respect, someone you can look up to. He's strong and quick, but his mind's sharp, too. He knows how to take care of himself. And he can take care of other people. He comes when you need him, and he does what has to be done. He's truthful, loyal and brave. He doesn't go back on his word."

Jessie's face had softened as she talked, until she looked almost dreamy, staring off into the distance, her eyes glowing.

"Somehow I feel this is a real man you're describing." Stephen's tone was sharp; he found her moony expression decidedly irritating.

She looked at him with wide, honest eyes. "I am. It's Sam. Samuel Ferguson."

"My brother."

"Yes."

"I'm glad to hear that my brother is such a paragon." Stephen wondered if Samuel knew that this strange young

woman was so enamored of him. Perhaps he did. Perhaps
he encouraged it. Her behavior might be strange, but there
was no denying that she was a pretty woman, with that
thick, flaming hair and big, brilliant blue eyes. Any man
might want her for his mistress—if he was able to put up
with her sharp tongue and outrageous ways. She would
never do in St. Louis or New York, of course, but out
here...

His mind turned away from the idea, reluctant to accept
her as Samuel's mistress. After all, she was a young girl
still, and despite her peculiarities, he suspected that she was
rather innocent. Her mother seemed every inch a lady. He
didn't like to think that his brother would take advantage
of Jessie's obvious admiration for him.

Jessie glanced at Stephen. She felt a little foolish for
having revealed her admiration for Sam. She hoped he
wouldn't make a joke about it to Sam. She couldn't imagine
why she'd said such things to him. Or, frankly, why she'd
said any of the other things she had. Joe, even Sam, would
probably have been appalled at her verbal attack on Stephen. However arrogant or sissified he might be, he was,
after all, their flesh and blood. And her mother! Jessie hated
to even think what *her* reaction would be.

She wasn't sure why she had gotten so angry. She had
expected him to get lost before she even set out. In fact,
he had done better and gotten farther than she had expected.
And what did it matter to her if he was an indolent, useless
ornament of a man? It was nothing to do with her.

It was just that she had had a little trouble finding him,
and she had even begun to worry that she might not be
able to. It had been scary coming through the stand of lodgepole pines, unable to follow his tracks on the carpet of
needles, and she had been swept with relief when she had
emerged into the mountain meadow and seen him. She'd
ridden toward him, smiling with relief. Then she had run
into the blank wall of his face.

Stephen hadn't been pleased to see her. You would think
that someone who was hopelessly lost would be happy to

see a rescuer. But not the high-and-mighty Mr. Stephen Ferguson. Oh, no. He'd just looked annoyed, as though she should have arrived earlier. Then, in that superior tone of his, he had accused her of wanting him to grovel and lavish her with thanks, and he had made a few sarcastic jabs about her lack of femininity. As if she weren't a woman just because she liked to wear comfortable clothes! Or maybe it was because she was more competent than he was that he thought she wasn't womanly enough.

His smug, biting comments had been like a torch to tinder, and she had immediately flared up. Jessie didn't understand how a nice man like Joe Ferguson could have such an exasperating son. She couldn't think of any other man who got on her nerves as easily as Stephen did. She thought he liked to do it.

Jessie squared her shoulders. Well, she wasn't going to give him the satisfaction of setting her anger ablaze again. Let him be as annoying as he liked. She would simply ignore him.

The rest of the ride to the lumber camp was a silent one.

The camp lay in a man-made clearing in the forest at the end of the narrow track Jessie had followed. There was a large, rough log building with a steeply pitched roof in the center of the clearing, and a smaller one to the side.

"That's the bunkhouse," Jessie explained, pointing to the bigger building. "And that's the cook shack. Over there are the stables, and that little house there is the headquarters. That's where Sam stays."

A man emerged from the cook shack and dumped a bucket of dirty water onto the ground.

"Hello, Cookee," Jessie called.

The short, slight man looked up and grinned. His hair was white and thinning, and half his teeth were missing. "Well, hi there, Jess. Wasn't expectin' ta see you 'roun' here."

"I made a surprise trip. Is Sam around?"

The man gestured toward a ramshackle building. "He's

in there, doin' some scribblin' and figurin'. I reckon he'll be glad for the interruption.''

Jessie grinned. "I reckon." She turned toward Stephen, and her smile died abruptly. "Come on."

She led the way to the building Cookee had indicated and jumped lightly down, tying her horse's reins to a nearby bush. Stephen followed suit. His heart was beginning to pound, and his throat swelled with excitement. Finally, after all these years, he was going to see Sammy again. He didn't know whether to grin or run.

He followed Jessie into the low building. A large, dark-haired man sat at a table near the window, his head bent over his work. He glanced up curiously at the sound of Jessie's entrance.

"Howdy, Sam," Jessie greeted him.

"What the hell are you doing up here?" Sam responded, jumping up. "Is Pa all right?"

Hastily Jessie reassured him that Joe was fine. There was a narrow bed against one wall, and a man lay on it. He was awakened by their voices and sat up. Stephen recognized him as the older man from the stage depot the day before. What was it Jessie had called him? Burley, he believed.

The old man stared at Stephen, and his mouth dropped. "Hellfire 'n' brimstone!" he exclaimed. "If it ain't the dude!"

Sam's eyes slid across to Stephen, really taking him in for the first time. He went utterly still as he gazed at him.

Stephen looked back. His heart was pounding in his chest. It was so strange to look at this man and see the resemblance to himself, to remember the boy he had been and see traces of that child in his face. Sam was about Stephen's height, with the same wide-shouldered build, though he was far more heavily muscled. His hair was dark, but still a shade lighter than Stephen's, and a black mustache spread across Sam's upper lip. His features were heavier and rougher than Stephen's, and his skin was weathered by the elements. Still, there was no denying the resemblance.

"Hello, Sammy."

"Stephen?" Sam's voice slid upward questioningly. "My God."

Sam started toward him, and Stephen thought he meant to hug him. But before he reached him, the dawning wonder on Samuel's face faded, and he hesitated, then held out his hand to shake Stephen's. The gesture was formal, even remote, and Stephen could see the wariness in his eyes. His brother wasn't too sure whether he liked having him return.

Stephen's heart fell a little. After his father's happy greeting, he guessed that he had expected too much from Samuel. Sam had been only a boy when he left; he had grown up without Stephen. No doubt Stephen was little more than a distant memory to him; being the older, he wouldn't have remembered him through the years with the warmth that Stephen had felt. Stephen wouldn't mean that much to him anymore.

Stephen managed a smile. There was really no reason Samuel should welcome him back with open arms. It had been the dream of a boy to think that he would.

"It's been a long time," Sam said slowly.

"Yes, it has. Twenty-two years."

They continued to talk awkwardly, their conversation filled with long pauses. Sam moved restlessly around the room, seemingly unable to stay still.

Stephen grew more and more uncomfortable. The two of them had little to say to each other. With Joe, the conversation had flowed fast and free, very naturally.

Stephen told Sam about their mother's death, but Sam expressed no sympathy. "Don't expect me to mourn her," he told Stephen. "She means no more to me dead than she did alive."

An angry retort in defense of his mother rose in Stephen's throat. He pushed it down and glanced away. He loved his mother, but, after all, he had experienced her gentle kindness and love all his life. Samuel hadn't really known her. No doubt the main thing he remembered of Eleanor was her leaving him. Stephen supposed that nothing could ever make up for that. He felt saddened and suddenly tired.

There was nothing else to say between them, Stephen realized. He took out the packet of envelopes Eleanor had left for Samuel and gave them to his brother. Sam took the ribbon-tied bundle and tossed it down onto the rough table without even looking at it.

Again there was a long silence. Behind Samuel, Jessie shifted uneasily. She shot a glance at Sam. She knew how he felt about his mother. That subject was a closed book, one he never opened. She understood; she couldn't imagine a mother who could so callously take off and leave her son behind. Worse yet, she'd taken one son, the favored one, and left the other behind. Unwanted. Unchosen. Sam had carried that pain within him most of his life, though, being the kind of man he was, he never talked about it.

She was sorry that Stephen had come along and reminded him of it. Still, she couldn't help but feel a little sorry for Stephen, much as she disliked the man. She knew well enough that it wasn't any fun to face that cold-fish stare of Sam's; it shriveled her right down to her toes. And, after all, Stephen wasn't responsible for what his mother had done. It wasn't his fault that Nora Ferguson had wanted him and not Sam.

Jessie had suspected that Sam wouldn't be as happy to have his long-lost brother turn up as Joe had thought he would be. But there was no point in letting the meeting degenerate into a fight, which was the direction Sam seemed to be heading in right now. Joe wouldn't like it for anything if she brought back his baby boy all bruised up at Sam's hands.

So she stepped forward, planting herself between the two brothers. "We'd better be going. I told Uncle Joe we'd be back before dark."

Stephen hesitated, then agreed. There was no point in prolonging this painful experience. Perhaps if Sam was given a little time he would come around. Stephen paused at the door and looked at his brother. "Goodbye, Sam. I'll see you again before I leave."

"No doubt you will. I'll be down in a few days. I make sure I see Pa every week or so," Sam said pointedly.

Stephen stepped off the porch behind Jessie and followed her to their horses. "Is he always that friendly?" he asked as they swung up into their saddles.

"Sam has his reasons." Jessie flared up in Sam's defense. "I don't reckon it would feel very nice to know that your mother didn't want you."

"It wasn't like that," Stephen began, then gave up. There was no reason to try to explain his mother to this girl. Instead he changed the subject. "I'm sorry. I had hoped to see something of the operation here. I know very little about the lumber industry."

Jessie rolled her eyes. "That's obvious. There's nothing to see here now. Chopping only goes on in the winter. Sam and the cook are just getting the camp set up for the men. They won't arrive until the first of next month."

"They work in the dead of winter?" Stephen looked at her curiously. "I would have thought it was just the opposite. How can they move the logs with all the snow?"

"They use the cold." Even though she didn't like this man, Jessie was never reluctant to talk about the business she loved. "The road monkeys water down the skid so it's icy, and the sleds carrying the logs just slide right down."

Stephen frowned. "I don't see how they would keep from wrecking, then."

Jessie was surprised that he understood enough to recognize what the problems would be. "That's why the hay men, the drivers' assistants, run along throwing hay on the road in front of the sleds when they need to be slowed down."

"I see. You certainly seem to know the business."

Jessie shrugged. "I grew up in it. My pa was a chopper, and after that Ma worked for the Fergusons. Now I do."

She continued to tell him about the timber business, explaining how the choppers felled the trees, using a double-cut saw and working in teams of two, and going on through the entire process until the logs were driven down the river after the spring thaw by the most agile and daring of the crew.

Stephen listened with interest and asked curious questions that surprised Jessie with their perspicacity. After she ran down on the subject of felling the tall trees, Stephen began to ask her about the vegetation around them. She identified the trees and bushes, pointing out the lodgepole pines, the elderberry bushes, the mountain willow trees that clustered along the banks of the streams and a dozen other things. Though his interest in the country amazed her, she was equally surprised by the fact that, even though he must be disappointed by Sam's unfriendliness, he did his best not to inflict his bad feelings on her, instead keeping up a lively discussion.

Here was a man, she thought, who kept his temper under control. It wasn't a characteristic she was used to seeing in men. She wasn't sure what she thought about it. It seemed false, yet it was also rather pleasant and warming to think that he would change his behavior so that it would not bother her. After their argument this morning, she had been certain that she hated Stephen. Now she wasn't quite as sure.

The sun was low, about to sink behind the mountains, and shadows broadened around them. They crossed a swiftly running creek, safely shallow at this time of year, and emerged from a grove of trees into a small clearing. Jessie turned to say something to Stephen, so she missed the glint of sunlight on metal that flashed on the hillside.

But she heard the crack that echoed through the valley, and she saw Stephen jerk, his face showing more surprise than pain. One hand flew up to his chest, where red suddenly blossomed on his new shirt. He'd been shot!

Chapter Five

Stephen's horse shied at the noise of the rifle blast, and as it did, another shot rang out.

"Get down!" Jessie screamed, leaping off her horse and pulling the rifle from the saddle scabbard.

Stephen's horse danced and reared, and Stephen fell heavily to the ground. The horses took off as a third shot slammed into the ground behind Stephen's body. Jessie darted to Stephen, firing her rifle as she ran. She threw herself across him, shooting blindly in the direction from which the shots had come, but she couldn't pinpoint the exact location, so she had no chance of hitting anyone. Her only hope was that her return fire might frighten their attackers away before they could finish off the job.

Beneath her, Stephen groaned and tried to rise. Unceremoniously, Jessie shoved him down. "You want to get killed? Lie still!"

"Get off of me! Damn it!" He managed to wiggle out from beneath her. "I'm not hiding behind a woman while she—"

Jessie ran out of bullets.

The air was suddenly, heart-stoppingly quiet. The scent of cordite burned in their nostrils. Jessie lay motionless, her body tense, waiting. Beside her, Stephen was equally still. Jessie knew she was out of luck if the shooting started again, for she had grabbed only the rifle from the horse, not even thinking of the extra ammunition in the saddle-bags.

"Come on." She grabbed Stephen's arm and jumped to her feet, trying to pull him up with her. "Run for it!"

Stephen staggered to his feet, and they ran, stumbling, across the clearing and into the trees. There were no shots. They melted deeper into the trees and stopped, staring at the hillside where their attacker had been. Seconds passed as they waited tensely.

Jessie drew a steadying breath. "He must have run off."

"Or decided to come down the mountainside and finish it close up."

Jessie shot Stephen a disgusted look. "You're a real cheerful—" She stopped short.

Stephen was leaning heavily against a pine, his face drained of color, his eyes narrow slits. Red stained the front of his shirt. When he was first shot, Jessie had been afraid he'd been killed, but when he'd started talking and moving and had even managed to run, she had assumed that the wound was minor. Now she realized how wrong she had been.

"Good God." She leaned the rifle against a tree and went to Stephen, swiftly unbuttoning his shirt and pulling the sides apart. He had taken the bullet in his left shoulder. His chest was bathed in blood.

She pulled his shirt the rest of the way off and tore it into strips. She wadded one up and pressed it against the wound. Stephen's breath hissed in, and his face turned paler, but he said nothing. With a shaking hand, Jessie took his arm and turned him so that she could see his back. There was no hole, which meant that the bullet was still inside him. Jessie held the bandage against his shoulder, waiting for the flow of blood to slow or end—and also for the shaking in her limbs to stop.

She couldn't let him die. She had to get him to town, where the doctor could care for him. Jessie glanced around, wondering if even now the assassin was circling through the trees, stalking them. She had to fetch the ammunition from her horse. She had to bandage Stephen's wound before he bled to death. What should she do first?

Jessie closed her eyes, concentrating on regaining her calm. She must have a plan of action. First things first. She couldn't go searching for her horse and leave Stephen here bleeding, or she'd be taking a corpse to town. Therefore, step one was to bandage him.

It restored her confidence somewhat to make the decision, and her fingers worked quickly and with only a slight trembling as she tossed away the blood-soaked pad and folded up a new one to replace it. "Here. Sit down while I bandage you."

She put his hand on the pad where hers had been and had him hold it. Then she tied the remaining clean strips of his shirt together and wrapped the resulting long strip tightly around his chest and over his shoulder several times. When she was finished, she sat back on her heels and checked her handiwork. It was a sloppy bandage, nowhere near her mother's quality. She had watched her mother work on wounded men over the years and had picked up what to do, but she had never been very good at it. However, the thing was tight enough to stop the blood flowing, and that was all that was necessary. Besides, it was all she had time for.

She glanced at Stephen's face. His eyes were closed, and his skin had a gray tinge to it. Jessie bit her lip. *Oh, please, God, don't let him die.* "I'm going after the horses," she told Stephen.

He gave a little nod to signify that he had heard.

"I'll be right back," she added, guilt swelling in her at the thought of leaving him alone and defenseless. But she had to find the horses, and she obviously couldn't drag him along with her while she did it! She couldn't even leave him a weapon; the gun was useless without the bullets. "Here." She laid the rifle beside him. "There aren't any bullets in it, but maybe you could scare him off."

"Sure." Stephen opened his eyes and mustered up a

faint smile. "He'd probably quake in his boots to see me holding a gun."

Jessie smiled, a little reassured. Surely he wasn't near death if he was able to joke. "Just rest. Maybe some of your strength will come back."

She knew she was lying—weakness from loss of blood didn't abate that quickly. But maybe he didn't know it, and her words would make him feel better.

Jessie rose lithely to her feet and peered around her. She could see no sign of their horses. The gloom was rapidly deepening beneath the trees. Before long she wouldn't be able to see her hand in front of her face.

She started off rapidly in the direction the horses had gone. Her eyes moved constantly, looking for any sign of the horses—or the killer. He could be sneaking through the trees right at this moment, looking for them. She had to make sure she saw him first.

Finally Jessie spotted a glimmer of white ahead of her. Her horse was a brown and white paint. She took the chance of whistling softly. There came a whinny and a movement. She could see the mare now. Jessie crept cautiously forward. She couldn't afford to spook her. She murmured the mare's name in a low voice, extending her hand as though there were a treat in it. The mare shook her head, setting the bridle jingling, and walked toward Jessie. The animal's fear had left her, and she was content to rejoin Jessie, snuffling against her hand for the nonexistent apple or carrot. She blew out and rolled her eye at Jessie accusingly.

"Sorry, girl. But you get us back to town safe and you can have anything you want. That's a promise."

She couldn't see a sign of Stephen's horse anywhere. Well, it didn't really matter. At least she had ammunition, as well as the pistol in the saddlebag, and they could get to town on one mount.

Jessie led the horse to where Stephen was. He sat in the same spot, leaning against a tree, his eyes closed. "Stephen." She bent down and said his name again, gently pulling his hands and taking the rifle from him. Stephen's eyes fluttered open, and he looked at her in confusion.

"It's me. Jess," she told him. "I got my horse. I couldn't find the other one, but we can both ride mine to Nora Springs. It's not far." As she spoke, she was reloading the rifle.

Stephen's eyes cleared, and he nodded. Good. At least he was awake and aware of what was going on. He got clumsily to his feet, wincing as his movements intensified the pain in his chest. Jessie put her hands under one of his arms and pulled to help him up. It occurred to her that Stephen had gone through it all—the shooting, her bandaging and now getting up—with hardly a murmur, even though his wound must be throbbing with pain. It surprised her. She never would have figured this man would show any signs of stoicism.

"Now you'll have to mount the horse," she told him, leading him over to the mare.

Stephen looked at her, his eyebrows rising. "I'm not sure I can." He grasped the saddle horn with his right hand, but then did nothing more than lean against the horse.

"Damn! Excuse me."

Jessie realized that Stephen was apologizing for cursing in front of her, and she had to clap a hand over her mouth to stifle a giggle at the absurdity of his unwavering courtesy even in this deadly situation.

"I feel so weak." He sounded faintly surprised.

"You've lost a lot of blood," she explained.

He nodded. "It seemed rather much. But then, you see, I've never been shot before."

Was this man real? Hysterical laughter bubbled in her throat. "Well, that makes two of us," she said crisply to quell the hysteria. "I've never seen anyone shot, either."

"Really?" He glanced at her. "My man Charles tells me it happens all the time out here."

"Not that I've ever noticed."

"Perhaps they usually refrain around ladies."

Jessie grimaced. "Do you plan to stand around here

cracking wise all evening, or are you going to get on this horse?"

"Actually, I was hoping to avoid it." Stephen's face was as white as paper, and sweat dotted his upper lip. "I don't think I have the strength." He stepped back. "Tell you what: you ride into town and get help. I'll wait here."

"Don't be foolish. He might come back."

Stephen didn't ask who. His head wasn't clear enough to figure out why, but it was obvious that someone had tried to kill him. "I know. But what good will it do for you to be here, too, still struggling to get me on this horse? He'd simply kill both of us."

"I'm not leaving you." Jessie tried to smile to lighten the moment. "Your daddy would kill me for sure if I left you behind to die. At least this way I have a chance."

Stephen shook his head but didn't argue anymore. Jessie glanced around and found the stump of a fallen tree a few feet away.

"Over here." She led him and the horse to the tree trunk. "You can use this stump for a mounting block. It'll work. I've often gotten up that way. You can put your hand on my shoulder to help you climb up on the stump. Don't worry, I'm strong."

He nodded, braced himself with a hand on her shoulder and stepped onto the stump. It was difficult, and it made his head swirl for a moment. Jessie reined the horse in close, and, still balancing with his hand on her slim shoulder, Stephen climbed awkwardly into the saddle. His feet dangled ludicrously below the stirrups, and he was slumped in the saddle, both hands around the horn, but at least he was on.

Jessie hopped lightly onto the broken trunk. "Scoot back as far as you can, so I can get on in front of you. Then you can hold on to me to keep from falling off."

Again he nodded, then moved back, his hands leaving the saddle horn. Jessie swung carefully into the saddle, her movements almost as awkward as his had been, for she had to bring her leg over in front to keep from kicking Stephen.

She settled gingerly into the saddle. It wasn't big enough for two people, even people as slender as they were. The saddle horn pushed into her abdomen and the tender mound of her womanhood, and her bottom was cupped by Stephen's legs and pelvis. She found the position acutely embarrassing. She had never felt any part of a man's body flush against hers before, especially *that* part!

She gripped the reins tightly, reminding herself that this was no time to be thinking of trivial things like that. If she didn't get Stephen to the doctor in time, he could die. She tapped the mare's sides, urging her forward. Jessie didn't dare ride fast, much as she longed to, for she knew that Stephen would never be able to stay in the saddle. As it was, he was curved over her back, his head against hers, his arms wrapped around her waist, using all his strength just to stay on.

The slow, rocking gait of the horse rubbed Stephen's body against her. She could feel his thighs, his chest, his arms, sliding up and down her with every step. And in front the saddle horn pressed into her intimately, rubbing in a way that was somewhere between pleasure and pain. Jessie's breasts tingled, and she could feel the nipples puckering, as they did in the cold. Good Lord, what was the matter with her? Had she lost her mind? She couldn't remember ever feeling this bizarre licentious glow deep within her. It seemed insane, horrifying, that she should feel it now, with a wounded man hanging over her back and a killer maybe on their trail. It must be the shock; the whole incident had rattled her so badly that her mind was flying off in strange directions.

But she couldn't ignore the fact that in reality it was flying off in only *one* direction.

She was enormously grateful when at last she glimpsed the dark bulk of the buildings of Nora Springs ahead of them. It was night now, but the moon gave enough light to follow the path and pick out the shapes of the town. Jessie continued the nerve-rackingly slow pace into town. She could tell from the laxness of his body that Stephen had lost consciousness. He was hardly even holding on to her now, and she knew he'd pitch off into the road if she moved any faster. As it was, he was beginning to list to one side, and she had to stretch one arm awkwardly backward to keep him in the saddle.

She rode straight to her mother's house, and as she drew near, she began to shout for Amanda. By the time she pulled to a stop in the street, her mother was on the porch, holding up a lighted kerosene lamp and peering into the dark. "Jessie? Is that you? What's the matter?"

"Yeah, it's me. Ma, get the doc. And send the men out here to get Stephen off the horse."

Amanda didn't waste time with questions but stuck her head in the door and shouted urgently to the men who roomed there, then hurried into the street, holding up her lamp to illuminate Jessie and her burden on the horse. Amanda drew in her breath when she saw Stephen Ferguson leaning so limply against Jessie's back. "Oh, no! Lord in heaven, what happened? Did he fall off his horse?"

"He's been shot."

"Shot!" Amanda gasped, but she didn't have time for any more questions. Several men were running out the door and across the yard in answer to her summons, and she whirled to them to issue commands. Within seconds, one of the men was racing down the street to Doc Holzworth's house, and several others were carefully pulling Stephen from the saddle.

Jessie felt his weight leave her back, and she relaxed gratefully. It was over. She had done all she could, and now the responsibility was lifted from her shoulders. She slid from the saddle and gave the reins wordlessly to one of the men. Every muscle in her body hurt, and she was embarrassingly close to tears.

She followed her mother into the house and up the stairs. She could have stayed downstairs, could have gone into her room and fallen into the utter softness of the big feather bed. She could have closed her eyes and let the fear and tiredness drain out of her, could have slept and left the care of the wounded man in Amanda's capable hands. Instead she found herself trailing after the little procession into Stephen Ferguson's room. Somehow she could not let go of her responsibility for his life.

The men laid him on the bed and stepped back to give Mrs. Randall access. Carefully she cut through the primitive bandage Jessie had stuck on his chest and peeled it away. The pad stuck to his wound, dried stiff with blood, and she had to soak it before she was able to pull it off.

Stephen's eyes flew open, and a groan escaped his lips. He looked at Amanda without recognition. "Jessie?" He glanced around. "Jessie?"

"I'm right here." She stepped forward into his line of vision. "We got back home all right. The doctor'll be here in a few minutes."

A smile wavered on his lips. "Good. You're—safe then? Nothing happened?"

"Nothing."

He nodded. His eyes slid toward Amanda. "And you're—uh, Mrs. Randall. Am I right?"

"Yes. But don't worry your head about it. You lie still and let me tend to this wound."

Stephen's servant shouldered through the crowd of men in the hall and stopped just inside the door. He drew in a shocked gasp and stared, frozen. "Master Stephen!" he exclaimed finally and moved forward. "What happened to him? What's wrong?"

Jessie glanced at him. He looked as though he might start wringing his hands and crying at any moment. Her mother answered him, her voice calm, "He was shot. But he'll be all right."

Charles gripped the back of a chair, his eyes fixed on his employer. "You'd be better off going back to your room and letting Ma tend to him," Jessie told him.

"No. No, I couldn't leave him."

Jessie shrugged and turned to watch her mother, ignoring the man. Amanda soaked a cloth and began to clean the blood from Stephen's chest until the small, dark red hole made by the bullet was clearly visible. Jessie watched her mother's deft hands work. How light her mother's touch was; she never gave unnecessary pain. Jessie hadn't bothered to learn such things, hadn't thought them useful. "Serving skills," she had dubbed them with scorn, much as she had her mother's cooking and cleaning. But now she could see how, at times like these, they could be worth far more than any strength or intelligence.

"Is he going to be all right, Ma?" she asked, her hands twisting together.

"I don't know. First that bullet needs to come out." Amanda glanced at the men still crowded in the doorway. "Tom, has anyone notified Joe Ferguson?"

"Yeah. Burton ran down to the mill right after Jessie and him rode in. We sent for the marshal, too."

"Good." Her gaze swept over the men, and she spoke with a quiet, almost maternal authority. "Why don't you men go back to what you were doing? You aren't helping this man any, standing here gawking."

"Anything I can get you?" Tom asked, as the others began to move away.

"Jessie'll get it for me." Amanda turned toward Charles. "Why don't you go, too? There's nothing you can do for him."

"I couldn't, ma'am."

Amanda shrugged and turned to her daughter. "Help me get these boots off him. We might as well make him as comfortable as possible."

Jessie went to Stephen's feet and began to pull off one of his boots. They were tight-fitting and difficult to remove, although the fine, supple leather helped somewhat. Jessie had never removed a man's boots before, and it felt strange to do so, almost intimate. She remembered the way his body had felt behind her, the heavy weight, the warmth, and color rose in her face. She hoped her mother would mistake it for the flush of exertion, not embarrassment.

"Here, Miss, Madam, allow me." Charles came up beside them. A touch of humor gave his drained face some life. "I think this is one thing which *I* can do better."

Amanda and her mother turned the task over to him and walked away from the bed. "What happened, Jessie?" Amanda asked in a low voice.

"Somebody shot him. I don't know who. They were hidden on the hillside in the trees. All of a sudden I heard a shot, and there was Stephen with blood on his chest."

"Someone hunting, do you think? An accident?"

Jessie shook her head emphatically. "No. It couldn't have been. Ma, he shot three times. Three times! He hit Stephen with the first shot, then he fired again. But Stephen's horse was jumping around, and Stephen fell off. Then the fellow shot again. Nobody fires at you three times by mistake."

"No." Amanda's forehead creased. "But who? Why?"

Jessie shook her head. "I don't know. Nobody even knows Stephen."

Joe Ferguson burst into the room. His face paled when he saw his newfound son lying still on the bed. "Oh, my God. I thought—I couldn't believe it when they told me. How—what—Jess, girl, what happened?"

Jessie started to repeat her story for him, but just then Rob McSweeney pounded up the stairs to the door of Stephen's room. He was frowning. "Miz Randall, the doc ain't there. His wife said today's his day to go to Ransom. He sees people there every other week. She said he always spends the night there, and he won't come back till tomorrow." He paused and looked at her. "What do you want me to do? Ride to Ransom for him?"

"No," Joe Ferguson snapped. "Stephen could die by the time you got there and back." He turned toward Jessie's mother. "Amanda, you'll have to do it yourself."

Amanda looked horrified. "Oh, no, no. I couldn't take out a bullet."

"Remember the doctoring you did at the camp in the old days? There wasn't a doctor then. You got to where you could do most everything. Hell, I bet you're better than a lot of doctors.''

"But it's been so long. I've forgotten how...."

"You don't forget skills like that. They come back to you, whenever you need them. Shoot fire, woman, remember the time Swede Gustafson got liquored up and shot Blackie Roscoe?"

"Yeah." Amanda snorted. "Over Delia Culbertson."

"And how about the time you cut that piece of wood out of Dave Wilson's leg and sewed him up again, good as new?"

"Yes, but...but what if I make a mistake and I kill your son?"

"Amanda, if you don't help my son, you'll kill him sure."

She looked at him for a moment. "You're right. I'll do it."

"No!" Stephen's valet shrieked. "No, you can't! You mustn't. You're not a doctor. You'll hurt him. Send for the doctor. Let him do it. Mr. Ferguson is a wealthy man. He can pay for any inconvenience, any—''

Amanda fixed him with a stern look. "No amount of money can bring that doctor here in time to save him. His father wants me to help him, and I'm going to. If you're going to argue and fuss, then Joe can put you outside. If you want to help Mr. Ferguson, then you shut your mouth and do what I say. Do you understand?"

"Let her do it." They all turned, startled, to look at the bed, from which the weak voice had come. Stephen's eyes were open, bright with pain but obviously alert. "I trust her, Charles. Mrs. Randall has my permission to take out the bullet."

Charles nodded and stepped back. Amanda turned to Jessie. "All right. Jessie, I'm going to need your help."

Amanda rattled off a list of the things she would need, and Jessie shot downstairs to get them. She worked quickly, trying not to think about what lay ahead. Her mother had had to practice a lot of rudimentary medicine when she cooked at the camp, and Jessie had helped her. But that had been several years ago; Amanda had given it up when Dr. Holzworth moved to Nora Springs. The thought of helping her mother get a bullet out of Stephen made Jessie queasy.

But she couldn't think about that. She had a task to do.

When she returned, she found Joe, the valet and her mother clustered at the head of Stephen's bed. The bedside stand had been pushed up tight against the mattress, and two kerosene lamps at full blaze sat upon it. Another lamp sat on the dresser. The room was a bright contrast to the dark hall outside. On the bedside table also sat a washbowl, several folded towels, a pair of tweezers and a threaded needle. Jessie's stomach pitched and turned, and she had to swallow hard.

She handed her mother the kettle of hot water and the two sharpened kitchen knives, then took the bottle of bourbon out of the crook of her arm. She poured a healthy shot into a glass. Her fingers trembled.

Jessie walked to Stephen's bed. He opened his eyes and looked at her. "You going to help her cut me open?" His voice was so faint she could hardly hear him. "Bet you'll enjoy that."

Jessie swallowed again. "Sure." She hoped he was too weak to notice the tremor in her voice. "You need to drink this. It'll make you feel better."

She slid her hand under his head and helped him lift it, and he drank from the glass. After a swallow, he coughed and shot her a disgusted look. "What the devil is that? Take it away. Cheap whiskey."

Jessie grimaced. "Sorry, I'm sure you're used to the finest brandy. But we can't always get it out here. Now drink again."

"Don't want to." He shook his head.

"You need to." She hesitated and glanced at Joe, then at Stephen. "For the pain."

"Oh, my God!" the valet gasped.

Stephen's eyes opened, and he focused on her. "What? Aren't you going to use chloroform?"

Jessie shook her head. "We don't have any."

"The doctor…"

"He took it with him. I asked McSweeney. This is—this is all we've got."

Jessie didn't know what she expected—crying or pleading or a sudden recanting of his decision to let Amanda take out the bullet—but she certainly hadn't expected what he did. Stephen gazed at her unblinkingly for a moment, then said, "Pour me another shot."

When she deemed him inebriated enough to take the edge off his pain, Amanda came forward, a small kitchen knife and the tweezers clutched in her white-knuckled hands. She looked at Joe. "You ready to hold him?"

He nodded. Amanda glanced at Stephen. His eyes were open, though foggy from the liquor, pain and loss of blood. He wet his lips, and Jessie could see him struggling to make his words come out sensibly. "Have a' it." His voice was slurred; his eyes wandered.

Amanda swallowed and bent over his wound. "All right. Hold him."

Charles, kneeling on the bed beside Stephen, bore down on his good arm to keep him from thrashing around, while Joe gripped his shoulder and arm tightly on the other side. Jessie stood behind her mother, watching, waiting to hand her whatever she asked for.

Amanda began to probe the wound, and a low groan escaped Stephen's lips. Jessie's stomach tightened.

"I'm going to have to make a cut," Amanda said, bringing the knife down to Stephen's skin. The valet made an odd noise, and his eyes rolled back. He fainted, collapsing on the bed beside Stephen.

"For Christ's sake." Joe swore and released Stephen to reach over and shove the servant aside. "Jessie, get up here and hold him."

Jessie crawled onto the bed and gripped Stephen's arm and shoulder tightly. She turned her head so as not to see the knife bite into his flesh, but she knew from Stephen's muffled oath and hissing breath when it did. Stephen's arm was taut and hard as stone beneath her. He was far stronger than she'd guessed. Each time her mother hurt him, the muscles beneath Jessie's hands bulged, and once, weak as he was, he raised her several inches off the bed.

It seemed as if it was taking her mother forever. Jessie glanced over and saw Amanda probing the wound with the tweezers. She turned away quickly. Another groan came from Stephen. Jessie found herself praying frantically inside her head. Abruptly Stephen's muscles relaxed beneath her. She glanced at his face and saw that he had finally sunk into blessed unconsciousness. Thank heavens!

A moment later her mother exclaimed, "Eureka!" Slowly, carefully, she removed the tweezers and held them up. A mangled, blood-smeared piece of metal lay between the prongs. Amanda laid the bullet on the table and wiped her hands on a towel, then picked up her needle, pressed the flesh together and began to sew with tiny, delicate stitches. Jessie continued to keep her face averted, wondering when her mother would finally be through.

"That's it." Amanda stepped back from the bed.

Jessie looked down at Stephen. The skin around the wound was bloody, but the wound was closed, held by small blue stitches. She began to tremble. Amanda went to wash the blood from her hands before she bandaged Stephen. Joe stopped her and enfolded her in his arms. Jessie crawled off the bed, hesitated for a moment, then hurried out the door. She ran down the back staircase and into the yard.

The evening air was chilly against her face, and she was glad to feel it. Amanda had done it. And Jessie had managed to stand her ground and do her job, too. But now her stomach turned and heaved, and she ran behind a bush to be thoroughly and violently sick.

It was some time before Jessie was composed enough to creep into the house and up the stairs. She went to her room and washed her face, then glanced in the mirror. Her skin looked sallow in the dim light, and her eyes seemed huge. She sat on her bed, took off her boots and lay against the cool coverlet. She still felt jittery inside, the result, she guessed, of the danger and fear she had faced earlier. She didn't think she could sleep.

She thought of Stephen and was embarrassed to remember how she had rushed out of his room. She hadn't even stayed to help her mother clean up. She wasn't usually that weak. Wondering how he was, she stood and went quietly down the hall to his room. The door to his room stood open a fraction, and she peeked inside. A kerosene lamp, turned low, lit the room dimly. Her mother stood beside the bed, smoothing out the covers. The lamp cast her shadow huge and dark against the opposite wall. Stephen lay on the bed, so still it made Jessie's heart beat a little faster in fear. Was he still alive? He looked so pale, so motionless.

She eased the door open and tiptoed inside. Amanda turned and gave her a little smile.

"How is he?"

"It's hard to tell. Right now he's resting comfortably. But when he wakes up, I'm afraid the pain will be fierce. And there's always the danger of a fever. However, he's a strong young man. I think he'll pull through all right."

Jessie came nearer. The sheet lay over Stephen's chest, but did not cover his shoulders and arms. A white strip of gauze came up over one shoulder, adding a touch of vulnerability to the masculine set of his shoulders. His eyes were closed in deep sleep; his eyelashes lay thick and dark against his cheek, absurdly beautiful. Something twisted in Jessie's chest. "I should have been watching better."

"Oh, honey, there was nothing you could do." Her mother slipped a reassuring arm around her shoulders. "You couldn't know someone would be hiding, planning to shoot him."

"Maybe not, but Joe asked me to look after him, and I promised I would. Then I didn't. I just showed him the

way. I didn't keep an eye out for danger. And I should
have. I was careless."

"I'm sure Joe doesn't blame you. How could you have
guessed that someone would ambush you? Even if you'd
been more alert, there's nothing to say you would have seen
the killer before he shot young Mr. Ferguson. It probably
would have happened exactly the same way."

"At least then I would have known that I'd done my
best. But now I have to live with the fact that I didn't."

"Maybe you weren't perfect. I don't think anyone ex-
pects you to be—except maybe you. But think about this:
that young man was lucky to have you along. If you hadn't
been there, he'd be dead right now. What if he'd gone
alone, or Joe had sent someone with him who wasn't as
quick or as sharp as you? You protected him. You chased
away the killer. You brought him home alive. You saved
him, Jessie. I think that's how Joe feels about it."

"I guess so." She gazed at the immobile face. How
handsome Stephen looked in repose, as though no flaw
could spoil his elegant features. He was very different from
Sam—up close, at least. She liked the way Sam looked
better, of course; harsh experience had given his face character. Still, there was no denying that this man was wickedly handsome.

He was also tougher than she would have guessed. He
had made that ride into town without a murmur of complaint, even though each step must have jarred his wound.
Then he had grimly endured Amanda's probing for the bullet in his shoulder, with only a bottle of whiskey to ease
the torment. Nor had he lost his head and panicked during
the shooting. He had gotten up and run with her to the trees
when she had told him to, and he had sat there gamely with
the empty rifle in his hands while she had searched for the
runaway horses. Stephen Ferguson had earned her grudging
respect tonight. Maybe there was some of Joe's and Sam's
iron in him, after all.

"I'll watch him tonight," Jessie told her mother. "You
go to bed."

Her mother glanced at her, surprised. Usually Jessie hated sickbeds and avoided nursing duties at all costs. "If you'd like."

Jessie nodded.

Amanda hugged her daughter, laying her head against the girl's bright red one. "He'll be all right. I know it. He can't die now, just when Joe's finally gotten him back."

Amanda slipped out of the room, closing the door softly behind her. Jessie pulled a straight-backed chair up beside the bed and sat in it. The lamplight flickered, casting shadows across Stephen's face. Jessie reached out tentatively and laid her hand across one of his. In his sleep, his hand turned over, and his fingers curled around her hand. Jessie settled herself to wait out the night with him.

Chapter Six

Stephen woke up and immediately wished he hadn't. His head was pounding, his mouth was dry, and his left shoulder felt as if it was on fire. He groaned and rolled his head to the side, closed his eyes and hoped that this was another one of the harsh, violent dreams that had been plaguing him all night long. But he knew it wasn't. The pain was too sharp, too real. He opened his eyes again. He was in a strange bedroom furnished simply and inexpensively.

His valet bent over the bed, his long, plain face concerned. "Sir? How are you feeling? Are you in pain?"

With some effort Stephen bit back an oath. "Of course I'm in pain. What do you think I'd be, with some woman cutting on me?"

He remembered now where he was and most of what had happened. He'd been shot while he and Jessie were riding to town. Then Jessie had dragged him home—what a courageous, quick-thinking girl! After he'd been shot, he had gone in and out of consciousness, and he had only jumbled memories of the ride home and being carried into the Randall house. Unfortunately he had come to quickly enough when Amanda Randall had started poking around in his shoulder, searching for the bullet. He remembered Jessie standing there, propping up his head, urging him to drink a bottle of rotgut whiskey. He had gotten drunk, though he couldn't recall that it had helped the pain; at least it had finally knocked him out.

It was no wonder his head was pounding and his mouth tasted so foul. He had a hangover as well as a bullet wound in his shoulder.

"I'm most sorry, sir." Charles looked deeply troubled. "I tried to stop them, but they insisted that it was the only way. They told me there was no doctor in the town. I never heard of such a thing."

Stephen remembered Joe Ferguson holding him down with all his force, Jessie helping him, while Mrs. Randall went to work. His father's face had been grim and his eyes almost tortured as he kept Stephen still. Stephen thought that nothing could have shown his love for his son more clearly than that expression.

"They are tough people here," Stephen murmured. He tried to imagine his lovely, delicate mother out here, and he failed. It was no wonder she had run to St. Louis. He couldn't picture her handing a man a bottle of whiskey and going in with a kitchen knife and a pair of tweezers to take a bullet out of him.

"Mrs. Randall left strict instructions to let her know when you awoke."

Stephen nodded. "Of course. Go tell her."

His servant left the room, and a few minutes later, Amanda Randall swept into the room, followed by Charles, who was carrying a tray. Stephen had expected to see Jessie with her mother, and he knew a curious sense of disappointment when she did not walk into the room.

"Well, now," Mrs. Randall said, smiling and coming over to the bed to pick up his hand. "I won't ask how you're feeling this morning, for I'm sure it must be awful. But I will say I'm terribly glad to see you awake and not feverish. It's a good sign." She was a soft, maternal woman, and her presence was soothing.

"Thank you." Stephen tried to squeeze her hand in his, though he found he was too weak to exert much pressure. "You were an angel to do what you did."

She chuckled. "That's not exactly what you were calling me last night, as I recall."

"I'm sorry. I was half out of my head. I don't know what I said. If I offended you—"

"Oh, no, no, I was only teasing," she hastened to reassure him, her kind face showing worry. "You were in pain, and I paid no attention to it. Believe me, I've heard much worse in my life—and not always from a man I was cutting a bullet out of."

Stephen smiled faintly. He felt unutterably weary. His shoulder throbbed. His eyes closed and fluttered open again. "Where is Jessie?"

"Jessie? Down at the sawmill. I tried to get her to sleep in this morning—she sat up half the night, watching you. But I couldn't reason with her. She said Joe would need her more now than ever. Maybe she's right. He was worried something fierce about you." Amanda smiled. "But I told him not to fret. I knew you came from strong stock. I figured you'd pull through, just like Sam would."

Stephen's eyes drifted closed again, and he opened them with an effort. "Sorry," he mumbled, fighting the exhaustion that threatened to overwhelm him. "I'm just so tired...."

"Of course you are. Sleep is exactly what you need. But first, I want you to eat a little broth. You lost a lot of blood last night, and you need to build it back up. I made you some good, strong meat broth. Charles, help hold his head up, please."

Stephen felt ridiculously weak. He couldn't even lift his head by himself. His valet had to put his hands under Stephen's head and prop him up while Mrs. Randall fed him a few spoonfuls of beef broth. At the first sip, his stomach almost revolted, but gradually it settled, and he was able to eat a little. Then Amanda let Charles lay him back down. Stephen was asleep before she got out the door.

"Do you know anyone who might wish to harm this Mr. Ferguson?" the marshal asked Joe. He stood with his hat pushed back on his head and his thumbs hooked in his belt, his face expressionless, as it had been all through Jessie's retelling of what had happened to her and Stephen on their ride home last night. Having told it to her mother and then to Joe, she was getting rather tired of relating the events, but Marshall Wayman, who had been given the facts by Joe last night, had insisted on coming by the sawmill this morning and hearing Jessie's story himself.

"No. It plain don't make sense." Joe shook his head, a perplexed look on his face. "I mean, he's only been in town a couple of days."

"Yeah," Jessie agreed. "God knows he's an irritating creature, but surely in so short a time he couldn't have gotten on anybody's nerves enough for them to want to kill him."

"Maybe it *was* an accident," Joe offered.

"Three times?" Marshall Wayman looked skeptical. "Didn't you say they shot at him three times?"

"Yes. They couldn't possibly not have realized they were firing at him."

"Maybe it's somebody that ain't from around here," the marshall suggested. "Maybe it's a fella that followed him from St. Louis to kill him. Something to do with something that happened back East."

"Why not do it there, then, instead of going to the trouble of following him out here?" Joe snapped.

The marshall shrugged. "You sure he couldn't't've been aimin' at you, Jess?"

Jessie shot him a disgusted look. "Well, he sure was a hell of a bad shot, if he was. He fired three times, and all of them were close to Ste—Mr. Ferguson. Not me. Besides, who'd want to kill me, either?"

"Well, I know a few people you've riled a mite now and then." Marshal Wayman gave a sly little grin. "But I wouldn't think it'd be enough to shoot you. More likely it was robbers. They saw that fancy city dude and figured he was easy pickin's, so they shot him and were going to ride down and take his money."

"There's only one problem with that. He didn't look like a rich tinhorn. He went out and bought regular clothes for the ride, and he looked just like you or me or—" She stopped abruptly, and her eyes widened. "Joe...you know who he looked like?"

Joe understood immediately. "Sam? You're saying somebody thought he was Sam?"

"Wait a minute," Marshal Wayman stuck in. "This Eastern relative of yours looks enough like Sam that somebody'd confuse 'em?"

"He's not just a relative, Marshal—he's my son. Sam's brother. They don't look exactly alike. Standing this close to him you'd never mistake Stephen for Sam. But they do favor. He's tall and has black hair and the same sort of frame."

"From a distance, it wouldn't be hard to mistake him for Sam," Jessie added. "Especially since it was getting on toward twilight. And he was riding with me. Everybody knows Sam and I are friends. Anybody could have seen me riding out in the direction of the camp that morning."

"Yeah, and I told several of the men at work that you'd gone to the camp," Joe added. "They asked about you 'cause they hadn't seen you around."

"So knowing I'd been to the camp and seeing this man who looked like Sam with me, naturally they'd assume it *was* Sam."

"They could have figured you had the payroll for the camp on you." The Marshall began to weave a story. "They followed you, and—no, that don't make sense. They'd've shot you when you were riding to the camp. They wouldn't figure Sam had the payroll when he was riding toward town."

"Maybe they weren't wanting to rob Sam."

"Ah, Jessie, now don't start that up," Joe groaned.

"Why not?"

"Start what up? Jessie, Joe, what's goin' on?"

"Somebody broke the main saw blade—on purpose." Jessie explained. "They're trying to hurt Joe."

"I thought that was an accident." Marshal Wayman looked confused.

"That's what you determined," Jessie said, unable to keep a trace of resentment and scorn out of her voice. "You said you reckoned it must have been an accident. There wasn't anything to show it had been tampered with."

"Yeah. So why do you say it had been?"

"'Cause it didn't just break. I know it didn't. It was fine the night before when the mill closed down. The next morning, first thing, it broke. And it broke so clean. No pieces of metal flying all over the place, just that big split right across the middle, so it fell into two pieces. Why would it break like that, unless someone weakened it along a line? Joe thinks so, too. He's been spending the nights in the mill since then."

The marshal swung his astonished gaze toward Joe. "Why didn't you tell me?"

Joe shrugged. "I got no proof, and neither does Jessie, no matter how convinced she is that she's right. It's all speculation."

"Well, it wasn't speculation that somebody took shots at a man who looked like your son. Now, who do you think might have broken that blade of yours? Who'd want to hurt your mill? Or you?"

Joe sighed. "That's just it. I can't think of anyone who would. Somebody with a big grudge against me or Sam, I reckon. Maybe he broke the blade, thinking that'd hurt our business so bad we'd be in real trouble. But when it didn't, when Sam just ordered a new one and we went on with the smaller one, then he might've figured he'd better hurt Sam directly."

The marshal shook his head. "This is hard to believe."

"I know. I been racking my brain, trying to remember if I've ever done anything to anyone that would make them this angry, make them want to take revenge on me. Especially something this serious—I mean, the saw blade was one thing, but trying to murder my son...!"

Wayman sighed. "I guess I'll have to ride out there tomorrow and look around, see if I can find anything on the hill to show who might've been there." He reached for his hat and started toward the door. He paused and looked back at Joe and Jessie. "If you think of anything, let me know." His face turned stern. "Especially you let me know if anything else strange happens. You understand?"

"Sure." Joe nodded. "I reckon the coward's already hightailed it out of here, thinking he'd killed Sam."

"Maybe." He didn't look convinced.

After the marshal left, Jessie and Joe sat silently for a moment. Then Jessie sighed.

"Maybe we ought to tell Sam now. I mean, there's no way to hide that his brother got shot. And if they're going after Sam, he ought to be on guard. Ready to fight back."

"Sam's always ready to fight back," Joe replied, his mouth curling up into a grin.

"You know what I mean. On the lookout for danger."

"Yeah. I thought of that. I don't want someone sneaking in on him at the camp and hurting him. But sure as fire, if I tell him, he'll be camping out at the sawmill. He probably won't even go get the blade because he won't want to leave me and the mill alone. He'll say Burley can go by himself."

"Well, we'll just have to convince him to go. After all, that fellow might try to stop Burley from bringing in the new blade. Sam ought to be there to make sure nothing happens to it."

"Right." Joe's expression lightened. "We'll use that argument on him." Then he frowned. "You know, that might just be the truth. Damn! There's no way to keep him safe. I'd rather it *was* an enemy chasing Stephen out here from St. Louis. At least Sam wouldn't be in danger—and Stephen wouldn't be lying there half-dead just because he came to visit us."

Jessie reached out and laid her hand on his arm. "It's not your fault that some lunatic is out to get you. Stephen was just unlucky enough to get in the way."

"And you."

"I didn't get hurt."

"Maybe not this time. But what about the next time? Suppose you get in the way? Or Stephen again? Suppose it's Sam?"

"Sure, any of that's possible. But what are you going to do? Give up? Leave town?"

Joe's face hardened. "You know me better than that."

"So what are you saying?"

"That I don't want you and my children in danger. Maybe you should stop working here."

"Look, Stephen will probably leave as soon as he gets well enough to go. I don't figure some city dude like him is going to hang around after getting shot at. But I'm not leaving. Sam can take care of himself, and so can I. You won't see the day when I start running scared. I'm staying right where I am."

Joe gave her a long, hard look, then grinned. "I reckon I knew that before we ever started talking."

"Then you might as well have saved your breath."

"Blast it, I want to know how a sweet woman like your mama ever managed to have a daughter as mule headed as you."

Jessie chuckled. "You don't know Ma very well if you think that. She may wear skirts and smile at you pretty, but underneath she's made of iron."

The older man's smile grew wider. "I reckon you're pretty right about that, too."

Stephen slept most of the day, and every time he awoke for a few minutes, there were Charles and Mrs. Randall, poking a few more spoonfuls of broth down him. He had no interest in eating, and his stomach remained unsteady all day. But Mrs. Randall wasn't about to let him get by without taking some nourishment. In the middle of the afternoon, the doctor came in, examined his wound and left him a bottle of laudanum for the pain. After Mrs. Randall gave him a spoonful of the liquid, the throbbing in his shoulder quieted down, and his sleep was easier and less troubled by the hot, fierce, senseless dreams he had experienced earlier.

When he awakened the next time, he could see by the darkened window that it was evening, and instead of Charles sitting in the chair beside his bed, it was Jessie Randall. He blinked, trying to clear his fuzzy mind. His shoulder was burning again. "Hello." He disliked how weak his voice sounded.

"Hi." Jessie rose from her chair and came over to the bed. She leaned down and placed her hand across his brow. Her skin was deliciously cool.

He liked the feel of her hand on his face. He wished she would leave it there. His eyes closed. Somehow he felt better with her there, silly as that seemed. Yet at the same time, it embarrassed him that she should see him so weak.

"You may have a bit of fever," Jessie said crisply. "I'll get you a cool rag."

She went to the washbowl and wet a rag, then wrung it out and placed it on his forehead. It was cool, but not nearly as pleasant as her touch.

"Are you feeling pain?" she asked. "Mama said you could take some more of the laudanum now, if you want."

"No. Maybe later." Actually, he would have taken the medicine gladly if it had been anyone else offering it. But knowing how poorly Jessie thought of him, he couldn't bring himself to admit to his pain. He could hold on for a while longer.

Jessie returned to the chair and sat, hands clasped together in her lap. She looked at Stephen. His eyes were closed again, and she wondered if he was sleeping. She wished that she had something to do with her hands, but she had never taken up any of the womanly skills of sewing or knitting or needlepoint, and she wasn't much for books, either. She was used to being up and doing things. The waiting was difficult. Sitting by a sickbed was something she wouldn't normally do, and she didn't know why she felt compelled to stay by Stephen's. She supposed it was because she had failed to protect him. She felt responsible for what had happened to him.

"Where's Charles?" Stephen asked, startling her.

"What? Oh. I said I'd spell him for a while. He's been looking after you all day long. I figured he needed a chance to rest and eat a little, maybe get outside for a walk."

"That was kind of you, to think of him."

Jessie shrugged. She wasn't about to tell him that she really hadn't considered Charles much when she had offered to relieve him of his patient-sitting duties for the evening.

To have something to do, she got up, rewet the rag on his forehead and laid it against his skin again. Stephen's cheeks were flushed, and there was a sparkle in his eyes. They were caused, no doubt, by the fever, but Jessie couldn't help but think how they intensified his handsomeness.

As she drew back, Stephen's hand came up and curled around her wrist, holding her there. Startled, Jessie went still, her heart speeding up strangely. His hand was warm around her wrist, and his grip was amazingly strong. With his hand wrapped around her arm like that, she felt, for a moment, strangely fragile.

"Jessie? Don't go just yet. I want to tell you something."

"I'm not going anywhere."

"Good." His fingers slipped from her arm almost reluctantly. "I want to thank you. For saving my life."

Jessie shook her head deprecatingly. "It wasn't anything."

A smile edged his lips. "It was to me. I'm rather fond of being alive."

"I didn't mean that. I just meant—I would have done it for—" She stopped abruptly, realizing how rude her response would sound.

"For anybody," he finished for her with a grimace. "I'm sure that's true. But you happened to do it for me, and I want to thank you. I'm indebted to you. You were quick

and smart and courageous. I don't think most people would
have thought or acted as fast as you did.''

Jessie shrugged, embarrassed. "I had a good teacher:
Sam Ferguson.''

Stephen was aware of a twinge of irritation. Her hero
worship of his brother was beginning to annoy him. He
gave a short nod and turned his head from her.

Jessie started toward her chair, then stopped and turned
to look at Stephen again. "I—I ought to tell you something,
too.''

Stephen glanced at her curiously.

"I—you hung in there, and you never even complained.
You were a lot tougher than I thought.''

Stephen's lips twitched. "I'll take that as a compliment.''

Jessie's eyes narrowed with suspicion. Was he laughing
at her? When she'd been trying to say something nice about
him! "Take it however you want.''

"No, wait. Don't get huffy. I appreciate what you said,
I really do.''

"Well, it doesn't matter. I wasn't looking for thanks or
anything. I just wanted to let you know. You were brave.''

He wondered if he had been as brave as Sam would have
been, but he kept the barbed thought to himself as he
watched Jessie return to her post in the chair. They stayed
in their positions for a long time, not saying anything. The
more time that passed, the worse his shoulder felt and the
more he thought about it. The more he thought about the
pain, the worse it grew. He felt hotter, too, all the time. But
he wasn't about to admit either of those things to Jessie—
particularly after her approval of his bravery, however
grudging.

After a while, Amanda came in with one of her unending
bowls of broth. She took one look at him and cast a stern
gaze toward her daughter. "Jessamine Randall, what are
you doing, just sitting there? Isn't it obvious that this man
is in pain? Not to mention running a temperature? Did you
give him any laudanum, like I told you?''

Jessie bristled. "He told me he didn't need it.''

"Oh, pooh! Men!" Amanda made a gesture of dismissal. "Their pride hardly ever leaves any room for sense. Of course he'd deny needing it. It's up to you to see that he takes it anyway." She nodded toward the tall chest in the corner as she set down the tray. "Fetch me that packet of powder over there, Jess. The doctor left it for the fever. Then get the laudanum and give him a spoonful."

Stephen was glad for Amanda's intervention. He'd been gritting his teeth against the pain for too long. He had been on the verge of giving in and asking Jessie for a dose. Now he struggled awkwardly up onto one elbow to take the spoonful of liquid that she poured and held out to him.

While Amanda was dumping powder from the packet into a glass of water and mixing it, Jessie took hold of Stephen's good arm and tried to help him into a half-sitting position, plumping up the pillows and stuffing them behind him. He didn't get comfortable—he didn't think that was possible—but at least he would be able to drink the other medicine and the ever-present thin soup.

Amanda held the glass to his lips, and he drank, grimacing at the taste of the powder, much of it still gritty in his mouth. "Good Lord, Madam. Are you trying to kill me?" he asked testily when Amanda took the glass away to allow him to breathe.

"Quite the opposite," she responded calmly. "Now finish the rest."

"I'm not sure I can."

"Of course you can." Amanda smiled coaxingly. "Now, open your mouth."

Stephen released a heavy sigh and made himself drink the rest. He considered heaving up the contents for a moment, but closed his eyes and breathed shallowly until his stomach calmed down.

Amanda smiled. "There. You did just splendidly." She glanced at her daughter. "See? You have to lead them a little and force them a little. Men make the worst patients. Now, you do the same thing with this broth."

Jessie looked at her uneasily. "But, Ma...I thought you were going to do it."

"I haven't time. There are the supper dishes to clean. And Joe will be coming up soon. We want our patient looking as healthy as possible for Joe, don't we?"

"Well, sure." Jessie looked at Stephen, half-lying, half-sitting in his bed. The thought of sitting on his bed and feeding him made her uneasy. "But I've never done this. I don't know how."

"You'll get the hang of it quick enough. It isn't hard."

Jessie picked up the soup bowl and sat down gingerly on the bed. She dipped the spoon into the bowl and brought it up to Stephen's lips. It seemed as if half the broth dribbled down his chin and onto the bedclothes.

"Oh, dear." Jessie looked at the spots in dismay.

"Not such a full spoon," Stephen said quietly.

"What? Oh. I see." Jessie blushed a little. She hated to look incompetent in any matter. Why had she agreed to do this? Or, to be more honest, why had she volunteered to relieve Charles? She took a more modest spoonful.

"Your mother sets the bowl in her lap and holds the towel under my chin."

It worked far better that way, Jessie quickly discovered, and after that it wasn't so bad. It was almost—well, not fun, of course, but enjoyable in some way. She had never taken care of anyone before, and she was amazed to find that it could actually feel good to do so, not as if she was a drudge. She cupped her hand beneath his chin, holding the towel, and tipped the spoon up to his lips again and again, all the while looking into his face. There was nowhere else she could look. She'd never stared at a man's mouth before. Stephen's lips were firm, the lower one a trifle full. Now and then a drop of broth settled on his lower lip, and his tongue came out to sweep it up. Once or twice he smiled at her, and she saw the flash of white, even teeth. The longer she watched, the more tightly she clamped her own lips together.

Finally Stephen shook his head and refused to take another spoonful. Jessie set the bowl and towel on the tray, but she didn't yet rise from the bed. Stephen lay watching her. His eyes were foggy, and Jessie knew that the laudanum was taking effect. She reached out and laid her hand to his forehead, as she had earlier, to check his temperature.

"That feels good," Stephen murmured, then was amazed that he had said it to her. His tongue was thick, and he had the disconcerting feeling that he wasn't entirely in control of his brain. He hoped that Jessie would leave her hand where it was. His eyes went unconsciously to her throat, exposed by the open collar of her mannish shirt, and to the soft swell of her breasts beneath the flannel. "You have a gentle touch," he commented. "I'm surprised."

Jessie jerked her hand back. She felt very awkward suddenly. Stephen's voice had been low and faintly slurred, almost...caressing. Something quivered deep inside her. She glanced around, annoyed to feel a blush rising up her throat. "Well, I'm surprised, too," she replied, struggling for a light, flippant tone. "I'm more used to working than sitting in sickrooms."

Stephen looked at her. He felt too tired to do anything else, even to turn his head away. Besides, she was pleasant to look at. Not pretty in that cool, cameo way that Elizabeth was. But there was something intriguing in the big, frank blue eyes and the wide mouth, the triangular face, the spattering of golden freckles across her nose and cheeks. Her hair was the color of flame, and even though she wore it pulled back tightly into two pigtails, she could not completely restrain it; fine hairs around her face had pulled loose and curled around her features. Stephen suspected that when her hair lay loose across her shoulders, it was a glory to behold. He wondered if any man had ever seen it loose. If any man had ever turned her soft.

"Why do you try to hide what you are?" he asked softly, almost as if he were thinking aloud.

Jessie stiffened, and her eyes turned suspicious. "And what's that?"

"A woman." His brain was growing more and more

numb, and he struggled to find the words to express what he meant. "You know, dressing like that. Acting tough."

"I *am* tough." Jessie crossed her arms over her chest and stared at him with blazing eyes. "I'm not trying to hide anything."

"But you're very pretty. You could look...enchanting."

Enchanting! The word stunned Jessie into silence. No man had ever even suggested such a thing. Finally she said, "You must be delirious. Your fever's worse than I thought." But her dry, cynical words came out a little breathlessly, and there was a funny, tight feeling in her chest.

Stephen smiled and shook his head. His eyelids drifted closed, and he pulled them open again. He wanted to say something else, to counter her self-deprecating words, but his mind had become too groggy. He wet his lips. "Jess..."

"Yes?" She leaned a little closer. His voice was slurred and almost too low to hear.

"What's your real name? Not Jess."

"Oh." Jessie grimaced. She had always disliked her full name. It was too prissy, too flowery. "Lots of folks call me Jessie."

"Not Jessie, is it?" His eyes were dark and velvety in the dim light of the kerosene lamp, the pupils huge. "Your real name?"

"No." She found she couldn't lie to a man who was lying there so weak. "No, it's not. It's Jessamine."

"Jessamine," he repeated, smiling. "Jessamine." Jessie squirmed under his repetition of her name. "Pretty. Pretty Jessamine."

He sank into sleep, a faint smile on his face.

Jessie sat through the evening, watching Stephen sleep. Normally she would have been bored silly, but tonight her brain was too active, returning again and again to what Stephen had said about her. "Enchanting." She wasn't used to men who used words like that. What had he meant by it, exactly?

It must have been the fever talking, she told herself. No one in his right mind would look at her in an old flannel shirt and denim pants and laced-up work boots almost to her knee and call her enchanting. Hell, she didn't even look like a woman, let alone a pretty one.

But, then, he hadn't said she *was* enchanting. He'd said she *could* be, if she tried. That meant if she'd wear skirts and arrange her hair up on her head and adopt a sweet, submissive face. Well, she wasn't about to do any of those things. Not for any man, and certainly not to impress one like Stephen Ferguson.

No doubt he liked women with lace frothing out of their cuffs and collar, and sweet little strings of pearls around their necks. He'd want the kind who flirted with him from behind their fans and who had all kinds of fancy, complicated rules for how people should behave, like those silly women in the books her mother liked to read. He'd thanked her for saving his life, but he still thought her unfeminine.

Jessie barely restrained a snort. She'd like to see how much good one of those frilly ladies would have done him last night on the trail when someone was shooting at them. Oh, no, he'd been glad enough then that she was tough and unwomanly and had gotten him out of there instead of falling into hysterics. But now, of course, he was rebuking her for her unfeminine dress and behavior. Well, let him. She shot a fulminating glance at Stephen's sleeping form. He was nothing to her. And what he'd said about her looks was nothing to her, either.

Still, a few minutes later, she couldn't stop herself from tiptoeing to the small mirror above the dresser. She turned her face from side to side, trying to see it from all angles in the poor light. *Enchanting.*

Jessie sighed. She couldn't see it. All she could see was carroty hair and thin red-brown brows and freckles splotched across her nose. Blue eyes were good; she'd always heard that men like blue eyes. But she didn't think that the direct, frank gaze in those blue eyes was what men wanted. No, it was vague, limpid blue orbs like Gertie Haskins down at the bakery had, the kind that glanced down modestly, then turned to gaze at a man with awe.

Jessie grimaced at her reflection. What in the world was she doing, mooning about in front of a mirror? She had far better things to do with her time than this. It didn't matter to her what Stephen Ferguson thought of her looks—or lack of them.

She returned to her chair and flopped down in it, stretching her legs out in front of her. She leaned her head back against the rocker and waited for Charles to relieve her. She didn't know what she was doing here, anyway.

Chapter Seven

By morning Stephen's fever was better, and he continued to improve all day. Even the burning pain in his shoulder subsided somewhat. By the time Jessie came home the next evening, he was awake and alert, and he had several questions to ask her about what had happened to him.

"Looks like you must be feeling better," she said when she came in, nodding toward where he sat against the headboard, propped up by pillows.

"Yes. Charles helped me sit. It improved my mood considerably."

Charles, like the well-trained servant he was, glided noiselessly from the room upon Jessie's arrival, leaving the door open slightly for decorum's sake. Jessie watched him go, then turned, shaking her head.

"Doesn't he ever say anything?"

"What do you mean?"

"Hello, excuse me, so long. That sort of thing."

"Of course, if he's addressed."

"Huh? You mean, he doesn't say anything unless you say something first?"

"Yes."

"Why?"

Stephen looked puzzled. "He's supposed to be unobtrusive."

"What does that mean?" Jessie wondered if Stephen always talked like this, or if he did it just to make her feel ignorant.

"Not noticed. You know. As if he weren't there."

"Why?"

"Because he's a servant. He's—it was part of his training." Stephen gave up trying to explain it to her. Obviously she would never understand being a servant.

Jessie shrugged. She walked to the bed, holding out an envelope. "You got a telegram. Mama said she thought you were feeling well enough to read it. It came to the telegraph office in Missoula, and they brought it on the stage today. They delivered it to the mill because those are the only Fergusons they know."

"A telegram?" Stephen frowned, reaching for the envelope. He tore it open and read through the message quickly. "Damn!" He read it again. It didn't make any more sense the second time.

"What is it?"

"My fiancée. She wired to say she's taking the train from St. Louis to Missoula. She's leaving tomorrow."

"Fiancée!" Jessie's eyebrows flew up. He was engaged! She didn't know why it surprised her so much, but she felt as if she'd suddenly lost her breath. "You're engaged?"

"Yes. But I can't think why she'd take it into her head to come here. Elizabeth's usually a very levelheaded woman."

Yes, and no doubt she wore expensive, beautiful, very feminine dresses and smelled like lilacs or attar of roses or some such thing. "Doesn't she say?"

"No. Just that she has to come and to please meet her."

"Maybe she figures you're running out on her."

Stephen gave her a repressive look. "Elizabeth would never be that foolish. She's known me all my life."

"Maybe she can't wait to see you. Maybe she's ready to get married."

Stephen's lips quirked up at the thought of calm, proper Elizabeth rushing out to the wilds of the Montana Territory because she couldn't bear to be away from him. "It seems unlikely."

Jessie glanced at him oddly. He hardly sounded like a man who was about to see his fiancée again. She would have expected him to be excited and happy, not calm, almost amused. "I don't understand."

"You'd have to know Elizabeth. She's very much a lady, very correct and—even dignified."

Dignified? It seemed even more peculiar for a man to describe the young woman he loved as "dignified."

"She simply wouldn't do something as rash as this without an extremely good reason." His frown returned. It must have something to do with Elizabeth's stepmother. Netta must have done something so intolerable that Elizabeth could not bear to remain in the same house with her until Stephen returned to St. Louis. But why hadn't she gone to stay with his grandparents? And how could he possibly meet her train in Missoula? "I can't let her arrive with no one there to meet her."

Jessie shook her head. "You can't ride a horse in your condition. You haven't even gotten out of bed yet."

That was true enough. He would be lucky to get up and walk around the room tomorrow, let alone ride a horse for several days. "But what will I do about Elizabeth?"

"Couldn't she take the stage?"

"By herself?" His eyebrows shot up. "Oh, no, I don't think so. Besides, she will expect me to be there. After all, she sent me a telegram days ago. I'm sure she had no idea how long it would take to reach me. And certainly not that I would be injured and couldn't meet her!"

"You could send a message to her. I know! Sam is going to Missoula with Burley and Jim Two Horses to pick up the new saw blade. He came into town this afternoon, and he'll leave for Missoula bright and early tomorrow morning. He could take a message to your fiancée. Better yet, he could bring her back here."

Stephen hesitated. It would be the next best thing to escorting her himself for Elizabeth to travel under his brother's protection. "But would Sam be willing to? He—I got the impression the other day that he wasn't happy to see me. That he wished I'd never shown up. He might not want the burden of looking after someone for me."

"No. Sam's somebody you can always count on. He wouldn't refuse to escort his brother's future wife, no matter—" Jessie stopped, suddenly realizing how tactless her words would sound.

"No matter how much he dislikes me," Stephen finished for her. "Right?"

Jessie squirmed a little. "I didn't say that."

"You didn't have to. It was obvious that Samuel's feelings toward me were, at best, ambivalent." Stephen's face was cool and polite, a social mask he had learned to wear long ago. "It's all right. It has, after all, been over twenty years. One can hardly expect a brother's feelings not to change. I was aware of that fact when I came here."

He was a cool one about everybody, Jessie thought. His fiancée. His brother. She wondered if he lacked feelings for anyone but himself or if he was simply very good at hiding what he felt. She was used to men who didn't talk much, especially about painful things, but at least they usually showed excitement and anger and happiness in their faces, if not in their words. She was having a hard time, though, guessing what Stephen Ferguson was feeling at the moment.

"Well," she said, "you might as well ask him. I don't know how else you're going to get the lady here if she can't ride the coach alone."

Jessie was right. Much as he hated to ask Sam a favor, given the way Sam had received him, it would be far worse to leave Elizabeth stranded in a wild Western town.

"Yes, you're right. I'll have to ask him."

"Then I'll send him up when he comes to supper." Jessie backed toward the door. She wasn't sure what to do. When she had come up here, she had expected to sit with Stephen through the evening, as she had the night before.

But he was so much better that it would be pointless for her to do so. It left her feeling awkward.

"Thank you." Stephen watched her make her way to the door. She looked almost as if she didn't want to leave, but he was sure that couldn't be true. It was simply that she was utterly lacking in social graces. He could imagine what Elizabeth's reaction to her would be. The thought was enough to make him smile.

Jessie left, and Stephen lay dozing, drifting in and out of sleep. Once, when he awoke, he remembered that in his astonishment and worry over Elizabeth's unexpected telegram, he had forgotten to ask Jessie about the circumstances of his shooting.

The next time he woke up it was because there was a knock at the door. He watched Charles go to the door and open it a fraction, blocking entry into the room. Stephen heard the murmur of low voices. "Who is it, Charles?"

His valet turned his head toward him. "He has not given his name, Master Stephen."

From outside the door he heard a rough, sarcastic voice say, "It's Master Samuel Ferguson of the Nora Springs Fergusons. Do I need an appointment to see my brother?"

Stephen smiled, and his chest felt suddenly lighter. Sam *had* come to see him. He had been afraid that he would not, despite what Jessie had told him. While Charles greeted Sam formally and ushered him into the room, Stephen pushed himself higher in the bed. He hated to look so weak before his brother.

Stephen dismissed his valet, and Charles exited the room quietly. Sam tossed his hat onto a chair near the door and came over to the bed. He stood, looking down at Stephen awkwardly. Stephen motioned toward the chair beside his bed. "Sit down, Sam."

Sam took a seat, clearing his throat. "Sorry about the ambush," he said finally. He sounded as if the words had been dragged out of him. "Somebody may have thought it was me riding with Jessie."

Stephen nodded. There was silence. "Does this sort of

thing happen often out here?'' He strove for a light tone, to break the ice.

"Not often, but occasionally." Sam looked at him. Suddenly a grin split his face. "Damn, but you sure had one hell of a welcome to the territory."

"I did at that," Stephen replied with a laugh, and they settled down to talk much more companionably.

By the time Sam left two hours later, they had learned a good deal about their separate pasts, though each carefully avoided any mention of their mother. Sam had also agreed to escort Elizabeth to Nora Springs, though Stephen had inadvertently upset Sam by offering to pay for the task. Sam was obviously very touchy. However, Stephen had smoothed it over with him, and they had parted on friendly terms.

Stephen smiled to himself. Sam wasn't an easy person to get to know, but they'd made a start. He was no longer the cold stranger he had been the other day at the lumber camp. It might take a while to reestablish their relationship completely, but at least now Stephen knew that he had his brother back again.

Stephen dreamed that night. He was in his home in St. Louis, but Jessie was there with him. They were in a dark hall. She was ahead of him, and he was hurrying to catch up with her. Suddenly, there was a man with her, struggling with her. She called Stephen's name, straining toward him, and he could see her pale, frightened face. He ran to help her, but for some reason he could not go forward. He ran desperately, reaching out for her, but she and her assailant remained in front of him. It was as if his feet were stuck in molasses, or as if the distance between them somehow grew. She screamed, and he called out her name, reaching, reaching...

The pain in Stephen's shoulder and side brought him to consciousness. He was struggling to sit up, reaching out one hand. His wound was on fire. He sucked in an agonized breath and flopped against the mattress.

It was a dream. Nothing but a dream. It had seemed so real and horrible. He closed his eyes. His heart was racing, and he was bathed in sweat.

The door opened, and a woman came in softly, hesitantly. She was carrying a glass kerosene lamp, and as she held it up to throw light over the room, he saw that the woman was Jessie. But this didn't look like the Jessie he knew. She was dressed in a long, heavy robe, belted at the waist, and when she moved across the floor, it separated in front to reveal flashes of pale nightgown beneath it. Her hair was loose, lying around her shoulders and spilling down over her back and breasts. Her tresses were a dark red in the dim light, flashing copper where they caught the light.

It was the first time Stephen had seen her dressed as a woman. And her hair—it was as glorious as he had suspected, a thick, rich fall that shone like satin. "Jessamine." Her name came out a whisper.

"Stephen?" She tiptoed closer. "Are you all right? I thought I heard you call out." She didn't add that it was her own name she had heard.

"Yes. I'm fine. I must have been dreaming."

Jessie nodded and set the lamp on the small table beside his bed. She reached across the bed and laid her hand on his forehead. It was damp with sweat, but not abnormally hot. She turned down the sheet to expose his shoulder and held the lamp closer to inspect his bandage. Jessie shook her head a little, tsking. "Looks like you tore open your wound a little." Her hair brushed against his arm and chest. It tickled his skin. It was as soft as the finest silk he'd ever touched.

She unwrapped the wound quickly, trying to keep her fingers light and steady, and pulled the bandage carefully away, grateful that it didn't stick. Then she folded up another bandage and placed it on him, winding a long strip of cotton around his chest to hold the pad in place.

Jessie felt uncomfortable, though she never would have admitted it. She was very aware of the fact that his torso was bare. She touched his skin time and again as she put the bandage in place. His flesh was smooth, and her fingers tingled strangely every time she brushed against it. She was also embarrassingly aware of her own attire. It wasn't proper for her to be here like this with a man, even if he was flat on his back with a gunshot wound. But that thought made her feel even more like a fool. Since when had Jessie Randall worried about whether what she was doing was proper?

"What did you dream?" she asked, hoping that conversation would diminish the awkwardness.

"I don't remember." Stephen wasn't about to tell her that he'd been frantically trying to save her. The helplessness of the dream still tasted bitter in his mouth. Besides, Jessie would only laugh and remind him that she didn't need anybody to save her, that she could take care of herself.

No doubt she could. She'd not only taken care of herself when the shooting started the other day, she'd taken care of him, as well. The thought galled him.

"Well." Jessie tied the ends of the bandage and stepped back, picking up her lamp. The bandage was a trifle loose and far sloppier-looking than her mother's, but she thought that it would hold until her mother could put on a fresh one. "That's done. I'll let you go back to sleep now."

She turned to leave, but Stephen reached out a hand and grasped her robe. "No, wait. Please."

Jessie turned, her face questioning. "What's the matter?"

"Nothing. I wanted to ask you something. I forgot to earlier."

"All right." She waited a little uneasily.

"That shot. How'd it happen? Who did it?"

"I don't know." She shook her head. "The marshal's investigating it."

"But—was it deliberate? Does the marshal think it was on purpose or an accident?"

Jessie squirmed inside. How was she supposed to answer

him? She didn't want to alarm or upset him, not in his condition, but she hated to lie. "He doesn't know yet," she equivocated finally.

Her silence had told Stephen what he wanted to know. "They meant to shoot me, didn't they?" His forehead creased in thought. "They shot at me more than once. Isn't that right? They kept on trying to kill me. It wasn't an accident."

Jessie hesitated, then nodded. "Yes. They kept on shooting. But we don't know who they were. Why would anybody in Nora Springs want to kill you?"

"I don't know. I don't know anyone here except my father and Sam."

"Well, it wasn't one of them." She shrugged, moving away. "We figure it might have been that they mistook you for Sam. You'd look enough alike from a distance."

"I know. Sam suggested that to me." He paused. "But does anybody hate Sam that much?"

"Somebody crazy. Anyway, we've been gossiping like crazy, Joe and Mama and me, getting the word out that you're not Sam. We figured then maybe he wouldn't try to shoot you if he saw you again."

"But what about Sam? He's still in danger."

"He'll be okay. There are two good men with him, and he's out of town. Joe and I figured he's about as safe as he can be."

"I see." Her words confirmed what he'd been thinking. Yet he sensed that she was still not telling him the truth, at least not all of it.

"Don't worry about it," Jessie assured him. "When the man who shot you learns who you really are, he won't try again."

"But what about Sam? What about when he gets back to town? The killer *will* go after him!"

Jessie nodded. "Maybe." She wasn't about to explain to him that she and Joe thought the attack was probably against the business rather than against Sam alone. Joe would have her head for worrying Stephen about such things when he was still so weak. He wouldn't like her telling Stephen as much as she had, but she didn't know what else to do, the way he kept asking her questions.

"Then something must be done. We have to find out who did it. What about the law? Is that marshal doing anything?"

"Sure. He's looking for the killer. He found where the man was hiding when he fired at you, and he followed the tracks for a ways, but he lost them."

"So he's learned nothing." Stephen frowned. "I don't like the sound of this. Perhaps I ought to send for a detective. We hired one in our business once, and he found the thievery we'd suspected right away. I could send a telegram to him."

"What good would he do out here?" Jessie asked scornfully. "A city man in the mountains?"

Stephen's lips twitched a little in irritation. It was obvious what she thought of the abilities of a man from the city. "Perhaps he couldn't track him through the wilderness, but I would think that finding motives and clues would be pretty much the same, whether one is located in St. Louis or Montana."

"Well, Joe and Sam wouldn't stand for it."

Stephen thought about his brother's prickly pride when he'd offered him money to rent a conveyance for Elizabeth. He suspected that Jessie was right. Sam would be too proud to let him pay for a detective, and he would probably be embarrassed that people might think he couldn't handle the matter himself. Being completely self-sufficient seemed to be the thing the people out here prized most. "All right. I won't send for the detective—yet. But in the meantime, we can find out some things on our own."

"Things like what?"

"Like who would have a grudge against Sam? Who's he fired recently? Or refused to hire? That's a good place to start. You handle the money records for the lumber company. You ought to be able to determine that."

Jessie tried not to let her surprise show. She would never

have guessed that Stephen Ferguson could come up with an idea that practical or sharp. Why, she hadn't even thought of it herself.

"Of course, it could be something personal." Stephen glanced at her uneasily. "Perhaps that's something you shouldn't delve into."

Jessie grinned. "Too nasty for my little ladylike eyes and ears?"

Stephen grimaced. "You, needless to say, don't think that's possible."

"I'll tell you what I think's possible. That my mother and your father will give me holy hell for talking to you about all this when you're supposed to be resting and mending. It's the middle of the night, you know."

"I know." His eyes flickered involuntarily to the neck of her bed robe, where the white of her nightgown showed above the collar.

One of Jessie's hands went to the top of her robe, clutching the two sides tightly together, and she colored a little. Her reaction surprised her, and she felt ridiculous for being embarrassed by nothing more than a man looking at her in her bed robe. Why, he hadn't even said anything suggestive. She made her hand relax and drop to her side, and forced her eyes to meet his coolly. "Good night."

"Good night." She started out the door. "Miss Randall!"

She paused and looked at him over her shoulder.

"Thank you for coming to see about me. You take good care of your patients."

His words warmed her inside, but Jessie just shrugged. She didn't know how to handle a compliment, especially from this man. "It wasn't anything. You go back to sleep now."

"I will. Good night."

She slipped out the door, and the room was plunged into darkness. Stephen lay looking out the window at the cold quarter moon. He wondered where Elizabeth was and why she was coming here. He wondered why someone had taken shots at him—or Sam. And he wondered what Jessie Randall looked like beneath that robe.

Stephen was a healthy young man, and he healed quickly. Soon he was getting out of bed with his valet's help and making his way slowly around the room. Every day he would sit up in a chair by the window, and with each day the time he spent there grew longer. But he still felt absurdly weak, and, to his impatient spirit, it was taking far too long to get well. His mind was fully alert and active despite his body's weakness, and he was bored.

Joe came by to see him every evening. They spent most of their time chatting about the sawmill and the lumber business. Stephen was curious about it, as he was eager to learn about most businesses, and Joe was more than happy to talk about it. Except for Sam, the lumber business had been Joe's life; he loved it with a feeling that ran far deeper than most men's attitudes toward their jobs. He was a part of it—the land, the trees, the vibrating hum of the mill. There was no job in the industry that he hadn't worked, no aspect of it he hadn't seen. And he loved every bit of it.

He told Stephen stories about the old days in the timber business, when the lumber camps had been smaller, primitive affairs, usually with only one building. He talked about the exhilaration and danger of driving the logs downriver, risking death with any slip of one's feet. He talked about starting the mill, and about the time it had caught on fire a few years ago, the sawdust sending it up in flames in an instant. It was one of the many hazards of the business, and he and Sam had simply started over. The more he talked, the more intrigued Stephen became. He chafed at his weakened state, feeling eager to get down to the mill again and take a tour with his father.

It was a wonderful thing to be with Joe, to be able to talk and joke with him. Stephen loved his grandfather, but Grandpapa was a distant, formal man, not given to affection or close companionship. Elizabeth's father had been the nearest thing he'd had to a father, and he had often gone to him for advice and sometimes even for comfort. But neither of them was the man Joseph Ferguson was; neither of them was the warm, laughing, rough yet tender father Stephen had known for the first five years of his life. They could not substitute for the man who had held Stephen on his lap and told him stories about daring, strong men and their impossible feats, who had whistled as he moved around the cabin, and who had been prone to burst into song on a long, cold winter's evening and grab his wife and whirl her around the room in a vigorous dance.

It was this man whom Stephen had never forgotten, whom he had held always in his heart, and it was like a miracle to be with him again. Sometimes Joe talked about his business or his love of the land; other times he recalled moments from Stephen's or Sam's childhood. He talked about his parents, long dead, and he talked about Eleanor as she had been when they fell in love. The more Stephen was with him, the more memories he dredged up from his youth, and with each new recollection, each remembered feeling and incident, he grew closer to his father.

Jessie visited Stephen, too, though not as often as Joe did. She rarely had much to say, just asked how he was doing and stood there awkwardly, until finally she left the room. Stephen felt like a fool at those times. Never before had he been so unable to carry on a conversation with a woman. He had been in hundreds of social situations, and he had always managed to keep the flow of talk going smoothly, no matter how tongue-tied or boring the other person might be. Every hostess in St. Louis considered him an asset. Yet here he was, unable to think of anything to say to a backwoods girl who dressed and acted like a man! It was absurd.

Stephen wanted to talk to her. Except for the visits from Joe, Stephen's days were deadly dull. Charles would have been shocked down to his toes had Stephen tried to chat with him, and Mrs. Randall was too busy to stay and talk. He quickly went through the single book he had brought to read, and he found that there were no books at all in

Mrs. Randall's house except for a few old schoolbooks. When he was able, he went down to the garden to sit, but the late September weather was already too cold for him to remain outdoors comfortably, and he usually returned to the house quickly. He spent most of his time sleeping or staring aimlessly out the window.

He would have welcomed any diversion. But that wasn't the only reason he wanted to talk to Jessie. He was intrigued by her. She was such an odd creature, and, for reasons he didn't delve into, he wanted to understand her. But he could think of nothing to say that would interest her. He was sure she would react with scorn to any of the customary polite chatter he used with women. Nor did she seem to be curious about any of the places he had lived or the things he knew. In fact, he wasn't sure what she would like to talk about, but he was certain that it would be something he knew nothing about. Given the silence and uncomfortableness that usually lay between them, Stephen sometimes wondered why she came to see him at all.

He didn't know it, but Jessie frequently wondered the same thing. It was obvious that Stephen was healing; there was no need to check in on him every night. And the visits certainly weren't enjoyable. Yet somehow, she couldn't keep her steps from turning to his room every evening when she came home—anymore than she could stop thinking about what he had said that night when he'd been dosed up with laudanum. He had said she could be "enchanting."

It was an idea that scared Jessie, yet it drew her, too. Before this, she would have said that she was utterly unconcerned with her looks. If anything, she wanted to be plain; it drew a lot less talk and jests from the men. But ever since Stephen had spoken that night, she found herself glancing at her reflection whenever she passed a mirror. Sometimes in the evening, in the privacy of her bedroom, she would go to her mirror and stare into it, studying each feature carefully. Was there beauty lying dormant there? Could that face, that form, attract a man? A man like Sam Ferguson?

Jessie had never fooled herself. She had adored Sam for years, first with the love of a kid sister and then with more adult, confused feelings, but she had never expected Sam to feel anything for her. She was a tomboy, slender, not billowing like the floozie she'd caught sight of Sam walking with one time. She had a redhead's skin, marred with freckles across her nose and cheeks, and her hair was the color of carrots. She wasn't feminine the way a man wanted a woman to be. Hell, she didn't even know how to pretend to be feminine. And she didn't want to be, not really. Not if it meant simpering and giggling like Mr. Swenson's daughter, Olga. Or wearing constricting skirts and silly hats. And yet…

She would never forget the shock in Stephen Ferguson's eyes when he had realized that she was a woman, not a boy. That horror galled her, ate away at her inside in a way that the other men's jokes and insults never had. Clear as day, he'd hardly been able to believe that she was a woman. He had been disgusted; she remembered just as well the cutting remarks he had made about her lack of femininity. Of course, she didn't *care* what someone like Stephen Ferguson thought about her. Still, it hurt; she couldn't deny the little ache in her chest. And she couldn't help thinking what pleasant balm it would be to her soul to have Stephen look at her with admiration. Was it possible that she could get him to look at her that way?

She couldn't help wondering if maybe she had missed out on something other women, like her mother, knew. She couldn't help thinking about how she would look in a dress, with her hair piled up on her head. What would Sam think if he saw her that way? Might he stop thinking of her as just an amusing little sister? What would it be like to have men glance at her in an entirely new way? Would they smile and flirt with her—or would they guffaw at the sight of her all gussied up?

Such thoughts occupied her mind more and more as the days passed. Once she even sneaked into her mother's room and tried on one of her dresses. But she couldn't tell much about how she would look, since her mother was a larger, more buxom woman, and the dress hung loosely on her, about as attractive as a sack. Obviously it wasn't something she could go at halfway. And it took more than a dress and a new hairdo; she knew that. It would mean acting differently, talking differently. She wasn't willing to do all that, of course, just for this silly whim. And even if she was willing, she wouldn't know where to start, or how to tell if she was making progress or just making a fool of herself. She would need help, and there was no one in the whole town to help her.

Except Stephen Ferguson.

Jessie rejected the idea as soon as it popped into her head. That was crazy. There was no way she'd let that snobby man view her stumbling, bumbling efforts to be feminine and pretty. If anyone would laugh at her, he would. Why, he knew beautiful and sophisticated women, the kind of women who bought dresses that cost more than her whole salary, and who draped themselves with jewels. He was used to women who knew how to flirt and what to say to a man, who knew how to make a man come running with merely a quirk of one eyebrow. Women like his fiancée. He would think Jessie was ridiculous, and that her efforts to look pretty were pitiful. Stephen Ferguson was the last man to whom she'd expose such foolish, fragile seedlings of hope.

On the other hand, she didn't care what he thought, did she? He didn't matter to her. And he was the kind of man who would know what she should be like. If she asked someone like Sam, he'd probably just shrug and say a woman was "like...well, a woman. You know." No, she didn't know. But Stephen Ferguson did.

He would be willing to help her, too. He was grateful to her for saving his life. If she looked like a fool in front of him, it wouldn't really matter, because he'd be gone in a few weeks.

The idea began to take root in her mind and grow. Finally, one evening, as she lingered by Stephen's door, unable to find anything to say yet reluctant to leave, she drew a deep breath and said abruptly, "Stephen, do you reckon you could make me into a woman?"

Chapter Eight

Stephen's jaw dropped. "Pardon?" She couldn't possibly have said what he thought she had.

"If I wanted to—*just if!*—I wanted to, you know, act like other women, could you teach me how? How to talk and act and everything?"

"Oh." For one flabbergasted moment, he had thought Jessie was asking him to take her to his bed. Of course she would never...and *he* would never...

"Well? Could you?" Jessie prodded, feeling more and more foolish for having asked. It had been a stupid idea. Stephen wouldn't do it. He couldn't; nobody could accomplish miracles. Besides, she didn't really want to change, anyhow.

"I—I don't know. You've deprived me of speech for the moment. I never dreamed..."

Jessie shrugged. "It's not important. You don't have to answer. I was just curious." She turned as though to leave the room.

"No! Wait. Don't go! It must have been important or you wouldn't have asked. I would think it took quite a bit of courage. Give me a minute to assimilate what you said. You want me to help in—in appearing more feminine?"

"I guess. I don't know. I just kept thinking about the things you said about me not being like a woman."

"I'm sorry. I shouldn't have said that. I was irritated with you, and I lashed out. You have a remarkable ability to irritate me." He smiled.

Jessie grinned back. "You're not the only one I have that ability with."

"I'm sure not." Stephen swung his legs off the bed and stood. He wore a dressing gown of heavy quilted satin over his bedclothes. He had another one, Jessie knew, of deep blue velvet, because she had seen him in it, too. Why would a man take two robes with him when he traveled? Jessie would have been surprised to learn that Sam had even one robe, let alone two. And certainly none like these! She had seen such rich fabrics only on the banker's wife, and then just on special occasions. The robe suited him, though; he looked more handsome than any man had a right to be, especially a few days past a gunshot wound.

Stephen walked over to her. "First of all, I'm not sure I can help you. I'm not privy to all the secrets and rules of ladylike behavior."

"But you know enough. You know that I'm not one. You must know how I should act."

"Perhaps some basics, but…are you sure you want to do this? Why, suddenly, do you want to act like a lady?"

Jessie's color rose. She wouldn't admit to him how intrigued she had been by his remark that she was enchanting. Nor was she willing to tell him that his insults about her lack of femininity had stung. And revealing the vague yearnings she had inside for a home, husband and family was out of the question. She shrugged and started to turn away. "If you won't do it, that's all right."

"Wait a minute." He reached out and grabbed her wrist, holding her still. "Are you always this difficult to talk to?"

She swung to face him, her chin up. "I reckon."

"Frankly, I don't see how I can help you if every time I say something or ask a question, you threaten to leave. I have to have your cooperation, you know."

Jessie looked at him suspiciously. "Does that mean you're going to do it?"

He sighed. "I'll do what I can. I'm not promising anything. I'm not a lady's maid or a deportment teacher. But I'll tell you everything I can think of. On one condition."

Her face closed up even tighter. "That's what I figured."

"And that is: you have to do what I tell you and not argue."

"Do what you tell me!" Her eyes opened wider. "What does that mean?"

"Nothing reprehensible, I assure you."

"Dang you, I can't understand half of what you say. What do you mean?"

"I mean, I have no intention of asking you to do anything wrong. But I refuse to put myself through the ordeal of arguing with you over every little thing I tell you to do. I've been around you enough to know that you will."

"I won't! Why would I ask you to teach me something and then not do it?"

"I don't know why, but I feel certain that you will. I'll tell you a lady does such and such, and you'll say, 'Why, tarnation, that's stupid!'" He mimicked her voice so effectively that Jessie had to giggle.

"So you're going to tell me to do a bunch of stupid things?"

"I imagine you'll think so."

Her expression wavered; then she set her jaw. "Well, I may not like it, and I may think it's stupid, but I won't argue."

"And you promise that you'll do it?"

"All right. I promise." Her mouth turned mulish. "But don't you go putting any jokes over on me, understand?"

"Jokes?"

"Yeah, like getting me to do ridiculous stuff, telling me it's what ladies do."

"Jessie! I wouldn't do that." He looked at her, puzzled. "Why would I want to make you look ridiculous?"

"I don't know. But men are always pulling that kind of thing."

"Well, I promise you that I won't. So, do we have an agreement?"

Jessie swallowed. She was scared of entering the unknown. Maybe she ought to forget the whole thing. But she couldn't. For whatever crazy reason, she knew she just had to do this. "All right." She wiped a nervous palm down her pants leg to remove the telltale dampness, then stuck out her hand. "It's a deal."

"It's a deal," he repeated and shook her hand. He'd never shaken a woman's hand before, only taken one to bow over it in greeting. Her hand felt odd, pressed palm to palm in his, so small and delicate, yet hardened with calluses and firm of grip, as well. He thought of how she had looked the other night when she had come into his room. He remembered the thick red hair hanging down around her shoulders like a silken cape. He had wanted to touch it. He still wanted to.

Stephen realized that he had held her hand longer than was customary, and he dropped it quickly. He backed up a step. It was crazy that he should feel even a twinge of desire for this girl. She wasn't at all feminine; she had none of the grace or culture Elizabeth had. They were as far apart as the poles. The only reason desire had rippled through him at the thought of touching her hair, he told himself, was that she was the only woman he'd been around for days, besides Mrs. Randall. It was only proximity and a lack of any other sort of female companionship.

He wondered what Jessie would do if he kissed her—or even ran a hand over her fiery hair. Probably send a right uppercut straight to his jaw. He smiled a little at the image.

"Well?" Jessie said brightly. "Where do we start?"

Stephen glanced at her. "You mean now? You want to begin right now?"

"Why not? No use wasting time. I mean, you'll only be laid up a few more days, and before long your fiancée will be here."

And Sam would be back. Stephen suspected that his brother was the man Jessie had decided to impress with her newly acquired femininity. He had seen the adoration in her eyes when she looked at Sam at the lumber camp. It made him feel a little strange to think that he was going to coach her so that she could pursue his brother. "All right," he replied, revealing none of his thoughts. "Where shall we start?"

"I don't know. That's why I asked you to teach me."

He crossed his arms and studied her. "Well, there are the obvious things. Your manner of dress, for instance. Ladies don't wear trousers."

"I don't have any dresses."

He blinked. "None?"

Jessie shook her head. "None that'll fit me. Last time I wore a dress was when I was fourteen years old."

"I see. Then, perhaps you could make one?"

He knew what her answer would be even before she began to shake her head. "Nope. I never learned."

"Well, it's hopeless if you aren't going to dress like a woman. We might as well save ourselves the trouble."

"I can wear some of Mama's clothes, I guess. And there's a woman in town who takes in sewing. I could pay her to fix up a dress for me."

"Good. That's a place to start. And you have to stop swearing. Ladies don't curse."

"I don't cuss all that much!" Jessie retorted indignantly.

"At all. Ladies don't curse at all. And your speech is—" he paused, groping for what he meant "—too rough. Too inelegant. You speak too bluntly and openly."

"I'm not sure I understand."

"We'll work on it. Also—and this is very, very important—ladies do not spit."

"Spit! I don't—" Jessie started to deny indignantly, then remembered her behavior when he'd met her. "Oh. Well, I don't do that normally. I just did it that day because you were so uppity."

"Uppity?"

"Yeah, you know—you acted like you were better than

anybody else. And you looked so—so shiny and polished, like a doll in a store. It got the better of me.''

"So you did it to shock me." Jessie nodded. "You did that, all right." He chuckled softly.

Jessie was surprised that he wasn't mad. Even as she was saying the words, she had been afraid he would explode. Instead, he had laughed. She found herself almost liking him.

"However." Stephen tried to pull his face back into stern lines. "Shocking people is not something ladies do, either."

"Sounds to me like ladies don't do anything."

"Of course they do things. They dance, sing, converse, laugh, have fun—but they do them in a softer, more genteel way. I think the difference is more one of attitude than conduct. I think you've tried very hard for years to make people believe that you aren't a woman. You've tried to think, talk and act like a man. Being a woman is natural to you, but you've done your best to hide it, even from yourself."

Jessie frowned. "I don't know what you're talking about."

"Take your name, for instance."

"What about my name?"

"Jessie. It sounds like a man's name. Sometimes it's even Jess. But, in fact, your real name is Jessamine. It's a lovely name, graceful and feminine. You've denied that name and substituted one that's masculine."

"The hell you say!"

"Jessie..." He looked pained. "I told you, ladies don't curse."

"Not even a 'hell' or a 'damn'?"

He shook his head.

"Not even sometimes?" Jessie frowned. "Well, he—I mean, what do they say when they get mad?"

He paused, nonplussed, trying to remember a time when he had heard his mother or Elizabeth angry. "I'm not sure.

The normal things, I guess. But they don't scream or curse. Or threaten to punch someone in the nose.''

Her eyes narrowed. "I never—at least, you never heard me say that.''

"Maybe not, but I suspect you have. Hitting people is not particularly ladylike, either.''

"I suppose shooting a gun isn't, either.''

"Not that I've noticed,'' he agreed.

"Then how does a woman protect herself?''

"That's what men are for.''

Jessie snorted. "Well, who else does a person need protection from, except men?''

"Not all men will protect a woman, of course. But a gentleman should protect a woman from danger and—and trouble, unpleasant things, the harsher aspects of life.''

"I reckon I don't know many gentlemen, then. 'Sides, I'd rather depend on myself. It's safer. I'd think a man'd get tired, always running to some woman's rescue.''

Amusement quirked one corner of his mouth. "Some women take less rescuing than others.''

"Yeah, and some never get rescued at all.''

"I'm sure you're right.'' He paused. "But I think we're getting a little far afield here. Aren't we supposed to be discussing how you should act?''

"Yeah.'' Jessie sighed. "I'm just not sure I'll like how I turn out.''

"You can always change back, in that case. Look, if you don't want to go through with it, we don't have to.''

"No.'' Jessie set her chin. "I made up my mind I was going to do it, and I will. Go ahead.''

"All right. Jessamine.''

Teaching Jessie how to be a lady was a slow and often frustrating task, but Stephen found that at least it kept him from being bored while he recovered. The next evening she appeared at his door after supper dressed in a calico dress that obviously belonged to her mother. It hung loosely on her shoulders, and the sash around her small waist made the material pucker and gather. It was not a pretty dress by any means, but it gave her a softer, more feminine look.

"Very nice," Stephen told her.

Jessie smiled a little at his words and entered the room. It occurred to Stephen that she was shy about being seen this way. She glanced into the hall and closed the door behind her, confirming his guess. "Do you really think so?"

"Yes. You already look more like a lady." But he couldn't help thinking of the way her denim trousers had outlined her legs and bottom. The dress hid everything except the daintiness of her waist.

"It's one of Mama's dresses." Jessie looked doubtfully at the garment, pulling out a piece of the loose bodice. "It's kind of big. I just took it out of her wardrobe and threw it on." She lifted the hem of her dress and petticoats to reveal her usual laced boots and, above them, the cuffs of her trousers.

Stephen pressed his lips together to hide his smile. "I'm afraid—" It was a struggle to keep the amusement out of his voice. "I'm afraid the shoes will have to go, too. It's hard to walk like a lady in work boots."

Jessie grimaced. "I figured that. But I didn't have anything else, and Mama's feet are smaller than mine. I guess tomorrow I could go buy some—some high button shoes."

Her cheeks were faintly flushed. "That embarrasses you, doesn't it?" Stephen asked in amusement.

Jessie shrugged and looked away. She didn't like to admit to weakness. "I guess."

"But why? You *are* a woman. Why would you be embarrassed to buy women's shoes?"

"I don't know. I guess I'm afraid they'll laugh."

"Believe me, no one who's trying to sell you a pair of shoes will laugh at you."

"Yeah. But they could tell other people. Somebody might see me doing it. And the men at the mill would snicker about it. 'Why, lookee there, ole Jessie's decided she wants to be a woman now!'" She mimicked a man's teasing voice. "'Reckon she's found herself a man?'"

"Oh, Jessie." Stephen impulsively took her hands. "What does it matter if a few buffoons laugh? All it proves is that they're ignorant, ill-mannered fools. How you look or what you do is none of their business. What *you* think is what counts. Besides, they'll get used to it in a few days."

Jessie looked at the floor. "I suppose."

"Come on." Stephen put a finger under her chin and tilted her face so she could look at him. "Since when is Jessie Randall scared of a few louts? I thought you believed in doing what you wanted and letting the devil take the hindmost?"

She smiled faintly. "Yeah. You're right." Her chin came out farther. "It's my business, not theirs. And if they want to make something of it, I'll pop 'em in the jaw."

"Oh, Jessie, no," he started, then saw the twinkle in her eyes and realized that she was joking. He chuckled, and Jessie joined him. He felt suddenly warm and close to her. He gave her hands a squeeze and let them slide from his fingers. His own hands felt strangely empty suddenly. "All right. Now you need to learn how to walk."

"How to walk! I already know how to walk."

"Not in a dress. You strode into the room like this." Stephen walked away with long, purposeful strides.

"Yeah, and these dang skirts and petticoats kept getting in the way."

"That's precisely my point. You don't walk like that in skirts. Your steps should be shorter, daintier, more—"

"Ladylike," Jessie finished for him in a singsong voice. She sighed. "All right. How's this?"

She came toward him slowly.

"Better. But you need to take short strides. You don't have to be so slow, just take shorter steps."

Jessie grimaced. "Sounds like more work to me." She tried a few mincing steps.

"Much better."

"I was joking."

"Well, it looked good."

Jessie rolled her eyes.

"Now, as you walk, you need to sway a little."

"Sway?" Jessie began to weave. "Are you crazy?"

"No, not like that. Like this." Stephen folded his hands demurely at his waist and began to walk, trying to gently swing his hips.

Jessie burst into laughter at his ludicrous portrayal.

Stephen turned and fixed her with a falsely stern gaze. "Please, I'm trying to be serious here." She responded with another hoot of laughter, and he grinned. "All right. All right. You know what I mean."

"Oh, sure," Jessie gasped. She managed to straighten up enough to walk across the room, swinging her slender hips exaggeratedly. Her skirts swished and curled around her legs. She paused, posing, one hip thrown out and her lips pursed in a mockery of seductiveness.

Stephen groaned. "No, no, no. I didn't say walk like a—a..."

"Slut?" Jessie suggested, ruining her pose by grinning. "Spoiled dove?"

Stephen shook his head. "You're hopeless."

"I think you're right." Jessie plopped down on the mattress in a very unladylike manner and hooked the heels of her boots on the side rail of the bed.

"No. I didn't mean that. You'll learn to do this—I intend to make sure of it. But you obviously aren't going to make my task any easier."

"Well, you started it."

"Started what?" Stephen asked with an air of accused innocence.

Jessie cast him a disgusted look and bounced to her feet. "Okay. Here we go." She began to walk carefully, taking short steps and making her hips sway back and forth. But she couldn't get the movement coordinated, and she stopped, crashing a heel onto the floor and growling, "Oooh! I can't do it!"

"Just keep on trying. Don't think about it too much, that makes you awkward." She began again. "Better. But you're still moving too much." Stephen came up behind her as she walked and put his hands on her hips to hold her down to exactly the right amount of sway.

Heat surged through Jessie; she was sure her face must be flaming. She couldn't think about anything but his fingers curled lightly across her hips, his palms flat against her. She lost her concentration and took a misstep, stumbling and almost falling. Stephen grabbed at her waist to keep her upright, his fingertips digging into her flesh. Jessie was aware of each separate finger; her skin was suddenly hot in each spot.

"Are you all right?"

Jessie nodded. But she wasn't, not at all. She had the strangest feelings running through her, all tingles and prickles and shivers, and she wasn't sure whether she wanted to giggle or run.

Stephen moved his hands down to her hips. "All right. Let's start again." His voice sounded deeper and huskier. Jessie wondered if he felt anything at having his hands so intimately on her body. She was amply protected, of course, by the padding of petticoats, skirt and trousers, but still, it wasn't the sort of place where people of limited acquaintance touched each other.

She began to walk, struggling to concentrate on her steps rather than on his hands. It wasn't easy. His fingers were long and slender, and there was a surprising firmness in his grip. Her flesh pushed against one or the other hand with every step.

"Good. Very good." His hands slid from her hips in a movement that was almost a caress. Jessie's heart jumped into a fast, irregular beat. Her skin burned where he had touched her. She kept her face turned away from him for fear that he would see in her expression how his touch had affected her.

"Now, when you are walking with a gentleman," Stephen said, coming around to stand beside her, "you put your hand on his arm, thus." He took her left hand in his and brought it up to rest on the inside of his arm, just above his elbow. He held his arm bent, his elbow jutting out from his body. Jessie curled her fingers around his arm. "That's right. Now, we will walk together."

They walked around the room. It took Jessie a few moments to get into the rhythm of walking with him. It was strange to be walking this close to a man, her hand on his arm. The fact that Stephen was wearing a dressing gown instead of street clothes made it even more peculiar. The satin was slick and cool beneath her skin; she had an urge to slide her hand up and down it, to sink her fingers into it. She had never felt anything this opulent. Her senses seemed more alive than usual, especially her sense of touch, and it took a great deal of restraint to keep her fingers from exploring the soft, alluring material.

Stephen looked at Jessie. She kept her eyes on her feet. "Look up, not down," he told her, reaching over to tilt her chin up.

She glanced at him. Her eyes were wide and luminous, the blue dark in the lamplight, and there was an open, soft quality to her face that Stephen had never seen there before. His breath stopped in his throat. She was lovely.

It was nothing to do with her dress or her newly acquired walk. It was an innate beauty that Jessie usually kept tamped down, under control. But something inside her was loosening, changing. For the moment her guard was down.

Or was it that his own guard was down? That he was seeing her for the first time without being deceived by her clothes and manner?

Stephen stopped abruptly, and Jessie followed suit, surprised. They gazed at each other for a moment that could have been one heartbeat long or a hundred. Stephen stared at her, seeing her soft, wide mouth and the glow of her skin, the curves and lines of her features.

Stephen broke the gaze first, turning his head away. Jessie came to with a start, for the first time realizing how close they had been standing and how long she had been looking into Stephen's face. She backed up quickly. He glanced at her and away, then cleared his throat.

"Uh, I, that's enough for tonight." Stephen felt suddenly, surprisingly weak, as he had when he was first recovering. "We'll try it again tomorrow."

"Of course." Jessie nodded. Stephen looked odd, as strange as she felt herself. "Are you all right?" She made a move toward him. "Is your wound hurting you?"

"No, I'm fine. Perhaps I overdid a little today. I feel suddenly tired."

"Shall I send for Charles?"

"No. I'll be all right. I'll simply rest for a minute." The last thing he wanted was to have his servant fussing over him.

"All right. Then I'll go. See you tomorrow night?"

He nodded, and she left the room. Stephen noticed that this time she swept right out into the hall without stopping first to see if anyone was there.

Stephen sank down into his chair with a sigh and closed his eyes. What a bizarre turn of events. He wanted Jessie. No, Jessamine. Surely that was who he desired, the woman hidden inside her. Not the prickly, pants-wearing, cussing tomboy Jessie. How could he desire a woman, a girl, really, who wore faded denim trousers and worn work boots? Who pulled her hair into tight braids like a schoolgirl? Who could handle a horse and a gun and account books with equal ease? She wasn't the sort of woman he was used to. She had no understanding of the world in which he lived. He felt sure she would have no interest in a good book or fine music. She had never attended a play or an opera; she hadn't danced at a ball. She didn't flirt; she didn't entice, even in subtle ways. No perfume drifted on the air around her to awaken his senses.

Then why had he felt that hot, bemused moment of desire? And, admit it, it hadn't been the first time; it hadn't come upon him without warning. There had been other flashes of passion. But why?

Stephen thought of the curve of her leg and derriere beneath her trousers. He thought of the way the denim pants cupped her body where her legs met, emphasizing the very threshold of her femininity. He squirmed in his seat. Damn! Just the thought of her was making him hot.

He remembered the intimacy of seeing her in her night robe, her hair down. Her hair had been a dark flame, thick and soft, and he had wanted to sink his hands into it. He had wanted to bury his face in it. He thought of her waist, cinched in by the sash of her mother's dress. Her breasts, with the soft flannel of her man's shirt pulled taut over them. The white column of her throat where she left the top button unfastened.

Jessie had hard edges, God knows. She was tough and smart, and she knew how to take care of herself. She was no fragile flower. Yet there was a sort of shining innocence about her. Wouldn't it be a sweeter victory to win her than an ordinary woman?

Stephen shook his head hard, as though clearing it of his thoughts. It was absurd to think this way. He might see something desirable in Jessie, but she wouldn't be interested in him. She didn't think of him as a man but as some sort of foreign dandy. She was in all likelihood in love with his brother. And even if those things weren't true, she simply was not the kind of woman for him. She would never fit into his world. Nor was she the kind of woman to whom a man could offer less than marriage. She might not personify his idea of a lady, but he knew that she was a woman of high morals. Most important of all, he was engaged to be married to another woman!

He thought of Elizabeth, whom he loved, whom he had asked to be his wife. She was the proper wife for him, the one who should be at his side throughout his life. He had loved her for years; they understood each other. Yet he couldn't deny that in all the years he had known Elizabeth, he had never felt that sudden, vibrant flash of desire that had ripped through him a moment ago when he looked at Jessie. He had to admit that while he loved Elizabeth, while he knew that they were suited to each other, he did not feel passion for her. But he knew many people who had not married for passion; among people such as himself and Elizabeth there were other considerations—matters of business and society and leading the right kind of life. There was the promise he had made to Elizabeth's father.

Stephen rose and went to his bed, unfastening his robe as he walked. He felt very weary. Perhaps it had been too tiring to teach Jessie; perhaps he should stop. Yet he knew he would not.

He got into bed and lay down. The wound in his shoulder itched beneath the bandage, and, tired as he was, he found it difficult to sleep. His mind kept going to Jessie. And to Elizabeth. He thought of his brother. Sam, he knew, wouldn't worry about the proper thing to do. If he didn't desire a woman, he wouldn't marry her. Nothing would stand in his way. Stephen wondered how it would feel to be like that, to operate on instincts, to always be the first man in a fight. And, for a moment, he wished he was his brother.

reading perhaps, but he knew many people who had not
married for passion; among people born as himself and
Elise, there were other considerations—matters of business and society and estate—the right kind of life. These
were the reasons he had made to Elizabeth's father.

Stephen rose and went to his bureau, removing his robe
as he walked. He lay down on the narrow, hard bed too
tired to reach her room anymore tonight. Yet he knew
he would not . . .

He got out of bed and pulled on his robe again. In his
robe pocket, his hand closed around a folded note. He found
a cheroot to smoke, his hand just going to relax. After so
long . . . He rubbed at his robe pocket, Stephen continued . . .

Chapter Nine

Stephen awoke the next morning feeling restless. He
dressed and went downstairs for his breakfast, as he had
done for the past two days. Everyone was gone except Mrs.
Randall, who was busy washing dishes in the kitchen. He
ate in solitary silence, plagued by a nagging boredom. Perhaps he ought to try a longer walk today. He had taken to
walking close to the house over the last few days, each day
stretching the distance a little farther. Yesterday he had
walked halfway to the mill. Maybe today he would go all
the way there.

A smile touched Stephen's lips. He liked a challenge,
and he was bored stiff with coddling himself. After all, the
doctor had said that his shoulder was almost completely
healed. It had been over a week since he'd been shot. He
needed to release the energy that had been building up inside him.

His valet helped him into his coat. "Sir, are you certain
you should venture out today? It seems rather cold for a
man just out of his sickbed."

"Yes, I'm certain. Don't fuss, Charles." Stephen thought
that it could be quite irritating having a servant help you
to dress. It would be so much faster to throw on his coat
himself rather than wait for Charles to bring it and hold it
for him. He wanted to be gone.

"Yes, sir."

Stephen sighed. "I'm sorry, Charles. I'm irritable these days. I'm tired of being cooped up."

"Yes, sir, I know. And, of course, I wouldn't presume, except that the weather here is unseasonably cool."

"I know. I didn't realize it would be so much colder than at home. Silly. We are practically to Canada. I must buy a warmer coat, I suppose."

"Here?" Charles looked appalled. "Oh, Mr. Ferguson, I'm sure this town couldn't possibly have a garment of the style and quality to which you are accustomed."

Stephen grinned. "You're probably right. But right now I'm more interested in warmth than style and quality."

"But—will we be staying that long?"

Stephen's grin widened. "What's the matter, Charles? Are you finding the West not to your liking?"

"Well, frankly, sir, it is a bit primitive. That wasn't apparent in the stories I read. And in the books it seemed much more—exciting."

"You mean my getting shot wasn't exciting?"

"No, sir, that was quite enough excitement. But I found that it was more frightening than enjoyable. In the stories, it was, well, it sounded different. Better."

"I've never read any of your stories, I'm afraid. But, you know, I've found that I like it better than I had imagined I would."

"Sir! But you were shot!"

"I didn't like that, of course. But there's something about this country that's...intriguing."

"Indeed." Charles's tone indicated that he found that highly unlikely.

"Indeed." Stephen smiled again and started toward the front door.

"Sir? Shall I accompany you?"

"No. I think I'd like to be by myself today. No need for you to go out in the cold, too."

"Thank you, sir."

Stephen stepped outside and started toward the mill at a

brisk pace. It was, in fact, colder than it had been the past few days, but he found the weather invigorating. He felt almost his old self again, healthy and strong, and there was a spring to his step. It made him happy to think of going to the mill. He looked forward to seeing his father and the surprise that would be on his face, to seeing the mill in operation after days of hearing his father talk about it. To seeing Jessie.

Not, of course, that that was why he was going.

Jessie found herself doodling on the paper before her and realized that she had been doing nothing for several minutes, just staring blindly at a letter and absentmindedly marking on it. She sighed in exasperation and seized an eraser to get rid of her drawing, an entwining of hearts, leaves and flowers. What a stupid thing to do!

She didn't know why she had been unable to keep her mind on business today. She had already made three mistakes in addition and had had to go over her figures countless times to find the errors. She had managed to waste so much time that she might as well not even have come to work. Thank goodness Joe had ridden up to the camp to check on it in Sam's absence and hadn't been here to see how poorly she had been working.

Jessie pushed back her chair and began to pace around the office. It was all that damned Stephen Ferguson's fault, she thought in irritation. No, she mentally corrected herself, that *darned* Stephen Ferguson's fault. Or maybe even *darned* was too harsh a word for a lady to use. What should one say?

Oh, hell, what did it matter, anyway? That was precisely the kind of thing that was getting her into trouble. All this worrying over what was proper and what wasn't and how she should act—all this *damned* lady-fying that Stephen Ferguson was putting her through.

Satisfaction poured through her at her mental use of one of the forbidden words, and Jessie smiled as though she had somehow outwitted her teacher. She conveniently ignored the fact that it was she who had asked Stephen to help her act like a lady. Instead, she recounted to herself the many sins that Stephen Ferguson had committed over the past few days, the humiliations and idiocies he had put her through. *"Do this. Don't do that."* Why, he had her so twisted around that she hardly knew whether she was coming or going!

She had stayed awake for hours last night, thinking about Stephen and his lessons, remembering his arm under her hand, his fingers digging into her hips as he showed her how to sway. Her nerves had been so jumpy and her stomach so churning that she hadn't been able to sleep. She felt strange around Stephen, confused and on edge. He was making her distracted and nervous, and if she had any sense she'd put a stop to all this "lady training" silliness right now!

The door to the office opened, breaking into her thoughts, and Jessie whirled around. Frank Grissom stood there. He grinned and leaned against the doorjamb, crossing his arms. "Why, Jessie, you jumped like a scared rabbit. What's the matter? Nerves jangling? I could help you relax."

Jessie grimaced. Grissom's leer raked her already irritated nerves. "There's not a thing on earth you could help me with!" she snapped and marched to her desk. "Now, what do you want?"

"Nothin' in particular. Just wanted to see you. Ain't seen you around much lately."

Jessie shrugged. "I've been busy."

"Yeah, I heard you been waitin' hand and foot on that sissy fella up at your ma's house, the one that got hisself shot. What happened? Did he shoot hisself in the foot tryin' to figure out which end of a gun was which?"

Jessie's mouth thinned, and she planted her hands on her hips pugnaciously. "No, we got ambushed, that's what happened to him, and you good and well know it. It's been all over town the whole week."

Grissom shrugged. "I don't much listen to gossip, leastways not about him. You're what interests me, Jessie, not some city slicker that can't take care of himself in the woods."

"I'd like to know who could keep from getting ambushed?" Jessie retorted hotly. "I was with him, and *I* sure couldn't do anything about it."

"For God's sake." Grissom pushed himself away from the door frame and started across the room toward her. "Stop yammering about that fool. I didn't come here to argue about him."

"I know. You came here to see me. Well, you've seen me. Now you can leave."

"You know something? You're a hard woman." Grissom stopped on the other side of the desk. His eyes moved slowly down Jessie's body, bright with lust. "But you've got a fine shape on you. I reckon you know that, the way you prance around in them tight trousers." His gaze fastened greedily on the V where her legs met, and his hand cupped his own crotch. "I reckon you know what you do to a man, walkin' around like that."

Jessie's throat went dry. The look on the man's face sickened her. "Get out of here, Grissom. And in the future, keep your dirty talk to yourself. I don't want to hear it."

"Like hell." His tongue crept out to wet his lips, and his eyes stayed glued to her body. "Why else you wear them pants, showing your body to the world? You're just crying out for a man."

Jessie swallowed. Her face flamed with embarrassment and anger. She had never thought of her attire in that way. It had seemed to her that dressing in a man's clothes was the opposite of being feminine, exactly the sort of thing that would *not* arouse lust in a man. "I've never cried out for anything, least of all you! Now get out."

"Uh-uh." He swung his big head slowly from side to side. "I ain't leaving. Not until we've got this thing settled. Joe ain't here to interrupt us, so you and I got plenty of time."

"Ha!" Jessie's lips twisted scornfully. "You and I have

no time.'' In her anger she leaned forward, planting her hands flat on her desk. ''I don't need Joe to protect me. I can do it myself!''

''Oh, yeah?'' Frank smiled. ''Good, then, let's go at it, just you and me.''

Faster than she could move, Grissom grabbed her arms and jerked her forward over the desk. His mouth came down hard on hers, and his arms went around her in a grip so crushing Jessie could hardly breathe. She struggled impotently. His grasp held her arms tightly against her sides, so that she was unable to move them, and the way he had pulled her across the desk left her feet dangling off the floor, able to kick nothing except her own desk.

Even though it didn't help, Jessie kicked, flailing her feet against the hard wood, desperately seeking some purchase that would give her leverage against Grissom. He bent her backward, making it even more difficult for her to breathe and starting an agonizing pain in her spine. His tongue pushed into her mouth, thick and wet, and Jessie shuddered in horror. She thought she might be sick. She felt the rumble of his laugh at her helpless struggles. He kept her pinned with one arm, and his other hand shoved itself between her legs, rubbing harshly.

Her legs thrashed even more wildly at his obscene touch, and he pinched her inner thigh hard. It hurt, even through the protection of her trousers, and tears sprang into Jessie's eyes.

Grissom lifted his mouth, and Jessie gasped for air. ''You want to play rough, huh? That's fine with me. You need somebody to take you down a peg. A man should have taken a hand to your backside a long time ago.'' His hand squeezed her bottom hard. ''I reckon I'm the man to do it. By the time I'm through with you, girl, you'll be begging me for it.''

Jessie sucked in another gulp of air and screamed.

Grissom chuckled. ''Go ahead. Scream all you want. You think anybody can hear you over the sound of that blade?''

His hand slid up and around to her breast, and he pinched her nipple. Then he shoved his hand down the front of her shirt, popping off several buttons, and clutched her breast. "Mmm. You got more of a handful than I thought, girl." He chuckled again. "You and ole Frank are going to have a good time, a good, long time."

Jessie shrieked again and again, writhing desperately. Why had she been so foolishly sure of herself? If only she hadn't leaned forward! Why hadn't she reached into the drawer instead and brought out the pistol she kept there?

There was a roaring in Jessie's ears, and she knew she was close to passing out. She had wasted her breath in screaming.

Jessie didn't hear the sound of footsteps running in the hall, but she felt the impact when something smashed into Grissom from behind. Suddenly his grasp loosened, and Jessie jumped back from him, panting. It took a moment for her jumbled mind to make sense of the scene before her. It was Stephen! Stephen Ferguson had come flying into the room and hit Frank Grissom hard enough to knock the wind out of him.

"Stephen!" Tears filled her eyes, and Jessie had to clench her teeth to keep back the hysterical, joyous laughter rising in her throat. Stephen had saved her!

Stephen's eyes flickered from the man he had just hit to Jessie. He wasn't fool enough to let his gaze remain on her for longer than a second, but it was long enough to see the fear still in her face and the state of her shirt, hanging open halfway down the front, the cotton chemise beneath it ripped. He had heard her screams when he stepped inside the mill, and he had run to her, fear pounding through his veins so hard he had forgotten his weariness. When he burst into the room, he had acted on instinct, slamming his fist hard into Grissom's side almost before his mind registered what was going on.

But now, realizing what Grissom had been doing to Jessie, a cold, fierce anger flooded Stephen, and he turned to the man, his hands tightening into hard fists, his body automatically falling into the loose, prepared stance of a fighter. Forgotten were the bullets that had laid him low for a week, and the long, tiring walk to the mill. The only thing in his mind was the determination to make this man pay.

Grissom recovered his breath and whirled, growling low in his throat. He was a huge man, and few men ever crossed him. Those who had had soon been laid out with a blow from his hamlike hand. It was rare that anyone even got a punch in against him, so that he was furious not only at the interruption of his plans with Jessie, but also at the idea that anyone would dare oppose him. When he saw who it was, his grin broadened.

"Well, now, is it a man? No, I think it's too pretty for that. You fool with me, boy, and you won't be neither one much longer. Come on." He raised his hands in a mocking come-here gesture, wiggling his fingers.

Stephen hardly heard Grissom's words. His eyes were intent on judging the man. He was big, but heavy. Stephen suspected that he would deal crushing blows, but would also move clumsily. Stephen came in slowly, circling, testing Grissom, waiting for the right moment to dance in and land his first blow. He had no doubt that he could beat him. Whatever advantage Grissom had on him in size, Stephen knew he made up for it in skill and speed. He had learned the manly art of fisticuffs when he was in college at Princeton, and he had been acknowledged the champion of the school. He didn't even think about his recent illness or the resulting weakness; there was too much angry strength pouring through his veins now.

But Jessie thought of it. He had barely healed; he was too weak to fight anyone, let alone a monster like Frank Grissom. Even if he hadn't been laid up in bed for over a week with a gunshot wound, she knew that Stephen would be no match for Grissom. Stephen was shorter and a lot lighter, and he would know nothing about fighting. He was, after all, just a gentleman who had been brought up in the lap of luxury. Grissom would kill him! "Stephen! No!"

Jessie's shriek distracted Stephen for a vital instant. Involuntarily he glanced at her, and Grissom lunged forward, his huge fist connecting with the side of Stephen's face. Stephen stumbled backward under the force of the blow and crashed into the wall. He shook his head to clear it and started to rise as Grissom lumbered in to finish the job.

"Frank, no! Don't!" Jessie ran across the room and flung herself between them, spreading her arms out to the sides as though to protect Stephen. "Please, no. Think, Frank! He's Joe's son. Sam's brother. They'll kill you if you—"

"Damn it, Jessie, what the hell do you think you're doing?" Stephen staggered to his feet and reached out to push Jessie aside. She was trying to protect him! She thought he was such a weak, useless excuse for a man that he couldn't even hold his own in a fight! Fury surged through him.

Grissom grabbed Jessie's arm and tossed her aside. "Can't hide behind her, boy. She's too skinny."

Stephen's mouth tightened, and he almost rushed the other man in his anger, but he controlled himself. He could not let Grissom take charge of the fight. He moved in lightly, feinting, and landed a jab in the other man's stomach, then bounced out of reach. Grissom's eyes widened in surprise, but he was a tough man, and the blow didn't affect him much. Stephen hadn't expected it to. He was merely sounding Grissom out, testing his reflexes, his timing, his skill.

A thin smile touched Stephen's lips, chilling in its coldness. Grissom had confirmed his opinion of the man's fighting skills. Stephen moved in, ready to start the fight in earnest. Just as he did so, a loud boom reverberated through the room, and something thwacked into the ceiling above them. Both men froze. A gun had gone off.

"Hold it!" Jessie shouted, leveling her pistol at Frank Grissom. As soon as Frank had shoved her aside, she had again remembered the pistol she kept in her desk drawer, and she had run to it and whipped out the gun. She whirled and fired into the ceiling to get Frank's attention, and now she aimed the gun with calm purpose at his midsection. "You stay right where you are, Frank. I've got this gun trained on your stomach, and you know you're too wide a target for me to miss."

Frank raised his hands in a gesture of surrender. "Now, Jessie, don't get in an uproar."

Stephen went white with humiliation and rage. He began to curse, violently and at length, too consumed with outraged pride and fury to even make a coherent statement.

Jessie ignored him, keeping her gun fixed on the other man. "All right, Frank. You go back to work and cool down. Then you think on it. You just might realize that I saved your hide from Joe and Sam. You know what Sam said he'd do if you came around me again. Think how he'd feel if you beat his brother to a pulp."

"Jessamine Randall!" Stephen thundered. "That's enough! More than enough. Put that gun down this instant, and—"

"Oh, hush, Stephen." Jessie didn't even spare him a glance. "This is no time to get on your high horse."

Stephen's jaw dropped, and for an instant he was speechless. Frank shrugged and sidled toward the door. "Okay, Jessie, I hear you. I won't hurt Pretty Boy." He threw a contemptuous glance toward Stephen, then looked at Jessie and grinned slyly. "You and me—we still got something to settle. We'll have our time. You wait and see."

"It'll be a cold day in hell before you get near me again!"

Grissom grinned and backed out the door, letting it slam to behind him.

Stephen stalked toward Jessie, his feet thudding down in grim emphasis to his words. "Just what the hell did you think you were doing? How dare you interfere between me and that—that throwback to the Dark Ages!"

His nostrils were pinched, and deep brackets tightened around his mouth. His eyes glowed red.

Jessie looked at him and sighed exaggeratedly. "Well, if that isn't just like a man! Here I save your hide, and you're yelling at me!"

"Save my hide! You didn't save anything! I had everything under control. I was going to—'' He made a noise of disgust and turned aside. "Oh, the devil with it. I can't expect a woman to understand the sport.''

"The sport? Sport? Are you calling brawling all over the office a sport? Having your head bashed in? Breaking your nose and splitting your lip? Being beaten black and blue and having your wounds reopened? That's sport?''

"*I'm* not the one who would have had his head bashed in. You don't believe I can do a thing, do you? You think I'm nothing but a weakling, a poor clumsy soul who cannot ride or fight or shoot a gun or do any useful thing. Isn't that right? You have to protect me. You have to jump into the middle of a fight, guns blazing, so that some oaf won't beat me to a pulp! Well, thank you very much, Miss Jessamine Amazon Randall, but I have somehow managed to take care of myself for over twenty-seven years without your protection. Damn it, woman, I came in here to protect you. I was in the process of teaching that scum a lesson for what he did to you when you decided to take over—''

"I didn't ask for your protection!'' Jessie retorted hotly, stung by his words, doubly so because she knew, with shame, that she *had* indeed needed help. "I can take care of myself.''

"Like you were doing when I came in? You screamed, and I took that for a plea for help. Next time, believe me, I won't bother!''

Jessamine's chin went up proudly. Stubbornly. "Please don't.'' Her hands curled around the front of her shirt, holding it together, but her expression was that of a queen dismissing a forward servant.

Stephen grimaced. He slapped the dirt off his trousers and started toward the door. The wound in his shoulder was beginning to throb. Damn, he'd probably reopened it. And, now that he thought about it, his muscles were queerly shaky all over.

Jessamine watched him until he was almost at the door. "Will you—'' she asked his back, and there was the slightest quaver to her voice "—that is, you won't tell anyone about—about this, will you?"

He swung to face her, shocked. "No! How could you think that I would?" He saw then that there was an odd glitter in her eyes, almost like tears. A small bruise had already formed on her neck. And her hands on the shirt's sides, holding it together, looked frail and pitiful. He swallowed, his anger seeping out of him. "I'm sorry. I lost my head. I apologize. I shouldn't have yelled at you. You've been through a horrible ordeal."

Jessie ducked her head, ashamed to let him see the tears in her eyes. "I'm all right."

"What nonsense." But his voice was light and concerned, no longer angry. "Did he hurt you? I mean, did he—"

Jessie shook her head quickly. "No! No! It was just that I was so stupid. I had a gun in the drawer, but I didn't pull it out when he came in. I never suspected that he would actually try anything like that!"

"Passion has been known to destroy a man's reason."

"But for me?" She tilted her eyes up at him comically. "Looking like this?" She swept her arms wide to indicate her faded, mannish trousers and too large shirt, the heavy work boots on her feet. But her gesture released the buttonless sides of her shirt, and it fell away, leaving her exposed to Stephen's gaze, with only the torn chemise for cover.

He could see the soft white top of her bosom, and where the tear in the chemise lay folded back, the full luscious curve of one breast was visible. Her nipples were darker shadows beneath the thin cloth. He gazed at her; he couldn't help it. His eyes seemed glued to the soft flesh. Her breasts were fuller than he had imagined; her large shirts had hidden them. And they were high and firm, the nipples large. He found himself wanting to slip his fingers beneath the torn edges of the cloth, to slide them down and around and cup the orb in his palm.

Jessie saw where his eyes had gone, and she blushed

fiercely and snatched the edges of the shirt together. Stephen looked away, and a faint line of red stained his cheekbones.

"He tore the buttons," she explained, her voice abnormally small.

He felt like a lecherous cad, enjoying the view that another man's bestial lust had exposed. "Forgive me." He shrugged out of his jacket and lightly draped it around her shoulders, pulling it to in the front. "I should have thought. You need a wrap."

Jessie swallowed. His kindness almost undid her where anger and harsh words had not. "Thank you."

Nor had he thought when he'd begun to fight the man, Stephen reminded himself. Now he considered her reputation, which should have been uppermost in his mind. No woman of good name would want to have a common brawl explode in the room with her standing there, her blouse ripped open, obviously the object of attempted rape. A gentleman didn't protect a lady's honor by forcing the knowledge of her near-dishonor on the world. What if the men in the mill had heard the fight and come in?

The incident would have been all over the small town in hours, and Jessie would have had to face the shame of being whispered about, no matter how innocent she had been. Stephen might not know this part of the country, but he knew gossip, and it was the same the world over. *It was her own fault,* people would say, shaking their heads. *Sashaying around town in those pants and working alongside the men in a sawmill.* They would sagely admit that they'd been surprised it hadn't happened long ago, that Jessie had been asking for it.

No, the last thing Jessie needed was for him to beat up that great hulk, with her virtue as the obvious reason. She had been wise to end it, however hurtful to his pride that ending had been. Now that Stephen was thinking more clearly, he knew that he must not follow Frank out of the office and demand satisfaction. No, he would bide his time, wait for an opportunity to arise—some insult or argument that had nothing to do with Jessie—and then he would make the man pay. He would see to it that Frank didn't get away with it, but he would do it discreetly, as a gentleman should.

Right now the important thing was to take care of Jessie. She had been so capable and so aggravating, as usual, that he hadn't even thought about how shaken she must be. "Come. I'll take you home."

His arm slid around her shoulders. Jessie, who until now had ignored the turmoil of emotions within her, surprised herself by leaning gratefully into his supporting strength for a moment. She closed her eyes, breathing in the reassuring masculine odors of tobacco and shaving soap and sweat. She couldn't seem to control the trembling of her limbs.

"Poor Jessie. I'm sorry." His lips brushed her hair. She couldn't identify the touch and wondered what it was; it seemed to make her tremble even more, but somehow in a different way.

Jessie drew a ragged breath and pulled herself upright. It was stupid to fall apart over something like this. After all, Frank hadn't actually done anything to her except scare her. She wasn't physically hurt. She had been scared before and lived through it. She would live through this, too. And she certainly wouldn't let the world know she had been frightened. Nor would Grissom find out. There was no way she was giving that snake the satisfaction of being intimidated.

"I'm all right," she told Stephen stiffly and stepped out of the circle of his arm.

He let his arm drop to his side, suddenly feeling empty. Jessie faced him squarely, her eyes looking straight into his. "I have to ask you another favor."

"Of course. What?"

"When I said, don't tell anyone, I meant *anyone*."

He frowned. "Not even my father?"

Jessie nodded emphatically. "Especially not him."

"But he would want to know. He would never allow that man to work here if he knew what he'd done to you."

"Exactly."

"And you want Frank to continue working here?" Stephen's eyebrows vaulted up.

"Not because I like him," Jessie snapped. "I assure you. Nor because I welcomed his—his advances."

"That was obvious. Then why do you want him around where he could try again?"

"Joe needs him here, especially while Sam is away. Joe often has to be up at the camp, overseeing that operation, and he needs someone here who knows the business and has complete control of the workers. Frank Grissom does. If Joe knew what Frank tried to do, he'd throw him out immediately. Then he'd run himself into the ground trying to manage both operations."

"Surely he could let one place or the other slide for a few days...."

Jessie shook her head firmly. "No. This is a very important time of the year. We have to get the trees in and sawed and shipped before we're shut down by the snows. Winter comes fast here. And when it comes, it's heavy. Joe can't afford to lose the time."

Stephen frowned. He couldn't believe that it was so important to get out every last piece of lumber, even to the point of risking Jessie's safety. "Will you promise to stay away from the mill?"

"No!" Jessie looked horrified. "Joe needs *me* here, too. I couldn't desert him now."

"It would hardly be deserting him." Stephen couldn't imagine why Jessie reacted so strongly to the thought of spending a few days away from the mill. "I don't understand."

"Of course not!" Jessie responded crossly, irritated that Joe had made her swear not to tell Stephen about his financial troubles. Without knowing that, she supposed it did seem a little bizarre that it was so urgent to keep the mill running at top speed. "You never had to work for a living, did you? You don't know what it's like to have to make money to keep food on the table all winter and warm clothes on your back. But there are those of us who don't sit around surrounded by piles of money waiting to be counted.''

Stephen grimaced. It was the very devil to try to talk to this girl sometimes. She seemed to be prickly about anything and everything, and one never knew when she was going to attack with some barbed remark. ''You haven't the faintest idea what I know,'' he responded, keeping his voice mild with some effort. After all, she had just had a bad time of it, and he must try to coddle her, however much she might shrug it off. ''All right. If it matters that much to you, I promise that I shan't tell Father.'' He would just have to figure out a way to make sure she was protected from the ruffian at the mill without letting Joe know, but he wasn't about to tell her that. No doubt she would rise up in anger at the thought that she might need protection. ''Now, will you allow me to take you home? You can take off at least a few hours from this job, I presume.''

Jessie shot him a fulminating glance for his sarcasm and, in answer, marched across the room and out the door. Stephen sighed and followed her. He suspected that it was going to be no easy task to keep Miss Jessamine Randall under his watchful protection.

Chapter Ten

Jessie slipped down the hallway to her small bedroom at the rear of the house, just beyond her mother's room. Fortunately, her mother was at work in the kitchen, and Jessie was able to make it to her room without Amanda knowing she was there. Jessie was grateful; her mother would have been full of questions as soon as she saw that Jessie was wearing Stephen's coat over her shirt. She was also glad that Stephen hadn't been full of questions and reproaches on the way home. She knew Sam would have chewed her out for getting caught alone with Grissom and then for not having the sense to pull her gun from the drawer before she faced him. But, except for his anger when she stopped the fight, Stephen had been only quiet and sympathetic.

It surprised her, now that she thought about it; she was actually glad that it had been Stephen and not Sam who had rescued her. Jessie slipped out of Stephen's coat and folded it carefully, then laid it across the foot rail of her bed. Her hand lingered on it for a moment. It was made of silk, soft and elegant. She had never owned anything made of a material that fine. She thought of Stephen and how he had looked in the suit jacket, the glossy brown color almost the same as his eyes.

She wondered if there had been many women back East who had their lures out for Stephen. There must have been, before he became engaged. No doubt he had been considered a fine catch—wealthy, impeccably dressed, handsome. Of course, such things didn't count with her, but they would be all that mattered to a city girl. A lady.

Jessie glanced at her gaping shirt, and her mouth tightened, thoughts of Stephen and the women in his life fleeing. Quickly she undid the last two remaining buttons and wadded the shirt up. She stuffed it in the rear of one of her drawers. Later she would pull it out and replace the buttons, but she couldn't bear to even touch it or see it now. It was too strong a reminder of Frank Grissom and what he had almost done to her. Hurriedly she unbuttoned the cotton chemise and shoved it into the drawer after the shirt. She would mend it, too, when she got around to fixing the shirt.

She poured water from the pitcher into the bowl and, taking up a cake of soap, lathered her hands, then scrubbed her chest and face, everywhere he had touched her. Damn that man! It made her skin crawl just remembering his hands on her flesh. She toweled herself dry, rubbing until her skin was red. Then she pulled another chemise and shirt out of her drawer and put them on. She sat on the bed. Now what was she going to do?

It was still an hour until supper, and she didn't want her mother to know that she was home. She couldn't go out and help Amanda in the kitchen, therefore. Nor did she feel like going into the sitting room, where the men gathered before supper. The last thing she wanted was to deal with their usual quips and teasing.

Jessie rose and walked to the window. How could she just sit in her room, twiddling her thumbs? She wanted to go somewhere, do something. She wanted not to have to think about Frank Grissom and his nasty, searching hands.

Her mind skittered away from that subject, and she thought of Stephen. She remembered the relief that had flooded her when he came in. Jessie grimaced. It wasn't any good to think about that, either. She shouldn't have been so happy to have a man rescue her; she should have been able to take care of herself. She felt ashamed that she hadn't. The only thing that made it bearable was that Stephen had been the one who found her. At least he hadn't thrown it up in her face. Most of the men around Nora Springs would have teased her unmercifully.

Then there was the heart-pounding fear she'd felt when Frank had knocked Stephen down. She liked to think of *that* even less than the other things. She had had a vision of Grissom pounding Stephen's face to a bloody pulp, and it had filled her with horror. She didn't want to remember it, and she certainly did n't want to consider why it had scared her so.

Jessie whirled away from the window. She didn't want to be alone with her thoughts, yet she hated the idea of talking to anyone, pretending that she was fine when all the while she was churning inside.

Stephen.

Stephen knew all about what had happened to her, and he had already proved that he wouldn't question or scold her. She wouldn't have to pretend for him; she wouldn't have to lie. And she had a reason to go to his room. He was instructing her in the art of being a lady. She could run up the stairs to his room and forget her problems by taking a lesson from him. She had found during the past few days that Stephen Ferguson always managed to keep her mind fully occupied.

Jessie plopped down on the bed and began to untie the laces of her boots. Ten minutes later, she was tiptoeing up the back stairs to his room, dressed in another one of her mother's gowns, with a pair of soft bedroom slippers on her feet. She tapped softly on Stephen's door and heard his voice bid her to come in.

Stephen turned toward the door, and his face went blank with astonishment when Jessie came into the room. He never would have dreamed that she would visit him for a lesson in gentility tonight, after what she had gone through this afternoon. Yet surely that was why she was here, given the fact that she was wearing a dress. "Jessie? What are you—are you sure you want to do this tonight?"

"Of course." She carefully kept her face cool and unconcerned. She would never admit that she was still frightened and nervous and didn't want to be alone, that she wanted something to take her mind off the events of the afternoon. "I'm not going to hide in a closet just because of Frank Grissom." She made his name a sneer. "I'm not afraid of him."

"But shouldn't you rest, or—or something?"

She cast him a disparaging look. "I'm tough, Ferguson. Remember?"

"How could I forget?" he murmured. "All right, then. Let's begin." He moved away from the window, where he had been standing since he returned home, blankly staring out, thinking dark thoughts about the future of one Frank Grissom.

Jessie looked better in this dress, he noted. It fitted her, at least, even though the style was years out of date. And she had slippers instead of boots on her feet, even if they weren't exactly what a lady of fashion would wear. He made a mental note to find a seamstress tomorrow and have her a proper dress sewn up, one that was stylish and fitted and of a color and material suited to her looks and youth.

"You look very nice in that dress," he told her. "Now let me see you walk." She sauntered slowly across the room, her skirt swaying gently. "Much better. Much, much better." He didn't add that the soft motion of her hips beneath the skirt started a fire in his loins.

Jessie turned and cocked her head saucily. "I'm turning into a regular lady."

"A veritable belle. A debutante."

"A what?"

He shrugged. "It's not important. The next problem is your hair."

Jessie sighed. "I know. It's the same color as smushed carrots. But there's nothing I can do about that."

"No. No. I didn't mean the color. The color is beautiful. It's the color of fire." He came closer to her, and his voice softened. "Or a sunset." He stretched out a hand to graze her hair. "Any man would be—" He stopped, realizing that he was getting himself into treacherous waters. "That is, it wasn't the color of your hair to which I was referring. It's the style. Pigtails are for little girls in short skirts and pinafores. Women wear their hair up."

"But it's a bother to do that. And it's always falling down. Isn't it?"

"Not that I've noticed."

Jessie's voice dropped, and she looked away. "I don't know how to do it."

"What?"

She turned, gave him a flashing glance and raised her voice defiantly. "I said, I don't know how to put it up. Where does it go? How?"

He gazed at her, nonplussed. How could a woman live as many years as she had without acquiring the most basic womanly skills? "Heavens, I don't know. I've never done it." He thought of the thick golden hair of an actress who had once been his mistress and how he had often brushed it, loving the silken, sensual feel of it gliding through his hands. "That is, well…" Stephen broke off, appalled at what he had almost blurted out. It was so easy to forget what he was doing with Jessie and just say the first thing that came into his head. He cleared his throat. "First, you must take it out of the braids."

"Oh, all right." Jessie made a face and grabbed her left braid, beginning to untie the bow. "I'll do this one. You get the other."

Stephen's eyes widened. He'd never thought that he might have to touch her hair. It wasn't a wise idea. Just thinking about her hair lying loose around her shoulders started his blood humming. It would be foolish to take it down. Too tempting.

Yet he could not seem to stop his fingers from moving to her long, burnished braid. He lifted the thick rope of hair in his hand and untied the knot of the flannel strip Jessie used in place of a ribbon. The ends of her hair slipped apart some, but the plait remained mostly intact. He would have to separate the strands with his fingers. Stephen noticed that his fingers were trembling slightly as he reached out. He sank his fingers into her braid, wiggling the strands free. Her hair was cool and thick, soft to his touch. It slid around his fingers silkily, and his breath came faster in his throat.

Her hair was lovely. The color of burnished copper. "How can you even think of disparaging the color of your hair?" he murmured. "It's like liquid fire. A man dreams of warmth like this."

Jessie glanced up at him, startled. His eyes were dark and intense, alive with an inner heat. Her thoughts scattered like leaves on the wind. She could only look at him.

His fingers drifted through her hair, and she felt the gentle tug against her scalp. Her eyes dropped to his mouth. It was a wide, generous mouth, the lower lip sensually full. She thought of that mouth against hers, and she wondered how it would feel.

Jessie tore her gaze away and moved apart from him. The funny, sizzling feelings inside her body shocked and alarmed her. What was the matter with her? Why did this man have such a strange effect on her? "I—I need a brush."

She glanced blindly around the room.

"On the dresser."

Jessie hurried to the dresser. A silver-backed man's hairbrush and a silver comb lay beside a shaving mug and silver-handled razor. Even the sight of such masculine toiletry articles shook her. She curved her hand around the brush. All she could think of was Stephen's hand on the same brush, lifting it to his own head. The silver was cool against her hot skin. She raised the brush with shaky fingers and pulled it through her hair. The curling, tangled strands were stubborn and caught on the bristles. In her haste, she jerked on the brush, bringing prickles of pain to her scalp.

She looked at herself in the mirror above the dresser. There must be something wrong with her, to even be thinking about a man's kiss after what had happened to her this afternoon. She looked at the bruise, already widening, on her neck. Her lips looked a little swollen, and there was a red, raw patch above her upper lip where Grissom's stubble had rubbed against the tender flesh. She thought of his wet, disgusting lips, of his tongue filling her mouth, and her stomach turned.

"Is it always like that?" she asked, her voice so low it was almost a whisper.

"What?" Stephen, watching her brush her hair, was brought out of his heated, sensual reverie with a start by the sight of her suddenly white face and wide, frightened eyes. He moved toward her instinctively. "Is what always like that?"

"When a man—when a man kisses you." She turned to face him. Her eyes were soft and vulnerable. "Is it like it was with Grissom?"

"Oh, Jessamine, no." His heart clenched inside his chest. She looked so achingly young and unsure. For all her air of unfeminine toughness, Jessie was really an innocent, naive girl. It was obvious that she knew nothing about the touch of a man. Desire coursed through him, and Stephen wondered how he could feel gently protective toward her and yet at the same time want to grind his body into hers and kiss her until her innocence fell away. "With a gentleman, a man who loves and respects you, it's entirely different."

"How?" She walked over to him and looked intently up into his eyes. "What's different?" Jessie could feel her heart hammering inside her, so loud she almost couldn't hear. She wanted to know about the other kind of kiss. She wanted to taste the kiss of a gentleman.

"Well, uh…" Stephen tore his eyes away from hers. It was almost too much for him to look into them, to see the questioning, the trace of anxiety left from Grissom's attack. "It's not rough. That is, well, perhaps sometimes it can be a little rough, but…but not in a hurtful way."

"What do you mean?" Jessie looked puzzled.

"Well, like—like when you love someone a lot and are very, very happy to see her, you hug her so hard that it hurts. But neither of you cares about the pain because it's so wonderful to hold her.''

"I understand. So you can kiss hard, but it feels good?''

Stephen could feel the heat rising in his face, and he wasn't sure if it was from embarrassment or passion. "Yes. It's, well, it's an expression of love. Of desire. A man who loved you wouldn't want to hurt you or to gratify himself at your expense. He would want you to enjoy it, too. He would make sure you did.''

"How would he do that?'' Involuntarily, Jessie's eyes flickered to Stephen's mouth.

He found it difficult to breathe. "He would...be gentle. Slow. He would say sweet things to you. Tell you what you did to his heart and mind. Tell you how he could think of nothing but you.''

"And then?''

"And then he would put his hands on your arms.'' His hands went to her arms and slid up them to her shoulders. "Gently, letting you know that if you didn't want him, you were free to pull away, to leave.''

"And if you didn't?'' Jessie breathed, staring raptly into his eyes.

"Then he would bend down, slowly.'' His actions followed his words. "And he would touch his lips to yours.''

Stephen's mouth brushed against Jessie's as softly as the touch of butterfly wings, and she shivered all through in a delicious way. Stephen spoke, his breath fanning her lips. "Then he would kiss you again.''

His lips closed the short distance between them, pressing into hers gently but insistently. It was nothing like Frank Grissom's kiss, she thought. Nothing. Then she was lost to all thought as his kiss deepened. She was aware of nothing but the scent and taste of him, the delightful fizz and sparkle that ran through her veins and along her nerves, the hot heaviness that mushroomed in her abdomen.

Stephen's mouth was searingly hot; his lips moved against hers, teasing them open. His tongue edged her lips and slipped inside her mouth. Instead of the disgust that had filled her at the touch of Grissom's tongue, Jessie felt only a delicious quiver of desire dart through her, and the heaviness in her abdomen leaped into flame. Her hands came up uncertainly and curled into the front of his shirt, innocently holding on to the joy that was sparking all through her.

Stephen's arms went around her, and he pressed her closer to him. Her arms went naturally around his neck. She could feel the hard warmth of his body all the way up and down hers, the strength of his thighs and the unyielding hardness of his chest. His arms were tight around her, but Jessie felt not even a flicker of fear. She liked the pressure of his arms around her body and the tightness with which he held her. Her body was like liquid, and she wasn't sure she could have remained standing without his support.

Stephen broke their kiss only to change the tilt of his head and kiss her again, his lips pressing harder against hers. His hands slid down her back, pressing her into him. The obviously inexperienced but hungry response of Jessie's kisses enflamed him. He was a man of the world, used to the skills and beauty of expensive prostitutes and sophisticated, restless socialites, but none of the women he had ever known excited him as this innocent, unfeminine girl did. He wanted her, here and now, with every fiber of his being.

"Ah, Jessamine," he sighed, his lips leaving hers and trailing down her throat, tasting its tender flesh. "Jessamine. Beautiful, beautiful Jessamine."

His mouth met the top of her bodice, which effectively stopped him. He felt like reaching up and tearing it apart so that his voracious mouth could reach her breasts. He wanted to pull her down on the floor and yank her clothes from her. He wanted to take her, to make her his. Just thinking about it made him tremble.

But he did none of the things he wanted to. Instead, his arms loosened around her. "Oh, God." He rested his cheek against her head and drew a long, steadying breath. "I'm sorry." He waited for his blood to cool enough that he was capable of pulling his arms away from her and stepping back. "I'm sorry," he repeated. "You...wanted reassurance, and instead I—I..."

"No! I wanted exactly that!" Jessie burst out, reaching out with one hand to take his. She squeezed his hand hard. "Don't apologize. Please, don't apologize." Her breath was unsteady, too, and she struggled to control it, to regain command of her mind and body. She wanted to tell him that she had been asking him to kiss her, to wipe away the memory of Frank Grissom, even though she hadn't been aware of it, but she couldn't get her tumultuous feelings shaped into thoughts and words. She felt as though she might fall into uncontrollable laughter or tears with equal ease.

Jessie raised a shaky hand to her face. Her cheek was as hot as fire. She swallowed, unable to think of anything to say. She could only stare at Stephen with wide eyes. In the space of a few minutes everything in her world had turned upside down—or perhaps she had just realized that it had been turning that way for the past couple of weeks. Ever since she had met Stephen Ferguson. "I don't know what's the matter with me."

Stephen shook his head. "It's my fault. I knew you were in a vulnerable state. It was the act of a blackguard to take advantage of that. I hope you will forgive me. In time."

He turned away. He thought that if he continued to look at her for another moment, his control would snap and he would pull her into his arms and not let her go until he had possessed her completely.

Jessie looked at his rigid back. Hurt sliced through her. He didn't want her; he had turned his back on her. She clenched her fingers in the folds of her skirts. At least that was something a dress was good for, giving one something to hold on to when one felt as if one might fall to pieces. She started to speak, but she couldn't, for there were tears swelling in her throat.

"Perhaps it would be a good idea if we discontinued our lessons," Stephen said stiffly, still turned away from her.

Jessie looked at him for a moment, then whirled and ran out the door.

Stephen heard her leave. His body went limp, as though all energy and life had drained out of him with her departure. He turned and looked into the empty hall. Slowly he walked to the door and closed it, then returned to his bed. He flopped down and lay back, crossing his hands under his head and staring at the ceiling. He was still on fire with longing; it would have taken almost nothing to have sent him running down the stairs after Jessie. God, he wanted her.

But he was engaged to Elizabeth! His duty, his love, his responsibility, were all to her. They must be. No matter how much desire he felt for Jessie, he could do nothing about it. Elizabeth was to be his wife; he was promised to her. He had given his word to her father, and Stephen never broke his word. He had betrayed both Elizabeth and Jessie by kissing Jessie; he had betrayed all three of them.

With a groan, he rolled off the bed and walked to the window. He was far too restless to lie still. He stared out sightlessly at the cold September evening. He wondered when Elizabeth would be here. He would marry her and leave as soon as Sam arrived with her. He'd tell Sam about Grissom's attack on Jessie and leave the girl in Sam's capable hands. He'd let Sam wreak revenge on Grissom. He could not stay to do it himself. He had to leave. He had to get as far away as he could—as soon as he could. Or he might just find himself forgetting all about honor and duty.

Their lessons in deportment might have to stop, but Stephen intended to start walking to and from work with her.

She came in to eat breakfast the next morning and saw him already sitting at the table, eating and talking with the other men and her mother. It surprised her. She had rarely known him to be up this early.

Jessie gave him a nod when he said hello, then slid into her seat. No doubt it was easy for him to talk to her as if nothing had happened, but she knew she wasn't sophisti-

cated enough to behave that way. She had spent half the
night tossing and turning and thinking about their kisses.
She had been aghast that she had kissed Stephen Ferguson—and even more aghast that she had enjoyed it so thoroughly.

How could she feel attracted to a man like that? He was
not a man she respected, not the kind of man she could
possibly love. Not a man like Sam. She had always thought
that a good woman was not supposed to feel desire for a
man she didn't love. Well, if the truth was known, Jessie
hadn't even known that such sizzling desire existed in a
woman. Certainly she had never felt it before. She wondered if that meant she was a wanton. Would she feel the
same about any man's kisses? Well, she hadn't felt that
way about Frank Grissom's kisses, that was for sure.
Maybe it was only with a man she liked.

But did she like Stephen Ferguson? She wouldn't have
said so, but now that she thought about it, she had to admit
that she did. Over the past few days, as he had helped her,
they had drawn closer. She had realized that there was a
kindness in him, a warmth, despite his rather formal manner. And one could get used to his politeness; it hardly
made her feel strange anymore for him to jump to his feet
whenever she entered the room or held her chair out for
her to sit down at the table or stood aside to let her pass
through a door first. He had a sense of humor, once she'd
gotten to understand it, even though he often still said
things she didn't understand. He had even shown some
depth of character when he'd gotten shot. And, God knows,
he was certainly pleasant to look at. She had gotten to
where she sort of enjoyed being around him. Well, face it,
she *did* enjoy being with him; she *did* like him.

But he wasn't the kind of man for this country. He
wasn't tough enough, hard enough. He wouldn't know how
to get by out here. He wouldn't stay for any length of time.

He was engaged to another woman.

It was that thought, which had kept coming back time
and again through the night, that had made her cry, much

to her chagrin. It had been wrong, very wrong, of him to kiss her when he was engaged to another woman. It showed a lack of morals, of honor, of respect for her. A good, solid man wouldn't kiss another woman if he was engaged, even if his fiancée wasn't around.

Of course, if that made him a scoundrel, what did it make her? Jessie didn't like to think about that. She had known that Stephen was engaged to that woman Sam was bringing home; Miss Elizabeth Hightone would be right here in town in another day or two. Why, she had been enjoying the kisses of an almost-married man! It was a horrifying realization that she hadn't even given that other woman a thought while he was kissing her. Hell's bells! She hadn't given anything a thought! She had acted like an empty-headed ninny. Jessie was ashamed of herself.

She was more ashamed because even though she was sitting several chairs away from Stephen, she felt not only the embarrassment she had expected, but also a new upsurge of those confused, exciting sensations she had known the night before. She blushed to her hairline and hoped no one was watching her. How could she, at this hour of the morning, right there at the breakfast table, be thinking about the way Stephen's arms had tightened around her, or the velvety pressure of his lips on hers? How could she actually feel the sudden tightening of her nerves all over and the heavy, heated yearning deep inside her? It didn't seem right.

She shoved her thoughts and feelings aside. The only thing to do was ignore them. She couldn't go around with this turmoil showing, especially not when Stephen was so cool and unconcerned, so natural-acting. It just went to prove that he must be a scoundrel inside, Jessie thought resentfully as she shoved a forkful of eggs into her mouth. A good man would be as embarrassed and awkward as she was.

It didn't take her long to eat. She had no appetite, and she was desperate to get away from the table, so as soon as she had made enough show of eating that her mother wouldn't start questioning her about it, she pushed her plate back and jumped up from the table.

"Are you off to the mill, Miss Randall?" Stephen said, rising from his place, too.

"Yes."

"Then I'll walk with you."

Jessie stared. "You're going to the mill?"

"Yes. I was going to talk to Joe."

"This early?"

Stephen shrugged. "It's as good a time as any."

Jessie frowned. What was this? Was he planning to try to sweet-talk her into something? But then, if he had evil designs on her, why had he stopped last night? She couldn't understand what kind of a game he was playing. Still, she was sure that he must have something up his sleeve.

"All right," she replied ungraciously. "I reckon you can come with me."

"Jessie!" Amanda reprimanded her, a shocked look on her face.

Jessie grimaced. Obviously Stephen had worked his spell on her mother. Jessie clumped out the door with Stephen behind her. When they got out of the house and were walking along the street toward the mill, she glanced at her companion. He was silent and appeared as cool and calm as ever, but she could see the tight lines around his mouth and eyes. He was feeling some strain in the situation, too. Then why had he forced himself into her company? It didn't make sense.

Stephen didn't talk to her much that day or the next, making only the few remarks necessary not to appear rude in front of other people. At the mill he spent most of his time in Joe's office, talking to him, or in exploring the sawmill with Joe, poking into all the different aspects of the operations. Jessie found his interest in the place distinctly annoying. Why should some rich Eastern dude find a poky little sawmill in Montana so absorbing?

However, it was even more annoying when he wasn't with Joe discussing the mill, for then he planted himself in the large outer office where Jessie worked and just sat there, saying almost nothing. Sometimes, when he sat like that, he watched her, and she found that the most unnerving thing of all. Finally, after five days of it, her nerves snapped, and she swung around to face him, snarling, "What in the blue blazes are you doing, sitting there? Why are you here all the time? Why don't you go home?"

Stephen's eyebrows rose lazily. "You don't like my company? I'm hurt."

Jessie grimaced. "You know good and well I don't like it, and you know why, too."

His face fell into a stiffly polite mask. "I assure you, you have nothing to worry about from me. I apologized to you for my behavior the other night. It was unforgivable. But I promise you it won't happen again. I'm not a Frank Grissom."

Jessie's eyes narrowed. "That's why you're here, isn't it? Because of Grissom! You think you're protecting me!"

"You have a strange way of putting it, but, yes, since you refuse to tell my father, I am obliged to watch out for you myself. I can hardly let you work here every day with that animal around, waiting for an opportunity to attack you again. I must afford you some protection. I can't always be sure that Father is in the office with you. He goes to the camp frequently."

"You can hardly let me work here?" Jessie repeated in a dangerous tone. "What makes you think you have any power to let or not let me do anything?"

"Of course, I have no rights over you, but I certainly have an obligation to see that you are not mistreated by Frank Grissom again."

"Why?" Jessie asked bluntly.

"Why? What do you mean, why? Because you are a lady, and I wouldn't be worth much as a man if I allowed a lady to be assaulted."

"I'm not a lady, and you know it. I wear pants, and I swear, as you yourself pointed out. But, more importantly,

I can take care of myself. I don't need you to protect me."
Her words mimicked his tone viciously.

"Mm. No more than you did the other day, no doubt.
As I recall, you found my protection then not quite so contemptible."

Jessie ground her teeth. It was just like him to remind
her of that. "I have a gun, and I will use it. I am on guard
now."

"So am I."

Jessie felt like growling. "You are the most annoying,
frustrating, bothersome man in the world! Why won't you
leave me alone? I don't want you hanging around all the
time!"

"It is not precisely enjoyable for me, either," Stephen
threw back at her. "As for frustration and bother, you have
no idea what that is until you've tried to deal with *you*!
There is no woman in the world as irritating as you are.
You're a wild, red-haired witch, and I wish to God I'd
never met you!" Stephen's voice rose thunderously. Never
before in his life had he yelled at a woman, but it seemed
as if Jessie could bring him to that loss of control in the
twinkling of an eye. His nerves were shredded because of
her. He'd hardly slept at all the past couple of nights for
thinking about her, wanting her and struggling to overcome
that desire. Then, during the day, he'd felt honor bound to
watch over her until Sam got back so that Grissom couldn't
attack her again. It was torture to be in the same room with
her the whole day. Yet, instead of appreciating what he was
doing for her, Jessie sniped at him for it! The most infu-
riating thing of all, what he simply could not comprehend,
was how he could desire a woman who was so thoroughly
exasperating.

Tears sprang into Jessie's eyes at Stephen's words, but
she blinked them away. Damn it! She was *not* hurt by his
open dislike of her; she had heard worse things than that
about herself from other men. She was just angry. He was
unreasonable and stubborn.

Stephen thought he saw the glimmer of tears in her eyes,

and his rage abruptly left him. Good Lord, had he made her cry? "I'm sorry." He wanted to go to her and take her hand, but he didn't dare. Touching Jessie was a dangerous thing to do. "You know, there's a simple way to get rid of me. Just tell Joe what happened."

"No! Absolutely not. He's worried enough as it is."

"Why?"

"Uh…" Jessie shifted. Now she'd done it. Joe would be hoppin' mad at her if she let Stephen know either of the reasons he was worried. "Well, he's anxious about the saw blade. He needs it."

"Jessie…" Stephen frowned. "Give me a little credit. I'm a businessman. I understand having to meet schedules. But I would never for a moment allow you to be in danger in order to do it. I can't believe my father would, either."

"He wouldn't. That's the point. He'd fire Grissom just when he needs him the most. But I don't want to be responsible for it."

"For what? Ferguson Mill's not sending out its last shipment of lumber for the year? It doesn't seem that important. And why has my father been so jumpy today? That frown hasn't left his face, and he must have been outside at least ten times." He stopped, realization dawning on him. He went cold inside. "It's something about Sam, isn't it? He thinks something's happened to Sam and Elizabeth."

"Now, wait, don't get in an uproar about it. It's bad enough to have Joe practically pacing the floor. They're just a little late, that's all. It's happened before. Normally Joe wouldn't even have worried about it. But he needs that blade so much. He knew Sam would do his best to get the blade here fast."

"How late are they?"

"Normally they would have gotten in yesterday. But Sam was going to push it and try to make it in the evening before."

"And they still aren't here. That makes them two days late."

"Men!" Jessie exclaimed disgustedly, shaking her head.

"You're exaggerating, too. They're only one day late, really, and there are all kinds of reasons for that. Just having a lady with them probably slowed them down."

"Even though Sam was trying to hurry?" Stephen sensed the underlying anxiety in her voice, despite her optimistic words. "He doesn't strike me as someone who'd let much of anything slow him down."

"Sometimes you can't help it." Jessie's voice lacked conviction. She was beginning to be worried, too. When Sam hadn't shown up yesterday, she'd simply blamed it on Stephen's fancy fiancée. But she knew exactly how much Joe and Sam needed that blade here, and she was certain that Sam wouldn't let some lady's silly fears or complaints slow him down this much. "All kinds of things can happen."

"I'm sure that's exactly why my father is worried." Stephen was swept with guilt. What if something had happened to Elizabeth—while he had been here in Nora Springs lusting after another woman!

Jessie looked at him. Stephen was sick with worry; she could see it in his face. She'd known he would be, but she had hoped she wouldn't have to witness it. He was afraid for the woman Sam was bringing. The woman he loved. Her own heart twisted inside her. Yet, at the same time, she felt sorry for him. She wished she could give him some comfort, say something that would make him feel better. But she couldn't think of anything, and after a moment, she returned quietly to her work.

The rest of the day and night dragged by. Stephen was tortured by guilt and worry. He kept picturing the terrible things that could have happened to his brother and Elizabeth—and all the while he had been so wrapped up in himself and the disturbing longings he felt for Jessie that he hadn't even realized it was past time for Sam and Elizabeth to return to town. Mentally he berated himself for so forgetting himself and his duty. Elizabeth was his responsibility, yet he'd hardly spared a thought for her since Sam left to get her. In fact, if he was utterly honest with himself, he knew that he had been happy that Elizabeth was not here yet, for her arrival would mean an end to his time with Jessie. He hadn't wanted to think about why she wasn't here or what might have delayed her.

Even now, as he worried over Elizabeth, he couldn't keep the thought of Jessie out of his mind. All too often, he found that his mind drifted off, picturing Jessie, remembering the softness of her lips beneath his, the yielding eagerness of her body. He was, he thought, an utter scoundrel to desire her when the only thing that should be on his mind was his fiancée.

He ought to get a horse and ride along the road to Missoula until he found Sam's party. But if he did, he would be leaving Jessie unprotected at the mill. He simply could not do that. He reminded himself that he had no obligation to Jessamine Randall; all his duty was owed to Elizabeth. Elizabeth would bear his name; she had had his love for as long as he could remember. But Jessie—ah, Jessie. He thought of her hair, the color of fire and the texture of silk. She sparked a wildness, an eagerness in him that Elizabeth never had. He wanted her with a thick, hot yearning. He felt torn between them and wicked for feeling that way, when there was only one path that was right and honorable. He lay awake far into the night, and when he woke the next morning, he felt as guilty and indecisive as ever.

Stephen walked with Jessie to the mill, as he had the past few mornings, and sat down to wait again. He found it almost impossible. Neither Joe nor Jessie seemed to be able to settle down to their work.

In mid-morning, there was the sound of a shout, barely heard above the pounding and whine of the mill machinery. All three stiffened, suddenly alert. They waited, listening intently. The sound came closer. Then there were boots in the hall, and one of the men who worked in the lumberyard stuck his head inside the door. "The wagon's coming! They're back!"

Stephen jumped to his feet. Relief flooded him. Elizabeth was safe. He looked at Jessie. The relief was joined by reluctance and regret. He knew that when he went out the door to meet Elizabeth, he would have to leave Jessie behind him forever. Suddenly he wished he could slip out the back way.

But Joe was already hurrying through the door, his face eager and happy. Jessie followed him. She turned and looked at Stephen. "Come on. They're back."

She stood there in trousers and a shirt, her hair hanging down her back in a thick, straight braid, and Stephen thought he had never seen anyone more beautiful or desirable.

"Yes," he said. "I'm coming." He started forward on feet that had turned to lead.

Chapter Eleven

There was a large freight wagon in the lumberyard, and the mill workers were crowded around it. As Stephen came out, two men, one an Indian and the other the bearded older man named Burley Owens, were climbing down from the high wagon seat. They laughed and talked to the men, gesturing toward the huge crate in the back of the wagon. The Indian went around to the back and began to unfasten the ropes that held the crate in place, while Burley shook hands with Joe and began to talk.

Stephen glanced around. There was no sign of a buggy. He frowned. He wouldn't have thought a light buggy would be slower than the heavily laden wagon. He walked out of the yard into the street, shivering a little when the cold wind cut into him. He looked up and down the street. Where were Sam and Elizabeth?

He turned back to the yard, where the men were busy unharnessing the team of mules and unloading the heavy saw blade. Joe, directing the unloading, turned and saw Stephen. He left the men and came over to him, smiling broadly.

"I should have known Sam would come through. They just got slowed down a little. Seems the stage line has a rival that blew up a bridge or two along the way, so Burley and Jim Two Horses had to come the long way around. Nothing to worry about.'' He chuckled.

"But where are Sam and Elizabeth?"

"Don't worry. They'll be here in a few days. Seems your fiancée got a little sick along the way, so Sam sent the wagon on without them. They'll be following in their rig.''

"Sick? What's the matter?''

"Don't get all het up about it. There's nothing to worry about. Burley says your girl's fine, just a mite under the weather. Seems she got a little boil or sore or something that made it hard to sit in the buggy all day. She just needed a few days to let it heal up, so she and Sam stopped at a homesteader's cabin, and Sam sent the men ahead with the blade. He knew how much we needed it.''

"I see.'' The tension oozed out of Stephen, and he smiled. There wasn't anything seriously wrong with Elizabeth. It was probably just that the trip had been a little too rough for her. But she was at someone's house, with the homesteader's wife to look after her while she got well, and with a little rest, she'd be fine. "Then there's no need to worry, is there?''

"Nope. None at all. Sammy'll make sure she's well before they set out again.'' Joe smiled broadly. He glanced at the wagon. "No, wait! Don't touch that blade!'' He loped to the wagon to supervise.

Stephen watched him go, aware of the new lightness in his chest. The only problem was, he wasn't sure if his relief was because he knew that Elizabeth was safe—or because it would be a few more days before he had to face her.

It was music to Joe Ferguson's ears when the new, bigger saw blade was attached and started up. Its shrill, mechanical whine shattered the quiet of the mill, and the men cheered. Quickly the first log was guided toward it in the log carriage, and the blade cut into the wood. Chips flew; sawdust filled the air. Joe turned to Jessie and Stephen, standing beside him, and grinned.

"We're in business again!'' he shouted.

They had to guess at what he said. The noise was deafening. The thrum of the machinery vibrated through Stephen, and the excitement of the moment gripped him. He knew, at least in part, how his father felt. He'd had moments of triumph in his business, but this was somehow more exciting, more immediate.

They watched for a few minutes, then turned and walked toward the office. When they reached the door, Joe turned to Jessie and Stephen and said, "You two go on in. There's someone in town I need to see." The grin that had rarely left his face from the moment the saw blade arrived flashed again.

Stephen glanced at him, surprised. He would have thought Joe would want to sit down with them and babble out some of his excitement over the new blade. But Jessie wasn't surprised; she knew exactly where Joe planned to go. He wanted to tell Elias Moore in person that the blade had arrived and the mill's note would soon be paid.

Joe left the sawmill and walked down the street, whistling. He didn't notice that he'd forgotten his coat or that the chill north wind was slicing through him. He pulled his watch from his pocket and looked at it. It was late in the afternoon; the bank would be closed. Well, old man Moore would simply have to open up for him. This was one bit of news that couldn't wait. He suspected Elias Moore wouldn't resent making this exception; after all, he stood to gain a few thousand dollars. The old skinflint.

Joe wondered if he would finally manage to put a smile on Moore's sour countenance. Probably not. He didn't think the man knew how to smile.

It took a few minutes of tapping at the bank's locked and barred door before a clerk showed his face, and then a few more minutes of talking before Mr. Moore himself finally opened the door and let him inside.

"What is it, Ferguson, that couldn't be discussed during business hours?" Moore asked crossly as he led Joe across the bank lobby into his office. "We were about to leave."

"Well, it's still business hours most places," Joe retorted

jovially. "The rest of the world works, you know, long after the bank closes its doors." He grinned. "I reckon that's 'cause we all have to sweat to make sure the bank gets our payments."

Mr. Moore frowned. He was a thin, spare man with a long, somber face. A large nose dominated his features, and atop it sat little spectacles. He had a habit of looking over the spectacles at someone until he began to shrivel and remember every sin he'd committed in his life. Mr. Moore tried the trick now with Joe Ferguson, but Joe grinned irrepressibly.

"I figured you'd want to hear my news. It might make your evening more pleasant."

"The only thing that would do that would be for you to pay off your note, which, as you well know, is already in arrears. If I don't receive your payment by the end of next month, I—"

Joe waved aside his words. "Hold your horses. No need to start threatening. You don't have to. You'll get your money. I came to tell you that we got the new saw blade today. It's in operation, and that means we'll get our shipment out in time."

Mr. Moore's mouth snapped shut. He blinked. "Well. I must admit you have surprised me." He smiled thinly. "Congratulations. Now both of us will profit." He rose and extended his hand to shake Joe's.

They continued to talk a few minutes about the new blade and Joe's estimation of how long it would take to finish their final shipment and receive payment. Then Moore escorted him to the front door. All the other employees had already gone, and the bank was empty.

The banker went outside with Joe and locked the door carefully behind him. Joe strode off toward the mill, and Moore began to walk in the other direction, toward his house. However, halfway there, he took a small detour down a side street. He took a piece of paper from inside his jacket and wrote a short note on it, then stuck it under the door of a small, shabby house.

That evening, after supper, when he was sitting in his study, there was a light tapping on the window. Moore arose and went immediately to the kitchen door to open it. A huge figure detached itself from the shadows and stepped inside.

"You wanted to see me?" Frank Grissom asked.

The banker glanced at him with cold eyes. "I can assure you that it was from necessity, not preference, that I sent for you."

"Huh?"

Mr. Moore grimaced. "Come with me. We can't talk here."

Grissom followed the thin man down the hall and into the study, his work boots clumping heavily against the hardwood floors. Inside the study, Moore locked the door and turned to his companion. "Well, you've certainly managed to make a mess of things."

Grissom shrugged. "I did what you told me. First I made sure the blade broke. Then you told me to take care of Sam, 'cause they couldn't meet the deadline without him. So when I saw Jessie ride out to the camp I reckoned Sam'd be coming back with her for the payroll. How was I supposed to know it was his brother? Nobody even knew there *was* another Ferguson kid."

Frank scowled. He wished he *had* killed the man, mistake or not. Then the weasel wouldn't have been around to interrupt him the other day with Jessie. Ever since then the dude had stuck to her like glue. Not, of course, that *that* would stop him from taking her if he wanted to. The city-bred Ferguson wasn't anywhere near his size, and it was obvious, looking at him in his fancy clothes, that he wouldn't last two minutes in a fight. Still, he was a bother. And what if he told Joe? Grissom sure didn't want to be kicked out while Elias Moore was willing to pay him for hurting the mill.

"I don't want any of your self-serving excuses." Elias's sharp voice intruded on Grissom's thoughts. "I want results! So far, you haven't shown me any. Sam went riding off to Missoula without a hitch, and now he's brought the blade back. Joe Ferguson was in the bank today, bragging to me about how he'd be able to pay off the note. Damn it, man, what do you think I'm paying you for? I want that sawmill shut down.''

"I can't see why you'd want to keep somebody from paying you."

Moore's lip curled. "You wouldn't. Just trust me—that mill is worth far more to me than what I'll be receiving when Ferguson pays off the note. Now, I want business at that sawmill to cease immediately. Do you understand?"

Grissom shrugged. "Sure. But it's gonna seem awful suspicious, after them other things."

"Make it look like another accident. No one will be able to tell for certain. That's what you should have done with Sam. Look, I don't care how much people suspect. Just don't get caught, and no one will be able to prove anything."

That was easy enough for *him* to say, Grissom thought resentfully. Moore wasn't the one risking his neck betraying the Fergusons. But he kept his thoughts to himself. "What do you want me to do? Mess up the new blade?"

"No. Too obvious. Besides, there's no sense in ruining a new saw—it'll add to the place's value." He thought for a moment. "What powers the blades?"

"Huh?" Grissom stared at him blankly.

Moore sighed. He hated dealing with fools. "What makes them run?"

"Oh. Well, the engine. The steam engine."

"One central engine?"

"Yeah. It runs everything."

"Could you put it out of commission?"

The big man shrugged. "Sure, I reckon. It wouldn't be too hard. And nobody knows enough about it to fix it, except maybe Sam."

"I thought Sam was back."

"Nah. He won't be in for a while. He got stuck on the

trail, something about his candy-ass brother's woman." He snorted. "I don't know what woman would have that one."

"All right." Moore ignored Grissom's extraneous comments. "That sounds good. Do something to the steam engine. Immediately."

"You're the boss."

Moore handed him a packet. "There's half the money, as usual. You'll get the rest when you've finished your job."

Grissom stuffed the envelope into a pocket of his jacket. He didn't like the way the banker paid, half and half. Last time the cheat had refused to give him the whole second half just because he'd shot Stephen instead of Sam. Hell, it was a mistake anybody could have made. Dealing with Moore was like handling a snake—a touchy one, at that. He'd be glad when he finished. He would have enough money then to get out of this town and start over someplace else. Considering the Fergusons, Grissom reckoned that'd be the safest thing to do.

Two nights later Stephen was awakened by the babble of excited male voices downstairs. He sat up, disoriented for a moment. It was pitch black, the middle of the night. He frowned and fumbled in the dark to light the oil lamp by his bed. By its dim light he picked up his watch from the table and opened it. It wasn't quite midnight. No wonder he felt so groggy. He'd been asleep hardly more than an hour.

Curious, he climbed out of bed and wrapped his heavy dressing gown around him, then went into the hall and down the stairs. In the back hall, he found a group of men clumped around one of the doors. Stephen had never been in this part of the house and wasn't sure what the room was. One of the men turned, saw him and stepped back.

"Oh! Mr. Ferguson. I'm sorry, sir. I didn't even think." Around him other men turned and drew back, opening a passage for Stephen into the room.

"What is it? What's the matter?" He walked past them into the room and came to a dead stop.

He was in a large bedroom, obviously a woman's room, but it was not a woman who lay on the bed. It was his father, stretched out on top of the covers, fully dressed, his eyes closed. "My God! What happened?"

Stephen covered the distance to the bed in two long strides. "Father? What's the matter with him? What happened to him?"

Blood clotted Joe's hair and oozed onto his forehead.

A woman reached out and gently took the lamp from Stephen's hand. He glanced at her and for the first time realized that Jessie was in the room.

"Jessie!" Instinctively his hand went out to her, and she clasped it tightly. "How—what?"

She shook her head. "I don't know. They just brought him in."

He noticed now that Amanda was there, too, on the other side of the bed. She was wringing out a cloth in a basin of water, and she leaned across the bed to dab at the bloody wound on Joe's head. Stephen saw tears in her eyes.

He drew a breath and turned to the men crowding into the room. Burley Owens stood at the foot of the bed, twisting his hat between his hands, his worried eyes on Joe's still figure. Stephen was glad to see him; from what little he had seen, Owens appeared to be a man of sense, however rough he might seem. "What happened?" he asked, directing the question toward Burley.

The man glanced at him; he looked every bit his age tonight—and more. "I don't know, rightly. I just found him like that. I went by late tonight, after the saloon closed to see Joe and maybe have a little celebration drink over the new blade. I went to his room at the mill, and he wasn't there, so I waited a while. Finally I got up, and for some reason I walked into the mill. Guess I wanted to see how the new blade looked. Anyway, that's where I found Joe. He was down by the engine, just layin' there. Like that. His head was bleedin', and I couldn't rouse him. Maybe the engine blew up on him or something, 'cause it was a mess, too. Or maybe he was tryin' to fix it and—'' He frowned and finished lamely, ''I don't know.''

At that moment the doctor elbowed his way into the room and hurried over to the bed. ''Well, Amanda, looks like I might as well set up residence in your house, too, the way you keep giving me business.''

He bent over the bed and probed gently at Joe's head wound. He opened one of Joe's eyelids. ''Concussion. What hit him?''

''We don't rightly know,'' Burley replied. ''Maybe it was a piece of metal from the engine.''

''Well, it didn't crush the skull. We can be thankful for that. With luck he'll wind up with nothing more than a gigantic headache.''

He dug in his bag for his supplies and began to clean the head wound. ''There's nothing any of you can do for him here. Might as well get out and go back to bed. It may be quite a while before Joe wakes up. I won't really be able to tell anything about his condition until he does.''

''He's right,'' Jessie said softly to Stephen. ''The men needn't stay here.''

Stephen understood what she didn't say, that all of them would be more of a hindrance than a help. ''Yes.'' He turned around, naturally assuming command. ''You men, go home and get some rest. Whenever we find out anything, we'll let you know.''

Several of the men nodded, and they began to file out the door. Soon the room was almost empty. The doctor turned toward Stephen. ''He was hit twice, whatever it was.''

''What?''

''There's a large bump on the back of his head, as well as this one closer to the front. The front wound bled more, so we noticed it first, but I wouldn't be surprised if the rear one was the harder blow.''

''It wasn't that the engine blew and he got hit by a flying

piece of scrap, was it?'' Stephen asked, watching the doctor's face intently.

Dr. Holzworth frowned. ''Well, I don't know if I could say for sure, but I think it's unlikely. There's the position of the two wounds. How could the engine, flying apart, hit him both front and back?'' He paused. ''If I had to make a guess, I'd say somebody hit him hard with something big and blunt. It looks like a lot of wounds I've treated. Somebody picks up a bottle or a gun and whacks another man on the head with it. There are no other cuts or contusions, no sign of flying shrapnel. Besides, wasn't the engine cut off?''

''Yeah. It should have been.'' Stephen glanced at Jessie, then at Burley. They both nodded.

''I don't see any way,'' Burley said in a low voice, '''cept some son of a bitch attacked Joe.''

The doctor shook his head. ''I'd say someone's after you Fergusons.'' He narrowed his eyes. ''You better watch your back, son.''

Stephen looked again at Jessie. She avoided his gaze.

''I've done about all I can for the present,'' the doctor went on. ''Or anyone else can, either. You might as well get some rest. Especially you, young man. As I remember, you're only a couple of weeks out of bed yourself. You need your sleep.''

Stephen started to protest, but Amanda cut in smoothly. ''I'll sit up with Joe tonight. Why don't you go to bed, Stephen? I'll wake you if anything happens.''

''No, I couldn't let you. It's too hard for you, ma'am.''

''Stephen…'' Jessie tugged at his hand, pulling him toward the door. He glanced at their linked hands, surprised. He didn't remember taking Jessie's hand, let alone holding it for so long. But it felt so good and comforting in his that he didn't let it go. ''Ma knows what she's doing better than you or me. She's the one to stay with him.''

''Yes, but that's too great a burden for her,'' Stephen protested. Then he remembered the way Amanda had looked at his father as he lay motionless in the bed. She loved Joe; Stephen was sure of it. She would insist on taking care of him. "All right. But she must let me relieve her later."

"Of course," Jessie assured him as she led him from the room. She, too, knew how her mother felt about Joe. She'd known it for years. More than that, she knew that right now, more than anything else, Amanda needed to be alone with Joe, to be able to cry and fuss over him without anyone there to observe. As for Stephen, for all his calm, there was a pale tightness around his mouth and eyes that she didn't like. He'd had a terrible shock. He had probably never seen a man injured before. Besides, he was Joe's son, his flesh and blood, however newly discovered; it must cut him more deeply. In Jessie's opinion, he needed the Western cure-all: a good, stiff drink.

Stephen followed her out of the room and down the hall to the kitchen. "Here, sit down," Jessie ordered, pushing him toward one of the plain wooden chairs at the small kitchen table, then went to the cupboard for a bottle of Irish whiskey that her mother kept hidden for Joe's occasional visits.

"She loves him, doesn't she?" Stephen asked.

"What? Oh. You could see that?"

"Yes."

"Yeah." Jessie found the bottle and uncorked it, then poured him a healthy shot of whiskey in a water glass. After a second's thought, she took down another glass and poured herself a small shot, too. "Does it bother you?"

Stephen glanced up, surprised. "No. Why should it? My mother's dead, and she'd been gone many years before that. There's nothing wrong in him finding happiness and love somewhere else."

Jessie set the drinks on the table, looking away as she said, "But she's not—not quality, like your mother was. I reckoned you might not think she was good enough for your father."

"Jessie!" Stephen's hand lashed out and grabbed her around the wrist, pulling her around to face him. "Is that what you think of me? That I judge people by whether or not they're in the social register in St. Louis? Amanda Randall is quality. And I've known women of great prominence in social circles who were no better than the most common tramp.''

Jessie's eyes flew up to his. It was on the tip of her tongue to ask tartly how he knew the state of those women's morals, but she clamped her lips over the imprudent words.

"Your mother is a lady. She's made of purest sterling. And so are you." Stephen's eyes bored into hers. "Don't ever think otherwise, Jessamine."

Jessie's knees trembled a little, as they always did when he said "Jessamine," and she sat abruptly to hide that fact. "I didn't know how you'd feel about it, especially if he'd—if they'd—"

"Slept together?"

Jessie nodded. "I don't know that they have. I just suspect. They're very circumspect. Joe would never do anything to damage Ma's reputation in town. But once I woke up in the middle of the night and heard his voice at Ma's door. They were saying goodbye." She glanced sideways at him, wondering what his reaction would be. She wasn't sure why she had told him; she had never revealed what she thought to anyone else, even Sam. But for some reason it was important to her to find out what Stephen thought.

"I'm happy for him, for both of them. Your mother is a generous and loving woman. And every inch a lady." Stephen reached out and took her hand, lacing his fingers through hers. He held on lightly, his thumb softly rubbing the back of her hand. "More to the point is how *you* feel about it. Whether you resent my father."

Jessie shrugged, surprised that he would even think of that side of the matter. She knew that it was always the woman who was considered immoral in such things, not the man. "Maybe a little, at first."

"I'm sure he meant no dishonor to her. He wasn't free to marry until Mother died."

She nodded. "Yes, but I didn't know that until you came into town. Mother certainly never talked to me about Joe or his marriage. And it was a forbidden subject with Sam. But I liked Joe, and I realized that he did his best to see that Ma was never hurt by it. He didn't treat her like a mistress. He made sure no one knew. He's a good man. And I was old enough, when I figured it out, to know how it is with a man."

Stephen grinned. "Oh? And how is it with a man?"

Jessie blushed and cast him a disgusted look. "You know what I mean." She jerked her hand away from his. The way he was caressing her made her feel strange inside, as if she wasn't quite in control of herself.

Stephen watched her, thinking how pretty she looked when she blushed. It made him want to lean over and kiss her pretty little upturned nose. And her forehead, her cheeks, her lips. Desire surged unexpectedly in him. He turned away and tossed down a slug of whiskey. What a time to be panting after a woman! His father was unconscious, possibly dying, in another room, and he was thinking about kissing Jessie!

He curled his fingers tightly around the glass, staring at its contents while inside the whiskey trailed fire down his throat and settled, flaming, in his stomach. "What if he dies, Jess? I've barely found him. What if he dies now?"

Jessie's heart went out to him. Stephen's usual polite social mask was gone, and there was stark pain on his face. She got out of her chair and went to him, bending to put her arm around his shoulders comfortingly. For a moment he was stiff beneath her arm. Then, with a hoarse noise, he turned to her, burying his face in her warmth and wrapping his arms tightly around her. He did not cry, but Jessie felt the shudders running through him as he fought to control his tears. Tears sprang into her own eyes, and she curled over him, laying her cheek against his head. His hair was soft beneath her skin.

"Don't worry," she whispered. "He won't die. Joe Ferguson is a tough ol' coot. It'd take more than somebody busting him in the head to make him give up the ghost. Once, when I was little, I saw a tree fall on him, and he got out with just a few scratches.''

Stephen nuzzled into her, seeking the warmth and sweet, feminine comfort she offered. For a moment he let himself float in that state. God, she felt soft. She smelled good. What bliss it would be to stay like this, wrapped together with her, to soak up her strength and warmth.

But he knew it could not last. At any moment someone could walk into the kitchen and find them this way. It would not matter that she was only comforting him; merely the position would compromise her. And Stephen knew that before long it wouldn't be mere comfort, either. Not with her body so soft and warm in his arms, and her skin separated from his lips by only a nightgown and robe. Not with her breasts pressing into him. Already his blood was beginning to course more warmly in his veins.

He straightened and released her. Jessie turned away, moving jerkily, as if someone was pulling her on strings. With her back to him, she picked up her glass and downed the whiskey. Stephen watched her. He'd never seen a woman drink whiskey before. He expected at least a gasp at its fiery strength. But there was no sound from Jessie.

Stephen smiled a little. Why would he expect anything else? Even if Jessie had never drunk whiskey, she would never let on. His eyes trailed down her back and caressed the curve of her buttocks, barely hinted at under her belted robe. He cleared his throat and turned away. This would never do. Could he not even accept her kindness without turning it into desire? Being around Jessie seemed to bring out the lecher in him—even with his father in such a grave condition.

He sipped at the whiskey and tried to focus his mind. There were many things that needed thinking about, things that needed to be done. Perhaps if he concentrated on them, he could keep his mind off his father's health—and off Jessie.

She turned to look at him. He wasn't watching her. It

must have been her imagination that she could feel his eyes on her. Imagination and her own wayward lust. She had gone to Stephen feeling only compassion and a need to help him, but when he had pressed his face into her, his arms holding her tightly, heat had sprung up all through her. Her skin had begun to tingle and her blood to race, and a hot, heavy knot had formed deep in her abdomen, aching and pulsing. She had wanted to turn Stephen's face up to hers and kiss him, kiss him deep and hard, as he had kissed her the other day. She had wanted to nip at his neck, to sink her fingers into his hair, to twist her body against him. How could she think of something like that at a time like this? Did she have the soul of a strumpet? Was this how her mother had felt about Joe all these years? Lord, if it was, she didn't know how Amanda had managed to keep from openly becoming his mistress.

The thought shocked her. Good Lord! Could she be thinking about becoming the mistress of this man? Throwing away her good name for the sake of a few days of passion with him? Why, only a couple of weeks ago she hadn't even liked him. She tried to summon up the way she had felt about him then, tried to recall that his elegant clothes and manner were sissified, that he wouldn't be worth a damn out here on his own, that he wasn't husky, hard, the way a real man was. He wasn't Sam, and Sam was her ideal.

No, he wasn't Sam. Jessie smiled a little. He wasn't like Sam at all. But she had never had feelings remotely like these for Sam. Right now, she had trouble remembering Sam's face. All she could see was Stephen.

"Well," she said, running her hands down the sides of her robe. Her palms were sweating. "I guess I'll go to bed. I'll trade watches with Mama after a while."

"Then call me to relieve you." He did not look at her, but kept staring into his glass as though it held the secrets of the world.

"I will." Jessie hesitated, then turned away and left the room.

Behind her, Stephen crossed his arms on the table and sank his head onto them with a sigh. *Ah, Jessie.* What was he going to do?

Chapter Twelve

"Stephen!" a voice hissed, and a hand shook his shoulder.

Stephen made a low noise in his sleep and flopped over onto his back. The persistent prodding at his shoulder continued, and finally his eyes opened a slit. Jessie was leaning over him. She was dressed in nightclothes, and her hair hung loose in vivid red waves. The ends brushed the covers over Stephen's chest.

Still foggy with sleep, not even thinking, he lifted his hand and wrapped it around several strands of her hair. Caressingly his hand slid down over the soft waves, letting them slip out of his palm. He didn't stop to wonder why Jessie was at his bed in nightclothes and with her hair invitingly unbound. He reacted instinctively. His hand went around her wrist and moved slowly up her arm. Jessie's eyes widened. She could have jerked back from his touch, but she did not. She stayed as motionless as a statue, barely breathing. His hand curled around her neck, then went up to curve over her cheek and jaw. He smoothed the hair from her face, and his hand remained there.

"Beautiful," he murmured, and his smile was slow and sensual.

A quiver ran through Jessie. All she could think about was lying down on the bed beside him. She wanted him to kiss her. She wanted to feel his hand on her skin. Suddenly her flesh was searing hot, as if a fire had exploded into life beneath her skin. Deep inside, a throbbing started, an aching emptiness that yearned to be filled.

Stephen's hand pulled her head down, and he rose up to meet her. For a moment, they were motionless, gazing deep into each other's eyes, their lips only a breath apart. It seemed like forever. The sound of her pulse roared in Jessie's ears as, gently, Stephen touched his mouth to hers. He kissed her, then kissed her again and again, pulling her onto the bed with him, until finally she was stretched out atop him, his tongue plundering her mouth. She dug her fingers into the covers, kissing him passionately.

All sleepiness burned away in the heat of his desire. Every inch of him was alive and alert now. But Stephen did not think of the miracle of Jessie's appearing in his bed; he did not consider the wisdom of what he did. He knew nothing but his need and her welcoming flesh.

He rolled over, pulling her beneath him. The bed covers lay between them, frustrating his desire to have her body directly against his, but he pressed into her, too eager and desperate to move away enough to pull off the covers. His pelvis ground suggestively into her, and even through the bedclothes, Jessie could feel the thick, hard length of his manhood. She whimpered and moved her legs restlessly, trying to get through the barriers that separated them. She twined her arms around his neck, clinging to him as they kissed endlessly, mindlessly.

With a growl, Stephen shoved the covers down to her waist, and his hand slid into her bed robe and cupped her breast. There was still the material of her gown between him and her skin, but it was thin, and through it he could clearly feel her heat and the hard tightness of her nipple. He caressed her breast, his breath ragged in his throat. He had to touch her, had to feel the satiny texture of her skin. With trembling haste his fingers unfastened the line of small pearl buttons down the front of her nightgown. He pushed the gown and robe off her shoulders and looked down at her.

Jessie's breasts rose up, full and firm, topped with the cherry points of her nipples. Her head was thrown back, her eyes closed, and her lips were slightly parted, moist and dark from his kisses. She was the picture of a woman lost in passion—erotic, seductive, compelling. Stephen caressed her breasts and cupped one in his palm. His fingers drifted teasingly over her nipple, and desire stabbed him, hot and intense, as the small bud hardened even more. He bent and kissed the supremely soft flesh. When his tongue came out to curl around the nipple, Jessie moaned aloud. The noise was a spur to his desire, and he pulled the nipple into his mouth.

Jessie arched her back, and her hands dug into Stephen's hair, clenching and unclenching with each new wave of desire that his mouth created in her. She writhed, lost to everything except the sensations shooting through her. She wanted to scream and cry. She wanted to feel him inside her. She wanted him to never stop touching and kissing her.

"Stephen. Stephen." Her breath was panting. Her hands slid down to his back and dug in.

Stephen groaned. His mouth widened, feasting on her breast.

There was the sound of a cough in the room next door, and Stephen stiffened. For the first time reason penetrated the haze of desire that surrounded him. He remembered where he was. He remembered that Jessie's body was not his to delight in and never would be.

He wanted to curse and rip the rest of the clothes from her; he wanted to make her his, so completely his that nothing could take her away from him. He wanted to damn the future and live only for this one moment.

War raged through him, reason and instinct struggling for control. As it always had with him, his mind finally won, and he rolled away from Jessie. He flung one arm across his eyes, blotting out everything, and a stream of vicious curses fell from his lips.

Jessie opened her eyes, dazed. She stared at him. A blush rose up her throat as she realized her nakedness. Hastily, ashamed, she yanked up her clothes and pulled them together across her chest. She scrambled out of bed, tears starting in her eyes. Once again she had forgotten everything under the force of passion. It had been Stephen who had had the strength and morals to stop—or perhaps it was only a lack of interest. That was an even more humiliating possibility.

"I came to wake you." Jessie spoke in a low, hurried voice. Tears clogged her throat. "You said you wanted to take over watching Joe. He's—I'm going to my room now."

She fled out the door and down the stairs.

"Jessie!" Stephen called after her, sitting up, but it was no good. She was already gone. He'd lost her. He'd given her up. He felt empty and aching inside. He wanted her so badly it was all he could do not to get up and run after her.

She must hate him. He'd handled things wretchedly. Never before in his life had he been so clumsy, so bestial, so lacking in smoothness and sophistication. It seemed insane that all his intelligence and skills should vanish when he was with the woman he desired more than he'd ever desired anyone. The woman he loved.

Stephen groaned and rolled over, burying his face in the pillow. Love. He couldn't be in love with her. It was too crazy, too horrible, too painful. He couldn't have her without marriage, because he loved her too much to disgrace her. Yet he could not marry her, because he was sworn and bound to marry another woman. And he could not bear not to have her.

No. It couldn't be love. It was just passion, if somewhat more extreme than what he usually felt. It could not be love. She was a strange, wild girl from the back of nowhere. She had no social graces to speak of and never worried about the correct thing to do. She had no use for fine clothes or food or art. She wore men's clothes and behaved in a completely unfeminine way. She never turned to him for help or gazed at him with soft, beguiling eyes. She was contrary, exasperating and stubborn.

She was also bewitching. Beautiful. Strong. Intelligent, impish and natural. She was warm and generous, kind. He could go on listing her attributes. It was easier to say what she was *not*, which was dull, boring and silly. Kissing her was like tasting the finest liquor—exciting, fiery, exquisite. No other woman had ever affected him so strongly, made him want her so much. But it wasn't only desire. It was far more than that.

Face it, he told himself. Admit it: you love her. He was in love with her in a way that wasn't even close to the lukewarm, fond emotion he had for Elizabeth. This love was intense and passionate, hot and unsettling.

It was also impossible.

He could not have her; he could not take their love to its final, right conclusion. He was engaged to Elizabeth, bound by his promise to her and his deathbed promise to her father. He had been reared in a society where honor and duty and doing what was right were the cornerstones of philosophy. A man did not run away from his responsibilities. The head ruled, not the heart. And wild, impulsive actions were avoided like the plague. Turbulent emotions were for common people, not people like the McClellans or the Caldwells. If one were unfortunate enough to feel such things, then one certainly did not act upon them. Emotions were never allowed to interfere with what had to be done.

He had to marry Elizabeth. To throw her over—especially now, when she had run away from St. Louis to marry him—would be the act of a scoundrel. Her reputation would be in shreds unless he married her; she would never be able to return to St. Louis. He would ruin her life if he refused to marry her. He could not do that to Elizabeth. His love for Jessie must be *his* burden, *his* pain, not Elizabeth's.

Stephen sighed and swung out of bed. He knew what he had to do, how he had to act. He had to avoid Jessie as much as possible, and when he was forced to be around her, he must not touch her; in fact, it would be best if he looked at her as little as possible. Stephen began to dress, sternly avoiding thinking about his decision. But inside his chest, his heart lay like lead.

It was broad daylight when Jessie awoke. The curtains across her windows were heavy, to help keep out the winter cold, but in spite of them the room was light. She jumped out of bed and ran to the window to shove aside the draperies. The pale winter sun was shining almost directly overhead. It must be close to noon! She couldn't remember when she had last overslept so badly.

She dressed hurriedly and ran downstairs, where she found the men already gathering for the noon meal. Good Lord, she'd missed a whole morning's work. She rushed into the kitchen and began filling her plate directly from the pots and pans before she remembered that there was no work this morning. The mill was shut down today, dead without the heartbeat of its huge engine. The engine was broken, and only Sam could fix it.

She ate some of her food, standing in the kitchen, then dumped the rest in the garbage pail. She no longer felt hungry.

Jessie went to her mother's room. The door was closed, and she eased it open and stuck her head inside. Joe was lying still on the bed, eyes closed, and her mother was sitting beside him, her hands busy with the sewing in her lap. Trust her mother to never be completely idle.

"How is he?" Jessie whispered.

Her mother turned and smiled. "Hello, dear," she answered in a normal tone. "No need to whisper. It would be far better if we *did* awaken him." She sighed. "He's no better, as far as I can tell. It's so awful. I can do nothing to help him!"

"I know, Ma." Jessie went over to her mother and patted her on the shoulder. "But he'll get better. Joe's tough."

"Of course. Of course. I'm being foolish."

Jessie stood for a moment, looking down at Joe. There was a battalion of questions inside her, all about confusing things like love and desire and the behavior of members of the upper crust. For once in her life, she had no idea what she should do or how she should act, and she needed her mother's knowledge and experience desperately. But she could not bring herself to ask Amanda such things now; they seemed so trivial compared to the life-and-death struggle going on in the bed before her. It would be cruel to burden her mother with questions at a time like this. She should be helping her, not adding to her problems.

So she said goodbye to her mother, pulled on her coat and, without really thinking about what she was doing, walked to the mill. As she moved down the hall toward the office, she heard a clanging sound in the huge room where the machinery lay silent. She stopped short. Someone was there. Why? Her heart began to pound. Could it be the person who had been causing all their problems?

Cautiously, Jessie crept through the double doors. The silence was eerie. There was another noise and a muffled curse. It came from the center of the room, where the steam engine was located. Jessie tiptoed closer.

In front of the engine was an oil lantern, burning brightly. A man sat beside it. He was dressed in rough clothes, and there were dirt and grease on his clothes, his hands and his face. Tools lay scattered around him. Jessie's jaw dropped.

"Stephen!"

The man glanced up. "Jessie! I didn't expect you to be in today." He rose smoothly from his cross-legged position on the floor.

"You scared me out of a year's growth! I heard a noise in here."

"Why did that scare you?" he asked.

Jessie hesitated. "Well, uh, because I thought it might be a stranger, and, uh…"

"Maybe you thought I was the person who did this." He gestured in the direction of the mighty engine.

"Did what?"

"Jessie…don't play games with me. There's no time for that. I'm not an idiot, though you seem to think I am. Apparently my father does, too. Why hasn't either one of you told me what's been going on?"

"I don't know what you're talking about."

"Will you please drop the act? When I arrived here, the saw blade had broken recently." Stephen began to tick off his points on his fingers. "A couple of days later you and I were ambushed, and I, who somewhat resemble my brother, was shot. Now, as soon as the new saw blade is brought in, the engine that powers the machinery is mysteriously disabled—and my father with it. It strains coincidence to the limit. Not only that, when I checked the engine, I found that it had obviously been tampered with. It didn't just happen to break. It had a lot of encouragement. My father must have heard the intruder and come to see what was happening, and the man hit him. Or perhaps he meant to put my father out of commission, too." Stephen paused. "Now…who is he?"

Jessie sighed and sat on the steps. "I don't know. I wish I did. Maybe I could have stopped it."

"How long have you known?"

"I suspected from the start, from the minute I saw that blade. The cut was too clean. It had been weakened deliberately. But Joe wouldn't tell either you or Sam. He didn't want you to worry, and besides, what could you have done?"

"Sam doesn't know about this, either? He thinks the blade was broken naturally?"

"I guess." Jessie shrugged. "But Sam's sharp. I imagine he'll put it together."

"Joe has no idea who's doing it?"

"Somebody with a grudge against him or Sam, I guess.

But we can't figure out who would have that much bitterness toward either one of them.''

''A grudge?'' Stephen looked skeptical. ''I don't think so. Maybe one incident. But three? It's hard to picture a mere grudge carrying a person to those lengths. My guess is there's another reason, and I suspect it has something to do with money. Things usually do. Who would profit by this mill being closed down?''

''That's just it!'' Jessie raised her hands helplessly. ''Nobody! In one way or another, most of the people in Nora Springs depend on the mill. They work here, or transport goods for us, or they sell things to the workers. The landowners sell us the trees, or lease us the timberland. Except for a couple of ranches in the valley, practically everything around here is connected to the sawmill. If it failed, the whole town would more or less die.''

''What about a business rival?''

''What business rival? There isn't another sawmill for miles and miles. And there's plenty of business for more than one mill in this part of the country. The demand for lumber just gets bigger.''

Stephen frowned. ''It doesn't make sense.''

''I know.''

Jessie looked so woebegone that Stephen wanted to take her into his arms and comfort her. Sternly he rejected the impulse. He had made a decision to stick to business whenever he was around her. If he got personal, he would be on dangerous ground. As it was, just looking at her, he was having trouble keeping his mind on the problem before them.

''All right. Let's start at the most basic level and build up. What will happen now that the engine's broken?''

She gave him an odd look. ''The mill can't run, obviously.''

''Ever?''

''Not until Sam gets back. He's the only one who knows enough about the engine to even figure out what to do.''

''So at least a few days.''

"Yeah."

"And if it needed a certain part, it could be two weeks, or even more."

"Sure, if a part had to be shipped here."

"So what happens if the mill is closed down for a few days or a few weeks?"

Jessie looked uncomfortable. "We couldn't fill our orders. They'd have to buy from somewhere else, and we'd lose a lot of business."

"And what would the result of that be?"

Jessie squirmed. "Why do you have to know all this?"

"Because I am trying to ascertain a motive. There has to be one, or someone wouldn't have tried three times to stop the mill from operating."

"Joe'll kill me if he knows I told you."

"Told me what?"

"If we don't make the deadline on our orders, we're out of business."

"Completely?"

"Yes. Joe and Sam have a note at the bank. They got it to make improvements a few years ago, and then, when the blade broke, Joe added to the note, borrowing money to buy the new blade. Right now is when our cash is the lowest, right before we get paid."

"And the note's coming up soon, and Ferguson Mill won't have the money to pay it unless they fill their orders, right? Which they can't do if they're shut down."

Jessie nodded. "Yeah. The bank would get the sawmill."

"Then someone would profit, or rather, some*thing*—the bank."

"Not really. The bank would get the mill, but they'd have to run it, and the people at the bank don't know anything about that. I would think they'd rather just get the money paid back, don't you?"

"Usually. Besides, it seems very unlikely that the employees would care enough about the bank's profit to do something like this. It's hard to imagine this as the work of an institution. Maybe—maybe it's someone who thinks that if Joe is facing ruin, he would sell the mill to him at a good price. Or that the bank would sell it to him at a good price, that they'd discount it.''

"Yeah, but nobody's tried to buy it. Wouldn't you think they'd at least make an offer before they set out to force him to sell?''

"Maybe. Maybe not. Well...'' He shrugged as though dismissing the matter. "At least I can take care of one problem. I'll make the note payment for my father.''

Jessie groaned. "He'll kill me. Joe doesn't want your money. He's afraid you'll think he was glad to see you just because he needed your money.''

Stephen grimaced. "I wouldn't have thought that. Did he actually believe I'd rather see him fail than pay a debt for him?''

"He's a proud man. He wouldn't like taking charity.''

"It's not charity. I'm his son. I'd give him whatever I had, and I think he'd do the same for me.''

"He would.''

"Then why should he object if I do it for him?''

"He's proud. Maybe it has something to do with your mama being rich, you know, and Joe taking her away from all that, then her going back to it.''

"But she didn't leave because Joe didn't have enough money for her. She didn't care about the luxuries. I think she was just too gentle, too soft a woman to survive here.'' He sighed. "But I can understand how my father feels.'' He thought for a moment. "Surely we could work something out, a business deal so my father and Sam wouldn't have to feel it was charity. I could lend them the cash—or maybe I could buy a share in the business. It would be an investment for me.''

Jessie brightened. "Hey! It might work. Joe might agree to that, as long as you were getting something in return.''

"Good. How much is the payment?'' Jessie told him, and he nodded. "That's fine. I have a letter of credit from my bank in St. Louis, and it will cover that.'' He paused, thinking. "But that may not stop the accidents from occurring. If it's a buyer who wants to force them to sell, he could continue to attack the business until Joe and Sam couldn't make a profit and would have to sell out.''

Jessie nodded. ''That's true.''

''And something else—if I make the payment, and because of that there are no more accidents, we'll never find out who has been causing them. Not for sure, anyway.''

''That's right. He would be able to get away with what he's done to Joe. And you.''

''Right.'' A devilish light danced in Stephen's eyes. ''What would you say about setting a trap for him?''

A wide grin split Jessie's face. ''Sure! How?''

''Suppose I don't pay off the loan until the last minute and don't make it known that I intend to? Whoever is doing this will assume that the loan won't be paid unless the mill manages to meet their schedule. Then suppose that the mill goes back into operation quickly? He would have to strike again.''

''And we'd catch him at it.''

''Exactly.''

''Let's do it!'' Jessie crouched beside him on the floor. ''We'll set up a secret watch, so he doesn't know we're here.''

''We? No. Absolutely not. *You* are not going to be on the watch. I will do it—and perhaps another man or two. Who can we trust?''

''What do you mean, I can't?'' Jessie exploded. ''There's nobody here you can trust more than me, and that includes you! Just because Frank Grissom got the drop on me the other day, don't think I'm no good in a fight. He caught me off guard, that's all, and I'll be prepared for this one. I can shoot a pistol as good as anybody, and I can—''

''For heaven's sake, I'm not questioning your ability or your trustworthiness. You won't be there because you might get hurt!''

''So might you, or anybody else. As I remember, you didn't fare too well the other day when you took on Frank Grissom.''

Stephen flushed. "I'm aware of your opinion of me, Miss Randall. I admit that the weakness from my injuries made me slow and careless, and Grissom did land a punch. However, I am quite recovered from my wounds now."

Now she'd injured his pride, Jessie knew. If she was her mother or one of those women Stephen had tried to teach her to be, she would try to placate him now. But, darn it, she didn't want to be cut out of his plan just because she was a woman! She wasn't about to sit meekly at home and hear about things secondhand. She crossed her hands over her chest and glared stubbornly at Stephen. "You can't keep me out. You have no right. I'm going to keep watch, too."

"You are not," Stephen ground out through clenched teeth.

"I am. You can't tell me what to do."

"Well, somebody certainly needs to."

"I'll come anyway, whether you say I can or not. You won't be able to keep me out without my creating such a huge fuss that the person who's doing this will guess something's up."

For a long moment they glared at each other mulishly. Then Stephen's lip began to twitch and, surprisingly, suddenly, he grinned. "Damn. I bet you would at that."

Jessie grinned back in a self-satisfied way. "You're right."

"You'll get yourself killed someday."

"Maybe so, but at least my life won't have been boring."

Stephen shook his head, half amused, half exasperated. "All right. You can watch with me. At least that way I can keep my eye on you and make sure you don't do anything too stupid."

Jessie chuckled. "And here I was going to say the same thing about you."

Her statement surprised a laugh out of him. "Oh, Jessie, what am I going to do with you?" He couldn't imagine having this sort of conversation with any other woman. She was so annoying. She was so lively and fun. Life with her would never be dull. What would it be like, he wondered, to wake up to Jessie each morning? To laugh and talk and fight with her? She made everyone else seem tame.

Sternly Stephen pulled his thoughts from the direction they were taking. He was not supposed to be thinking this way. He had promised himself last night that he would avoid Jessie. That was one reason he had come down to the mill this morning to look at the engine. Yet here he was, wanting to kiss the impish grin from her face and thinking about spending his life with her.

He turned away and jammed his hands in his pockets to keep them from reaching out for her. *Damn it! Keep your mind on the subject.* "What about the others?" he asked in a remote tone. "Who else can we trust?"

Jessie felt suddenly deflated. "Well, uh, Burley Owens, of course. He's been with Joe ever since the beginning. If we can't trust him, there's nobody we can trust. And Jim Two Horses. Sam likes him and trusts him."

"Okay. Good. We'll switch off with them, then."

"Wait a minute. Don't you think we're getting ahead of ourselves? I mean, what's the point of all this planning? The mill's crippled with the engine down. There's no way to get it operating again quickly."

"That's simple. Repair it."

"How? Sam's the only one who knows anything about the engine. I could probably repair half the machines in here myself, but not the steam engine."

"Ah, that's why you're lucky I happen to be here."

"*You* know how to fix a steam engine?" Jessie stared.

"Yes. Don't look so astonished. It's impolite."

"But you—you're so fancy!"

Stephen glanced at the rough garb he was wearing, now liberally smeared with dirt, oil and grease, then looked at her sneakingly. They both laughed.

"You know what I mean, though! You're rich. You don't work with steam engines."

"I do work, contrary to what you think. I've worked in

my grandfather's business since I was fifteen. And before that I was always hanging around it. Do you know what my family's fortune is founded on?''

Jessie shook her head.

"Shipping. *Steam*ships."

"Oh." Her mouth opened, and hope rose in her eyes.

"That's right. Oh. I've been inside the engine rooms of more steamships than you can imagine. Large and small. When I was a boy, I was fascinated by the machinery of the ships far more than by their cargo or their profits. I spent a lot of time with the men who worked them, and I managed to learn a good bit. This engine is not precisely like the ones I am accustomed to, but it's close enough. I've found the problem, simply a damaged pipe or two. I think I can repair it easily enough. I may not be able to put it in perfect condition—we'll need to order a part to replace the damaged one. But I can put something together so that it will work until the new part gets here.''

"Oh, Stephen!" Jessie wanted to throw her arms around him with joy and kiss him soundly. But she made herself stay where she was, letting her happiness show only in her blazing smile. "That would be wonderful." She clasped her hands together tightly. "Joe will be so happy.''

"How is he? Is he awake?''

She shook her head. "No. He's the same. I'm sorry.''

Stephen returned to the engine and picked up a wrench. He squatted and began to work. Jessie stood for a moment, watching him. There was no reason for her to stay, but still she lingered, unwilling to leave him. She watched his hands as they worked. They were stained with dirt and oil, no longer carefully manicured. His fingers were long and slender, supple. They moved quickly, his touch delicate and deft. Jessie remembered the way they had felt on her skin, exploring her with the same gentleness and care.

Tendons moved and tightened in his hands and arms as he turned the wrench forcefully. There was strength in him. Jessie had felt the same strength in his arms last night as he had held her. When she had first met him, she had thought that Stephen was soft and weak, but she had been wrong; she knew that now. She had been fooled by his lean build and his manner, by his clothes and too-handsome face. She had been wrong, too, about his uselessness; he was not an idle, ignorant rich man. He had worked for a long time; he had experience and knowledge. He also had grit, determination and courage.

Nor was he the ice-cold man that his carefully controlled expression usually indicated. Jessie was positive of that, passion burned in him like a sawdust fire—fast, explosive, searing. She smiled, thinking about that passion. It had raged nearly out of control early this morning. But at the last minute he had been able to stop it.

She should be glad, of course. After all, he was an engaged man. He loved another woman, would marry another woman. There could be nothing more for them than a few nights' pleasure, so it was far better that they had stopped. Still, she couldn't help but feel a little piqued that Stephen had pulled away from her. She couldn't help but wonder why. Had it been out of love for his fiancée? She found that that idea caused a burning, itching sensation somewhere in the region of her heart. Or had it been because he would not dishonor her? That thought was much more attractive. Of course, there was still another possibility—that he simply didn't find her desirable enough. Jessie didn't like to think of that at all.

"Stephen? Why did you stop kissing me last night?" Jessie had always been a direct and honest person; she saw no sense in beating around the bush on any subject.

Stephen's wrench fell to the ground with a clatter. His head snapped around. "What? What the devil kind of a question is that?"

"I don't know." She shrugged. "A simple one?"

He made a noise of disbelief and bent to pick up the dropped tool. "Nothing is ever simple where you're concerned."

"Me? Are you joking? I think I must be painfully plain compared to the women you're used to. All those things they have to remember about walking and talking and everything, the hundreds of little tricks and deceits.''

"I'm more accustomed to them. But you—well, usually I find myself lost." He went back to his work.

"Well?"

"Well what?"

"Aren't you going to answer my question?"

He sighed. "That's not the kind of question you ought to ask a man."

"Why not? It's what I want to know." Jessie leaned forward, staring at him. "Stephen Ferguson! Are you blushing?"

He shot her a scornful glance. "Of course not."

She chuckled. "Yes, you are! I thought you were supposed to be a man of the world."

"I'm not generally accustomed to being asked such questions. Hasn't anyone ever pointed out that you're too bold?"

"Mmm, lots of times. Now, quit trying to wriggle out of it and tell me why you stopped."

"All right." He set the wrench aside and turned to face her seriously. "You're a beautiful woman, Jessie, and I want you very much. But it would be wrong for me to take advantage of you. You're an innocent. If I seduced you, I would be a cad, a scoundrel. Surely you can see that."

"Because you love someone else."

He hesitated, then said carefully, "Because I am pledged to someone else. I gave her my promise, my word. I can't go back on that. I can't marry you. And a woman like you should settle for nothing less."

A bubble of emotion swelled in Jessie's chest. She wanted to cry, but she wasn't sure if it was out of sadness or pleasure. She ducked her head and blinked back the tears. "Thank you." She forced a smile. If she asked for the truth, it wasn't fair to start crying when she got it. "You're a good man, Stephen Ferguson."

"And you're a beautiful lady, Jessamine Randall." For

a moment they gazed at each other. Finally Stephen pulled his eyes away and went back to his job.

Jessamine stood, dusting off the seat of her trousers. "When shall I tell the men to start work again? I imagine most of them will be dropping by today."

Stephen frowned at his work. "Tomorrow morning. I'll be finished tonight. And we'll have a guard to make sure nothing else happens."

"All right."

She walked out of the room and down the hall to the office. The quiet was eerie. She thought that if she was alone she might have been a little afraid, given the strange things that had been happening and the emptiness of the place, but it was comforting to know that Stephen was not far away. He would come running if she called.

Jessie shook her head. She must have lost her senses. Never before had she wanted a man's protection. And even if she was scared enough to want protection, she wouldn't have figured that Stephen Ferguson would be the man she'd pick to provide it.

Most of the workers dropped by throughout the afternoon, inquiring after Joe's health, and Jessie told them that they would be able to start the mill again the next day. Frank Grissom didn't drop by, and Jessie was glad. She didn't relish being alone with him, even if she did have her pistol close at hand.

But Grissom showed up the next morning, and the moment Jessie saw him, she knew that he brought trouble. She had awakened early and hurried to the mill, carrying a couple of cold biscuits in a napkin for her makeshift breakfast. She was nervous about running the mill without Joe, and she wanted to be there to meet the men as they came in the door, to reassure them that she was responsible and in charge. Another, unexamined reason for her early departure from the house was that she didn't want to have Stephen walk with her to the mill as he had done ever since Grissom's attack. She had thought about the matter long and hard the night before, and she had come to the conclusion that Stephen was right. There could be no possibility of a romance between them. Therefore, the best thing for her to do was to avoid being around him as much as possible.

Now she stood at the front door of the mill, greeting the workers as they walked up the stairs. The early morning air was chilly, even though she had on her heavy wool jacket and cap, and her breath crystallized in the air in front of her. In a few more weeks the snow would start falling, beginning the process that closed them in for the winter. The men seemed in good spirits, calling out greetings to her and each other, joking and laughing. She guessed that they must be grateful to be able to work; they must have feared, as she had, that the mill would be shut down for weeks. No one questioned her authority.

Until Grissom came up. She saw him approaching out of the corner of her eye, but she didn't turn to look at him. If she was lucky, she thought, she'd manage not to have to speak to him.

She wasn't lucky. Grissom walked straight to the bottom of the stairs and planted himself in front of her, his fists bunched on his hips pugnaciously. His eyes burned with resentment.

"What the hell do you think you're doing, anyway?" he roared. "Ordering my men back to work without a word to me!"

"I wasn't aware that you were in charge of whether or not the mill employees worked."

"I'm the foreman here, and with Joe down, I'm the one who'll be giving the orders. Not some split-tail in pants!"

"Is that right? Well, I never saw anything that put *you* in charge, either. I'm taking over until Joe is well enough to come down here himself, and I'm doing it because I'm his assistant. I know what Joe wants."

Grissom uttered a coarse curse. "You don't know nothin' missy, or you'd have talked to me before you went around telling all the men to come back to work. 'Cause I'm ordering 'em out of here!"

Jessie straightened, her eyes shooting sparks. "They

aren't going. They're not your employees—they're Ferguson Mill employees. And why are you so all-fired eager to make these men lose another day's pay?''

"I'd rather see them lose a day's pay than an eye or a leg or maybe their life.''

"What a ridic—''

"The hell it is,'' he charged on. "I heard that engine was stone dead. Who fixed it? I'll tell you who—that stranger! That fancy pants from back East. What does he know about a sawmill? There's no telling what he did to rig that engine back up to work. It'll probably explode any minute. I don't want my men working in a dangerous place.''

More and more men had gathered around them, some stopping on their way into the mill and others coming out to find out what the ruckus was. Jessie could sense their growing restlessness, and she knew that the men were leaning toward Grissom's side. They didn't want to lose pay, but they distrusted the city slicker, and Grissom had gotten them thinking about the possible danger. Panic rose in Jessie. What could she say to make them stay?

"Mr. Ferguson may not know much about sawmills, but he knows steam engines. He fixed it, and it'll run as good as new.''

"Well, I don't know, Jess,'' one of the men put in slowly, pausing to spit a stream of tobacco over the railing. "I ain't sure I want to risk my life on that young feller's say-so. I'm thinkin' we might orta wait till Sam comes back.''

"That could take days!'' Jessie protested. "Look, I'm telling you, it's safe now!''

"That's what *he* says.''

"I don't know as how we can trust him.''

"Maybe we better wait.''

The statements came from all around her, and the men began to shift, moving away. Jessie dug her nails into her palms, watching helplessly. Damn that Frank Grissom! He would spoil everything with his hardheadedness.

"Wait!" The clear, confident male voice carried across the lumberyard. "I believe I'm the subject of this discussion. Perhaps you gentlemen should be talking to me, instead."

Jessie swung around. Stephen stood at the entrance to the yard. He looked cool and calm, and his clothes were as neat and elegant as always. He looked like a gentleman of leisure out for a stroll. But his eyes were hard and cold as he stared across the yard at Grissom. "Grissom, do you have some complaint? I realize that you would probably rather bully a young woman, but I suggest that you take any problems you have with this mill or that engine up with me. Am I making myself clear?"

"Yeah." Frank grinned ferally. His eyes were lit with an unholy light. "I'd be real happy to take this up with you." He started across the yard toward Stephen, his fists doubling into knots.

Chapter Thirteen

Stephen waited for Grissom calmly. Jessie's heart began to thunder in her chest. Grissom wanted to fight Stephen; she had seen the blood lust in his eyes when Stephen appeared. If he managed to goad Stephen into a fight, Frank wouldn't stop until he'd maimed or killed him. Grissom was the biggest, meanest man in the area, and no one would dare to make a move to stop him.

Grissom stopped directly in front of Stephen and stared into his face. It was an intimidation tactic he had used successfully in the past. Stephen, however, did not flinch or look away. He simply gazed back, and there was something in his face, a kind of smug superiority, that made Grissom's blood boil.

"The engine is in good working order. It's perfectly safe. I give you my word."

Pointedly Grissom turned aside and spat on the ground. "Your word?" He laughed. "Well, now, ain't that something? I always would trust the word of some fancy-pants stranger." His eyes narrowed, and his voice turned harsh. "Who the hell are you to be coming down here trying to fix things and handing out orders about when we'll work? Who are you to tell us that the engine's safe? What gives you the right to stick your nose into our business?"

"Our?" Stephen repeated, his tone faintly amused. "I

wasn't aware until now that Joe Ferguson had taken you on as a partner." He dismissed Grissom with a glance and turned toward the other men, his gaze sweeping over them slowly, confidently. "My name is Ferguson, and that's what gives me the right to get Ferguson Sawmill running again. It is my father's business, no one else's. Ordinarily he would give the orders, and if he couldn't, then my brother, Sam, would. But Joe has been struck down by the vicious person who tried to ruin the steam engine. The person who is trying to stop Joe Ferguson's mill from running. If Sam was here, he wouldn't let that happen. But he's not here. So that leaves me. I'm Joe's son, and, just like Sam, I intend to make sure that whoever tried to kill my father and ruin his business won't succeed. That's what gives me the right. I don't think there's anyone here who has a better one."

His eyes settled on Grissom, cool and challenging. The men began to shift uncertainly and murmur among themselves. Jessie smiled. He had a beautiful way with words, that Stephen Ferguson. He'd obviously made the men start to rethink their decision to leave with Grissom.

"I realize that you men don't know me," Stephen went on after a moment. "But I am a Ferguson, and I think that name stands for something around here. I have done and will do nothing that will lessen that name. Now, if any of you are interested in putting in a day's work and getting paid for it, let's go inside."

Stephen started to move around Grissom toward the mill, but Grissom planted himself in front of him again, blocking his path. "Just hold on a damned minute! You can't go giving my men orders!"

"I will if they're working for me. That includes you, if you want to continue to work here."

"You can't fire me!"

"You want to stay and work? Fine. I'd like to see you do it. I was under the impression that you were refusing to work. That you were too scared to."

Jessie sucked in her breath. Now he'd put the fat in the

fire. Grissom was already on the verge of exploding. Why was Stephen goading him? Didn't he realize what Grissom would do? He wouldn't stop just because Stephen was Joe's son, not if he was mad enough. He'd pound him into a pulp.

"What?" Grissom's voice was deadly. Stephen gazed at him, contempt tinging his face.

Despite what Jessie thought, Stephen knew exactly what he was doing. It was obvious that Grissom would use his influence with the men to keep them from obeying Stephen and Jessie. He could stop the mill more effectively than any tinkering with the engine had—unless Stephen cut his power out from under him. His power was his brute strength; let Stephen beat him in a fight, and the men would swing over to him, not Grissom. Stephen had seen as soon as Grissom arrived at the mill that this confrontation would have to end with one of them establishing superiority over the other. What was more, this was a perfect opportunity to give the boor the thrashing he deserved for his attack on Jessie without exposing Jessie's name to any scandal.

Stephen was ready for Grissom to swing at him. He wanted it.

"Are you calling me a coward?" Grissom went on.

Stephen shrugged, letting his body fall into a relaxed, even careless posture, while inside every sense was alert, every muscle and nerve ready and waiting. "You're the one who kept talking about how frightening it would be to work in the mill. I would say that speaks for itself."

Grissom's eyes flared red. "Nobody calls me a coward!" he roared. He swung his huge fist at Stephen.

Jessie's heart leaped into her throat. She wanted to cry out to Stephen to watch out, but she didn't dare distract him. She gripped the railing and leaned forward.

Grissom's fist would have knocked most men to the ground—if it had hit. But when it reached Stephen's face, Stephen was no longer there. He bobbed aside, and as he moved, he sent his fist into Grissom's belly with all his strength. Air whooshed out of Grissom, and he looked comically surprised.

Stephen stepped back and shrugged out of his coat and the suit jacket beneath it. A man in the crowd reached to take them from him. "There, that's more suitable attire for fisticuffs," Stephen said, raising his hands and taking a professional stance. "Well?"

Grissom recovered his breath. "Why, you little son of a—" He charged, lowering his head to butt his opponent, a tactic that usually resulted in at least a broken nose for the other fellow, but once again Stephen neatly sidestepped, and this time Grissom stumbled past him and fell to the ground.

He jumped up and whirled around immediately, rage pouring from him. Still cursing, he came at Stephen, punching.

"Stop!" Jessie screamed. She looked around frantically for help and caught sight of Burley and Jim entering the lumberyard. They stopped, interested, and began to watch the fight. Jessie wanted to scream at them for their stupidity. Why didn't they do something? Didn't they realize what was going to happen? Not even glancing toward the fight, she hurried down the stairs and pushed her way through the spectators to get to Owens. "Burley! Burley, please, you've got to stop it. He'll kill him!"

Burley shrugged. "That's no loss to the world. I never did like him anyway."

Jessie's mouth dropped open in horror. "No! You can't mean that. He's Joe's son! Sam's brother."

Burley gave her an odd look. "I didn't mean Ferguson. I was talkin' 'bout that bastard Grissom. Looks ta me like Ferguson's goin' ta clean his clock. Ain't that right, Jim?"

The Indian grunted his agreement, intent on the fight.

Still Jessie stared. "What? You mean Stephen's—" She whirled around. She couldn't see through the tightly packed crowd. She scrambled up onto the gate to see the fighters.

There was a livid red spot on Stephen's cheekbone that would soon turn into a bruise. But Frank Grissom's face was far worse—bruised and smeared with blood, one eye swelling badly. He was huffing like a locomotive, while Stephen was barely breathing hard. He danced in and out, dodging Grissom's heavy fists while he jabbed and punched. He was fast, and his fists hit hard. Grissom looked dazed, and he swung wildly, his blows rarely landing.

Burley was right. Stephen was winning the fight!

It was difficult to absorb that fact; it was so completely the opposite of what she had expected.

"Damn good fighter," Burley commented beside her. "I reckon he must have trained for it." He chuckled. "Well, that'll surprise ol' Sam, I guess."

No more than it surprised her, Jessie thought, numbly watching as Stephen hammered at Grissom. Burley was right. Stephen must have studied with a professional. She had seen men get into countless brawls over the years. Some were better than others, but she'd never seen a man, even Sam, who fought with Stephen's precision and speed.

Stephen landed a hard right to Grissom's jaw, and the other man staggered and fell heavily to the ground. He didn't get up. Silently, calmly, Stephen rolled down his sleeves and retrieved his coat and jacket from the man who had held him. All around him the ring of people stood, openmouthed, staring at the body of Frank Grissom stretched out on the ground. Stephen could barely restrain a chuckle at the looks of amazement on everyone's face. It was clear that no one had expected him even to put up a decent fight, let alone knock out the local bully.

He climbed the stairs to the mill entrance and looked back. "Now, I'm ready to work. Who else wants to earn an honest dollar?"

"I'm with you, Ferguson!" shouted a man in the crowd below. "Hell, anybody can see you're ol' Joe's son, through and through."

"Good. Then let's get to it." He turned and strode through the door, and the men pushed through behind him.

"Sit still!" Jessie snapped, dabbing at the scrape on Stephen's cheek. "I'm just putting some medicine on you, for

Pete's sake. You'd think that after you'd whipped Frank Grissom into the ground, a little sting wouldn't bother you."

"Ow! Don't you think you're applying that a trifle roughly?"

"Don't be such a baby." Jessie gave his face a final dab and stepped back. "There."

"I'd rather face ten Frank Grissoms than one woman with a medicine bottle." Stephen grinned and slid off the desk.

Jessie grimaced and slammed the bottle down.

"You know, one might almost think that you were sorry I didn't lose that fight," he told her teasingly.

She shot him a flashing glance. "That's silly. Of course I didn't want you to lose."

"You don't act like someone who's happy."

"I'm happy. I'm very happy." She stalked to her desk, then whirled to face him. "Why didn't you tell me?"

"Tell you what?"

"That you could fight like that? Why, I'd almost think you earned your living doing it."

"Hardly. I doubt I could even stay in the ring with a professional pugilist. But I did study it when I was at Princeton." He struck a pose. "The noble art of self-defense. I had an excellent teacher. We used the Marquis of Queensbury rules, of course. But the tactics are the same, even when you're in a street fight."

"You knew you could whip Grissom."

He shrugged. "I guessed it. The brief sparring match we had in this office told me what kind of a fighter he was. He depends on his strength. He has no speed. He gets in close and batters his opponent. I knew that if I made him move, if I avoided his punches, I could get in enough blows of my own to eventually get the best of him. If nothing else, I'd tire him out."

"But you didn't bother to tell me! Why? Did you want

me to worry? I guess you thought it was really funny when I pulled a gun to protect you from him.''

''No. I didn't think it was funny. Jessie...what is it? Are you mad because I didn't tell you earlier?''

''Oh, no! Why should I be mad? Just because you didn't bother to inform me that you could defend yourself against that brute. Just because you let me worry and stew about how to make sure Grissom didn't jump you and beat you into a pulp. Just because—''

''All right, all right. I'm sorry. I didn't realize it would upset you so.''

''Upset me! Damn it! I was scared today! I thought for sure that I was going to see you beaten to death right in front of my eyes. I could picture the blood all over you, and—'' Her voice broke, and she turned away.

''Oh, Jessie...'' Stephen came up behind her and put his hands on her arms. He leaned down to rest his cheek against her hair. ''I never thought. It was stupid of me. I didn't realize you cared.''

Her heart began to hammer in her chest. His breath ruffled her hair, and she felt it along every nerve ending in her body. ''Not care!'' she exclaimed, trying to keep her voice even. She *would not* let him affect her so. She had promised herself that she wouldn't get herself in this position again. She had been furious with him only moments before. How could she now feel as if her bones were melting and all she wanted was to turn in his arms and press her body against his? In the past few minutes she had flown from fear to anger and now to desire. It was all too fast for her. She felt breathless and shaken and vulnerable. It wasn't a way she was used to feeling.

''Stephen, please.'' She pulled away from him.

Stephen's arms fell away from her quickly. He had gone to her and held her so instinctively that he hadn't really realized what he was doing. He recalled his vow to stay away from her. How soon he had broken it! He was going to have to be much more disciplined from now on if he intended to keep his promise.

The problem was that she had felt so good in his arms. He had been flushed with victory, still pumped full of energy and excitement. He had wanted so much to share it with her, to make her smile and laugh and enjoy his winning as he did. It had seemed right to hold her, and for that moment everything had been perfect. But now his arms were achingly empty. The knowledge that he was doing the correct and honorable thing didn't begin to fill the void.

He turned away, shoving his hands into his pockets because it was difficult to keep them from reaching for Jessie. He cleared his throat. "I'm sorry. It won't happen again." For a moment there was silence.

Then Jessie said in a businesslike voice, "Well, we'd better decide what we're going to do now, since we no longer have a foreman. How will we keep the mill running?"

Stephen turned, relieved to have a topic to pursue. "I don't think we'll find that there's another man who can do the job equally well, so we'll simply have to make do without a foreman. We'll keep a close eye on the men ourselves. After all, these jobs are skilled. The men know what they're supposed to do. The foreman is there to make sure they work and to resolve whatever problems might arise. I think for a few days, until Father's better, you and I could do that. You know all the facets of the business, don't you?"

Jessie nodded. "Yes. I know how everything works and what everyone is supposed to do, though many of the jobs require such strength that I've never done them. I'd know if the workers were shirking or doing something wrong. But the problem is that they won't want to take orders from me."

"But they will from me. I've earned their respect in the quickest way possible—beaten the man they feared. So if you need to order someone to do something, I'll do it. We'll be a team, and together we ought to be able to fill one man's shoes, don't you think?"

Jessie thought of spending all her time with Stephen for the next few days, working closely with him. It was exciting and scary. She wasn't sure she could handle it. Yet she knew she wouldn't pass it up for anything in the world.

"All right," she replied, hoping that what she felt didn't show on her face. "Let's do it."

Jessie and Stephen spent most of the next two days together, until Joe finally regained consciousness. Unfortunately, he was unable to give them any information about the person who had attacked him. He had heard noises in the mill and gone to investigate, and someone had struck him down from behind with a heavy blow to his head. Joe remained weak, foggy and plagued with violent headaches for several more days and was unable to return to work, so Jessie and Stephen continued to carry on the business for him.

They walked through the mill several times each day, checking on the speed and quality of the work. To Jessie's surprise, the men worked as well as they had when Frank Grissom was overseeing them. If anything, they seemed to go a little faster. Perhaps they were doing it because they liked Joe and were aware of his financial problems. Or maybe it was more pleasant to work without Grissom's presence. But she also was sure that the men felt respect for and confidence in Stephen, despite the fact that all of them knew more about sawing lumber than he did. Jessie had thought that Stephen would be remote and dignified around the men, but she found that he had a friendly, easy manner, though he always retained a certain bearing that proclaimed him the man in charge.

Every moment that Jessie didn't have to spend working she spent trying to teach Stephen the business. She took him through the mill, explaining each process. Though Joe had taken him on a tour of the sawmill before, he hadn't shown him everything in such detail. She showed him the bookkeeping records, the payroll work and the correspondence that constituted most of her job. She explained who the mill's customers were and how much each usually bought, and she showed him the mill's bills for various expenses.

Fortunately, Stephen was sharp and caught on quickly. Also, he clearly had a base of business experience that enabled him to grasp "all those damned number things," as Joe called them. Stephen enjoyed learning the business. In fact, he soon had ideas for improving it buzzing around in his head.

For Stephen, perhaps the headiest, most wonderful sensation came from working so closely with Jessie. They worked together well, each one often seeming to sense what the other was thinking, and they spent endless hours discussing things. One of the things Stephen had always liked about Elizabeth was that she was a woman he could converse with intelligently, but even she had been bored by conversation about the steamship line. But Jessie was happy to talk about the mill—or dozens of other things that he had never dreamed of discussing with a lady, such as his interest in boxing, or mechanical things. She even asked him to draw a diagram and explain the workings of the mill's steam engine to her, and they were lost in the subject for one entire evening, oblivious to the fact that everyone else had left the mill long ago and that they were missing supper.

At night they often went back quietly to the mill to stand their watch for the culprit who had hurt Joe and tried to wreck his business. They had collected a group of four trusted men besides themselves and set up watch in three groups of two. Stephen and Jessie took the first shift each night, sitting silently in the darkened mill or talking in low whispers. Nothing untoward happened, but Stephen found that he enjoyed his time in the quiet dark with Jessie. It seemed almost as if they were the only people in the world; everyone and everything else were far away.

He couldn't deny that he was happy, though he felt guilty for feeling that way when Joe was ill and they were struggling to save his business—not to mention the fact that his brother and his own fiancée still had not arrived. Still, he awoke every day with a sense of excitement and eagerness. There were times when he daydreamed about remaining in Nora Springs. He imagined waking every morning to the fresh, pine-scented air and walking to work at the mill. He would buy into the business with Joe and Sam and spend the rest of his life here. He would marry Jessie and build a beautiful house for her. He would…

But it was only a dream. In reality it couldn't happen. Because in reality Elizabeth would be arriving any day now, and he would be marrying her, as he had promised. There would be no happy life with Jessie in Nora Springs or anywhere else.

That realization kept him in constant turmoil. He had never known before how important a woman could become to a man, how he would rack his brain for a witty remark just to see her smile, or how just the sight of her could raise his spirits. But that was how he felt about Jessie. He wanted to be with her all the time, and when he wasn't with her, he thought about her. He loved to watch her, to talk to her, to see her flash him a grin. He loved her thick red hair and her eyes as blue as the Montana skies. He loved, in short, everything about her. All the things he had once found irritating or even horrifying now struck him as endearing, intriguing, challenging.

So, loving her and placed by fate in direct contact with her daily, yet having to refrain from caressing her, kissing her or telling her of his feelings, was torture for Stephen. He found himself infected with a strange possessiveness; he wanted to snarl at any man who stood too close to Jessie or looked at her with too much interest. He couldn't stop himself from watching her as she worked. When she stood or walked, his eyes were drawn like magnets to her slender, shapely legs, perfectly delineated in the worn denim trousers, and his hands ached to reach out and slide over the pert curve of her derriere. Inevitably his thoughts became more and more lustful, until he was thinking of sliding his hand between her legs and up the smooth cloth all the way to the top, and then of unfastening the trousers and peeling them down, his fingers exploring her soft flesh. By that time, of course, he had become so heated that it took several minutes of concentrating on numbers before he could even decently leave the concealment of his desk.

Always, without ceasing, even when he wasn't clutched in the hot talons of desire, there was a low, constant thrumming in his blood, a banked fire ready to flame up at the slightest provocation. Stephen had never known such tormenting, insistent passion before, a lust strengthened and multiplied by the love he felt for Jessie. Before this, he would have scoffed at the idea of such desire. But now he knew exactly how real it was and how much he was at its mercy.

He would have been astounded to learn that Jessie was suffering much the same torture that he was. She had known that she desired Stephen, but she hadn't even guessed that she loved him until his fight with Grissom. Then, with fear and panic surging through her, blinding her to what was happening in the fight, she had realized that she had fallen in love with Stephen. It had been easier to deal with her desire.

How could she love a man who was so different from any she'd ever known, any she'd ever thought she could love? What about Sam? She had believed for years that she was in love with him. Had it not been true? Worst of all, how was she to control this alien, explosive feeling?

She spent time sifting through her emotions, trying to figure them out. When she was fourteen or so, she had developed a crush on Sam. The intense emotion had quickly worn itself out, but she had continued to love him. Jessie realized now that the love she had felt for Sam had not been romantic love, as she had thought. She had been naive and inexperienced. What she had felt for him didn't have the same spark, the same excitement and rushing joy, that blossomed inside her when she thought about Stephen. Perhaps she loved Sam more as a sister loved an older brother.

She looked at Stephen and remembered the man she had

thought he was when she first met him. She had assumed he was idle, incompetent, weak and foppish. But he had shown her that he was tough and enduring. He had courage and determination. He was honorable; he was hardworking; he was inventive. The things she had held against him had been only appearances, not his inner spirit. She had simply been too prejudiced and set in her ways to see that. But now she knew that he was exactly the kind of man she could love.

All that was beside the point, of course. It didn't matter how much she loved him. The fact remained that he was engaged to another woman. No doubt he loved his Elizabeth; no doubt she was a beautiful, feminine creature who would not embarrass him in the elegant world in which he lived. Even if Elizabeth hadn't existed, Jessie knew that marrying Stephen was out of the question. He might desire her, but he would never accept anything less than a lady as his wife. And Jessie was not a lady, never would be. She couldn't live in the city, in his world. She couldn't wear skirts all the time and sit just so and keep her mouth shut about the things that were improper for a woman to have an opinion on—or even to know!

She had no chance of winning Stephen's love, or being his bride. And she had too much pride to settle for anything less! She would not allow herself to be his mistress, even if she did love him. She could not sleep with him. Therefore, she had to avoid getting into situations like the one the other night, when her passion had been so aroused that she hadn't even thought of stopping him. Unfortunately, she couldn't remove herself from temptation. What with working together and standing watch at the mill, they spent almost every waking minute of every day in each other's company. But Jessie was careful not to touch him, not to reach out and place her hand on his arm when she had something to show him, for example. She kept as much space as possible between them as they worked.

She had never dreamed it would be so difficult. There were times when Stephen would come and stand beside her, leaning over her, to see something she was working on. He would plant one of his hands flat on her desk and the other on the back of her chair, bending down so that his head was near hers. She could see the impossibly long curl of his eyelashes, the curve of his cheek, the faint shadow of his beard late in the afternoon, only inches away from her. She could smell the tang of his cologne and the subtler scent of his skin. She could feel his strength, his masculinity. And she longed to reach out and stroke her fingers down his face, to follow the curve of his eyebrows or the line of his mouth. She wanted to touch his thick hair, black as midnight. She wanted to stretch up the few inches it would take and press her lips against his.

She knew how his mouth would feel on hers, how warm and coaxing, how tender and passionate. She knew how his arms would tighten around her, pressing her into him, all the way up and down their bodies. He would pull her up out of her chair, his mouth digging into hers, and...

Then Jessie would shake herself out of her dream. She would tighten her fingers around her pencil and will her body to obey her head. After a moment Stephen would walk away, leaving her shaken to the core. She kept telling herself that with practice it would become easier. Instead, it seemed as if the opposite was true. With each passing day, she wanted him more.

The longer she was around Stephen, the more she talked and listened to him, the more she watched him, the more she fell in love with him. She saw him as he was: curt and harsh with a shirker, compassionate with an aging worker who could no longer keep up the pace of his job, smiling, swearing, frustrated, eager. And she loved him. At times he had an almost childish enthusiasm for learning this new business. At other times he exhibited a shrewdness that was deeper than that of most men twice his age. He was not a simple man; Jessie suspected that she could spend years with him and still discover new things about him. But she would never get that chance. Her time with Stephen was limited to mere days.

Her heart ached at the thought of letting him go, of watching him walk away with another woman. She wanted to reach out for him and pull him into her bed. She wanted to beg him to make love to her, to hold him and bind him to her in any way she could. Her attitude amazed her. Surely this was not really her, thinking of using her body, feminine trickery, *anything*, to keep a man with her. She wouldn't do it, of course. She couldn't live with herself if she did. She couldn't bear to face Stephen, knowing what an honorable man he was. But even the fact that she felt tempted was shocking to her. She would never have believed that she could feel such torment and longing for a man.

At night Jessie lay in her bed and thought about Stephen, dreamed of lying in his arms, and she smiled a little, secret smile. Then she would think of the long, lonely years stretching ahead of her, and she would turn her face into her pillow and weep.

Chapter Fourteen

Jessie raised her head from the row of figures she was adding and stretched, rolling her head to ease the tension in her shoulders and neck. On the other side of the room Stephen chuckled. "Are the numbers beginning to cross your eyes?"

Jessie smiled. "No. Though they are getting blurry." She wasn't about to add that the long columns of figures in the ledger weren't the only things that had made her tense. She was all too aware of him sitting in the room; often this morning she had thought she felt his eyes on her, though she refused to look up. It was hard to keep her mind on her work when Stephen was around.

She made herself glance at him impersonally. It was harder to pull her eyes away. After a few days of working in the mill, Stephen had given up wearing his flawless suits, which were often covered with sawdust or spattered with dirt or grease by the end of the day. He had begun wearing the heavier, rougher clothes that most of the men wore. Today his legs were encased in denim, and he wore a flannel shirt with a heavy sweater over it. His hair was getting a trifle long and shaggy. He looked rougher, looser—happier.

That thought surprised her. She hadn't thought of Stephen as being unhappy when she first met him. But there was an elusive something in his face now—a sparkle in his eyes, a relaxation of his mouth, an expression of interest in his features—as if he enjoyed life. It had not been there before.

Realizing that she must have been staring, Jessie jerked her head away. She rose and walked to the window to cover her awkwardness. Suddenly she gasped. "Look!"

"What?" Stephen was by her side in an instant. "Why, it's snowing!"

Fat, puffy white flakes were floating down outside, most of them disappearing as they hit the ground.

"But it's too early." He turned his head toward Jessie. "Does it usually snow here this early?"

She shrugged. "Not usually, but sometimes there'll be a snow in late September or early October. I thought this morning that it looked like it might be snowing higher up in the mountains."

"I imagine it's beautiful here when it snows."

Jessie smiled. "Oh, yes. When the mountains are covered with white, and snow hangs on the pines and the firs, it's lovely—especially when it clears up, and the sky's blue, and the sun makes everything sparkle. Everything looks brand-new and clean then, even this dirty old mill." She turned impulsively and took his hand. "Come on."

"Where?"

"Outside." Jessie pulled him down the hall. By the time they reached the door, they were almost running, and they burst outside gasping and laughing as the frigid air hit them.

They hurried down the steps and into the yard, away from the protection of the building. Snowflakes splashed them, wet and cold. Jessie tilted her head back to let them catch her full in the face. Stephen watched her. Her cheeks were pink with the cold, her skin glowing. The snowflakes kissed her skin and clung to her eyelashes. She was beautiful, and he thought of kissing the snowflakes from her face. He could almost taste her warm skin and the icy contrast of the snow, feel the wetness on his tongue, melting.

Desire stabbed through him, so fierce that he almost trembled from the force of it.

Jessie opened her mouth to catch a flake on her tongue, and Stephen shivered, though not from the cold. At the moment all he felt was the heat rushing through him. He thought of kissing Jessie, his tongue following the snowflake into her mouth. He thought of opening her shirt and seeing the snowflakes touch her breasts, her nipples hardening in the cold. He would take each snowflake from her skin with his mouth, coming at last to her nipple....

He swallowed and whirled away. Lord! In another moment he would embarrass them both by seizing her and kissing her right here in public, where anyone walking by or glancing out the window might see them. Her reputation would be in shreds. And he might very well be lost to all reason.

He cleared his throat. "It's cold out here."

Jessie turned to him, making a face. "Sissy! I always knew you fancy Eastern dudes couldn't take it."

Her face was laughing and warm, teasing. He ached to respond. He wanted to grab her, knowing that she would start to run and he would chase her. He could feel the excitement bubbling in him, the laughter that would tumble out as they ran like children playing tag. But they weren't children, and he knew what he would do, what he would not be able to keep himself from doing, when he caught her.

He shook his head slightly. "Let's go inside."

There was disappointment in Jessie's face, and something else, too—the knowledge of why Stephen had stopped her. "All right."

Jessie turned and walked into the building with Stephen following her. He hated himself for causing the laughter and light to die out of her face. For all that he loved her, he had brought her nothing but unhappiness.

They worked through the rest of the afternoon, hardly speaking or looking at each other. Stephen immersed himself in some of the files, Jessie in her ledgers. Neither of them paid any attention to the snow falling harder and harder outside. However, late in the afternoon, the sharp whining of the wind around the corner of the building at last penetrated Jessie's consciousness.

She looked up, frowning. "Did you hear that?"

"What?"

"The wind." She pushed her chair back and walked to the window. What she saw outside was a different world from what it had been a few hours earlier. The snowflakes were no longer drifting down. They were falling so fast they almost obliterated the leaden sky, and a wind blew in spurts, swirling them around. She frowned. "The wind's really kicked up."

Stephen joined her at the window. Just as he did so, the office door opened and Will Coggan stepped in. Will was the head sawyer, the most highly skilled worker in the mill, and he had more or less assumed the role of representing the workers since Frank Grissom's abrupt departure. He nodded toward Stephen and Jessie. "Mr. Ferguson. Jess. The weather's gettin' right bad out there. We're thinkin' it's nigh onto a blizzard. Maybe we oughtta shut down early and get on home whilst we kin still see."

"Is it that bad?" Stephen asked.

"Yes, sir, I'm afraid it is."

"Then close it down, of course. Let the men go home."

"Yes, sir. Thank you, Mr. Ferguson."

Coggan hurried out the door, and Stephen turned to Jessie. "Perhaps you should go, too."

"I'll wait for you. I know the way better."

Stephen stared. "Really, Jessie, I'm not a complete fool. I've walked the route a few times now."

"No, don't take it that way. I know you're anything but a fool." For a moment her eyes rested on his face in a soft, caressing way that made his heart speed up. "But you don't know how disorienting a blizzard can be. Things get confused with all that snow whipping around. It's easy to get lost, even right on the street."

Stephen still looked a little disbelieving, but he said only, "All right. We'll both go. Let me put up the files."

While Jessie closed her ledger books and straightened her desk, Stephen replaced a stack of files in the cabinet. He went to his desk to pick up the stack he had not yet read and glanced at the top file. Written in his father's large, scrawling handwriting were the words "Moore Note." Stephen's hand paused in the motion of picking up the stack of files. He frowned at the folder for a moment, then reached for the file and opened it.

"What did you say the banker's name was?"

"The president of the bank? Elias Moore. Why?"

"I'm not sure." Stephen flipped aside a page of numbers and began to read the legal-looking documents behind it. "There's something strange here."

"What?" Jessie walked over to him, intrigued. "Something about the loan?"

"Yeah. Didn't you say the loan was with the bank?"

Jessie nodded. "Sure. That's where Joe's always gotten money."

"Not this time."

"What? What are you talking about?"

"Look." He held out the file for her to read. "See this? It's a promissory note signed by Joseph Ferguson, but it's not made out to the bank. It's to Mr. Elias Moore personally. And see the deed of trust?" He flipped the note up to expose the security agreement. "This property is put up as security for that loan. To Elias Moore, not the bank."

"I don't understand."

"I'm not sure I do, either. Here, hold this." He shoved the file into her hands and strode over to the filing cabinet. He pawed in the drawer for a moment, then pulled out another brown folder. He opened it and quickly flipped through it's contents. "Here it is. The note to the bank was cancelled earlier this year. July 6."

"That's when he added to the loan. When the saw blade broke, and he had to borrow more money to replace it."

"Then he must have signed a new note to replace the

old one." He turned the pages, his eyes scanning them quickly. "Yes! Here's a letter from Elias Moore explaining that the bank cannot add to the present loan, as the security is insufficient. But he knows Joe Ferguson and knows that he will repay the debt, so he offers to lend him the money *personally*."

Jessie snorted. "I'll bet it's at a higher rate of interest. That old goat never did anyone a favor."

"No. It's at the same rate." Stephen looked up at Jessie. "Moore isn't a friend of my father's?"

"No. I mean, they've done a lot of business over the years, but that's all. Joe doesn't especially like him. In fact, he usually calls him an old skinflint."

"I think we're onto something."

"What? I don't follow you. What difference does it make whether the bank or Mr. Moore gave Joe the loan?"

"It could mean a great deal of difference." Stephen took the file she held and put both folders on the desk. In his excitement, he took her hands in his. "Remember the other day when we were talking about who might want to ruin my father's business? You said that the bank would get it if they foreclosed because he couldn't repay the note. But it seemed too crazy, remember?"

"Of course. Why would anyone go to all that trouble and take all that risk just so a bank could get a piece of property? I mean, the whole bank couldn't be in on a conspiracy to ruin Joe."

"Right. Even if Elias Moore would profit from his business getting the property, it's still very indirect. But it's an entirely different thing if he has made the loan himself. *He* gets the mill if he forecloses, not the bank."

"Of course! That makes it much more likely! It gives Moore a better reason." Jessie's face lit up; then she frowned. "But Elias Moore? I can't see him creeping around in the dark dismantling steam engines or breaking saw blades—or hiding in the brush and ambushing us, either."

"It doesn't have to be him doing it. He's a wealthy man. He can hire someone."

"Who?"

"I don't know. Maybe someone with a grudge against your father. Or just someone without scruples."

"You think you know who, don't you?"

"I have no way of knowing, but I suspect someone, yes."

"Who?"

"The person who's been a troublemaker ever since I arrived here. A man who covets you and probably resented Joe and Sam for standing between him and what he wanted."

"Frank Grissom?"

He nodded.

"But why? If he stopped it, he wouldn't get paid—oh, of course. If Moore was paying him enough, he wouldn't care about his salary."

"And if anything happened to Joe or Sam, he'd have the added benefit of getting you."

Jessie snorted. "No man would do something like that to have me."

"No?" Stephen glanced at her, and suddenly the light in his brown eyes was hot. "I think there are any number of things a man would do in order to have you."

Jessie suddenly found it difficult to breathe. She swallowed and glanced around, trying to think of something to say. The room was silent around them; she could hear the blood thrumming in her ears. Then she realized how odd it was to hear the quiet in this room. "The machines are off. I forgot, everyone must be gone."

"Yes." Stephen dropped his eyes from her face. "I'm afraid I got so interested in the files I forgot what we were doing."

"We probably should leave now—the snow."

Stephen nodded and glanced at the large clock on the wall. "Of course. We've been here much longer than I thought.'' He set the files in one of the cabinets and locked the drawer.

They pulled on their coats and hats and left, carefully locking the office behind them. They walked to the front door, and Jessie reached out to push it open. It didn't budge. She turned the handle again and pushed harder. The door opened a few inches, then slammed shut again in her face.

"What the devil?" Stephen asked, coming up to help her.

"It's the wind. It's gotten worse. It must be blowing against the door."

Stephen put his hands on the door and pushed against it with her, and it began to open. Suddenly it snapped wide open, nearly breaking its hinges, and Stephen and Jessie tumbled into the snow. It was already thick on the ground and stairs, and it swirled around them blindingly.

Stephen bit back an oath. "I can hardly see a thing."

"I know." Jessie had to cup her hands around her mouth to make her voice carry to him in the wind. She groped forward to the railing and began to carefully feel her way down the stairs. Behind her Stephen struggled to close the door. When he turned, Jessie was nowhere in sight.

"Jessie? Jessie, where are you?"

"Right here!" she called from the stairs. "I'm three steps down."

"I can't even see you!"

"Feel your way down with your feet and hold tight to the railing."

"That's fine here, but what about when we reach the yard?"

"Maybe it'll be a little clearer down there."

Stephen doubted that, but he shrugged and followed Jessie down the steps. When at last he reached the ground, he was able to see Jessie who was standing just in front of him, her hand around the bottom post of the rail. She looked at him, and he could see the doubt in her eyes.

"It's bad!" she shouted through cupped hands.

The icy wind cut through Stephen's coat and the sweater beneath. He already felt chilled to the bone. He wondered if he'd be able to reach Mrs. Randall's house before he froze. "Can you find your way?" he yelled.

"I'm not sure." Jessie edged away from the stairs. The swirling, stinging whiteness swallowed her up.

Icy, unreasoning fear clenched around Stephen's heart when she disappeared. "Jessie!"

"Here!" Stephen couldn't tell how far away she was. In another moment she appeared in front of him. "It's no use! Go back!" She motioned up the stairs.

"What? But—" Stephen realized the futility of discussing their situation out here in the cold and wind, and he closed his mouth and turned to climb the stairs.

It was as slow going up as it had been going down, and it seemed to take even longer to pry the front door open wide enough for them to squeeze through. Inside, they stamped their feet and brushed at their clothes to get rid of the snow, shivering in delayed reaction to the cold.

"We can't make it," Jessie said, her teeth chattering slightly.

"But we have to."

"I can't see a blessed thing. Even knowing the way home as well as I do, I'm not sure I can keep on track. We could walk a few steps off course and get so muddled we would wind up freezing to death right on the street. Believe me. It would be like asking to get killed to try to walk home in this. We'll have to wait until it stops, or at least slows down."

Stephen thought of spending hours alone with Jessie; he couldn't stand the temptation. He started to protest that they could make it, but then he remembered the fear that had seized him when she had disappeared in front of him in the snow. She could get killed trying to get through the blizzard. It was insane to risk that. He nodded. "Of course."

They went to the office, and Jessie lit the lamps. Stephen stoked up the fire in the cast-iron stove and added more wood to it. "Well, at least we have plenty of wood for the fire," he joked lightly, sweeping his hand toward the lumberyard outside. "We won't have to freeze."

Jessie smiled slightly. "That's true. But I'm afraid it doesn't help my stomach." She patted her middle. "I'm already hungry." She, too, was very aware of the fact that they were the only two people in the place and that it could be hours, perhaps the whole night, before the snow and wind died down enough for them to make another attempt to leave. She wanted to keep the light, inconsequential chatter going.

"I am, too, but I imagine we won't be here long enough to starve."

"No." She glanced around. "I suppose, since we're stuck here, we could get back to work."

"Yes. You're right. I'd like to look over those notes again more carefully."

The two of them settled down to work. Jessie found it difficult to concentrate on her figures, however. The room was unnaturally quiet. She was used to the pounding of the machines and the steam engine, and the high-pitched whine of the huge buzz saw. The complete silence made her even more acutely aware of Stephen's presence. She could hear his every movement—each stirring in his chair, each rustle of a page turned, each sigh from his lips.

"How're you doing?" she asked, turning to look at him, unable to sit still any longer and pretend to be adding up numbers. She had to talk to him; anything was better than this nerve-racking waiting.

Stephen shrugged. "There's really nothing here that we didn't see before."

"There's still something I don't understand. Why would he want the mill? How would he profit? Mr. Moore doesn't know anything about lumber or running a mill. He doesn't know the men. Why wouldn't it be a better deal for him to collect the interest?"

"You're right. It'd make more sense if there was someone who wanted to buy it at a high price." Stephen sighed and pinched the bridge of his nose. "I'm through reading, anyway. The lamps don't provide enough light."

He was right. The light from the windows was growing even dimmer as evening approached, and their two lamps made only small glowing circles in the huge darkness of the room. The office simply wasn't equipped for the night-time work.

Jessie closed her ledger book. For a moment they looked at each other. She was afraid that he might hear the terrible pounding of her heart from where he sat. Why did being alone with him have to have such an effect on her?

Suddenly she brightened. "I just thought of something! I'm so stupid. Why didn't I think of it earlier?"

"What?"

"Joe has a room downstairs. You know, he's been staying here the last few weeks. He brought in a stove and some furniture. I'd lay you odds he also has some food stashed there."

"You think so?" Stephen stood. "Let's check. At least it'll give us something to do."

After extinguishing one of the oil lamps, Stephen picked up the other one to light their way, and they ventured into the darkening hallway. At the end of the hall there was a small staircase down to the floor below. There, walled off from the machinery at the other end of the building, was a small hall with a few doors opening off it. One of them proved to be a supply room, and another was a small closet containing brooms, mops and cleaning materials. The third door led into a small room where someone had obviously been living, at least part of the time.

There was a round table with a single chair against one wall, and directly across from it was a set of shelves containing a few books and several jars and cans. In the center of the room stood a small Franklin stove, with wood piled beside it. There was also, across the back wall of the room, a narrow iron bed topped with blankets. Stephen's eyes went immediately to the bed, and he glanced away again just as quickly. Seeing the bed had brought flashes of thoroughly indecent pictures, all involving himself and Jessie, to his mind. He hoped the thoughts didn't show on his face.

Since he avoided looking at her, he didn't see that Jessie's reaction was much the same as his. A flush climbed in her cheeks, and she looked away from the bed, glancing at everything in the room except it.

Jessie went to the stove and began to build a fire. Stephen walked to the shelves, hoping to put the bed out of his mind, as well as the insidious, insistent thought that he and Jessie were alone in the building. "You're right. He does have some food. There's even a plate and some utensils. Let's see." He bent and began to pick up the jars and cans, examining them. "Beans. Pickled beets. Something I can't identify—and don't care to. Chokecherry juice. That doesn't sound too promising, does it?"

"Oh, no, chokecherries make good juice. Syrup and jelly, too. That looks like some of Ma's. That's wonderful—we need something to drink."

"I suppose." He gave the jar another doubtful look and set it down. "This appears to be preserves of some sort." He picked up a squat jar and read the label. "Barb. jelly?"

"Creeping barberry. That's Ma's, too. It makes delicious jelly. We can put it on these crackers. Look, a bowl of hard candies." She smiled. "Joe obviously didn't want to pass the long nights without something to nibble on."

"Doesn't make for a square meal, exactly, but at least we won't go hungry."

They opened the jars and cans and put them on the table, then sat down to their odd repast. There was only one of everything, so they shared the plate, and Jessie took the spoon, Stephen the fork. Half the time they used their fingers. There was only one battered tin cup, which Jessie filled with chokecherry juice. She drank from it first and held it out to him, smiling, the juice slightly staining her lips. Stephen took the cup and drank from it, very aware of the fact that her lips had just touched it. He knew he should drink from the opposite side, but he couldn't bring himself to. He wanted even this hint of her taste.

It was an intimate meal. They couldn't rid their minds of the fact that the narrow bed was the major furnishing in the room. With only one chair, which Stephen politely gave to Jessie, he had nowhere else to sit except on the edge of the bed. At first he stood, but that was awkward, and besides, he would have to sit on the bed sometime. He couldn't spend the whole evening standing up or sitting on the cold, unwashed floor.

He watched Jessie eat, watched her lips part and her white teeth bite into a piece of what looked like crisp, uncooked okra. He could almost taste her mouth, almost feel it. It was all he could do to stop from running his tongue across his lips. He thought of her earlier this afternoon, catching a snowflake on her tongue, and of how he had wanted to kiss her, to feel the tantalizing combination of the warmth of her mouth mingling with the icy snow.

Jessie glanced at him. "What?" she asked doubtfully.

Stephen shook himself from his reverie. "Pardon?"

"Why were you staring at me?"

"I was, uh, wondering what that was you were eating."

"Oh. Pickled okra. Want one?"

He cocked an eyebrow. "I don't think so."

"Come on, try it." She smiled and held out the remainder of the okra to him.

His heart slammed in his chest. The thought of her feeding him was something he couldn't resist. "All right."

He opened his mouth, and she slipped the crisp morsel onto his tongue. Her fingers brushed his mouth, and he wanted to close his lips over her fingertips, to take them into his mouth, too, and slowly, gently...

Stephen turned his head away. He had to stop thinking like this. He would never last the evening if he continued to conjure up erotic images of Jessie. On the other hand, he couldn't imagine being this close to her for hours without conjuring up erotic images.

He chewed the tart, crunchy vegetable and swallowed. "Thanks. I think I'll stick to what I have on my plate."

"Coward." She held up a small, reddish-purple beet. "Sure you wouldn't like to try one of these?"

"It's pickled, too? No, thank you."

Jessie giggled. Beet juice was beginning to drip down her finger, and she scooped it up with her tongue. Desire sizzled through Stephen. All he could think of was that pointed pink tongue snaking across his skin.

Jessie bit into the beet, and the purplish juice stayed on her lips for a moment. Stephen clenched his hands on the bed beneath him to keep from leaning across and licking the drop from her lips. He could feel his mouth loosening, his blood pumping thick and hot through him, his manhood pulsing—the signals of his desire, the warning that it would soon carry him away if he wasn't careful.

"Come on." Jessie held out the beet again, almost to his lips. There was something a little hot and reckless in her eyes, too. She touched the food to his lips, moving it a little.

Stephen opened his mouth and seized the beet, and as he did, his tongue ran across her fingertips. Jessie's eyes widened a little. They continued to stare into each other's eyes, their breathing turning rapid and uneven. Then, silently, Jessie extended her fingers toward his mouth, bending them a little as if showing them to him. Traces of the purplish liquid still clung to the tips of one finger and her thumb.

Neither of them spoke, but their eyes burned into each other's. Still without a word, Stephen opened his mouth and closed his lips around her finger, sucking the drop of juice from it. His tongue circled her finger greedily, tasting the tartness and the salt and the unique taste of her. He turned to her thumb and did the same.

His heart was slamming wildly in his chest. He wanted to grab Jessie and pull her across his lap. He wanted to hold her and kiss her until she was limp and moaning in his arms. He wanted to roll onto the bed with her and make love to her so thoroughly that neither of them would ever forget it.

Jessie gazed into his eyes, unable to look away, her lips

parting slightly. She wanted him to kiss her. She wanted to feel his hands on her body. She wanted—oh, a hundred things so wild and wanton she hardly knew what they were. But she knew how much her whole body hungered for them.

Stephen's eyes went to her lips. It was impossible to look at that soft, sensuous mouth and not want to kiss it. He wanted her so much that he felt as if he might explode. It was hard to breathe. Hard to think. "Ah...I...maybe we should check outside. See if the snow's died down."

Jessie nodded slowly. "Yes."

Neither of them made a move to leave.

Stephen stretched out his hand and laid his fingertips lightly on her jaw, and Jessie's eyes fluttered closed at the gentle, intensely sensual touch. His fingers drifted down her neck, and her skin flamed to life. He touched the hollow of her throat, where her flannel shirt met her skin, and paused for a moment; then his fingers moved lower, onto the shirt, down to the swell of her breast. Caressingly, his hand rounded her breast. Jessie moaned low in her throat.

"Jessamine." Her name sounded like poetry when he said it. "You are so damnably beautiful. A man could consign his soul to hell for you."

"I...wouldn't...ask that of you." Her breathing was labored and uneven.

"You don't have to ask." His hand tightened slightly, and his thumb rubbed across the center of her breast. His eyes glazed with desire. God, he had to touch her, had to taste her. Had to see her.

He reached out for her and pulled her into his lap. "Please stop me, Jessie. Stop me," he mumbled as he buried his face in her neck.

"I don't want to," she whispered, moving her head so that more of her neck was exposed to his predatory mouth.

It was an invitation he hadn't the willpower to resist. With a groan, Stephen began to kiss the soft flesh of her throat, arching her back over his arm. His free hand came up to cup her other breast, kneading and stroking until her nipple was a hard button pressing through the cloth of her shirt. Jessie whimpered and squirmed on his lap. Passion burst white-hot in him, and suddenly he was past all hope of stopping.

He murmured her name over and over as his hand gripped the back of her neck and turned her lips to his. He kissed her fiercely, deeply, his tongue laying bold claim to her mouth.

Jessie quivered, and her hands curled into his shirtfront, holding on. They kissed again and again, their mouths clinging hungrily, tongues twining in a dance of love. Stephen pulled back, sucking air into his lungs, and for a moment he just looked at her, drinking in the sight of her face, warm and relaxed with love, her eyes glowing up at him. There was love in her face, and beauty, everything a man could ever hope for in a woman.

His fingers went to the long braid that hung down her back and tugged loose the tie that held it. He sank his hand into her hair, separating the thick strands until her hair tumbled down in waves, filling his hand and spilling over it like molten fire. It was almost surprising that her tresses felt cool against his flesh, not hot. He clenched his fist, crushing the soft hair between his fingers.

"I love your hair." He brought his hand to his lips and gently kissed her hair. "I love it down. It's like fire. Like satin."

He combed his fingers through it. It fell past her waist, long and thick. He nuzzled into the hair at her neck, burying himself in its scent and texture. Passion pounded through him, heavy and hard. He knew in the back of his mind that the next morning he would regret what he was doing. But he also knew, with an instinctive, unthinking certainty, that right now there was no chance that he would turn away and not make love to her. In this moment she was his, and he was hers, in the most primitive and basic way. There was no room in him right now for refinement or courtesy or codes of ethics; there was only a driving need to love her that pushed everything else aside.

Stephen kissed Jessie's hair, her neck, her ear. His breath, hot against her skin, sent shivers running through her. Tentatively, her hands slid up his chest and onto his neck, gliding up the column of his throat to where his hair brushed her fingertips. She wasn't sure what to do; she felt clumsy and inexperienced. But she knew she had to touch him, had to feel his skin beneath her hands.

Stephen drew in his breath sharply at her touch, and Jessie froze. "No," he murmured hoarsely. "No, don't stop. Please."

"I wasn't sure. I wanted to—touch you."

"I want you to." His reply was shaky. "It's just—" He drew another breath. "It feels so good. Ah, Jessie..." He moved his head against her hand, seeking her caress.

Jessie moved her hands into his hair. It was thick, and softer than she had thought it would be. She combed her fingers through it, letting the strands slide across her skin, delighting in the sensations that ran through her.

Stephen nuzzled her neck, and his lips slipped downward to the hollow of her throat. His tongue rimmed the indentation and dipped into it. But when his mouth moved lower, he was stopped by her shirt. His hand went to the top button, pausing to curve over her breast on the way. He glanced up at her face, and there was a question in his eyes.

"Love me," Jessie whispered, answering his unspoken question, assuring him that she wanted him to take away her maidenhood. She raised her lips to his, murmuring again, "Please love me."

He kissed her long and deeply. His fingers shook a little on her buttons as he unfastened them. Jessie dug her fingers into his hair, passion surging through her, and she kissed him hungrily. His mouth dug into hers as if he would consume her. Jessie began to tremble, and she clung to him, awash in a sea of emotions and sensations that were entirely new to her.

Stephen parted her shirt and pushed it back on her shoulders, then raised his head and looked down at her. Beneath the shirt Jessie wore a plain white cotton chemise with only a single narrow strip of lace across the top. He had seen sheerer undergarments than this, and ones far frothier with lace or fashioned of the finest silk. But none had ever stirred him as this simple shift did. The cotton drifted across her breasts, exposing the soft, tremulous tops, and beneath the material the darker circles of her nipples showed, the tight little buds pressing up against the cloth.

He drew a calming breath, forcing himself to go slowly. He bent forward and drew a circle around her nipple with his tongue. Jessie stiffened, arching up a little. His tongue continued to play with the fleshy button through the cloth, teasing it into greater hardness. Softly he blew upon the wet fabric, and again Jessie tightened all over, a tiny moan escaping her lips. He went to the other nipple to work the same magic on it. Jessie stirred restlessly, moving her legs. He slid his hand down her stomach and between her thighs. She made a sound of surprise low in her throat, but her legs closed around him, squeezing.

He lifted his head to look at her. Her eyes were closed, and her head lolled back. He moved his hand rhythmically between her legs, and her hips rolled with him. Where the chemise was wet over her nipples, it was almost transparent, and he could see the buds clearly. They rose up, taut and eager, hard with the desire he had aroused in her.

His own desire swelled in him. He was hard and ready. He wanted to thrust into her immediately and ride out his passion. But he knew he must go slowly, for Jessie's sake. Sternly tamping down his desire, he slipped her shirt the rest of the way off her body. He pulled down the straps of her chemise, uncovering her breasts completely. For a moment he simply looked at her, drinking in the sight of the lush, rounded globes that he had been thinking about, dreaming about, for weeks. Then he bent and pressed his mouth against the soft, quivering flesh. He trailed kisses over the curve of her breast, moving ever closer to her nipple, until at last his lips closed around the throbbing, puckered flesh.

He pulled the bud into his mouth, sucking and stroking

with his tongue, teasing until Jessie was writhing beneath him, her breath coming in ragged spurts. His hand went to the buttons of her trousers and unfastened them, then slipped into the hot, damp center of her femininity. Gently his fingers explored the slick folds of flesh and slipped inside her.

Stephen groaned. He was on fire, and it was the most exquisite torture to hold back. Jessie moved her hands restlessly over him, digging into his arms, his back, his hair. She lifted her hips and moved against his hand, seeking a deeper fulfillment. Stephen wasn't sure he could wait any longer. He had to be inside her, had to know her completely.

Abruptly he stood, setting her on her feet on the floor, and Jessie blinked at him. Her eyes were dark and dazed with passion, and she looked the very picture of a woman lost in the throes of desire. The image sent a shudder of longing through him, and he had to reach out and cup her breasts in his hands once more and caress the jewel-like tips. He bent and kissed each nipple lightly, then pulled away from her.

"Stephen? What—" Jessie felt bereft and lost. Surely he could not mean to stop! He could not leave her like this, poised on the edge of—well, she wasn't sure what, but she knew it was something grand, something magnificent, something she wanted more than she'd ever wanted anything in her life. She was aching and empty inside.

Stephen yanked his sweater over his head and began to unbutton his shirt, his fingers fumbling in their haste. A smile spread across Jessie's face. He was stopping to undress. She watched him as he took off his shirt and dropped it on the floor. His chest was leanly muscled and covered with a sprinkling of curling black hair. She wondered what it would feel like to touch it. She thought of running her hands across his chest, of circling those small, flat, masculine nipples. Would they tighten and ache as hers did when he touched them?

He struggled to pull off his boots, still standing up, then

shucked off the rest of his clothes. He stood before her completely naked. Jessie looked, her heart skittering around in her chest like a wild thing. He looked primitive and powerful, no gentleman now, but a man intent on claiming his woman. And Jessie felt in her a breathless eagerness to be that woman, to receive him and pleasure him and make him forever hers.

She held out her arms to him, and Stephen crossed the space between them in a single stride. He swooped her up in his arms and kissed her, a dizzying, eternal kiss. She clung to him as to an anchor in a spinning world.

He lowered her onto the bed and undressed her, his hands lingering over the soft, white flesh he revealed. His hunger was so great that he wanted to tear the garments from her, but her body was so beautiful that he could only move gently over it, pausing again and again to caress her.

At last she was naked, and he shifted on top of her. Jessie drew in her breath at the feel of his hard, masculine body stretched out full length against hers. He was all bone and muscle, so different from her, so excitingly different. She twined her arms around him, seeking to pull him even more tightly against her. She wanted more, wanted all of him.

Stephen entered her slowly and gently, restraining himself with great effort so that there would be little hurt to her. Jessie moaned, arching her neck. There was some pain, but far greater than that was the intense pleasure, the satisfaction of feeling him inside her. He filled the center of her ache and her emptiness, stretching her unaccustomed flesh. She dug her fingers into his bare back, breathing his name as she thrust her hips up, opening herself more fully to him.

He shuddered at her welcoming passion and had to pause for a moment to regain his shattered control. Then he began to move slowly, thrusting with long, unhurried strokes, building their passion ever higher. Instinctively Jessie moved with him, with a combination of innocence and passion that vaulted Stephen past all reason and control into a realm of white-hot, shattering sensation. He thrust into her wildly. Pleasure exploded deep in Jessie's abdomen and swept outward, undulating through her. Stephen cried out, shuddering, as he poured his seed into her. They clung to each other, lost together in a swirling, mindless ecstasy.

"Jessie," he murmured. "My love, my love."

Chapter Fifteen

A shaft of light from the small window above the bed fell onto Stephen's face, and his eyelids fluttered open. He lay for a moment in groggy contentment. He was squeezed against the wall, a warm body snuggled against his. Red hair tumbled over the pillow beside him, and a few stray strands had drifted across his cheek. Jessamine.

He closed his eyes, luxuriating in the smell and feel of her, in the delicious, satisfied languor that permeated his body. They had awakened twice during the night, each time making love again. It was impossible to awake with his hand curved around Jessie's breast and not want to make love to her again. In fact, he wanted to right now.

But it was morning and light, and somehow it was no longer possible to hide from the truth. He must not make love to her. He had been the lowest form of scum to do it last night. He was engaged to Elizabeth, bound to her. He could not marry Jessie; he could only dishonor her.

And he had done that.

Stephen sighed and sat up, running his hands through his hair. What was he going to do? He could not refuse to marry Elizabeth. He had a duty to her.

He looked at Jessie, still asleep, red hair spilling over her naked white skin. He drew his hand along the curve of her spine and hip. How soft her skin was. How vulnerable she looked.

She belonged to him. She was his. He had taken her body, her innocence. He had a duty to her, too. But there was more than that. For a few moments, the two of them had been joined in a way he'd never known with any other woman, no matter how desirable or skillful she had been. In one shattering instant, he had really possessed her. And she had possessed him. It had been as if they were a single body, an entwined heart and soul. How could he possibly give that up and settle for a lifetime of something less?

He groaned, digging his fingers into his scalp. Damn it! Why had he done it? Why had he given in? He wasn't usually that weak.

But then, he had never before been tempted by Jessie. He had never been tested by love. He continued to look at her, and a small smile touched his lips. He couldn't regret what had happened between them. It had been the most beautiful night of his life, the most thrilling and satisfying. He wondered how he could live without ever experiencing it again.

On the other hand, how could he marry Jessie? Even if he were to ignore the deathbed promise he had made to Elizabeth's father, if he were to abandon her and his honor for the sake of love, he could not marry Jessie. They would never suit. They were too different. Why, hardly a day passed that they didn't have an argument about something. Jessie didn't even know how to have a genteel argument. She didn't freeze up or talk in a furious, low tone, as most of the women he knew did. She expressed herself loudly and often wound up yelling or pounding something or even, on occasion, picking up an object and throwing it on the floor—or at him. Her eyes flashed, and her cheeks turned red, and her fiery hair seemed to crackle. She didn't stop to consider propriety or the presence of anyone else within earshot.

Of course, there was also the fun of talking to her, of watching those fine eyes light up with excitement or anger, of listening to her clever ideas or the funny things she said. She was so easy to talk to, so easy to be with; there was no constraint or awkwardness with her. There were even times when he found that he enjoyed their fights.

But that wasn't enough. Love wasn't enough. He had to think of how Jessie would feel. He couldn't marry her and take her home. She would never fit into his world; she wouldn't want to. She would be miserable in St. Louis or New York, as miserable as his mother had been here.

Careful not to awaken Jessie, he slipped out of bed and dressed. It was terribly cold in the room, and he went to the small metal stove and stirred up the coals inside. They sparked and glowed red hot, and he stuffed in a few sticks of kindling, then set some larger logs on top of them. Holding his hands out to the fire, he waited for it to warm him. And he thought.

With each passing moment, his guilt weighed more heavily upon him. His actions had been unpardonable. Lust, even love, was no excuse for the wrong he had done to both women. The two women in the world whom he loved. He had been foolhardy, selfish, unthinking.

By the time Jessie awoke, he had worked up an enormous case of self-hatred. He dreaded having to face her. In the sanity of daylight she was bound to regret what she had done. She was certain to despise him. Stephen didn't think he could bear to see her look at him with contempt.

When he heard her stirring, he was tempted to hurry out of the room. But he forced himself to stay. He deserved whatever she chose to do or say. After his base actions, the least he could do was let her vent her wrath on him. He made himself turn toward the bed.

Jessie's eyes were open, and she was watching him. Stephen thought he'd never seen anyone look as desirable as she did that morning. Her tresses were tumbled over the pillow and sheets, vivid against the blank white, and her eyes were big and luminous, the color of a spring sky. Her bare shoulders were visible, soft and curving, hinting at the naked body below. Even as contrite as he felt at the moment, Stephen couldn't suppress a sharp twinge of longing.

"Good morning," Jessie said softly. She felt shy and uncertain. It was strange to awaken naked in a room with a man. It was also exciting. Her body still ached a little in unaccustomed ways from what they had done last night. This man, in some ways still almost a stranger, knew her in a way that no one else in her life ever had. Ever would, for that matter, for Jessie was certain that she could never feel this way about any other man. Last night had been glorious and wild. Still, when she thought about what she had done, she couldn't help but blush. What did he think of her now? Had she been too bold, too brazen? Or had she been too inexperienced and clumsy? Last night he had seemed as enthralled, as dazzled, as passionate as she had been. This morning she wasn't so sure. She wanted reassurance.

"Good morning." Stephen's voice was low and rough, his words clipped. He sounded…almost angry. Jessie tightened up inside, bracing herself. "Jessamine, I—Lord, I'm sorry. I'm so sorry."

"Sorry?" Jessie sat up, which made her feel less vulnerable. She clutched the covers to her chest, covering her nakedness.

"Yes." Stephen looked away, unable to meet her eyes. "You must hate me."

"Hate you?" she repeated. She sounded like an idiot, she thought. A parrot!

"Yes. I quite understand if you cannot find it in your heart to forgive me."

"Forgive you for what?" Her voice sounded leaden.

"For—for what I did. For taking you. Despoiling you."

"Is that what happened?" She fought to keep the tears back. Was that how he viewed what had happened between them? Just lust and dishonor? To her it had been beautiful, thrilling; their lovemaking had seemed to touch her very soul. Yet Stephen apparently found it contemptible. "You were a blackguard out to steal my virginity from me?"

"Jessamine!" Her bluntness still had the power to startle him. "Of course not. I—" He stopped himself. This was no time for a declaration of love. That, too, would be the act of a scoundrel, to say he loved her when he could offer her nothing. It would only be self-serving; it wouldn't help her. "I'm sorry. What I meant was that to do what I did when I am affianced to another..."

Jessie's chin went a little higher. Her eyes were clear and dry, and her voice trembled only slightly as she said, "You are going to marry someone else. I knew that. I went into it with my eyes open. I wasn't exactly the victim of your wiles."

"You were an innocent. I was responsible. I knew. What I did was wrong. To place you in this kind of position, knowing that I could not do the honorable thing—it was despicable."

"The honorable thing!" Jessie flared. "Damn your eyes! I'm no obligation, no duty for you to perform so that you can still lay claim to the title of gentleman. Perhaps I was innocent physically. But I knew what I was doing. I was fully aware of the fact that you would not marry me. I love—Elizabeth." It was difficult for her to choke out the words. She had to pause a moment to take a deep breath. "I did not believe that being in your bed meant being your wife. You didn't deceive or seduce me. I wanted to. There's no need for you to do the honorable thing. I don't want you to. The fact is, I wouldn't be your wife if you had a gun to my head!"

Anger surged through Stephen, burning away his guilt and self-recrimination. "Is that right? You slept with me, yet you wouldn't marry me! What do you think that makes you?"

"A free woman!"

"Free! Alone is more like it."

"Maybe that's the only way a woman can be free."

Stephen was filled with a rage so intense, so fierce that he almost shook beneath its force. He wanted to roar, to grab Jessie and shake her until she admitted that she loved him, to force her to agree to be his wife. It was all he could do to keep himself from crossing the room and hauling her out of the bed. Instead, he swung around and slammed his fist against the wall. He stood for a moment, his back to her, battling his anger. The violence, the sheer magnitude of his feelings shocked him.

Finally, when he was sure he had himself under control again, he pushed himself away from the wall. Without turning to look at Jessie, he said in a flat tone, "I'll leave so you can dress. Then we'd better return to the house."

"Of course."

The evenness of her voice caused another small geyser of anger inside him, and he strode from the room, slamming the door behind him.

Jessie stared after him, filled with righteous indignation. Here she was absolving him from all obligation—how dare he think of her as a duty!—and all he did was get furious at her! It was enormously unfair. He acted as if she didn't care, as if *she* had hurt *him*. Yet *he* was the one who hadn't said a word about the beauty of what they had done, instead just talking about honor and obligation and how sorry he was. With a muffled, frustrated shriek, Jessie grabbed the closest thing to her, a book, and hurled it across the room. There was nothing else to throw, so she gripped the iron bedstead and shook it with all her might. Then she burst into tears and sagged against the headboard, weeping her heart out.

When Jessie joined Stephen in the office sometime later, she was white and silent. Neither of them said a word about what had happened last night or this morning; both were churning with new and volatile emotions, too confused to be able to speak coherently. They trudged home through the snow in a vast, uncomfortable silence, not even noticing the serene white beauty of the snow-covered town around them.

When they got back, Stephen was surprised to find that Amanda had little interest in their halting explanation of why they had been gone all night. "I figured that was what happened. I kept telling Joe you'd stay at the mill instead of trying to make it home through the blizzard. Come on up and see him. He's been worrying like a hen with one chick."

Joe was pacing the floor in the rear sitting room, and when Stephen and Jessie came in, he grinned widely and walked over to hug them both. Stephen tightened his arms around his father. He found himself wanting to pour out his troubles to Joe, but he reminded himself quickly that Joe was the last person he could tell about Jessie and what had happened. She was like a daughter to him.

Stephen stepped back. "How are you feeling?"

"Better. A lot better. Damn headaches have finally stopped. I'll be coming back to work now." He smiled and glanced toward Jessie's mother. "You haven't told them yet?"

Amanda blushed and shook her head. She crossed the room and slipped her hand into Joe's. "No. I'll let you."

Joe raised her hand to his mouth and kissed it. He looked at Stephen. "Amanda and me are gettin' hitched."

"Married!"

"Oh, Mama, that's wonderful!"

Jessie flew across the room and hugged her mother. Stephen looked surprised, then smiled and reached out to take Amanda's hand and bow over it in a courtly manner.

"I can't think of a more lovely addition to the Ferguson family," he told her. "I can only wonder why it took my father so long to ask you."

"I've been thinking about it ever since you came to town and told me about your ma." Joe shrugged. "I guess when I came to the other day, I realized how crazy I was to be shilly-shallying around about it."

"Congratulations." Stephen shook his father's hand. "I'm very happy for you."

Joe winked and squeezed his hand. "Thanks, son. Now, as soon as that rapscallion brother of yours gets back, we can have us a wedding."

"You can have a double wedding," Jessie suggested brightly, but there was a brittleness underlying her tone that caused her mother to glance at her sharply. "After all, when Sam gets back, he'll have Stephen's fiancée with him."

"Why, that's right." Joe was looking at his future wife and therefore didn't see the frozen expression on Stephen's face. "What do you say, Amanda? Shall we horn in on the young folks' hooplah? It'd be a bang-up celebration."

Amanda glanced at Stephen. "That's not really for us to say, is it, dear? Perhaps Stephen's fiancée wouldn't want to share such a precious moment."

"I'm sure it will be fine with Elizabeth," Stephen said tightly. "She's a very amenable woman." He couldn't keep from shooting Jessie a sideways glance. She was watching him, her mouth tight and her face as pale as a marble statue. She set her jaw even tighter at his words, and her eyes flashed. She whirled away.

"Well, I reckon I better find something suitably grand to wear for such an occasion," she commented and strode out of the room.

Amanda excused herself and slipped out after her daughter. Stephen let out a sigh and sat on the bed beside Joe.

"Anything wrong, boy?"

Stephen shook his head. "Of course not. I'm glad for you and Mrs. Randall." He paused. "Have you remembered anything about the man who attacked you?"

Joe shook his head disgustedly. "Nope. I wish I could. If I ever get my hands on that son of a bitch—"

"Why didn't you tell me?" Stephen asked quietly.

Joe sighed. "It wasn't anything against you. I just didn't want to worry you."

"You mean you were too proud to let me know you were having a problem."

Joe scowled. "I don't want any of your money, if that's what you're thinking of doing."

"Jessie told me you'd balk."

"What's the matter with that girl, anyway? She was acting awful peculiar a while ago, not like herself at all."

"Don't try to change the subject. I know you don't want any favors from a stranger. But it hurts that you consider me a stranger."

"It ain't that! And don't you go trying to manipulate me, neither. I'm not taking your money."

"Not even as a loan? I'll make the same arrangement you did with Moore—you can even put the mill up as security. Or I could buy into the company. There's nothing wrong with a third Ferguson having a share in Ferguson Mill, is there?"

Joe considered it. "Well, no, I reckon not. That is, not if Sam is agreeable to it. But what would you want with part of a mill so far away from where you live?"

"I've become rather interested in the business, actually. I wouldn't mind li—" He paused and seemed to mentally pull himself back. What was he thinking of? He couldn't live here. There was Elizabeth. There was his business. There was his obligation to his grandfather. "You're right. I would be far away from it. However, I think I could trust you and Sam to manage my share for me."

"Of course you could."

"Then it's settled." Quickly Stephen explained his plan to conceal his intentions of paying off the note in the hopes that they could catch the man who had engineered the mill's "accidents."

With the matter settled, he started to leave the room, but Joe stretched out a hand to him. "No. Don't go yet. There's something troubling you, isn't there? Why don't you tell me about it? Maybe I can help."

Stephen shook his head. "No. It's nothing."

"Is it the young lady you're worrying about? Your fiancée? Are you afraid she might be trapped out in this snow?"

"No." Stephen's eyes widened. "Good God, no! I hadn't even thought about it!" He was flooded with guilt. He hadn't even thought once about Elizabeth being caught in the blizzard. "If they were caught outdoors, they could have frozen by now. I must go look for them." He started toward the door, then stopped. "No. I haven't the slightest idea where to look. A search party, then. We should send out a search party."

"Now, now, I didn't mean to get you all het up. Just calm down. What I was trying to say was that you didn't need to worry. Sam's no fool. He knows this country. He'd have seen the blizzard coming. He wouldn't have missed the signs, and he'd take shelter. A cabin, a cave…if nothing else, he'd build a lean-to. She'll be all right."

"Are you sure?"

"Positive. Think I'd be so calm about my son lying out in the snow somewhere frozen? They're all right. The storm will just delay them for a while. But you'll see—give 'em a few days, and they'll come ridin' in, big as you please. No need to send out anybody to look for them. Nobody knows these mountains as well as Sam. Besides, we don't know where in tarnation they are. Burley said they had to stay off the road 'cause of the bridges."

"Good. Thank heaven."

Joe studied his son shrewdly for a moment. "Well, if that wasn't it, what was making you frown so? Something's gotten under your skin like a burr."

Stephen shook his head. "It's nothing I can talk about."

"It's Jessie, isn't it?"

Stephen's head shot up. "How did you know?"

"Lucky guess. But it looks like I was right. What is it, boy? Did something happen between you two last night?"

Stephen cast him an agonized glance. "Yes. You'll hate me—and with good reason. I took advantage of the situation last night. Of Jessie."

Joe stared. "You aren't meaning to tell me that you forced her!"

"Good God, no! What do you think I am!"

"Then what happened? She was willing?"

"Yes." Stephen's voice was so low that Joe had to strain to hear it.

"It doesn't sound like it's all your fault. Sounds like Jessie had something to do with it, too."

"That's what she said." Stephen sounded exasperated. "But, damn it, I should have been more responsible. I should have kept the situation under control."

Joe smiled slightly. "I'd like to see anybody try to control Jessie. You know, son, I think you'll find women out here are a mite more independent than what you're used to. Especially Jessie. She's used to making her own decisions."

Stephen stared. "But don't you care? Aren't you angry with me? What I did was dishonorable."

"Of course I care. I'm fond of Jessie. But I know she does what she wants. And I know that when a man's in love, he doesn't always think straight." He paused, and his face became uncertain. "You do love her, don't you?"

"Of course I love her! How could I not love her? She's beautiful and generous and unaffected. She's strong, smart, funny. I want her so much I can hardly think straight when I'm around her. But what can I do about it? I'm engaged to another woman. Elizabeth and I grew up together. She trusts me, depends on me. Her father was—well, I was very close to him, and when he died, I promised him that I would marry Elizabeth. How can I break that promise? How can I fail Elizabeth? What kind of man am I if I turn my back on a woman who's given up everything and come halfway across the country on my word that I'll marry her?"

His father nodded. "I see your problem. Now, I don't hold much account with deathbed promises. They always seemed like threats to me. But you've made a commitment to that woman, and you owe her something. Only, tell me this, do you owe her the rest of your life? Is it going to make her happy for you to be miserable? A marriage without love is a sad way to live."

"But you and my mother loved each other, and look what happened."

Joe sighed. "Yes. Maybe it doesn't always work out. But I don't see how in the hell it's got a chance if you don't even have love. I've been fortunate enough to be loved by two wonderful women in my lifetime. Sometimes it was enough to break my heart. But I wouldn't have traded it for a loveless, bloodless marriage. Think about it, son. Duty is a fine thing, and so is honor. But they'll never keep you warm at night, and they'll never make a December day seem like April. Only love can do that.''

Jessie and Stephen did their best to pretend that nothing had happened between them. Jessie was cool to him, but polite, and Stephen was the soul of courtesy toward her. But neither of them could look at the other without thinking of the night they had spent together and the soul-shattering passion they had shared. They could not speak without feeling the familiar upswelling of love inside them.

They were wise enough to keep their distance. Stephen moved into Joe's room at the mill, so he wouldn't have to sleep only a flight of stairs away from Jessie, and she no longer kept watch with him at night. But she often awoke, sweating and aching, from erotic dreams of Stephen's lovemaking. And during the day she found herself staring at him as he worked, remembering the smooth play of his muscles beneath his skin or the heat of his mouth on hers.

She wanted him. She loved him. There was no denying either fact, much as she might want to. But it was just as undeniable that he was bound to another woman. He might desire her, but his love was given elsewhere.

One afternoon, two days after their night at the mill, Jessie left work early, unable to remain in the same room with Stephen for another minute, and tromped home through the snow. Inside the parlor, she found Harmonia Taylor, the widow who earned her living as a seamstress in town, sitting waiting for her, a large box on her lap.

Jessie stared at Miss Taylor in surprise as the woman bounced up and shoved the box into her hands. ''Oh, Miss Randall, I'm so sorry,'' the woman twittered, her girlish voice at odds with her hefty frame. ''I had this finished three days ago, but I couldn't get over here earlier because of the snow.''

"Of course. That's perfectly all right. But what is this? I didn't—"

The other woman smiled archly, managing to look both ingratiating and annoying in the peculiar way she had. "Of course not. It's a surprise. A gift for you."

"A gift?"

"Yes. There's a note inside. He left it for you."

"He?" Jessie was still puzzled.

"Yes." Harmonia smiled again and almost giggled. "That fine gentleman."

Jessie's eyes widened. "Mr. Ferguson?"

"Yes. Mr. Ferguson. Mr. Stephen Ferguson."

Jessie took the box upstairs, hardly waiting long enough to bid Mrs. Taylor a polite farewell. She laid the box on her bed and pulled off the lid. She drew in a sharp breath. Inside lay a dress of ice-blue velvet. With trembling fingers, she reached in and drew out the garment. She held it up in front of her and looked into the mirror.

It was beautiful. She had never owned anything of such richness and elegance. Champagne-colored lace frothed at the cuffs and accented the neck. The skirt was pulled back into a saucy bustle in the rear, and there, too, row upon row of lace tumbled down, just as it did below the draped velvet skirts in the front. Mrs. Taylor must have used up every scrap of lace in Swenson's store on this dress! And the velvet! It was so soft and rich, and it was the exact color of her eyes. Had Stephen realized that? Had he planned it?

She looked at her face in the mirror. Her eyes were huge, her mouth soft. She smoothed the dress against her body, her hand running lightly over her breast and stomach onto her abdomen.

Jessie froze. What was she doing?

She tossed the dress onto the bed. This was the kind of gift a man gave to a woman he knew intimately, to a wife...or a mistress. Stephen was trying to appease his guilt, she thought, to make up for taking her virginity when he could not marry her. Or perhaps it was a payment for her services.

She picked up the lovely dress and crumpled it into a ball, then heaved it across the room. Bitterly she cursed Stephen. Then she cursed herself for being the fool that she was. Finally, she plopped down in the chair beside the window and sat for a long time, staring out. She thought about Stephen and the night they had shared together. She thought about the beautiful dress lying in a mess on the floor. She thought about her mother and the years she had spent loving Joe Ferguson, as faithful and loving as a wife, with never a public claim on him. Had her mother's heart ached as hers did now? Had she cried into her pillow at night and awakened feeling empty and lonely? She wondered if her mother had thought it was worth it. She must have, even before he asked her to marry him. Jessie had never heard Amanda speak a word against Joe or show in any way that she resented her position.

The day darkened before Jessie's eyes as she sat there thinking. She heard the sounds of voices and cutlery in the dining room and knew that supper had been served, but she didn't move. She wasn't interested in food. She just sat, staring blindly.

It was a flicker of movement outside on the lawn that finally caught her attention, a furtive gliding that was different from the normal passage of people along the street. She straightened and leaned forward a little, wondering exactly what it was she had seen.

For a moment she could discern nothing but shadows; then one of the shadows dislodged itself from a tree, and she realized that it was a person. A man, lurking beneath the tree. She peered out, squinting her eyes, glad she had not bothered to light the kerosene lamp in her room as the day had dimmed. There was something so secretive about the man's stance that it sent a frisson of alarm up her spine. He was standing looking at the second story of the house, still and waiting.

The front door opened and closed, and Jessie heard the

sound of steps going down from the porch. The shadow melted under the tree. She saw a figure leave the front yard and turn up the street. It was Stephen. No doubt he was going to sleep in Joe's room at the office again. A moment later, the shadowy man slipped out of the yard after him. For an instant the shadow's face was clear in the moonlight.

It was Frank Grissom.

Jessie stiffened, her breath hissing in. Frank Grissom was following Stephen, and she couldn't think of a single good reason in the world for him to do that. Fear stabbed through her. Frank hated Stephen; Stephen had bested him before everyone, had humiliated him. Stephen had fired him. And if Frank was, as Stephen thought, the one who was responsible for the mishaps at the mill...

Jessie jumped out of her chair and hurried to pull on her boots and coat. Stephen might be able to beat Grissom in a fair fight, but, knowing Frank, Stephen wouldn't have a chance this time. There wouldn't be anything fair about it. She ran down the stairs and pulled her mother from her dishes to whisper where she was going and why. Then she hurried into the snow and down the street toward the mill.

The mill yard was dark and silent when Jessie walked up. She moved across it quickly, her eyes alert for any sign of Frank Grissom. Her feet were silent on the stairs, and she opened the mill door and closed it behind her just as quietly. She paused for a moment, listening. She heard nothing.

She tiptoed down the hall to the office, unlocked the door and went inside. Aided by dim moonlight coming through the window, she made her way across the room to her desk and opened the top right-hand drawer. The revolver was there. She checked to make sure it was loaded, then tiptoed out of the office and down the stairs to the bottom floor.

If Frank Grissom had not followed Stephen, she was going to feel very foolish, she thought. Her heart was pounding like a hammer in her chest, and she felt slightly sick with tension and fear. Sliding along the wall, she made her way toward the light that spilled out of the open doorway of Joe's room. Still there was no sound.

Jessie stopped at the doorway and cautiously peered around the frame into the room. An oil lamp burned on the small table. The room was empty.

Suddenly, with a roar, the steam engine sprang to life somewhere behind her. Jessie jumped at the abrupt violation of the silence. She slumped against the doorway, her heart slamming inside her chest. Thank heavens, it was just the machines. The noise had nearly scared her to death.

But what were the machines doing running at this hour of the night? An even greater fear clutched at her stomach, and she ran down the hall to the mill. She jerked open the door, and as she did, she glanced at the floor. On the floor, liberally streaked with sawdust as it always was, was a cleared path. Something had been dragged along this way.

Stephen!

She burst through the door, heedless of any noise she made. The din inside the mill was too great for anything she did to be heard. There was a light inside, and she ran toward it. The high—pitched whine of the huge buzz saw filled the air.

Jessie saw a man's shape outlined against the glow of a lantern. He bent and hoisted the limp form of another man onto his shoulder and lumbered across the floor toward the log carriage. For a moment Jessie was struck numb with terror. Grissom was carrying Stephen, who could only be either unconscious or dead.

Grissom turned slightly, shifting his load, and the lantern light flickered across Stephen's head. His hair was wet and matted, and scarlet blood stained his face. With a grunt Grissom threw Stephen's body onto the log carriage. Then he turned to the lever and shoved it away from him. The log carriage began to rumble forward toward the buzz saw.

The sight freed Jessie from her momentary paralysis, and she screamed, "Stop! Grissom! Stop it!"

Grissom whirled and saw her. His jaw dropped; then he

grinned. "Come to see your lover sliced up?" he shouted across the noise.

Jessie leveled her gun at him. "Stop it. Now! Or you're a dead man."

Grissom began to laugh. "Or you're goin' ta shoot me? Go ahead! A woman ain't got the nerve."

The carriage moved inexorably onward, carrying Stephen. Jessie knew she had to stop it. She drew in a breath, sighted and squeezed the trigger.

The crack of the pistol shot barely rose above the thunderous noise of the carriage and saw. The bullet hit Grissom in the chest, knocking him backward. Red spread across his shirt, and he stumbled and fell. Jessie didn't pause to watch. As soon as she fired, she started running forward. She reached the saw mechanism and threw the lever to stop it. But that wasn't enough, she knew; Stephen would still be carried right into the saw's deadly sharp teeth, even if they weren't whirling. She ran on, not sparing a glance for Grissom, who was scrabbling around on the floor, trying to rise.

She passed the moving carriage and ran alongside the track to the lever that would stop it. She grabbed the handle and pushed. It didn't budge. Frantically she pushed again. Finally, lowering her head, she planted her feet, wrapped her hands around the handle and threw her entire weight against the lever. It snapped forward, and the carriage shuddered to a halt.

Jessie leaned against the long handle, her knees suddenly weak. She turned, trembling, and looked back. The carriage—and Stephen's head—lay less than a foot from the sharp points of the saw. She wiped the sweat from her forehead. The muscles in her legs felt like rubber. She glanced at Grissom. He had given up his attempts to get up and had flopped onto his back. Blood soaked his shirtfront.

"Damn!" he whispered. "I never thought you'd do it."

Jessie wet her dry lips. It took all the strength she had to keep her voice even. "You're just lucky the light's bad in here. I was aiming for your head."

She turned and climbed onto the carriage. She would have to pull herself together enough to tie Grissom up and go for the marshal and the doctor. But first she had to see Stephen.

She bent over him and picked up his hand, pressing her fingers against his wrist. His pulse was uneven, but it was there. Thank God. He was alive!

Chapter Sixteen

Stephen came to groggily. The room was dim around him, the only light coming from a kerosene lamp on the table, its wick turned low. A groan escaped him. His head was splitting.

His father was immediately beside his bed, grinning at him. "Stephen! You're awake. Well, it's a good thing you've got a harder head than I do. You've only been out a couple of hours."

"My head feels as if there are a hundred little men inside with hammers."

"That's to be expected. Frank Grissom can really crack a head open." He rubbed his own head ruefully. "I ought to know."

"Frank Grissom? He hit me? What happened?"

"You up to hearing the story?"

Stephen nodded, then immediately regretted the move. "Yes," he whispered. "Tell me."

"Well, you were at the mill last night, sitting at the table working on some accounts."

"Yes, I remember that."

"You had your back to the door." Joe clicked his tongue against his teeth in reproval. "That's something a man's got to learn out here: never sit with your back to a door, especially when you've acquired an enemy like Frank Grissom."

"He hit me over the head?"

Joe nodded. "Yep. Then he dragged you down the hall into the mill."

"Why?"

"Seems he wanted to get rid of you. It would have shut the place down, too, but I reckon he'd gone past carin' about that. Main thing he wanted was to get shed of you."

"What happened?"

Joe related the story of how Jessie had seen Grissom and followed him to the mill, then saved Stephen's life. "Burley and Jim arrived not long after that, and they hauled Grissom over to the doc's."

"He's still alive?"

"Yeah. Reckon he'll stay that way, too. Jessie says she's been kicking herself 'cause her aim was off. But it's better this way. When Grissom got to the doctor's he confessed everything. Said he'd arranged all the accidents at the mill, and your shooting. And he laid it all at Elias Moore's doorstep. So the marshal hustled over to ol' Elias's house. It seems that there's going to be a railroad spur coming up here from Missoula, so one of the big lumber outfits got interested in acquiring timber around here, and the person they checked with was the local banker. Our Mr. Moore. He didn't waste any time telling them that he would soon foreclose on a mill, and would they be interested in buying it? Seems they were. So Moore got busy setting me up." Joe chuckled. "Only he's the one that got caught. The marshal's still up there talking to him. I reckon he's thinking ol' Elias might have been involved in some other havey-cavey dealings along the way."

"A railroad. Of course. I should have realized. I was just thinking the other day about what we could do if we put in a railway line." He rubbed his hand across his forehead, frowning. "Where's Jessie?"

"Don't fret about her. She wanted to stay with you, but

the marshal insisted on her coming down and telling her story. I tell you, that was one wrought-up young lady.''

Stephen's eyes drifted closed. ''I'd like to thank her.'' His voice began to slur.

''Sure. In the morning. Right now you go back to sleep.''

He took a second look at his son. Stephen had already followed his advice.

When Stephen awakened the next time, his head felt much better. There was no one else in the room, and he cautiously slipped out of bed. His head spun for a moment, and his stomach rolled, but then everything settled into place. He went to the curtain and drew it back. It was obviously morning. He dressed, moving with great care so as not to disturb his head, and went downstairs. There he found only Amanda and her maid, bustling around in the kitchen, cleaning the breakfast dishes.

''Why, there are is! I was just going to come up and see about you.'' Amanda directed him to a chair at the kitchen table. ''Sit down. Feel like breakfast?''

''Maybe. A light one.'' He glanced around. ''Where's Jessie?''

Amanda shook her head. ''That girl. I finally made her go to bed. I told her you weren't bad enough off for her to be sitting up watching you. She lay down around dawn. If I know her, it shouldn't be too long before she's up again and coming in to see you.''

Stephen was disappointed. He wanted to see Jessie and talk to her, and every moment's delay seemed a huge waste of time. ''Oh.''

The biscuits and bacon Amanda set down in front of him helped calm his queasy stomach, and the headache powder she gave him did wonders, as well. By the time Stephen left the kitchen, he was feeling almost normal.

He climbed the stairs to his room and found his valet inside, fussing over one of his suits. Charles cast a look of disdain at the plain denim trousers, boots and shirt Stephen had put on.

"Is that what you're planning to wear today, sir?" he asked in a dreadfully polite voice.

"Yes, I rather think so."

"Very good, sir." Charles turned away and hung the suit in the wardrobe.

"I've found that sturdier clothes fare better here."

"Of course, sir."

"Charles...am I safe in assuming that the West has lost its appeal for you?"

Charles turned. "I have found it to be—rather different from what I expected, yes."

"Then you would be happy about going back to New York?"

The valet's somber face lit up. "Indeed, sir, I would consider it a privilege to leave this place."

"Good. I thought so. Well, you'll be getting your wish any day now, as soon as Miss Elizabeth arrives."

Charles couldn't suppress a smile. "Very good, sir. I will be happy to accompany you and Mrs. Ferguson to the—"

"Oh, not me. Or, at least, I hope I won't have to escort Elizabeth all the way to New York. That's one reason I want you to accompany her, to make sure she has a safe and pleasant journey."

"I beg your pardon, sir?"

"I won't be marrying Miss Elizabeth, Charles."

"You mean you won't be marrying her now? Here?"

"Now, here and forever, anywhere."

Charles stared, bug-eyed. "Sir!"

"I've had a change of heart, Charles—and mind, and most everything else, as well."

Charles pulled himself in order. "Yes, sir. Very good, sir." He bowed and left the room.

Stephen removed his boots and flopped on the bed, linking his hands behind his head. He winced a little at the soreness, but then he forgot it. He lay gazing at the ceiling, making plans and smiling.

It was some time later that there was a small, tentative knock at his door, and Jessie slipped inside, closing the door after her. She stood for a moment, looking at him. He stared back.

She was wearing the pale blue dress he had hired the local seamstress to sew for her. He had almost forgotten about it in the hectic events of the last few days. She looked even more beautiful than he had envisioned.

It fit her as her mother's dresses had not. The waist nipped in snugly, and the cloth outlined the generous curves of her breasts rather than hiding them. The velvet and lace added softening touches to her beauty, as did the way she wore her hair, piled loosely on the crown of her head, with curling wisps drifting down beside her face. She looked feminine and lovely, and her face glowed.

"Hello, Stephen." Her voice sounded oddly small and shy.

"Jessamine." He stood, pulled to his feet by the force of her beauty. "You are...beautiful," he said simply.

She smiled, dimpling, and color washed her cheeks. "Thank you. I'm so happy to see you up and looking so...so well."

"Thanks to you. You saved my life. Again. And don't say it was nothing. It was quite something to me."

"It was quite something to me, too." Jessie's voice was soft and slightly shaky as she continued. "I love you, Stephen. I came here to ask you to make love to me."

Desire clenched in his gut. "Jessie..."

Jessie wet her lips. Her hands were ice cold, and she couldn't recall ever feeling quite this scared. "I know you swore not to, that you were sorry about last time. But this time, you don't have to feel guilty for seducing me. I'm no longer inexperienced. And you aren't leading me astray. I want to."

She reached up and pulled the pins from her hair. It cascaded in rich red waves upon her shoulders. She smiled at him, and it was the knowing, beckoning smile of a seductress. Stephen could not speak, could only stand and watch her, his pulse throbbing, as she wove her spell of enchantment around him.

Her fingers went to the small pearl buttons that ran down the length of her dress, and she began to unbutton them, revealing first her throat, then the soft, tremulous tops of her breasts, and finally the white lacy camisole beneath. Stephen's eyes followed the path of her fingers, dwelling on the satiny skin and the clinging, revealing garment covering it. The cloth moved with every breath she took, tightening and loosening over her full breasts. Her aureoles were wine-dark circles beneath the sheer white, and the nipples hardened, pushing against it.

When her dress was unfastened, she shrugged out of it and let it fall to the floor. Then she unfastened the ties of her petticoats, and they crumpled to the floor atop the dress. She stood before him clad only in her underthings and stockings. Keeping her eyes on his face, she reached up and untied one of the pink bows that held her camisole together. Her fingers slid lower, and Stephen's eyes followed as she undid the next small satin ribbon. The garment gaped wider with every breath she drew, so that the beauty of her breasts was revealed little by little, shadowed and mysterious.

Desire sizzled through Stephen, enflaming every nerve, heating every vein. "You don't know what you're doing."

"Oh, yes, I do." Jessie's voice was low and breathy, arousing him even more. She strolled across the room to him, stopping only inches away. "When I saw you last night I didn't know whether you were alive. I've never been so scared."

She began to unbutton his shirt, her fingers slow and caressing. "I knew then that I loved you more than anything on earth. I can't live without you."

Jessie slipped her hands into his shirt and opened it, baring his chest. Stephen sucked in his breath. She looked at him. His eyes were glittering, his face flushed with desire. She knew that if she moved her hands down, she could touch the sure proof of his desire for her. He wanted her; that was all she needed to know.

She stepped closer and pressed her lips against one of

his nipples, nestled in the hair of his chest. Stephen jerked and groaned. "Jessie..." Her name was half laugh, half moan.

Her tongue flicked out and circled the small bud. She could feel the heat flooding his body. "I wanted to do this the other night, but I wasn't sure if you would like it."

"If I would like it! You're going to make me explode."

"Good." Jessie smiled and began to nibble at his skin. "That's what I want to do. I don't want you to think about anything but me. I don't care about my name or my reputation. I know I cannot be your wife. But I can't leave you. I can't live without knowing your lovemaking again. Make love to me, Stephen." She lifted her clear eyes and gazed deeply into his. "Let me be your mistress. I'll follow you back East. I'll live wherever, however you want me to. Just love me, and let me love you."

Her eyes were luminous, her face glowing with love and desire. Her lips were moist and very kissable. Stephen was shaken to the core with lust and love. He bent and kissed her, his hands clutching her hair. His lips dug into hers; his tongue possessed her.

He kissed her again and again, murmuring her name and soft words of love and passion. They pulled off their clothes and joined together stormily in his bed, wild with a hunger restrained so fiercely for days. They rolled and tumbled, kissing greedily, their hands exploring, stroking, gripping. Finally he moved between her legs, opening her to his loving invasion, and plunged deep within her. Jessie gave a soft cry and wrapped her legs around him, moving with him, until at last their passion exploded, hurtling them into the momentary oblivion of satisfaction.

Later, damp with sweat and shaken by the depths of their lovemaking, Stephen lay curled up with her, cradling her in his arms. Jessie nestled against him, utterly at peace.

"I love you," Stephen whispered.

She smiled faintly and kissed his chest. "I love you, too."

"But I have to turn down your offer."

Jessie stiffened, and her eyes flew open. "What?"

"I don't want you to be my mistress."

Hurt flooded her face, and she turned away, scrambling to leave his bed. Stephen's hand lashed out and fastened around her arm.

"No! Wait! I said that clumsily."

Jessie shot him a flashing glance. "How could you say it smoothly?"

"No. I didn't mean that I don't want you. I do. I want you and love you with every fiber of my being."

She paused, bewildered. "Then what—"

"I love you too much to make you my mistress. I would never dishonor you that way."

"Honor be damned!"

His mouth quirked into a smile. "Would you please let me finish what I'm trying to say? I love you. I don't want to spend my life sneaking out to see you, hiding you away from the world. I want to spend every moment with you. I want everyone to know that I love you. I want you to be my wife."

Jessie's jaw dropped. "What?"

"I want to marry you. Will you marry me?"

For a moment she couldn't speak, could only gape at him, astonished. "But—but—what about Elizabeth? What about your promise?"

"I've been thinking a lot over the past few days. Last night, almost dying—well, it crystallized my thinking. It made me realize what an idiot I was. I don't love Elizabeth. I can't marry her, no matter what promise I made her father. I can't condemn myself to a lifetime of boredom and misery because it's the 'proper' thing to do. I won't let you go, and I certainly wouldn't ask you to bear the shame of being my mistress. Elizabeth is a good woman, and she doesn't love me any more than I love her. She will understand; she's been my friend for years."

Jessie looked doubtful. "I don't think I'd understand your choosing another woman. I think I'd slug her."

Stephen chuckled. "You probably would. But not Elizabeth. She doesn't want me. All she wants is to be able to live free of her stepmother. I do have a responsibility to her, but I realized this morning what I can do. I will explain it all to her, and I'll send her to New York. Charles is eager to leave here, and he can escort her. In New York, she can live with Isabelle Clampton. I don't know why I didn't think of it before. Isabelle is a distant cousin of Elizabeth's father and is living now as a companion to her sister. She hates her position, but though she is quite genteel, she has only a small portion from her father's will. She will be a perfectly acceptable chaperone for Elizabeth, and they will get along well. They're both educated and intelligent.

"Elizabeth has an income from the trust her father left her, and, as I am one of the trustees, I can easily increase the amount so that she and Isabelle can live comfortably. No one in New York will know that she ran away from her home in St. Louis in order to marry me. Her reputation will be secure. Perhaps Elizabeth will even find a man there whom she can love as she doesn't love me."

Jessie gazed at him for a long moment. "You're serious, aren't you?"

"Yes! Of course I am!" He kissed her hard. "Well? Will you marry me?"

Jessie began to laugh. She threw her arms around his neck and covered his face with kisses. "Yes. Yes, I'll marry you, you crazy man! And you'll see—I won't embarrass you when we go to St. Louis. I'll learn all about being a lady. You can teach me. I promise I won't cuss or throw things or shoot a gun."

"Whoa. Wait. Hold it." Stephen set her away from him, gripping her by the shoulders and gazing intently into her eyes. "We're not going to St. Louis."

"What?"

"You heard me. I'm not taking you to live in the city. Do you think I'd pull up a beautiful wild rose by its roots and stick it in a glass vase, just to watch it die? I'd never do that to you. We'll get married and live right here. I like

Montana. I like the business. I don't have to go back to St. Louis. Joe will let me buy into the mill, I think. And if he and Sam don't want that, well, I'll find something else I can do. It's a brand new land. I can do anything I want to."

"But—but won't you miss it? Won't you be sorry?"

He shook his head. "No. I'd like to get to know my brother and father again. I'd like to help build something. There's nothing for me back home, except a stale life that someone else created for me. My grandfather will manage without me. He can find someone else to run the company. Maybe he'll sell it. I don't know. But I do know I can't live for him. Here, with you, is where I've really lived. And I guarantee you, I won't miss anything or anybody as long as I have you."

Tears brimmed in Jessamine's eyes. "You are the best and kindest of men. And I love you to distraction. I love you."

She threw her arms around him and kissed him again, and for the next few minutes, both of them were pleasantly lost.

It was some long time later that they finally rose and pulled their clothes back on, talking and laughing softly. They had trouble keeping their hands off each other, and Stephen pulled Jessie back time after time to kiss her. When they were finally dressed, they strolled downstairs, hand in hand. Amanda, seeing their linked hands, raised her eyebrows but said nothing. They wandered into the parlor and sat down. They talked together quietly, making plans for their future, studying their linked hands with all the intensity that only new lovers have.

It was late in the afternoon, and Stephen and Jessie were still lost in each other's eyes, when there was the sound of feet pounding up the front steps and Burley Owens burst into the house. "Miz Randall! Where's Stephen?"

"In here, Burley."

Burley stuck his head into the parlor. "Say, you're

lookin' mighty good for a man what almost got sawed up into two-by-fours last night."

"Why, thank you, Burley...I think. What's your news?"

"I was down at the mill. Guess who just rode into town? That ringtail rascal Sam Ferguson, that's who," he continued, answering his own question. "And he's got your fi—" He glanced at Stephen's and Jessie's linked hands, and his voice faltered. "That is, well, Miss Elizabeth's with him."

Stephen and Jessie looked at each other. Jessie's stomach tightened in fear, and suddenly she was afraid that this afternoon had been only a dream, that Stephen would stand up and walk out of her life.

But he smiled and squeezed her hand. "Come on. We'd better go face the music. Don't worry. She'll be fine."

He stood, pulling Jessie with him. "I'm glad they've finally arrived. All safe, I take it?"

Burley nodded, seemingly unable to speak.

Jessie hung back. "Stephen...are you sure?"

He turned, smiling slowly, and his eyes held a hot promise. "Yes. I'm sure. I love you, and I want to marry you. Damn the consequences." He leaned down and kissed her thoroughly. "Now, shall we go?"

Jessie's grin was dazzling. "Anywhere."

She tucked her hand in his arm, and they walked out the door together.

* * * * *

THE HELL RAISER

Dorothy Glenn

Prologue

Montana Territory 1866

"Run up to the house and fetch that little leather pouch of nails, Sammy."

Sammy, engrossed in pulling long, wiggly worms from the soft, damp earth, didn't hear his father's deep voice because he spoke softly, absently. Nor did the father look to see if his son obeyed.

Joe Ferguson grasped the curved handle of a big wooden plane and began shaving the rough edges from the plank he had cut. For Joe work was a way to relieve his troubled mind. His wife, Eleanor—Nora—more precious to him than life, had defied her affluent family in Saint Louis to come to the Montana wilderness with him. She had become more and more withdrawn during the past few weeks, and he was worried. She seldom spoke to him, or to their sons for that matter, unless it was absolutely necessary. A nagging dread had been eating at Joe for weeks, and he worked every minute he could spare, hoping to make life easier for her.

Today he was building a platform for his wife to step

onto to dip water for her wash pot. Nora had never washed her own undergarments until she married him. Now she scrubbed the family's clothes in a tub beside the creek in the summer and hung them on the bushes to dry. In the winter she scrubbed in the kitchen and hung the clothes over the cook stove.

While he worked, thoughts tumbled around and around in Joe's mind. If he made it easier for her to draw water for her washing, if he trapped enough mink to make her a coat, if he took her to visit the neighbors more often, if he told her that he knew how much she had given up to become his wife, if he told her how much he loved her...

"Sammy!"

"Yeah, Pa."

"Run fetch the nails, son."

"Then can I go fishin' down by the flat rock?" Sammy scooped up a handful of worms and crammed them into the pocket of his britches.

"Sure, but fetch the nails and tell your ma where you're going."

"Look at this'n, Pa." The boy pulled a thick worm from his pocket. It wiggled out of his small, dirty fingers and fell on his bare foot. He quickly retrieved it. "It's a mean one, Pa. I'll catch a big'n with this'n, and Ma'll cook it for supper."

"You might at that."

"I'll take Stevie fishin' with me. He likes to fish."

"You'd better ask your ma about that. Stevie's only five, and he needs watching."

"I'm ten," Sammy said as if it was something he had accomplished all on his own. "I'll watch him."

"Ask your ma."

Sammy picked up the long wooden plane Joe had inherited from his grandfather, who had been a master craftsman. Unser Ferguson could build anything and build it better than anyone else, or so his grandson thought. Joe had a wooden trunk Unser Ferguson had built. It was grooved on the ends and pegged—truly a work of art.

"You said I could use this sometime."

"Aye, I did. But not today, son. Be gone and fetch the nails."

"Why are nails square, Pa?"

Joe paused and looked at this son of his who always had a headful of questions and who liked working with his hands.

"Because they're hand-forged. That means they were made by a blacksmith."

"You used these before, didn't you? You pulled 'em out of the old cellar door."

"Aye, and I greased 'em so they wouldn't rust."

"I'm goin' to grease my nails like you do, Pa."

That brought a smile to Joe's craggy, weathered face. He cupped his big hand around the boy's head and hugged it to his side for a brief instant.

"And I'm going to grease your bottom with my hand if you don't fetch the nails."

Sammy broke away and grinned. "You gotta catch me first." It was a game they played in the winter when the ground was covered with snow. "Catch me, Pa. Catch me," Sammy would scream as he raced into the woods with Joe in pursuit. When Joe caught him, he would roll him in the snow, then throw him over his shoulder and tickle his ribs as he carried him home.

"Not today, son. I've got work to do."

The boy turned up the path toward the comfortable three-room house set amid tall pines. He dragged his bare toes in the dirt and wiped his nose on his sleeve. He wished his pa had time to play and go fishing. Stevie never sat still long enough to catch a fish; he just wanted to play with the worms. Sammy decided on the way to the house that when he grew up he was going to be just like his father and build things with that big plane that made wood as smooth as doeskin. He was going to be a logger like his father, too. His father could cut down a lodgepole pine quicker than any man in all Montana Territory, Samuel thought proudly.

At the back of the house he stopped to pick up the fishing pole, then stepped carefully around his mother's wildflower garden. He pursed his lips and whistled a gay Irish tune. When he heard a horse stamping and a harness jingling, he instantly forgot fishing, forgot everything in his belief that someone had come to visit.

At the corner of the house, the grin left his freckled face. It wasn't a neighbor's wagon. It was *their* wagon and *their* horses hitched to it. Stephen sat on the wagon seat. Sammy smiled again, then frowned; he'd have to wash up. They were going visiting. Why hadn't Pa told him?

When he heard a small cry behind him, he turned to see that his mother had come out of the house. She was wearing her hat and carrying a valise. Her startled eyes were on his face, her hand over her mouth.

"Where we goin', Ma?"

Eleanor tore her eyes from her son's face and hurried to the back of the wagon. It took all her strength, but she managed to throw the valise in over the gate. She turned and caught Sammy's face in her hands and kissed him. Then she pulled up her skirts and climbed the wagon wheel to the seat.

"Come on, Sammy! We're goin' to see Grandpa. I'm takin' my whistle," Stephen yelled.

"Ma!" Sammy ran to the side of the wagon. "Where'er you goin'? Can't I go?"

His mother looked at him, mumbled something and shook her head. He could see tears on her cheeks.

"I want Sammy to go!" Stephen wailed, and began to cry.

Eleanor took up the reins and slapped them against the backs of the horses. "Giddyap!" Her voice came out in a screech.

Sammy began to panic. Something was wrong. Suddenly he knew—his mother and brother were leaving and were not coming back!

"Sammy come! Sammy come!" Stephen screamed as the wagon turned to leave the yard and head down the trail through the thick pines.

"Ma...ma! Don't...go!" Samuel ran after the wagon. "I got worms, Stevie. See..." He dug his hand into his pocket and brought out the fistful of worms. "Don't go, Stevie! I'll take you fishin'..." The wiggly, wet worms slipped through his fingers, but Sammy didn't notice, didn't care.

"Sam...my..." Stephen cried between sobs, turning to watch his brother run behind the wagon. "Sam...my..."

Eleanor whipped the horses into a trot, and Stephen had to cling to the seat.

"Come...back, Ma...ma—" Sobs burst from Sammy's throat as he ran. "Mama...come back!"

Although the wagon pulled ahead, Sammy ran as fast as he could. Through the blur of his tears he could see his mother's straight back and his brother's hand stretched toward him.

The boy ran after the wagon until he was weak and gasping for breath. When his legs would no longer hold him, he dropped on the dirt track, buried his face in his arms and sobbed his anguish. Somehow he knew that his life would never be the same.

He lay in the dirt for an hour or more and cried as though his heart was breaking. Then his father was kneeling beside him, lifting him. Sammy wound his small arms tightly around his father's neck.

"Ma...ma's gone," he sobbed.

"I know." Joe held his son, and they cried together.

Later, a long time later, he lifted Sammy in his arms and carried him to the house.

Chapter One

Montana Territory 1888

The logging camp, high in the mountains above Nora Springs, was quiet in mid-September. Only a handful of men were in the camp. Soon the five-month cutting season would begin. A half a hundred men would descend on the camp and stay until the ground thawed in the spring. To some of the loggers one bunkhouse or another was as much of a home as they wanted. They decorated the walls with pictures from the *Police Gazette* and stored their belongings beneath their bunks.

Awakened at dawn by the cook ringing a cowbell and shouting "Roll out! Breakfast on the boards," the woodsmen would tumble out of bunks, dress in the freezing temperature and hurry to the cookshack. Grub at the Ferguson logging camp was famous among the lumberjacks. The owners, Sam and Joe Ferguson, believed a well-fed man made a contented, productive worker.

Evenings at the camp would be spent at the grindstone, as the men prepared their axes for another day's work. The double-bitted ax was used by expert choppers who commanded the best wages in camp. No work was done on Sundays, and those who were sober did their laundry or cut one another's hair. Some even shaved, although most of the men allowed their beards to grow until spring. When these tasks were over, time was spent in horseplay or hazing a newcomer.

Sam Ferguson stood in the doorway of the camp headquarters and gazed at the soaring lodgepole pines surrounding the camp. This was his life, and he had never given a thought to doing anything else.

Soon the swampers would arrive to prepare the roads. For the past few years he had used the Michigan lumbermen's idea of driving tank sprinklers along the trail to insure a heavy coating of ice in the ruts made by the sleds. Great loads of logs then could be slid along the ice-coated ruts.

Each year Sam looked forward to the start of cutting season, and each year he looked forward to the end. He was like all the other lumberjacks: a creature of the forest. He grumbled and swore about the isolation, but by autumn the call of the forest was in his veins, and he was as eager as any lumberjack to put in thirteen hours a day in weather twenty below zero.

Sam was tall. His arms and shoulders were thick with muscles from years of swinging an ax. He handled the cutting end of the lumber business he and his father had started twelve years ago when Sam had finished his schooling in Missoula. Joe Ferguson ran the mill in Nora Springs. They had prospered during the past twelve years and had put all their profits into the mill.

Sam watched Burley Owens come toward him from the cook house. The cook had told Sam at breakfast that the old man had come up from Nora Springs the night before, eaten and gone straight to the bunkhouse.

"You sick or something?" Sam called as Burley approached.

"Hell, no, I ain't sick. Do I look sick?"

"You're usually in here complaining about something the minute you hit camp, so naturally I thought you were sick."

"Well, I ain't."

Burley sat on a bench and leaned against the side of the building. Sam lifted a booted foot to the bench, rested his elbow on his thigh and waited. He had no doubt that Burley had made the trip for a reason, and Sam could wait to find it out.

"Hot, ain't it?" Burley said.

"We have a hot day now and then up here."

"Yore just dyin' to know the news, ain't ya?"

"Yes, Burley, I'm just dying to know the news, but I know you're not going to tell me until you're damn good and ready."

"Well, I'm ready. First off, Joe said he'd got word 'bout the new saw blade. It'll be in Missoula in a couple of weeks. He thinks ya ort to go with me an' Jim to get it, that is if'n there's somebody here ya can leave in charge."

"Someone should go with you two lunkheads." Sam smiled at the old man affectionately. "You grizzly old buzzard, you're not fit to be turned loose in town by yourself."

"I whipped yore hind oncet, boy. I can do it again."

Sam laughed. "Does Pa think he'll have time to finish the contract?"

"He's thinkin' so. 'Twas a hell of a time ta break the

big blade. I'm thinkin' he ought not to be givin' a cut in price if he don't fill the bill in time."

"Well, he will. He'll fill it in time and pay off the loan to the bank. Any news from town worth repeating?"

"Yeah, a dab. Yesterday the stage come in with Jessie ridin' on top. She'd been visitin' down south a ways. It pulled up big as ya please, and two dressed-up city fellers got out." The old man shook his gray head, and his rounded shoulders shook with laughter. "Lordy mercy! They was so sissy-lookin' me 'n' the boys was makin' bets that they'd squat ta pee. Well...it 'ppears that one of 'em was a val...et to the other'n. Anyways, that's what the driver says. The val...et set about waitin' on the other fancy dude hand 'n' foot. While he was bowin' 'n' scrapin', Henley from the livery pipes up 'n' asks if we reckon that valet wipes the dude's butt." Burley laughed until tears came to his eyes.

"Why didn't you ask him?" Sam laughed with him. Because he knew how much Burley enjoyed telling a story, he listened attentively.

"Like I said, Jessie was on the stage. The dude thought she was a boy. She had on them britches she's always wearin', 'n' totin' her rifle. The dude says, 'Hey thar, boy, carry my trunk.'" Burley stopped to laugh again. "Jessie's eyes spit fire. She flung off her hat, 'n' that red hair came fallin' out. She flew into him like a scalded cat." Sam had to wait for Burley to stop laughing. "Well, that dude backtracked a-plenty. The val...et loaded himself up with stuff, but he warn't no stronger than a pissant."

"What did Jessie do?"

"She bent over 'n' grabbed up them bags. The dude 'n' the val...et got a eyeful of her rear in them britches."

"Jessie's been wearing britches too long. She shouldn't have toted the dude's bags. Amanda should've put her in a dress and taught her to sew and knit instead of packing a gun and spittin' like a man."

"She was only showin' up the dude."

"That's another thing. She's too old to be showing off. She needs her butt whipped."

"Why don't ya do it? She's been runnin' after ya like a hound dog after a bone since she was dry behind the ears," Burley said dryly.

Sam watched the old man. Burley had been pushing Jessie at Sam for the past couple of years. Beside his pa, Burley, along with Jessie and her mother, Amanda, were the closest things to a family Sam had known since the day his mother had left with his brother, Stephen. Amanda's husband, Jessie's father, had been killed in an accident at the logging camp, and Sam and Joe had been looking after the two women ever since. Now nineteen years old, redheaded Jessie had given up everything feminine to try to prove she could take care of herself and her ma without help from anyone.

"What's the dude doing in Nora Springs?"

"I never got around ta findin' out. Joe wanted me ta come on up here. Ya got any decent coffee? I could make better coffee out of shoe leather than that cook ya got."

Sam sat at the table working on his maps while Burley snored on a bunk, but his mind was not on his work. It was on Jessie. It was time she started wearing a dress and acting like a woman. He had snatched her out of enough scrapes. Sam was thinking that her shapely little butt in britches had invited comments from every newcomer in town. Suddenly the object of his thoughts stuck her head in the door.

"Howdy, Sam."

"What the hell are you doing up here?" He got to his feet, suddenly fearful she was bringing bad news. "Is Pa all right?"

"Uncle Joe is fine. I brought someone to see you." Jessie stepped into the room, followed by a stranger.

"Jessie, you know I've already hired the crew."

Burley reared up off the bunk. "Hellfire 'n' brimstone! If it ain't the...dude!"

Sam met the man's brown-eyed stare. Something about him stirred old memories. The two men looked at each other for a long while as the silence wore on. A strange feeling started in the tip of Sam's toes and worked upward. His heart pounded in his chest, sending weakness instead of strength throughout his body.

Both men were tall, brown-haired, brown-eyed. Sam was just a bit taller and heavier. His features were rougher from days and weeks spent outside in all kinds of weather, and he had a slash of silky mustache on his upper lip. His hair was streaked from the sun and grew long on his neck. The face of the man who stared at him was smooth. His hair was glossy, neatly cut and just a shade darker than Sam's. His clothes were obviously new, from the general store in Nora Springs, and his hands looked as if they had never done a hard day's work.

"Hello, Sammy."

The words almost knocked the legs out from under Sam. No one had ever called him that but...

"Stephen?" He didn't know how he managed to say his brother's name.

"My God!" They both said at the same time.

Stephen stepped forward and offered his hand. Sam took a step to meet him, seemed to hesitate, then took his hand in a formal handshake.

"It's been a long time."

"Yes, it has. Twenty-two years."

"More than a lifetime for some people. I suppose you've seen Pa," Sam said.

"Of course he's seen Uncle Joe," Jessie said, looking from one man to the other. "He was determined to come up here. I had to bring him. Uncle Joe was afraid he'd get lost in the woods and the bears would eat him," she added dryly, and waited for a reaction from Sam. He ignored her.

"I've seen Father," Stephen said. "I was anxious to see you."

The silence was awkward. Unaware of his movements, Sam went to pour coffee into a graniteware cup and found the pot empty. Moving restlessly, he went to his worktable and shuffled papers. Years ago he had blocked his mother and brother from his mind. It was unnerving to be suddenly thrust into a past he wanted to forget.

"Sit down," he said, suddenly remembering his manners.

Stephen remained standing. "Mother died a few weeks ago."

"Really?" Something inside Sam's throat began to swell until it almost choked him. "Is that the reason you came to see Pa?"

"One of them. I came to see both of you. I thought you'd want to know."

"Don't expect me to mourn," Sam said harshly. "She means no more to me dead than she did alive."

"Ya durn clabberhead!" Burley exclaimed. "That's a mean thin' to say 'bout yore ma."

"Shut up, Burley. You're butting in where you have no business." Sam had never spoken so harshly to the old man and was immediately sorry when he saw the stricken look on Burley's face.

"I had another reason for coming." Stephen's voice filled the embarrassing silence. He reached into his inside coat pocket and pulled out a small packet of letters tied with a narrow ribbon. "Mother left these for you. She did some things that were wrong, but she wasn't a bad person. She loved *both* her children."

Stephen held out the letters until Sam was forced to take them. He tossed the bundle onto his worktable without looking at it.

"I'm not much of a reader," he said curtly.

"Mother let me believe that you and Father had died," Stephen said, looking his brother in the eye. He pulled an envelope from his pocket. "While she lay dying, she wrote me a letter. I'd like for you to read it."

"No, thanks."

"Suit yourself." Stephen's voice carried a hint of irritation. He put the letter in his pocket.

It was hard for Sam to believe that this tall, well-spoken man was his younger brother, yet the resemblance to his father was there. Too much time had gone by for Sam to greet this stranger with open arms. He remembered him, but he remembered more his father walking the floor those first few weeks when they were alone. He remembered the tears on his face, remembered seeing him age prematurely from grief. Joe had never ceased to love the woman who had deserted him and their son. He had named his town Nora Springs after her. Sam hated the name; it was a constant reminder of a mother who did not want him.

Sam thought about how he had put his own hurt behind him and tried to make up to his father for his loss. It had not been easy. Now, on seeing his brother, all the old resentment boiled up inside him.

"We'd better be going. I told Uncle Joe we'd be back before dark." Jessie edged toward the door.

"I plan to be here for a while, Sam. I want to get to know you and Father before I return to Saint Louis."

"Well, enjoy yourself at the local saloon. It's about all we have in the way of entertainment, unless Jess takes you to the spelling bee at the school. There'll be a hurrah over at Gogg's Flats, Jessie. I hear they've got a fiddler now that's got more than two strings on his fiddle."

"Sam Ferguson, you make me so mad I could... spit!" Jessie tossed her mane of red hair and glared at him.

Stephen stood beside the door with his hat in his hand. He had a puzzled look on his face.

"Goodbye, Sam. I'll see you again before I leave."

"No doubt you will. I'll be down in a few days. I make sure I see Pa every week or so," Sam said pointedly.

After they left, Sam sat at the table and stared at the clenched hands in front of him.

"Well, ya shore do know how to make a ass o' yoreself, don't ya?" Burley exclaimed.

Sam looked up. "Get yourself gone, old man. I don't want to talk about it."

Sam was scarcely aware of Burley's leaving. He picked up the bundle of letters. His first impulse was to toss them in the fire. His second impulse was to hide them from his father. Joe had been hurt enough. Sam took his saddlebags from the peg on the wall, buried the letters in them and tried his best to forget them.

He stayed in the cabin all evening, not bothering to go to the cook house for supper. His thoughts were a jumble. He thought of his brother and how it had been twenty-two years ago. Times had been hard for the family. The country had been sparsely settled when he had last seen Stephen. For the first time in years, Sam heard in his mind the small, sobbing voice of his brother on that morning his life had changed forever. *I want Sammy to come!* He remembered the small hand that had stretched out to him as he ran behind the wagon, and how his mother had ignored him.

Hell! Stephen had been only five years old. He had been a victim of their mother's callousness as much as Sam had been. Stephen was not responsible for breaking up the family and for ruining his father's life. Stephen had suffered the loss of his father and his brother. But he had grown up surrounded by wealth, had been educated in the finest schools and stood to inherit a shipping business from his grandfather.

Stephen had wealth and education, but Sam thanked God that he had been left with his father. He loved his life amid the trees, the cold, fast-moving streams, the snowy winters and the warm, fragrant summers. His life was here where he had worked alongside his father building the Ferguson Lumber Company from scratch.

Sam rode down the mountain to Nora Springs on a bright autumn day. As he approached the mill, he could hear the whine of the powerful spinning saws as the steel teeth bit into the butt of a log. The metallic scream of the blades was as familiar a sound to Sam as his father's voice. He left his horse at the stable and walked into the office.

Joe got to his feet, a broad smile splitting his face. He was a big man, like his sons, but the years had thickened his middle and streaked his thick black hair with gray. The shoulders of his plaid flannel shirt, which was tucked into his duck trousers, were sprinkled with sawdust. Joe closed the door to muffle the sound of screeching machinery.

"How's things going at camp?"

"All set. I left Gordy Sunner in charge."

"Sunner's a good man."

Father and son looked at each other. Both men knew that things were not the same. It was no longer the two of them. A stranger who was son and brother had appeared and rocked their world.

"I suppose you heard about Stephen?" Joe sat on the end of the desk.

"Jessie brought him up to the camp, but you know that. She said you sent her with him."

Joe's face took on a puzzled frown. He got to his feet. "You haven't heard that...he was shot after he and Jessie left camp?"

"Shot? What the hell!"

"He's all right. A bushwacker shot him out of the saddle, would've killed him if not for Jessie. She fired a few shots and chased him away, then got Stephen back in the saddle and brought him home—that is, brought him to Amanda. He was hit high in the chest. They dug the bullet out and have been taking care of him."

"Who would have a grudge against Stephen?" Sam asked.

"Damned if I know."

"He could have been mistaken for me. I turned away

a few soreheads while I was hiring for the winter's work.''

"I couldn't believe my eyes when I saw that boy, Sam. Twenty-two years is a long time.''

"He's hardly a boy, Pa. He could have gotten in touch with us a long time ago if he'd wanted to.'' There was a sharp edge to Sam's voice.

"Don't blame him, Sam. I've spent many hours getting reacquainted with him. He's told me all about his and Eleanor's life since they left here. She told the boy we were dead, thinking it would be easier for him.''

"Eleanor thought it would be easier! Hell, Pa—''

"Don't say a harsh word about your mother,'' Joe said quickly. "That's all over and done with. She suffered, too.''

"Bull! While she was *suffering*, she was sleeping on a feather bed and being waited on hand and foot.''

"Samuel!'' Joe thundered, then softened his voice. "Meet your brother halfway, son. The two of you are all I have.''

It had been more than five years since either man had mentioned the woman who had left them. Joe was just as forgiving as ever, and Sam was just as resentful. It was a subject better left alone. Both men were grateful for Jessie's interruption.

"Hello, Sam.''

Jessie stood in the doorway, slim and boyish and smiling. She had never understood why she was expected to wear cumbersome skirts when she could wear the simple boys' clothing she bought at Swenson's Mercantile. Britches and flannel shirts were comfortable and warm. She saw little advantage in dressing like a woman. It was the men who had the adventure and the fun.

"Hello, squirt.''

"Did Uncle Joe tell you that Stephen wants you to meet his fiancée when you go to Missoula?"

"Meet his...what?" Sam's eyes snagged his father's before Joe could look away. "All right. Spill it, Pa."

"I told Stephen you were going to Missoula to get the blade coming in on the train, and I said I was sure you wouldn't mind escorting the woman back here."

"Hellfire!" Sam sputtered. "What do you mean... escort? Didn't you tell him there was a stage?"

"He knows that," Jessie put in. "He came in on it. He says that Miss Elizabeth Caldwell is a gentle-born woman—whatever the hell that means—"

"Hush up your swearing, child," Joe said gently.

"Sorry, Uncle Joe." Jessie mouthed the words but didn't look one bit sorry.

"I'll put her on the stage," Sam said. "She can't ride the freight wagon with Burley and Jim Two-Horses."

"Stephen says he'd rather *dear* Elizabeth travel under your protection. *He* made the trip by stage, and *he* don't think that a woman of *her* upbringing should be subjected to that mode of travel. She's been sheltered all her life." Jessie's voice was heavy with sarcasm, and in spite of himself, Sam had to grin.

"If she wants to ride the freight wagon with Jim Two-Horses, Burley can ride horseback."

"He knows you're here," Jessie said. "I told him I saw you ride into town."

"Just a regular little know-it-all, aren't you, squirt?" Sam teased Jessie while a worried frown covered Joe's face.

"I've spent every evening with him, son. Your brother understands your bitterness, but he wants to be friends."

"Settle down, Pa. I don't hold anything against Stephen. I'll admit I was taken aback at first. Lord! It's been twenty-two years. Did he expect me to greet him with open arms?''

''Why not?'' Jessie said. ''Uncle Joe did.''

''Someday I'm going to paddle your butt for mouthin' off, squirt.'' Sam jerked a strand of bright red hair as he left the office.

Sam went up the stairs at Amanda Randall's boardinghouse and knocked on the door of his brother's room. It was opened by a man in a white shirt, black tie and coat. The man raised his brows in question, and for a moment Sam stared at him stupidly.

''Yes?''

''Yes, what? Who the hell are you?''

''Charles, who is it?''

''He has not given his name, Master Stephen.''

''It's Master Samuel Ferguson of the Nora Springs Fergusons,'' Sam said sarcastically. ''Do I need an appointment to see my brother?''

''Come in, Sam. Charles, this is my brother, Samuel.''

''Pleased to make your acquaintance, sir.''

''Likewise, I'm sure,'' Sam said dryly, and tossed his hat onto a chair.

Stephen lay propped up by plump pillows, a writing table over his lap and papers scattered on the bed.

''I'll not need you, Charles.''

''Very well, Master Stephen.'' The servant went out and gently closed the door. Sam thought of a comment he'd like to make about the val…et, as Burley called him, but stifled the urge.

''Sit down, Sam.''

''I'm sorry about the ambush. Someone may have thought it was me riding with Jessie.''

''Does this sort of thing happen often out here?''

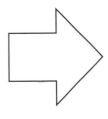

NO COST! NO OBLIGATION TO BUY!
NO PURCHASE NECESSARY!

PLAY "LUCKY 7" AND GET FIVE FREE GIFTS

HOW TO PLAY:

1. With a coin, carefully scratch off the silver box at the right. Then check the claim chart to see what we have for you—FREE BOOKS and a gift—ALL YOURS! ALL FREE!

2. Send back this card and you'll receive brand-new Harlequin Historical™ novels. These books have a cover price of $5.99 each, but they are yours to keep absolutely free.

3. There's no catch. You're under no obligation to buy anything. We charge nothing—ZERO—for your first shipment. And you don't have to make any minimum number of purchases—not even one!

4. The fact is thousands of readers enjoy receiving books by mail from the Harlequin Reader Service®. They like the convenience of home delivery...they like getting the best new novels BEFORE they're available in stores...and they love our discount prices!

5. We hope that after receiving your free books you'll want to remain a subscriber. But the choice is yours—to continue or cancel, anytime at all! So why not take us up on our invitation, with no risk of any kind. You'll be glad you did!

THIS SURPRISE MYSTERY GIFT CAN BE YOURS _FREE_ AS ADDED THANKS FOR GIVING OUR READER SERVICE A TRY!

"Not often, but occasionally."

The second meeting between the brothers was less strained. In the next few hours they talked of many things, carefully skirting any mention of their mother.

"I got a wire the other day from my fiancée, Elizabeth Caldwell, Sam. She's on her way to Nora Springs and will arrive in Missoula a week from tomorrow. There's no way I can go to meet her. I'm sorry to have to ask, but I would greatly appreciate it if you would meet Elizabeth and bring her here. Father told me you were going to pick up a blade for the mill. Something extremely important must have happened to cause Elizabeth to make the journey. She's not a flighty woman."

"We're taking a heavy freight wagon to get the blade and other supplies. Burley and Jim Two-Horses are going with me. I'll meet her and put her on the stage. That way she'll get here a couple of days before we will."

"I'd rather you didn't do that. Hire a carriage in Missoula with a top and good springs. If you can't find one for hire, buy one, regardless of the cost."

"That isn't necessary when there's a stage that runs from Missoula to Nora Springs."

"I don't think you understand, Sam. Elizabeth isn't used to being in a situation where she must cope with ruffians and the like. I expect to pay you for your trouble. Charles will give you money for the buggy."

Stephen realized he had said the wrong thing when he saw Sam's eyelids half cover his eyes and his lips thin. When Sam spoke, his voice was so cold, so angry, that Stephen realized this brother of his was a dangerous man when crossed.

"This might come as a surprise to you, but out here money doesn't solve everything. No amount of money will buy a favor if the person doesn't want to give it."

"Good Lord! I didn't mean to insult you!"

"Pa and I aren't rich, but we're not poor, either. You might say that we've got more pride than money. I'll meet your prissy-tail woman who's too good to ride the stage, and I'll bring her here."

"I'm sorry, Sam. I'm used to paying for everything. People in the East expect it."

Sam shrugged. His manner was casual, but he was still angry and seething with resentment, as his next words indicated.

"I don't think Nora Springs has accommodations suitable for such a high-toned *lady*."

Stephen met his brother's eyes steadily. "You took my meaning wrong. Elizabeth is a *lady* through and through. She's intelligent, sweet and kind. We grew up together, and our families have always planned that we marry, and we will before the year is out."

"Why couldn't she wait for you in Saint Louis? Why is such a woman coming to the wilds of Montana Territory? You of all people should know that *gentry* don't adapt to this country." There was heavy sarcasm in Sam's voice.

"Elizabeth said she would explain. I know her well enough to know that she does not act impulsively." Stephen was determined not to let his brother rile him.

"Maybe she's so in love she couldn't wait a few weeks to see you again." *Maybe she wants you to bed her. Maybe she's like an ordinary woman under those fancy skirts.*

"Regardless of her reason for coming, I'm responsible for her. And I know she will be safer with my brother than with anyone else."

"Thanks for the confidence, but it's not saying much

for your judgment. You don't know a damn thing about me.''

"Oh, but I do. Father has told me a great deal about you."

Sam snorted. "A father's not likely to tell one son the other son is a no-good son of a bitch!" He slammed his hat on his head. "I'll see you before I leave for Missoula."

Sam left the room. He didn't see the look of regret on his brother's face.

Chapter Two

"Jehoshaphat!"

"What's griping you now, old man?"

"Ya'd think that was the last bottle o' whiskey in Missoula the way yore guzzlin' it. I ain't never seen ya down the stuff like that before."

"This might surprise you, Burley, but there are a lot of things you haven't seen." Sam's voice had an edge. "And that's pure gospel."

"Yore right as rain 'bout that. I ain't seen much, but you ain't seen much, neither."

The old man eyed the younger man, affection and disapproval competing in the expression on his lined face. He had seen Sam in this mood before. He was in his don't-cross-me-or-I'll-twist-your-tail mood—and had been ever since they'd left Nora Springs to come to Missoula. Before the night was over, Sam Ferguson would be in a hell-raising mood.

Sam pushed his hat to the back of his head and poured another drink. His face reflected boredom, but that didn't fool Burley. He had known Sam since he was knee-high to a duck. The shock of seeing his brother after twenty-two years had drawn Sam's nerves as tight as a bowstring. One of two things could happen. The whiskey was going to loosen him up or he was going to turn mean and hurt someone.

"How long have you known Pa, Burley?"

"Long time. You know that."

"You knew...*her*, didn't you?"

"If yore meanin' yore ma, you know I did."

"She was a bitch!" Sam's voice was low and hard. He spit the words out as if they were nasty in his mouth.

"She warn't no such thin'. She was a nice, pretty woman."

"Nice? Bullshit!" Sam snarled. "She ran off and left me and Pa. She took Stephen and told him Pa and me were dead." Sam emptied his glass in one gulp and poured another drink.

"She had her reasons. Yore pa don't hate her. Why do you?"

"I've not thought about her enough to hate her. She wasn't that important to me." Sam's words were cold and hard as an icicle to hide his hurt. Burley had no desire to argue with Sam about his mother. That was a subject he and Joe left alone.

Sam's thoughts turned to one of the two reasons he and Burley and Jim Two-Horses had come to Missoula. The big saw blade at the mill had been damaged, and they had been forced to use a smaller blade to try to complete an order that would pay off their bank loan, which was due in a month. The new blade they had ordered from the steel mill back east had come in on the afternoon train. It was already loaded on the freight wagon.

Joe had assured Sam that things were going along well at the sawmill and that, with the new blade, they would finish the contract in plenty of time. Sam did not like

Frank Grissom, the mill foreman, although Joe insisted Frank did a good job. Frank had his eye on Jessie. She had made it plain to the man she was not interested. If that bastard bothered her while he was away, Sam thought, he'd take care of Grissom when he got back.

Suddenly Sam got to his feet and went through the bat-wing doors of the saloon. He walked with a steady, easy stride. One would never guess he had consumed almost a full bottle of whiskey. He stood on the porch, leaned casually against a post and looked up and down the rutted street of Missoula. He wondered what Stephen, who had lived in a city the size of New York and had gone to school in the East, had thought of Missoula when he stepped off the train.

He wondered, too, what that prissy, high-toned woman of Stephen's would think when she arrived. She was too persnickety to ride the stage. Damn Stephen! He should be here to meet his woman.

As Sam stood on the porch of the saloon, the conversation with Stephen played over in his mind. Remembering only made him more curious about the highfalutin Miss Elizabeth Caldwell. *She was not used to ruffians.* A cocky grin widened Sam's mouth. Maybe he should give the hoity-toity baggage a trip with a real, honest-to-God Western hell raiser. It would give her something to talk about while serving tea to the garden club after she returned to the mansion in Saint Louis.

Sam looked up the street toward the hotel where he had a room, down the street toward the tin shop, the mercantile and sundry other shops that made up Missoula, a railroad town that serviced the logging camps and ranches in Northwest Montana Territory. It was dusk, suppertime. Soon things would liven up. The town had its share of saloons and whorehouses. Sam thought about going to one but realized he wasn't drunk enough...yet. He went into the saloon, picked up a bottle from the bar as he passed it and headed for the table where Burley sat.

Mike, the bartender, ran the wet cloth over the bar and watched Sam Ferguson. Sam had first come into the Emporia Saloon with his pa when he was a stripling. He took no pushing, drunk or sober, and was known to jump into a fight among strangers just to even the odds. He was drinking more than usual this trip, and before the night was over, he just might take it into his head to let off steam.

Sam hooked a chair with his booted foot and sat.

"Where in the hell is Two-Horses? I told him to see about getting a rig to carry Miss Prissy-tail."

"He'll be along." Burley pounded on the table with his empty beer mug, and the bartender brought him a full one.

"When? Next week?"

"Soon as he sees to the wagon and the mules...and the rig," Burley said patiently.

"When's the next train?"

"From the east?"

"Of course from the east. Dammit, Burley, are you awake?"

"Four days. Why?"

"If Miss Prissy-tail's not here, she can find her own damn way to Nora Springs. I'm not waiting here four days."

"Have ya checked the hotels?"

"I'll do it in the morning."

"I thought we was leavin' in the mornin'."

"We are. If she's not here, we go without her."

"Hellfire! You can't do that."

"Who's going to stop me?"

"Oh, bull fiddle!" Burley exclaimed. Sam had consumed his limit of whiskey and was no longer reasonable. From here on it was hell-raisin' time.

Jim Two-Horses was part Sioux, part Mexican and part something else that no one had bothered finding out about. He was small, wiry, of undetermined age, and extremely loyal to the Fergusons as they were to him and Burley. He came to the table, pulled out a chair and sat down.

"Mike," Sam shouted. "Bring Jim a whiskey or a beer. Bring him the whole damn barrel if he wants it."

Jim's bright, dark eyes met Burley's. They looked at each other and shook their heads as Mike made his way to the table. He stood close to Sam and spoke in low tones.

"Now, Sam, you know we can't serve Indians."

"Then don't serve the Indian part of him, damn you! Serve the Mexican part."

Jim got to his feet. "I got ta go see—"

"Sit!" Sam placed a heavy hand on his shoulder and shoved him down in the chair. He poured whiskey into a glass and set it down so hard in front of Jim that it splashed on the table. He glared at the bartender threateningly. "*I'm* serving him. You got something to say about it?"

"No. I don't reckon I do."

As Mike passed Burley on his way to the bar, he gave the older man a nudge. Burley got the message. If Sam caused trouble, Mike would call in the marshal. It wouldn't be the first night Sam had spent in jail. Burley remembered the time Sam had gotten in a fight with a town tough because of a remark the man made while they watched an Irish funeral procession pass. The man had said something about dirty mick. Almost as soon as the words left his mouth, they were followed by a few teeth, courtesy of Sam's rock-hard fist. The fight that erupted between the mourners and the bystanders resulted in broken windows, broken porch posts, broken noses, several broken arms, one broken leg and two runaway horses. Sam had had to dig up a hundred dollars to pay his share of the damage.

Burley filled a glass from the whiskey bottle and waited for Sam to look the other way. He set the glass in front of Sam, and Sam picked it up. The sooner Sam became so drunk that he was manageable, the sooner Burley and Jim would be able to get him to the hotel room, and maybe, just maybe, they would avoid trouble.

Elizabeth Caldwell wondered if she had taken leave of her senses when she left the security of her hotel room and ventured onto the street alone. She had seen quite a few new towns on the journey west, and Missoula was no more primitive than the others: a hodgepodge of painted and unpainted buildings strung out along a dusty street. Feeling more lonely and more frightened than she had felt in her life, she walked sedately down the boardwalk to the restaurant. The rigid training of her school years and the required behavior of the daughter of a socially prominent family forbade her to show her fear. She had to eat; her stomach had been complaining for hours.

At the restaurant she was served a huge slab of partially cooked meat, fried potatoes and onions, cold biscuits and bitter black coffee. The sight of blood from the meat on her plate had almost turned her stomach. After forcing herself to take a few bites of the potatoes and biscuit, she had placed her fork on the edge of her plate and taken a few sips of the coffee.

When the woman came to take away the dishes, she looked so concerned that Elizabeth had forced a smile.

"The long train trip, the smoke and all, has taken my appetite."

"It does that, dearie." The raw-boned woman clicked her tongue sympathetically. "But don't you fret none. In a day or two you'll be hungry as a bear. Just passin' through?"

"Yes."

The woman lingered, plainly curious. The sight of such a fancily dressed woman alone in Missoula was rare. The top of Elizabeth's high-necked gray suit fit perfectly over generous breasts and a waist that looked no wider than a man could stretch his two hands. A row of tightly spaced pearl buttons ran from neck to waist, where the bodice flared over curving hips. The soft kid gloves that lay on the table were decorated with a row of small pearl buttons, miniatures of those on the suit. The serving woman's eyes kept returning to the pink silk rose, nestled in a cluster of gray veiling, attached to the brim of Elizabeth's hat. It was the most beautiful thing she had ever seen.

"Waitin' fer the eastbound? It'll be comin' Saturday." When Elizabeth gave her a noncommittal smile, the woman said, "Well, you come back, hear? We'll have steak 'n' eggs 'n' biscuits in the mornin'."

"Thank you." Elizabeth took some money from her purse and placed it on the table. "Is this enough for the meal?"

"Yes, ma'am, it's aplenty."

Thinking about the supper as she hurried toward the

hotel, Elizabeth didn't think she would ever again be hungry enough to eat meat.

She was a woman of medium height, and she appeared to be perfectly confident as she ignored the stares of the passersby who turned to gawk at her. Dressed all in gray, from the soft, high-buttoned shoes to the felt hat that set on her high-piled dark curls, she looked as out of place as a rose in a patch of dandelions. Back straight, chin held high, she continued on her way, her skirt swaying gracefully as she walked.

It was almost dark. From inside a saloon she was passing she heard a woman's tinkling laughter, then crude, slurred words in a loud male voice. The woman laughed again, and Elizabeth felt the blood rush to her face. How could the woman laugh at that lewd suggestion?

Music from an out-of-tune piano drifted across the street. Light streamed from open double doors. Two couples were galloping around the plank floor while shouts of encouragement came from the men lined up at the bar.

Most of the porches in front of the businesses were lined with benches, which were occupied by an assortment of men of all ages and, by their attire, all occupations. Indians with long braids and black flat-crowned hats watched as she passed. There were drovers with spurs on their boots, and railroad workers wearing heavy work shoes. Elizabeth avoided looking directly at any of them, but some tipped their hats as she passed. It was all very frightening to Elizabeth—this newness, rawness, wildness.

She stepped off the boardwalk, crossed the dusty street and climbed the split-log steps to the porch of the hotel. A handsomely dressed man in a dark frock coat lifted his bowler hat. His eyes roamed her figure boldly, and when he smiled, white teeth showed beneath a trim black mustache. He moved to approach her, but she entered the hotel, quickly crossed the lobby and started up the steps.

On the first landing she stopped and looked back. The lobby was clear. The man had not followed her in. She sighed with relief as she slowly retraced her steps to the desk where a young man in a white shirt with a stiff celluloid collar and black sleeve bands stood watching her. As she approached, he lifted his palms and smoothed his already slicked-down hair. It was parted in the middle with a flat curl on each side of the part.

"I'm expecting my fiancé, Mr. Stephen Ferguson from Nora Springs. When he comes in, will you tell him I have arrived?"

"Your...fiancé? But, ma'am, he arrived this afternoon, shortly before you did." The clerk moved his finger along a line on the register. "S. Ferguson, Nora Springs, Montana."

"Oh, but that's wonderful! Did he ask if I was here?"

"No, ma'am. But this isn't the hotel the train passengers usually stay in. They stay in the one nearest the depot."

"The conductor said the Baltimore House was the nicest."

"It is. But most passengers want something cheaper."

"What room is Mr. Ferguson in?"

"Room 208."

"Thank you." Relief caused her to forget herself, and she allowed her shoulders to slump momentarily. She smiled at the young man and turned to go up the stairs.

"He went out."

Elizabeth paused. "He went out to dinner?"

"He went out this afternoon just after he arrived."

"Oh? When he comes in, please tell him that I'm here and that I'm anxious to see him."

The train conductor had recommended the hotel, saying it was the best in town. Even at that, it was lacking in the accommodations Elizabeth was used to having. She unlocked her door, leaving it open so that she could see to light the lamp in her room, then closed the door and locked it. She removed her gloves, pulled the hat pin from the crown of her hat, removed the hat, replaced the pin and set the hat in a hatbox. She was meticulous with her person and her possessions. Elizabeth patted her hair into shape with her fingers before she removed her suit jacket and hung it in the wardrobe.

The small number of bags, boxes and a small trunk was evidence of her hasty departure from Saint Louis. Glory! What had possessed her stepmother, Netta Caldwell, to act as she had? Stephen would understand why Elizabeth had come when he heard about Netta's latest scheme. Dear Stephen. Only two years older than she, he had grown up with her. Her father had considered Stephen the son he never had. Papa and Eleanor, two of the dearest people in the world to Elizabeth, were gone. Only Stephen remained. Knowing that he was in Missoula, Elizabeth no longer felt so alone.

Elizabeth pulled back the window curtain and looked at the street, searching for Stephen's familiar figure. He would be wearing his black bowler, and Charles would be with him.

Her attention was drawn to a building across and down the street from the hotel. A woman had come out onto an upper porch and was calling to someone on the street. The light from the window shone on her bright yellow sleeveless dress. She had yellow feathers or ribbons—Elizabeth couldn't tell which—in her hair. A man stood on the sidewalk with his hands on his hips and called something to the woman. She turned, bent over and flipped up the back of her dress before she flounced inside. The man on the walk laughed and slapped his thighs with his hands. He was joined by some other men. They all laughed and looked up at the empty porch.

This was a strange new world for Elizabeth. She had seen a side of life, during her trip, that she had not known existed. The people in the West seemed to enjoy life to the fullest. They took an uncommon interest in their fellow man. The serving woman at the restaurant was concerned because Elizabeth hadn't eaten her food. The conductor on the train found someone to take her and her bags to the hotel. In a way, they were as uninhibited as children. She thought of the cowboy on the train who had suddenly burst into song. No one had seemed to think it strange. He sang about "dogies" and "mavericks" and the girl he left behind him. The other passengers applauded, which encouraged him to sing song after song. Elizabeth had to admit she had enjoyed the diversion.

A half hour went by while Elizabeth watched the activity on the street. Finally she pulled up a chair and sat by the window. During the next hour only a few people came into the hotel, and none of them was Stephen or Charles. Finally her attention was drawn to a trio coming down the boardwalk. Two men were helping a third, who seemed to be very drunk. The drunk was a good head taller than his companions, and every so often he refused to take another step. Elizabeth giggled in spite of herself when the three staggered up the split log steps. Then the tall man backtracked and stood in the street laughing at the other two.

She looked up the street to where a crowd had come

out of a saloon. One man had been thrown into the street. Several men jumped on horses, fired their guns in the air and raced out of town. When she looked back, the drunk and his companions were not in sight.

Elizabeth heard people going down the narrow hallway, doors slamming and the low murmur of voices. She was tired. She looked longingly at the bed and suppressed a yawn. She couldn't imagine what Stephen would be doing at this time of night, unless he had found someone who enjoyed a game of chess as much as he did. When he was playing chess, time meant little to him.

She would write a note and slip it under his door. They could meet in the morning for breakfast, and she would tell him the news. The decision made, Elizabeth opened her small trunk and took out her writing materials. She wrote Dear Stephen, then paused and thought about him.

Stephen had been excited when he left Saint Louis. He was eager to meet the father and brother he hadn't seen for twenty-two years. Elizabeth had known Stephen for all that time, although she was too young to remember the first few years. She thought her father might have been in love with Eleanor Ferguson in his younger days. But she was sure that Eleanor had considered him a friend and nothing more. What had caused Eleanor to leave one son and bring the other home to her parents? Eleanor had refused to talk about that part of her life.

Stephen had taken Elizabeth to her first party and given her her first kiss, even if was a mere peck on the cheek on her sixteenth birthday. Heavens! That was almost ten years ago. Could she be twenty-five years old, going on twenty-six? No wonder Netta was anxious for her to marry and leave home. It made Netta seem older having a spinster stepdaughter living in the house. There was no one Elizabeth would rather marry than Stephen. She loved him, had always loved him. It wasn't the kind of passionate love she had read about in novels. It was a comfortable love. They understood each other, liked the same things, knew the same people.

"Oh, shoot! I'm so tired I'm thinking in circles," she muttered, and covered her mouth to hide another yawn.

After penning the note in neat script, she folded it, picked up her drawstring purse and unlocked the door. She went out, relocked the door, dropped the key in her purse and looped the strings over her arm as she went down the hall in search of room 208. She turned, went down a short hall and found the room on the right. The light in the hall shone on the brass numbers. As Elizabeth stooped to slip the note under the door, she heard a sound inside the room. She stood and listened. Had Stephen returned while she was writing the note? She heard another sound, crammed the note in her purse and gently rapped on the door.

No sound came from the room. She rapped harder. "Stephen?"

The door was suddenly flung open.

Elizabeth gasped and backed up a step. The man who stood there was…*shirtless*. He stood on legs that were not quite steady. His face had a growth of dark beard, his hair was in wild disorder and his shoulders seemed a yard wide.

"I beg…your…pardon," Elizabeth stammered. "I thought…this room—"

"S'all right, swee'heart—" He reached out, grasped her wrist and yanked her into the room. "Guess I'm drunker'n I thought. Don't remember tellin' Bertha ta send me a woman, but I sure am glad she did."

"Oh..." Elizabeth shrieked in fear and pain. Her arm had almost been yanked from her shoulder. A red tide of fear washed over her. She tried to jerk free of the hand holding her. "Let go!"

"What's your name, honey?" The man dragged her to the bed, sat down and jerked her onto his lap. "Hellfire! You're stiff as a board—"

"Help! Help!" Elizabeth shrieked, and hit him on the head with her purse. "Let go of me!"

"You wantin' to get right at it, hon? I don't know if I can, just yet. Let me kiss ya a little, then we'll..." His arms wrapped around her waist so tightly she could hardly breath.

"Help!"

"Gimme a kiss—"

"Help!"

"You're strong for a skinny woman. Stop wigglin'—"

"Help!"

"Hell, woman! You got on a corset!"

Elizabeth worked her arm free, and with strength brought on by desperation, jabbed him in the stomach with her elbow.

"You...beast!"

Abruptly the man stood, dumping Elizabeth off his lap and onto the floor. For a second she was stunned and lay there, looking up at the giant. He towered over her, holding his stomach with his two hands. Suddenly he reached for the bowl on the washstand and retched as she tried to scramble away. On her hands and knees, screeching her revulsion, she tried to crawl to the door, but the man took a step, and his booted foot was planted firmly on her skirt, pinning her to the floor.

"Dear God!" Elizabeth closed her eyes briefly. The

odor of vomit filled the room. Fear churned her stomach so that she was afraid she would swoon before she could get out. She tried to call for help again, but only a squeak came out of her tight throat.

The door was jerked open, and Elizabeth saw two booted feet take two steps into the room and stop. On her hands and knees, she looked up through the hair that tumbled over eyes that were blurred with tears of frustration, rage and fear.

"Help me!" she pleaded, and burst into loud sobs.

"Jehoshaphat! Sam! What the thunder are ya doin'?" Burley looked at the woman, then at Sam, bent over and holding his stomach.

"Get 'er out. I never called for a...woman—" Sam's stomach erupted again.

"Oh, dear God!" she wailed.

Burley stepped over Elizabeth and shoved Sam, onto the bed.

"Dammit, yore standin' on her dress. Lordy! Look what ya've done. Let me help ya up, miss. I ain't never seen him so drunk he couldn't hold it afore." Burley helped Elizabeth to her feet. "What'd ya come in here for anyhow? Who sent ya?"

"Nobody *sent* me!" She didn't understand what he was talking about. Then the meaning of his words hit her like a brick. *He actually thought that she was a whore!*

She had to get back to the safety of her room. In a sudden movement she darted for the door and ran into a man who stood there. This man's hair was black and hung to his shoulders. *He was an Indian!* She cowered and looked wildly for a way out.

"We ain't goin' to hurt ya none, miss." Burley didn't know who she was, but he was certain she wasn't who

Sam thought she was. "This's Sam's room, ain't it, Jim?"

"That's his saddlebags, ain't they?"

"Please...let me go—"

"Ma'am, we ain't keepin' ya. We're plumb sorry—"

"My purse! It's got my room key."

Elizabeth looked for her purse and saw it on the floor, where she had lost it when she fell. She looked helplessly at the short man with the sparse gray hair. She saw the concerned look on his wrinkled, weathered face. Then she looked at the big shirtless man sitting on the bed.

This was a nightmare. It had to be.

The bare-chested giant who had dragged her into the room sat with his head in his hands. The drunken, low-life, worthless creature had not even the decency to apologize.

Sudden anger washed away Elizabeth's fear and humiliation. How dare that vulgar man do this to her! She took the steps necessary to reach her purse and picked it up. Then she picked up the large crockery water pitcher from the washstand and carried it to the bed and calmly poured every last drop of water in it on the drunk's head. He sat there as if nothing was happening. He didn't move a muscle. Elizabeth glared at him, hating him, then threw the empty pitcher on the bed beside him.

Miss Elizabeth Caldwell of the Saint Louis Caldwells had never done such a thing in all her life, but then she had never been in such a situation before. With all the dignity she could muster, she turned to face the Indian and the short, gray-haired man.

"For what it's worth to you," she said with her chin in the air, "your drunken friend dragged me into this room when I rapped on the door, thinking it was my fiancé's room. I am not a loose woman to be insulted by the likes of...him! Room 208 is the number the clerk downstairs gave me. Now stand aside and let me pass or I'll scream my head off. Even in this uncivilized place there must be someone within hearing distance who has some decency."

"That clerk made a mistake, and that's sure, ma'am. This is Sam Ferguson's room. Ya can't be a blamin' him fer—"

"Sam Ferguson?"

"Yes'm. He's here to meet his brother's betrothed and take her to Nora Springs."

"What's his brother's...name?" Her voice sounded small and weak. She felt small and weak.

"Stephen. Stephen Ferguson, a fine—"

"No! Oh, no!"

"Do ya know him? Oh, Lordy—"

Elizabeth pushed past Jim and walked rapidly down the hallway.

"What's she in a snit for?" Jim asked.

"Whadda ya think, ya dunderhead? It's *her*! Stephen's woman. Go after her," Burley urged.

"You crazy?"

"Hellfire!" Burley ran after Elizabeth and caught up with her as she was fumbling to open her door. "Miss," he called. "Are ya...are ya Stephen's woman?"

"I'm Mr. Ferguson's fiancée." Her voice trembled with the effort not to scream at him.

"I'm shore sorry, miss—"

"You said that."

"Yeah, well... My name's Burley Owens. I been with Joe and Sam Ferguson since Sam was no bigger than a...well, I been with 'em a long time."

Elizabeth looked him straight in the eyes. "Why did

Stephen send that...inferior piece of humanity to meet me?''

"Piece a...what? Well...we was comin' ta pick up a saw blade 'n' he asked Sam to fetch ya 'n' carry ya back.''

"And that's all? Stephen is all right?''

"Right as rain!'' Burley said cheerfully. No sense in telling her that her man had been shot, Burley thought. Sam had already scared the life out of her.

"Mr. Owens, is Stephen aware that his brother is... that sort?''

"Sam ain't like *that* all the time.''

"Well, that's a relief. Regardless, I'll stay in Missoula until Stephen comes. Good night.''

"Ya can't do that, miss. Ah...'' *Bang.* The door slammed in his face. "Damn!'' Burley stomped down the hall to the stairs. "I'm too old fer this,'' he muttered. "Too damned old ta be messin' with drunks 'n' high-toned women.''

Chapter Three

"I did what? Stop mumbling, Burley."

"Ya nearly puked all over her."

"Don't shout." Sam gritted his teeth. "I thought you said I puked on someone."

"Almost—on Miss Caldwell."

"Damn! My head feels like someone was beating on it with a hammer."

"I wish they was," Burley muttered.

Sam stood at the washstand, splashing water on his face with his cupped hands. His head hurt, his mouth tasted like the bottom of a cave and his stomach lurched, but there was nothing more to come up.

"What the hell was she doin' in here?"

"Ya dragged her in. I'm guessin' ya thought she was a whore."

"Damn!"

"The clerk told her S. Ferguson was in this room. She thought it was Stephen."

"I didn't...hurt her?"

"She was on the floor. Ya was standin' on her dress, pukin' into that bowl."

"Oh, Lord!"

"She's the high-toniest woman I ever did see, but she's spunky. Afore she left she dumped the water pitcher on ya."

"I'm relieved to know that. I thought I'd wet the bed. Phew! This room stinks. What time is it?"

"Six."

"That late? Go tell somebody to shag their butt up here with some hot water. I've got to clean up. We're leavin' here in an hour. Knock on that woman's door and tell her to be ready. See that Jim brings the rig around."

"She said she warn't goin'. Said she'd wait for Stephen."

"She's goin' if I have to hog-tie her. Tell her that."

Sam began to dig clean clothes out of a carpetbag as soon as Burley was gone. *Puked right in front of his brother's future wife!* He didn't care about the woman, but he wondered what Stephen would think. The first and only thing his brother had ever asked him to do, and he had to go get drunk and make a fool of himself. What the hell happened? He never puked when he was drunk. The last thing he remembered was Burley and Jim helping him up the steps to the hotel porch. He had raised a lot of hell in this town, but this was the first time he'd drunk himself senseless.

Burley said the woman was really peeved. In a way he didn't blame her, and in another way he thought it was her own damn fault. He would apologize in time, but he'd be damned if he'd grovel at her feet. It would depend on her attitude. He didn't owe her anything. Hell, he was entitled to let off steam once in a while. She just happened to be in the wrong place at the wrong time.

Burley returned with a bucket of hot water.

"Did you tell her?"

"Yeah."

"Well...what did she say?"

"She said to tell ya that she wasn't goin' on the say-so that ya was Stephen's brother. She said that Stephen was a gentleman 'n' couldn't possibly be related to an *atrocious degenerate* such as ya be. What does them fancy words mean?"

"It means she doesn't like me much. Hell! I forgot the letter." Sam dug into the carpetbag again, found an envelope and held it out to Burley. "Take her this. Tell her to be downstairs in half an hour, or I'll be up to get her."

"Take it yoreself. I ain't yore delivery boy." Burley stood with his hands on his hips, his chin jutting stubbornly. He had not had much sleep, and he was in no mood to play nurse.

"Come on, Burley. I know I gave you and Jim a bad time and I'm sorry for it. I'm not making excuses, but things just piled upon me and I acted the ass."

Burley snatched the letter from Sam's hand. "Ya did, fer a fact. That woman's a nice woman. She don't have nothin' ta do with yore feelin' for yore ma. Ya best treat her right, or ya'll hear from me." He stomped off down the hall.

While he shaved, Sam thought about what Burley had said. His mother had been a high-toned woman who had everything she wanted until she married his pa. His pa had given her his all, worked his fingers to the bone, but it wasn't enough. It was a good thing Stephen had his business in Saint Louis to go back to. This woman wouldn't last out here as long as his mother had. Within a year she would be running back to the soft life in Saint Louis.

Sam dressed and packed his bag. He looked around

the room. Hell. He'd never left a room in such a mess before. Burley and Jim had cleaned up some of the mess, but there was plenty left. He would give the clerk an extra dollar for the cleaning woman when he paid his bill. Before he went out, he paused to look at himself in the mirror above the dresser. He assessed himself critically even though his head pounded so hard he could scarcely focus. He looked tired, and his eyes were bloodshot, but otherwise he looked his usual. He picked up his bag, closed the door gently and walked down the hallway, trying not to jar his head.

Elizabeth folded her nightdress and packed it in her trunk. She was wearing a maroon gabardine traveling suit and a soft pink blouse. Matching gloves lay on the bed beside a pink parasol and a small travel bag. Pink silk roses adorned the narrow brim of the maroon fedora that sat atop high-piled inky black curls. Elizabeth inspected herself carefully in the mirror. She was satisfied that the hat pin held her hat firmly in place and that she was neatly and properly dressed for travel.

Just before she was ready to leave the room, Elizabeth read for the third time the note Burley Owens had handed her.

My dearest Elizabeth,
This letter will introduce you to my brother, Samuel, whom I told you about before I left Saint Louis. At the present time, due to a slight accident to my shoulder, I am unable to come to Missoula to meet you. Samuel is coming to pick up a blade for his sawmill and will escort you to Nora Springs. He will see to your needs. You will be perfectly safe with him.

I am looking forward to seeing you and showing you this beautiful country. I trust you are well and that the long journey has not been too tiring.

Your devoted Stephen

Elizabeth wondered how well Stephen knew his brother. *Perfectly safe, my hind foot!* She snorted. She would be about as safe in a bed of rattlesnakes as she would be with him. Thank goodness she wasn't totally at his mercy. The little pistol in her travel bag might persuade him to behave like a gentleman and treat his brother's intended wife with respect. She would keep the bag close at hand. Stephen would not knowingly put her in danger, but obviously he did not know his degenerate brother very well. She felt the long hat pin in the crown of her hat and smiled. She had two means of protecting herself. If Samuel Ferguson as much as laid a hand on her arm, he would get something he would not soon forget.

Carrying her hatbox, travel bag and parasol, Elizabeth went to the hotel desk. The clerk was older and fatter than the one she had spoken to the night before.

"I'm Miss Caldwell, room 201. I'd like my trunk and two valises brought down."

"I get 'em."

Elizabeth had not noticed the Indian she had seen the night before in Samuel Ferguson's room until he spoke. Already he was taking the steps two at a time.

"Does he work here?" she asked.

"An Indian work here? Heaven forbid! This is a first-class hotel."

"Oh?" Elizabeth lifted her brows and gave the man a haughty stare.

"He's Sam Ferguson's man."

"What do I owe you?"

The clerk backed up a step or two and looked at her. "Mr. Ferguson paid for your room."

Elizabeth was shocked into silence by his words. Was that a smirk on his fat, pasty face? Damn and double damn! This stupid fool thought...thought...that she had...

Denying the anger that bubbled up in her, she kept her features calm and pleasant as she gave the clerk one of her sweetest smiles.

"How very nice of Mr. Ferguson." She placed the room key on the counter, went to the door and out onto the porch, muttering threats of torture and death to the louse, reprobate, blackguard—

"Ya say somethin' ta me, ma'am?" Burley jumped from the bench where he had been waiting.

"Good morning, Mr. Owens. Yes, I said that I'd like to break Mr. Ferguson's unwashed body and feed it to the buzzards." Elizabeth was shocked by her own words. What was this uncivilized country doing to her? "Do I have time to eat something before we leave? I don't wish to disrupt your schedule."

"Yes'm. Sam said feed ya. He ain't stoppin' till noon."

The street was almost deserted. A heavy freight wagon, filled to capacity and covered with a tied-down canvas, was on the street. The four mules hitched to it waited patiently. In front of the hotel was a light buggy with a red and white striped top edged with a fringe of red balls. The seat of the buggy was black, the base and footboard apple-green. Hitched to it was a big-footed sorrel that looked as if it could pull a locomotive. The whole outfit was disgustingly tacky, garishly ugly, the gaudiest rig Elizabeth had ever seen. She turned her back on it and handed her hatbox to Burley.

"Excuse me. I'll go have some breakfast."

Burley scratched his head and watched her as she made her way down the walk to the restaurant. She was the proudest, most high-flown woman he'd ever seen. He scratched his head again. He wasn't sure if she was just putting on airs, or if she was really the way she seemed. Was she going all the way to Nora Springs dressed like she was going to church or to wherever rich, grand women went when they got gussied up like a trussed-up turkey ready for Thanksgiving? Fiddle and be damned! 'Bout the first time they splashed across a creek, or she stepped out on a fresh cow pile, she was going to be fit to be tied. Pink gloves! Lordy! Pink roses on her hat! Fiddle! A pink parasol! Holy hell! Was this what they called civilization? Sam was going to laugh himself sick.

Sam was surprised that he could eat. After he downed two cups of strong black coffee, his stomach settled and he ate a plate of eggs and biscuits. With something in his stomach, his head eased and he was able to move it without groaning. He kept trying to think of what he had drunk last night. He had started out with good Irish whiskey. After that he'd had beer. He must have had a hell of a lot of both.

Sam was mopping his plate with his last biscuit when he heard one of the serving women hiss to the other.

"Psst! That's her. The one I told you about."

Sam looked over his shoulder to see who they were talking about.

"Ain't them the fanciest clothes you ever did see? She ain't got on nothin' she had on last night."

The woman who stood inside the door, waiting to see if she should seat herself or if someone would come to seat her, looked like a picture from *Godey's Lady's Book*.

"Last night it was gray gloves, shoes, everything. She's got a pink rose on this hat, but it ain't as big as the one on the gray hat."

Sam looked Miss Elizabeth Caldwell over as she pulled off her gloves, one finger at a time. He looked at *her*, not at the clothes that so impressed the serving women. Her hair was black and shiny and pulled to the top of her head. The skin on her face was porcelain white, making her eyebrows and lashes appear to be black as coal. Her eyes were the only beautiful feature on her face when he looked at each feature individually. Her eyes were green. God, they were green, large, tilted up at the corners. They gleamed from between rows of thick, dark lashes like new oak leaves in the spring. They were beautiful. When he looked at them, he didn't notice that her mouth was a trifle too wide, her nose a trifle too short, her chin tilted too high. *Elegant* was the way to describe her. Elegant and confident. So this was Miss Prissy-tail Caldwell, the one he had mistaken for a whore last night.

Head held high, looking neither left nor right, she passed Sam and went to a vacant table in the back of the room. He caught a whiff of sweet-smelling perfume that, for some reason, only added to his dislike of the fancy woman. He got to his feet as soon as she passed him, placed some coins on the table and hurried out.

Holy hell! Stephen had picked himself a straightlaced, stiff-necked prude of a woman who looked like a clotheshorse in a dressmaker's window. Stephen said she was two years younger than he was. That would make her twenty-five or twenty-six, long past the age when most women married. It was no wonder the grande dame was an old maid. She would put off any red-blooded man who came near her with that hoity-toity attitude of hers.

The devil inside Sam began to jab at his sense of humor with his tiny pitchfork. The prissy-tail woman thought he was a hellion. It wouldn't do to disappoint her, now, would it? It was time she knew a little of the hardships the women in this country endured—that is, those who had the guts to stick to their men. She would learn that out here people took each other at face value. She could put on all the airs she wanted to, but they wouldn't mean doodle-dee-da!

There was a chance, a slight one, that by the time they reached Nora Springs, she might unbend a little, settle down and act like a soft, honest-to-goodness woman. Sam grinned when he thought of what Jessie would think of her. Jessie was a woman to winter with, as the old-timers used to say. She was worth six of this prissy old maid.

When Sam saw the buggy and Jim strapping trunks and cases on the back, he laughed heartily.

"God almighty, Jim! Where did you get *that*?"

"Wagon shop." Jim continued to work at the straps.

"Is that all they had?"

"Nope. Storm surrey with three seats 'n' a funeral wagon. Ya said good springs 'n' a top." Jim finished tying a canvas over the luggage and stepped onto the walk.

"What did you do? Take parts from two buggies and put them together?"

"Purty, ain't it?"

Sam reached out and shook the frame. The buggy was sturdy and the springs were strong, even if it did look like a buggy the circus would use to carry the fat lady. Sam couldn't keep the grin off his face, and when he saw the heavy, big-footed horse, he laughed out loud again.

"You done good, Jim. Real good."

The Indian's usual stoic features creased with a smile. He reached out and flipped some of the red tassel balls with his forefinger.

Burley came from around the building, stopped and swore. "That's the gawdawfullest lookin' thin' I ever did see. That ain't no fit rig fer Miss Caldwell."

"I like it. Do you want to drive this morning or do you want Jim to do it?"

"I ain't drivin' that thin'!" Burley made a complete turnabout, went to the freight wagon and climbed the wheel to the seat.

"That leaves you, Jim. Burley will drive tomorrow."

"Not me!" The Indian tried to wiggle past Sam, but Sam dropped a heavy hand on his shoulder.

"Yes, you! I'm boss, remember?"

"You ain't that much boss." Jim ducked under Sam's arm and darted across the walk to the freight wagon. "You boss, you drive snotty woman."

"Cowards!"

Burley unwound the reins as soon as Jim was aboard, slapped them against the backs of the mules and yelled, "Hee yaw!" The heavy wagon with the saw blade and various other supplies for the mill pulled away, turned in the street and headed out of town.

"Cowards!" Sam yelled again.

Elizabeth took her time eating breakfast. The biscuits and honey were delicious. The eggs were another matter.

She had asked for soft eggs and was served eggs that resembled shoe leather. The coffee was freshly made, hot and strong. She sipped at it and dabbed at her mouth with her handkerchief. She had not been supplied with a napkin.

"I see ya et more this mornin'. Stomach not actin' up as much?"

The serving woman had edged over to the table after pouring another patron's coffee from a big graniteware pot. A rag was wrapped around the handle of the pot, and she rested the smoked bottom on the table.

"No. I feel fine. The honey is the best I've ever had, and the biscuits are delicious."

"I'm proud to know it. Made 'em myself." The woman flushed with pleasure. "Leavin' today?"

"Yes. Would it be possible for you to pack a few biscuits, buttered and spread with honey? I see you have apples. I'd like one of those, too."

"Why, shore, hon. Ya just sit right there and I'll fix ya up a bait to carry along with ya. Anythin' else I could fix ya to take?"

"No. That will be all."

Elizabeth had noticed the glances cast in her direction. Surely she wasn't the only stranger here. This was a railroad town, and strangers must stop here all the time. Maybe they were just curious because she was alone. As she waited for the woman to bring the biscuits, she thought about Samuel Ferguson. She would accept his apology—for Stephen's sake—if he had the decency to offer one. The two brothers had been raised at opposite ends of the earth, and that accounted for one brother being an uncouth hell raiser, the other a perfect gentleman.

After paying her bill, Elizabeth left the restaurant and walked leisurely down the walk toward the hotel. She was late, but after the way Samuel had treated her, he deserved to wait. The gaudy-looking rig was still parked in the street. Now, however, it had a saddle horse tied behind it. The porch of the hotel was empty. She paused. They would not dare go off and leave her. She took a few steps inside the hotel lobby. There was no sign of Mr. Owens or her luggage. She went back to the porch and looked up and down the walk, her brow wrinkled with concern.

"Hey, Liz!" The male voice came from somewhere close by. "Shake your butt, gal, we got miles to go."

Elizabeth turned toward the voice. A man leaned out of the buggy and looked at her. His hat was pulled low on his forehead. His knees were spread, his booted feet on the footboard. The cigar between his teeth was tilted upward.

"Were you speaking to me?" she asked with a lift of her brows.

"Ya don't see nobody else, do ya? C'mon, honey bunch, we ain't got all day. Shake your pretty little fanny, girl, and climb in."

Elizabeth took a deep, unsteady breath. She was incensed that he dared speak to her in such a crude, familiar manner, but she was determined not to give him the satisfaction of knowing he had offended her.

"And who are you?" she asked even though she knew he was Stephen's less than desirable brother. He was as disgustingly crude this morning as he had been last night. The brown eyes, lashes and brows and the shape of his face were like Stephen's. The hair was the same texture, only a shade lighter. His voice held the same deep tone as Stephen's. But he was *nothing* like Stephen.

"Samuel Ferguson at your service, ma'am." Sam saluted cockily and grinned around the cigar. "But we already met. Remember?"

"How could I possibly forget?" Her eyebrows rose. "Where is my luggage?"

"Tied on the back."

Elizabeth went to the back of the buggy and checked her luggage. Then she placed her traveling purse, the package from the restaurant and her parasol on the floorboard. Ignoring her, Sam looked down the street as if there was something that held his attention.

Lifting her skirt, Elizabeth placed her foot on the highstep and grasped the seat to pull herself into the buggy. She didn't make it on the first attempt. She tried again, and this time Sam reached for her arm and hauled her onto the seat with such force that she fell across his thighs. Her hat tilted over her ear when her head slammed into his chest.

"Now, now, Lizzie, babe. If you're wanting to ride on my lap, you'll have to wait until we get out of town. I got my reputation to think of." Sam held his cigar to the side and tapped off the ashes.

Elizabeth righted herself, knowing that her face was scarlet, hating it…and hating him. She moved as far as possible from him and repinned her hat. Sam sat hunched over, his knees spread so far apart that he took up two-thirds of the seat. He held the reins loosely in his hands.

"Ready, hon?" He looked at her, grinned, then turned and lifted the reins. The horse lifted her tail. "Yupsy! We'll have to wait for the old gal to do her business. Isn't that just like a woman?" he muttered as if to himself. "They always have to go at the wrong time." The horse held her tail high and big globs of solid waste came tumbling out while Sam took a couple of puffs on the cigar. "Didn't see any reason to scatter it down the street." A wide grin split his face as he looked at Elizabeth's flushed cheeks. He spoke to the horse in a confidential tone. "Finished, girl? Then let's go." He stung the mare on the rump with the whip. "Giddyap!"

The horse took off so suddenly that Elizabeth's head was jerked back. She grabbed the side of the seat to keep from tumbling out. The buggy sped down the middle of the main street, bumped across an intersection, careened around a corner and headed for open road.

The miles down the narrow green valley stretched before them, and in the distance jagged mountain peaks were muted by a soft purple haze. To Elizabeth, the mountains seemed a million miles away.

"Whee!" Sam shouted, and flicked the reins. The horse settled into a fast, lumbering pace. "Ain't this great, Lizzie? There's nothing like a good fast buggy ride to clear the head after a wild night of whiskey and fast women." He slapped her knee with the palm of his hand. "Right, Liz?"

They hit a rut in the road, and Elizabeth's head hit the side of the buggy. Her hat went askew again and tilted over her eyes. She gritted her teeth. For the first time in her life she muttered an obscenity, one she had heard used by a stable hand when he smashed his thumb.

I hate him! I hate him! When I get out of this buggy, I'm going to kill him!

Chapter Four

Sam kept the horse moving at a fast pace until they caught up with the freight wagon, moving up close. The dust stirred up by the wagon settled around them like a cloud. Sam appeared to be unaware, but Elizabeth, choking on the dust, loosened her hold on the side of the seat long enough to pull a handkerchief from the tight sleeve of her jacket and cover her nose so she could breathe.

The big horse pulling the buggy had begun to sweat. Sam was sure this plodding animal had not had a good run in months. His horse, tied behind, was not even winded. He glanced at the woman beside him. Sitting stiff as a board, looking straight ahead, she had not uttered a single word since they left town. He suspected that she was wearing one of those corset things women laced themselves into that cinched their waist and pushed their breasts up. He had seen pictures of them in the catalogs and wondered how the hell a woman could stand to be in such a contraption.

"Dust bothering you, Liz? Up ahead there's a place where we can go around. By whoopee damn! Here it is. Hold on, we'll give 'em our dust!" He flicked the mare's rump with the tip of the whip and swung around the freight wagon. "How about a race?" he yelled when he was even with the lumbering wagon.

"You crazy or somethin'?" Burley shouted angrily. He looked down, then gave his attention to holding the suddenly excited mules. The buggy pulled ahead and put distance between them. "Crazy half-sloshed clabberhead!" Burley yelled once he had the mules under control. "Ya ain't got the brains of a pissant. Yore actin' like a drunk hoot owl! If'n ya turn that buggy o'er 'n' hurt that thar woman, I'll take a whip ta yore butt!"

"Boss gone loco." Jim Two-Horses spoke matter-of-factly and hunched his shoulders in resignation.

"He's got a burr under his tail, that's certain," Burley grumbled.

Sam slowed the horse to a walk, turned and grinned at Elizabeth's set profile. She sat as still and as straight as a statue. Thick dark curls had come loose from the pins and now lay curled against her cheeks. She lifted a gloved hand and looped them over her ears. The wind had whipped some color into her cheeks.

"I've got to walk the old girl for a while or she'll give out on us."

Elizabeth turned a calm face toward him. "How far is it to Nora Springs?"

"Miles or days?"

"Either."

"Six or seven days."

"Is that all? I thought it would take longer." Proud of the unconcerned way she answered him, she stuffed the handkerchief in her sleeve, folded her hands in her lap and looked straight ahead toward the mountains.

Behind the calm facade her thoughts were filled with turmoil. Besides the physical torture, she didn't know how she would be able to endure the presence of this crude creature for six or seven days. How could Stephen have done this to her? She would have spent weeks or even months waiting for him in Missoula rather than spend six or seven days in the company of his brother.

Elizabeth moved slightly to tilt some of her weight to her left buttock. She had first noticed a sore spot when she sat on the hard chair at the restaurant. Even now, on the soft buggy seat, she felt some discomfort. Her corset strings may have come loose and the metal end worked into her drawers. Elizabeth had worn a corset every day since she was thirteen years old. She was absolutely certain that the whalebone stays had never dug into her flesh as they were doing now.

And she was hot. If not for this poor excuse of a man beside her, she would remove her gloves and suit jacket. She simply would not give him the pleasure of knowing how hot and miserable she was, or that the dread of the days ahead was settling like a rock inside her. On the train coming out, she had been told that it was cold in the mountains, that sometimes it snowed in late September. It certainly wasn't cold in the foothills. Elizabeth decided that she would bear up until they stopped, which surely they would have to do by midmorning in order to water and rest the horses.

They met two horsemen heading for town. Both men gaped in open-mouthed amazement as the buggy approached. They reined in their horses and gawked.

"Howdy." Sam lifted a hand in greeting.

"Howdy." The two men spoke in unison, then whooped with laughter after the buggy passed. "I ain't never seen nothin' like that in all my born days!"

The loud words drifted to Elizabeth. Embarrassment sent waves of heat to her already hot face. She had no doubt that Sam Ferguson had hired this gawdy rig to humiliate her. She glanced at him. He had removed his hat, revealing thick, light-brown hair that waved back from his forehead. The deep opening of his shirt showed hair darker than his mustache. His brows and lashes were dark and thick, and no shadow of a beard lay beneath his sun-browned skin. The thought came to her that he was not unpleasant to look at, but looks were only skin deep. Some of the most atrocious crimes had been committed by handsome men. After all, John Wilkes Booth had been a fine-looking man.

Sam pulled a gold watch from his pocket and pressed the top of the winding stem to flip open the lid. Could it be only a quarter till ten? It had been one of the longest two and a half hours of his life. An hour ago, when he failed to get a rise out of Miss Prissy-tail, he had given up trying. Now, lolling against the side of the seat, he had loosened the reins. The animal was used to pulling a buggy and stepped along at an even gait without being prodded. The buggy was so comfortable that Sam had almost forgotten how ridiculous it looked until he heard the remark.

Overhead a lone eagle soared, its screech audible in the midmorning silence. As Sam watched the magnificent bird, he envied its untamed freedom, its ability to fly, to go where it chose to go. The golden bird screamed again and plummeted from sight behind a dense stand of spruce, its talons outstretched as it prepared to scoop up its prey and carry it away for a feast.

For a split second Sam wanted to share the drama with his companion. He turned to see her looking at him with a haunting wariness in her wide green eyes. Then quickly her expression changed as if a shadow had suddenly crossed her face, leaving her finely sculpted features without any indication of what she was feeling or thinking. What a poker player she would make, Sam thought when she had turned away to give him a view of her profile once again. He forgot about the eagle, forgot about needling her as he watched her soft mouth compress into a taut line and her chin tilt a fraction higher because she knew he was looking at her.

If Sam had one redeeming quality, it was that he was exceedingly fair-minded. Damn! he thought, this can't be easy for her, either. He analyzed his actions, and decided he had played the fool because he was embarrassed about what had happened the night before. Seldom had he been so drunk that he didn't remember anything. He had to take Burley's word for it that he had grabbed her, dragged her into his room and... Damn it to hell! What would Stephen think when she told him?

Burley was right when he said it was not Miss Caldwell's fault that his mother had deserted him and his father. Why was it that he was compelled to blame her for something that had happened twenty-two years ago? Elizabeth Caldwell and Eleanor Ferguson were as alike as two peas in a pod, that was why. They were cut from the same cloth, his inner self told him. But, he reasoned, Elizabeth Prissy-tail Caldwell wasn't his problem; she was his brother's. His job was to get her to Nora Springs all in one piece, so to speak. With that in mind, he tried to think of something to say to her that would make the journey a little more pleasant.

"We'll stop soon. You can get out and rest awhile."

She nodded.

"There's a creek up ahead that comes right down out of the mountains. You can get a cool drink while we water the horses. We'll not stop again until noon."

She turned her cool, green eyes on him and nodded politely.

"The noon stop is halfway between Missoula and the first stage station, where we'll stop for the night."

Again she looked at him and nodded, then turned to look toward the mountains.

Hell! He wasn't good at carrying on a conversation with a woman, much less a one-sided conversation. His thoughts turned dark again. Prissy-tail, highfalutin old maid! She could sit there like a dummy in her tight corset with her mouth buttoned up like a miser's purse all the way to Nora Springs and it would suit him just fine. Even if she wasn't his brother's intended, she'd have nothing to fear from him. He liked women who were soft when they were supposed to be soft, attentive and amusing women who acted as if they enjoyed a man's company instead of looking down their hoity-toity noses at everything and everybody.

What was he up to now? Elizabeth wondered. If he thought for one minute that she'd be a friendly traveling companion, he was sadly mistaken. Uncomplaining, *yes*. Friendly, *no*. Definitely *no*, after the way he'd acted last night and this morning. His actions were a reflection of his character, and a person's character did not change in a matter of a half hour or so. She vowed silently that she would die of thirst, swelter in the heat or freeze to death before she would utter a single complaint. With that resolve firmly in mind, she shifted her weight slightly to ease her left buttock, which had gone numb, and winced when she put her weight on the sore spot.

Sam pulled off the main road onto a trail that led to a crop of aspen along a creek bank. The leaves were turning yellow. A birdcall rang clearly from across the creek, the shrill notes seeming to float on the crystal-clear air. Reflectively, Sam puckered his lips and imitated the call. Startled, Elizabeth looked at him and was surprised to see the intelligence and humor that gave depth to his coffee-colored eyes. His smile faded when she failed to respond.

Sam stopped the horse and without a word climbed down, walked up the creek and disappeared. Elizabeth sat in the buggy, not knowing what to do. She needed privacy, but didn't know how she was going to manage it. She saw the freight wagon pull in. The men climbed down, unhooked buckets from the side of the wagon and went to the creek for water. They returned and set a bucket in front of each mule.

Elizabeth removed her gloves, then her hat and jacket. The cool breeze felt wonderfully refreshing. She watched Sam approach. It was the first good look she had had of him. He was taller and heavier than Stephen, and he moved differently. His long body seemed to flow over the uneven ground, and one look at his sharp eyes gave testimony to his alert state. She wondered how often he used the gun that was strapped to his lean waist, if there was a woman who loved him, if he was a father of children...and if Stephen really knew him.

"Climb down, Liz. I scouted the creek bank. There's no Indians hiding in the bush to carry you off and no bears to eat you for dinner. If there were, you'd have nothing to worry about—bears are fond of sweets." He grinned wickedly. He had not intended to be brash, but the disapproving look on her face as she'd watched him approach had goaded him into it.

His words were no surprise to Elizabeth. They were what she had come to expect from him. It also was no surprise that he went to the back of the buggy and untied his horse without offering to help her down. She waited until he was leading the horse away before she carefully backed out of the buggy and eased herself to the ground. After waiting a minute or two for her legs to steady, she hooked her small travel bag over her arm and walked a distance along the creek bank before she paused and looked over her shoulder to see if she was out of sight.

Elizabeth looked around her. It was hard to believe that two weeks ago she'd been home in Saint Louis where she had only to walk down the hall from her room to use the water closet. Now she was traveling with strange men in the wilds of Montana, getting ready to squat in the bushes to relieve her aching bladder.

She lifted her skirt, feeling inside the split in her drawers to find the loose corset string she had been sitting on. Surprised to find there was no loose corset string, she searched her buttock with her forefinger and found a hard knot beneath the skin that was sore to the touch. She wondered if she had been bitten by a spider. Knowing that there was nothing she could do about it, she relieved herself, straightened her clothes and walked along the path.

Sam had taken the buggy to the creek so the horse could drink. Burley Owens came to her with a canteen of water.

"Drink, ma'am?"

"Yes, thank you. I have a cup in my travel bag." Elizabeth dug into the bag and brought out a small tin circle that telescoped into a drinking cup.

"Well, ain't that fancy," Burley exclaimed. "Are ya sure it won't leak?"

"I'm sure. Try it." She smiled at him while he filled the cup then drank the cool water gratefully. "I'll have more, if you don't mind."

"Any time ya want a drink, jist reach for the canteen. I'm leavin' it with ya."

Sam led the horse to the track leading to the road and handed the reins to Burley. Without a word, he mounted his horse and turned toward the road.

"It seems that Mr. Ferguson has washed his hands of me. I can drive, Mr. Owens, if you lead the way."

"I'd not hear of it! Let me help ya on up in there." He went around to the other side of the buggy, held out his hand and gently pulled her up. "Jist let me get my rifle. Dang young pup," he muttered as he walked away. "He ain't got no manners at all no more."

They reached the open road. Sam was riding slowly up ahead. For the first time since they left Missoula, Elizabeth relaxed and could appreciate the view of the mountains.

"How far away are they, Mr. Owens?"

"The mountains. 'Bout twenty miles. The goin'll slow down when we get there. Ever little bit we got to rest the mules on the uphill."

"Will we be there by night?"

"Yup. We stay at the stage station. Sam's got it mapped out where ya can spend the night. He don't plan for ya to have to sleep in the open."

"That's nice of him," she said dryly. "Do you know the nature of Stephen's injury, Mr. Owens?"

"Yup. Somebody shot him."

"Sh-shot him? Oh, my word!"

"It ain't nothin' to get in a lather over. Jessie and Amanda dug the bullet out 'n' are fussin' over him like a hen over a chick."

"Who are Jessie...and Amanda?"

"Well...Jessie is Amanda's girl. They run a boardin' house 'n' Jessie works for Joe some. Joe, that's Sam 'n' Steve's pa. Joe 'n' Sam got a sawmill 'n' lumber business. That Jessie is somethin'. Feisty as a cat on a hot stove. She got the reddest hair ya ever did see. Purely looks like a sunset.'' Burley grinned and spit tobacco juice over the side of the buggy. ''Anybody messes with Jessie's got Sam to reckon with, that's certain.''

''Is she his wife?''

''Wife? He ain't got no wife. But women's chasin' after him right along. Hell! He's always a gettin' pie, cake 'n' offers for washin' 'n' ironin' 'n' stuff like that. Jessie'd like ta be his woman, ta my way of thinkin'. I figger they'll marry up someday. She's growed up right under his nose 'n' thinks he's 'bout the grandest thin' ever hatched.''

''Poor, misguided girl,'' Elizabeth said softly, but Burley's sharp ears heard the words.

''She ain't poor. She 'n' her ma's doin' fine. Joe 'n' Sam see to it.''

''Who shot Stephen?''

''Don't know. Sam thinks 'twas somebody turned down for a job. Jessie had took Stephen to the loggin' camp to see Sam. Jessie got in a few shots.''

''Sam Ferguson is certainly nothing like Stephen.''

''I reckon not. About what happened last night. Sam carouses some when he comes ta town, but he ain't never been that drunk afore. Me 'n' Jim poured the drinks in ta him, so's ta get him outta the saloon afore all hell broke loose. He's ashamed of the pukin'. Course I don't reckon he's goin' ta say so.''

''Why not?''

''It's cause yore the same kind of a woman as his ma was.''

''He could not give me a higher compliment than to compare me with Eleanor Ferguson,'' Elizabeth said staunchly. ''She was a dear, sweet person.''

''Sam's hurtin'. Been hurtin' fer a long time. Him 'n' Joe went through a bad time after his ma left.''

If Burley thought to dredge up sympathy for Sam and

make excuses for his behavior, he failed. Elizabeth felt not one ounce of pity for the man riding ahead on the buckskin horse. The man was a bore, an uncouth bore, and the sooner she saw the last of him the better. She and Stephen would be married, leave this uncivilized place together and go to Saint Louis. Elizabeth was so caught up in her thoughts that she unconsciously shifted her weight to her right buttock and winced.

At noon they stopped beside another stream. Burley explained that water was plentiful in this country.

"In places there's too dang many rivers ta cross. Course, waterways is what loggers need. Ya just ort ta see them logs comin' down river ta the mill when the gate's lifted. Sam's the best log herder I ever did see. He'll dance over them buckin' logs, a pushing 'n' a bumpin' till he gets 'em sucked into the current 'n' on their way—"

"Sounds dangerous," Elizabeth said, because she felt she had to say something.

"'Tis. A man can slip away real fast on a rollin' log. Lose a few ever' year."

Not waiting for assistance, Elizabeth backed out of the buggy and reached for her jacket. It was surprising how fast the air had cooled.

"No bears, no Indians," Sam said softly as he rode past Elizabeth and looked down on the lustrous black swirls pinned atop her head. Without the silly hat she looked softer, more like a real woman. He wondered what she would do if he combed her hair with his fingers, scattered the pins and let the hair tumble around her face and down her back. He grinned. She would probably be outraged. Poor Stephen. Sam didn't envy Stephen marrying such a prude.

When Elizabeth returned from taking care of her bodily needs, Burley was staking out the mules and horses to munch on the grass, and the Indian was squatting over a small fire. A smoked coffeepot sat over the blaze. Elizabeth went to the buggy for the biscuits and apple she had brought from the restaurant.

Sam came from the creek, where he had dunked his head. He combed water out of his hair with his fingers, slammed his hat on the grass and squatted beside the fire.

"What are we eating?"

Jim handed him a hunk of bread with a piece of meat on it, and a tin of peaches.

"Is this all?" Sam glanced at Elizabeth, who was leaning against the buggy. "Ever had smoked possum, Liz?"

Jim snorted. "Ain't possum."

"What is it? Rattlesnake?" Sam's eyes, filled with a mischievous light, stayed on Elizabeth's carefully controlled features.

"Elk. You loco?"

"Tastes like rattlesnake to me," Sam said between mouthfuls. "Want to try it, Liz?"

"No, thank you." Elizabeth poured water from the canteen into her cup, carried it to a deadfall and sat. She opened the packet and took out one of the biscuits, determined to get it down, although she had never felt less like eating. She had a splitting headache and her bottom hurt.

Burley flipped back the top of the coffeepot to see if the coffee was boiling, then removed it from the fire and poured in water from a tin cup to settle the grounds. He waited a minute or two then poured coffee into a graniteware cup and carried it to Elizabeth.

"It's not the best, but it's hot 'n' it's strong."

"Thank you."

"Ever had camp-fire coffee, Liz?"

"Dang bust it, Sam. Yore pa didn't raise ya ta be disrespectful to women folk."

"What's the matter, Burley? Don't you want me to call her Liz? She's going to be family. After she hooks...after she and my brother are married, I can't be calling her Mrs. Ferguson, can I? I think Liz suits her."

"It's all right, Mr. Owens. Don't fuss. I'm used to being called Liz. My father had a brother who was a rotter, a drunken ne'er-do-well, an insensitive man who lived on other people's charity without a considerate thought for anyone. He called me Liz...too."

Burley failed to get the thrust of her remarks. He nodded agreeably and went to pick up the bread and meat Jim had laid out. Sam, however, understood exactly what she meant. He kept his eyes on her face. When she looked at him, he didn't look away, nor did she. Brown eyes and green ones did battle for several long seconds. Then she calmly looked away from him as if he was of no consequence. That, more than her words, infuriated him.

Sam ate and drank in silence. When he finished, he walked out of the clearing and was soon out of sight behind the thick growth of brush that grew along the creek bank. Jim put out the camp fire, then he and Burley hitched the mules to the freight wagon and the horse to the buggy.

Elizabeth was hoping that Burley wouldn't leave her at the mercy of Sam Ferguson. He didn't. He assisted her into the buggy and climbed in beside her. They led the freight wagon out of the clearing and onto the trail.

A half hour went by before Sam rode past and took up a position ahead of the buggy.

Chapter Five

It was twilight when they finally stopped. As soon as the sun went behind the mountains, the air became cool. Elizabeth was chilled to the bone. She had looked forward to a warm, cozy inn, and was keenly disappointed when Burley stopped the buggy in front of a long, low building made of logs and rough timber. It squatted along the roadside among tall pines as if it had grown there. Smoke rose from a stone chimney, but no light shone from the open door.

Sam was waiting for them. He stood beside the doorway with a heavily built bearded man in loose, baggy pants held up with wide suspenders. He was so short he had to tilt his head to look at Sam. When Sam motioned to Burley, the old man grumbled.

"Sit right here, ma'am, 'ppears that somethin' ain't quite up ta snuff."

Burley, then Jim, joined Sam and the other man. Sam stood with one shoulder against the building. Elizabeth waited impatiently in the buggy. She sensed that whatever they were talking about was important. Her anxiety goaded her to ask Burley when he came to help her down.

"Is something wrong?"

"Bridge is out up ahead. The stage won't be runnin' till it's fixed." ·

"Then we can't go on?"

"We'll go 'round. It'll take a mite longer is all."

Burley untied her luggage and set it on the ground. The bearded man, his hands on his hips, looked at the buggy then at Elizabeth. She suspected that behind the beard he was laughing, but she was so miserably cold she didn't care. She lifted her hatbox and fixed him with an icy stare.

"I would like a room for the night."

"Sam's already told me, ma'am. Sorry I am that my woman ain't here to meet ya. She went down to Missoula to visit her ma, thinkin' we'd have no lodgers till the stage run again. Come in. Come right on in."

Elizabeth followed him into the building, passing Sam without a glance. She waited beside the door while the innkeeper lit a lamp. The room he led her through, according to the tall counter along one side and several tables with chairs along the other, was used as a barroom. The floor was slabs of warped plank that made walking perilous for one used to smooth floors. The air was fouled by the odor of stale ale. They passed through a wide doorway and into a newer part of the building, which served as kitchen and dining room in one. The stove was shiny black, the long table scrubbed, the floor even. A delicious aroma came from a pot on the cook stove. This was a woman's domain.

They entered a short walkway and then stepped into a small room. The landlord placed a lamp on a shelf beside the door and flattened himself against the wall so Burley and Jim could bring in her luggage.

"Bed's clean, ma'am. My woman keeps the mattress

clear o' bedbugs with a regular dose of coal oil.'' He turned to follow Burley and Jim out, then turned back. ''I'll get ya a fresh bucket of water and rustle ya up some supper.''

''Thank you.''

Elizabeth waited for him to leave. She didn't know what she was going to do if there wasn't a chamber pot under the bed. As soon as the plank door closed, she lifted the patchwork quilt and there it was—a low, squat china pot with a tin lid. Relieved that she no longer had to worry about that, she looked around. The room was a ten-foot square. The window was shuttered and fastened on the inside with an iron clasp. The door had a bar to drop across.

Elizabeth gripped the end of the iron bedstead. It seemed to her that she had suddenly been transferred to another world. Wanting only to sink on the bed and rest, she set about doing what had to be done. She shook the dust from her jacket and put it away, brushed the dirt from her hat and placed it in the hatbox with the gray hat and a flower-decorated one she planned to wear at her wedding. From her trunk she took a washcloth, a towel and an ivory box that held a bar of scented soap.

The rap on the door and the innkeeper's voice came simultaneously.

''I got ya some water, ma'am. A bucket o' warm 'n' a pitcher o' cool spring water.''

Elizabeth opened the door and stood aside. The man carried the bucket and the pitcher to the washstand.

''Thank you.''

''Stew's on the stove, ma'am. It'll be ready when ya want some.''

Elizabeth nodded, closed the door and dropped the bar.

It was good to be alone, and it was heaven to take off her dusty clothes, remove the tight corset and wash in the warm water using the fragrant soap. She dried herself on a soft towel and dusted her body with fragrant powder. Then she pulled on a soft flannel gown with a high neck and long sleeves, relishing the warmth as it fell to her ankles. Sometime during the past half hour she had decided that she would rather do without eating than get dressed again. That decision was made before she heard the sound of running horses and loud male voices coming from the front of the building.

Elizabeth removed the pins from her hair. The heavy mass of dark curls fell to her shoulders and down her back to her waist. She massaged her scalp with her fingertips then picked up her brush. The long, even strokes through the cloud of thick dark hair were soothing. Curly hair, she had been told, was a blessing. At times like this, when it curled around her fingers as if it was alive, sprang up from her forehead, thick and lustrous, she thought it was. At other times, when she wanted to wear it slick and neat, it was a curse.

The sore spot on her bottom worried her. She had tried to see it in her hand mirror, but the angle was not right. It felt hard and hot to the touch. *Please, God, don't let it be a boil.* She had not had a boil in years, but she remembered the agony she had endured as a child when, one hot summer, one appeared beneath her arm.

Elizabeth lifted the bed covers and inspected the sheets. The landlord was right: the bedding was worn and mended, but it was perfectly clean. A wave of fatigue washed over her. She lay on her stomach on the bed. She heard the murmur of male voices and occasional loud laughter as if they came from a great distance.

A knock on the door jarred her out of near sleep. She slid off the bed and called, "Who is it?"

"Sam. Open the door."

"Ah...what do you want?"

"Open the door."

"I'm not dressed, Mr. Ferguson."

"Then dress, dammit. I'm not going to attack you."

"Just a moment." Elizabeth took a heavy wool robe from her trunk, slipped it on and belted it. Before she lifted the bar she looked to be sure she was completely covered. "Yes?"

Sam, shocked speechless, gazed at the pretty black-haired woman. This couldn't be the stiff-necked Miss Prissy-tail Caldwell who had sat so prim and proper beside him, who had compared him to her drunken, good-for-nothing uncle. She looked young, terribly young and defenseless, with her hair hanging over her shoulders, curling around her white face.

He watched her lift a hand to brush away a curl that was stuck to her cheek. Inquiring green eyes merged with inquiring brown ones. Was it fear or uncertainty that clouded her eyes? Whatever it was, it jerked at Sam's conscience, and he pulled his brows together into a frown. *My God!* He couldn't take his eyes off her. She was the epitome of all that was soft, sweet and feminine. The fragrant scent of her body drifted up to him. He felt something begin to coil in the pit of his stomach as the memory of his treatment of her came back to haunt him.

"Yes?" Her inquiring voice came from softly parted lips.

"I just wanted to tell you not to come out to supper. A bunch of rowdies rode in and are boozing it up in the barroom. It may be...unpleasant."

"I wasn't coming out."

"They were pretty well liquored up when they got here and the barkeep says they're a fighting, cussing bunch—"

"I wasn't coming out," she said again.

"I'll bring your supper. Burley's getting it ready."

"You don't need to. I've got a biscuit and an apple left from this morning."

"A biscuit and an apple? You've got to eat more than that," he said gruffly, then spun on his heel and walked away.

Elizabeth closed the door and leaned against it. *The pot was calling the kettle black.* The irony of it, she thought, laughing softly. One reprobate protecting her from other reprobates!

She could still see the surprised look on his face when she opened the door. Why had he stood gawking at her? She looked at herself again. She was completely covered; not a line of her body showed beneath the thick robe. He couldn't have been shocked by her lack of covering.

She *was* hungry, and she was grateful for this temporary respite of thoughtfulness on the part of Stephen's brother. Sam was handsome when he was behaving himself. He exuded strength and something that was primitive and...sexual. Lordy! Where in the world had that thought come from?

Abruptly Elizabeth sat on the bed and leaned over to take her weight off her buttock. With gentle fingers she felt for the sore spot on her bottom and wished the innkeeper's wife was here so Elizabeth could ask her for something to put on it.

Sudden boisterous laughter came from the front of the building, followed by a crash, thumps on the floor and yells from the innkeeper.

"Outside! Fight all ya want, but ya'll do it outside! Ya break up my place ya'll pay! Hear?"

This was a raw, violent land, and the men in it were even more raw and more violent. Elizabeth wondered if she would have left the security of home had she known what she was getting into. Yes, she decided, even this was better than what Netta had planned for her. She shuddered at the thought being held against Judge Thorpe's big belly and being touched by his pudgy, soft hands.

Elizabeth went to the door when she heard a thud near the bottom of the solid slab. "Yes?"

"It's me. Sam."

When she opened the door, he stood with a plate of food in one hand, a small pitcher of milk in the other. He smiled into her eyes. It was not the sarcastic grin she had seen so often today, but a friendly smile that crinkled his eyes and tilted his wide mouth. She returned the smile, admitting she had been more than correct about him being a handsome man.

"I had to kick the door since I have only two hands."

"Most people do."

"Haggerty's wife cooked before she left. Where do you want this?"

The heavy china plate he was holding was filled with small chunks of meat, potatoes and carrots all swimming in rich brown gravy. It looked and smelled delicious. She smiled into his eyes.

"It looks a lot better than what I had at the restaurant in Missoula." She stood back and swung the door open wide so he could angle his large frame through the doorway. "Over here on the bureau. It's the only place."

"I didn't bring a glass for the milk. I remembered you had that folding thing you used today." Sam set the plate and pitcher down, reached into his shirt pocket for a spoon and a three-tined fork and placed them beside the plate. "The coffee has been sitting on the back of the stove for a week. It tastes worse than boiled acorns."

"I'm glad you brought the milk. Thank you."

Sam went to the door, passing so close to her that his arm accidently brushed the robe she was wearing. In the confines of the small room, the air was filled with the scent of her—the sweet, woman scent of her. With his hand on the door, he looked back. Their eyes meshed. She seemed small, standing there...alone.

"You're the most polite woman I've ever known. What does it take to ruffle your feathers?"

She studied his face and realized that he looked amazingly like Stephen at this moment, yet different. The thought left her as the most incredible warmth washed over her. A sheltering warmth. With Stephen, a woman need never fear anything.

"Is being polite against the law out here?" she asked, scarcely realizing what she was saying.

"No. But that doesn't say much. There's not much that's against the law out here."

"I appreciate your bringing me the food. I wanted to rest more than I wanted to eat. I'm sure that I'll get used to the travel in a few days and not be so tired."

"It'll be a rough ride tomorrow. We've got to make a detour around the bridge that's out. Eat and get a good night's rest."

"Thank you. Good night."

As Sam turned to go, she started to close the door. His hand came out and stopped it. Their eyes met. Elizabeth couldn't look away from velvet eyes glowing with a mischievous light. He smiled, and creases appeared in his cheeks. *Why had she not noticed them before?*

"Let me give you a little advice, Liz. You'll be a lot more comfortable if you leave off that damn corset you wore today. No one out here gives a hoot in hell if your waist is two inches smaller, if your breasts are shoved up a little higher, or if your stomach sticks out a bit."

Sam pulled the door closed, but not before he saw her eyes widen with shock and a flush cover her cheeks.

He couldn't keep the grin off his face as he went through the walkway to the kitchen, climbed over the sturdy bench and sat at the trestle table where Burley and Jim were eating second and third helpings of stew.

"I ain't likin' that look on yore face one bit, ya young scutter," Burley said, making jabbing gestures at Sam with his spoon. "Ya done somethin' mean ta that woman, didn't ya?"

"No, I didn't, so don't get high behind, old man. I was very nice to the lady up to a point, then I told her a simple fact for her own good." Sam reached for the bread then dug his knife into the butter crock.

"Well," Burley had stopped eating, but Jim continued to eat as if he was going to be hung come morning and this was his last meal. "What'd ya say to her? Spit it out."

"I said—" Sam took a bite, deliberately chewed a long time and swallowed before he continued "—that she'd be more comfortable if she left off that bone-crushing contraption she laces herself in."

"God almighty, if ya ain't the limit! Ya ain't been talkin' ta that lady 'bout her…corset?"

"Why not? It's true."

"True or not," Burley sputtered, "it ain't yore place ta be sayin' it."

"Pass the salt."

"Yore brother'll think yore dumb as a stump."

"Pass the bread."

"But maybe she won't tell 'im."

"And the butter."

"That's a nice woman! Dad burn it! She's been raised up gentle like, 'n' ya got no business talkin' ta her 'bout her corset."

"I'll have more coffee."

"Hellfire! Ya ain't listenin'!"

"What are you getting all riled up for, Burley? Settle down. We've got more important things to discuss."

"Bridge didn't just fall down." Jim spoke.

"We know that." Burley gave Jim a disgusted look. "Haggerty thinks someone's got it in fer the stage line."

"We can go around this one, but I'm wondering how many more are out. What if the one is out up around Bitterroot?" Sam mused.

"It'll snow any day," Jim said.

"What'd you say?" Sam asked, turning concerned eyes on the Indian.

"Said it'd snow soon."

"Well, now, ain't that jist fine 'n' dandy," Burley exclaimed, taking what the Indian had said without question, knowing that if Jim said it would snow in the mountains, it was almost sure to snow. "It ain't goin' ta be easy getting that wagon up them mountain roads when they're slicker'n goose grease."

"Then we've got to make every hour count." Sam took a sip of coffee. "We'll start at dawn and go till dark."

"Ya mean forget 'bout stoppin' at the stage stations?"

"There won't be any stage stations if we leave the main road. You know that, Burley. We'll go as far as we can each day and camp."

"What 'bout Miss Caldwell?"

"What about her?"

"Good Lord! She can't camp out!"

"She'll have to. She can't stay here with Haggerty's wife gone."

"We can take her back to Missoula, is what we can do."

"Burley, you know as well as I do that we've got to get that blade to the mill. It's going to take twenty-four-hour shifts to complete that order as it is. I mean to disappoint that old bastard at the bank if he thinks we're not going to fill the contract and pay back the loan."

Two men came reeling into the room, laughing and pushing each other. They grabbed tin plates from the stove and filled them so full of stew it sloshed onto the table when they sat. They laughed as if it was a great joke and began to shovel quantities of food into their mouths. The one nearest Sam reached across him and speared the loaf of bread with his skinning knife without as much as a by-your-leave. Their clothing, hands and faces looked as if they had not seen soap and water for months. Neither man had bothered to remove his hat.

They slurped the food in silence, then refilled their plates before one of them spoke.

"Hey, Pete, did ya see that fancy buggy out back with them little red balls hangin' on it?"

"Yeah. Looks like a Injun's rig ta me."

Jim's spoon hesitated for a fraction of a second on its way to his mouth, then he continued to eat.

"Shore does. Injuns like them little red balls goin' flip-flop, flip-flop." The man who spoke stood, poked his knife into the butter crock and dragged it across the table toward him, grinning at Burley and Sam.

"That yore rig out there, Injun?" Pete asked.

"Don't reckon the Injun talks white man's talk," his friend said when Jim remained silent.

"I'm talkin' to ya, Injun. I ain't likin' ta be ignored by no blanket-ass," Pete said angrily.

"Don't get riled. Maybe he ain't hearin' ya. Maybe he's deaf as a stone."

"And maybe he ain't."

"Reckon we ort ta find out?" Pete's friend cupped his hands around his mouth, leaned toward Jim and yelled, "Boo!"

Pete laughed so hard, he spit food onto the table. "Ya scared the blanket-ass!"

Sam nonchalantly placed his palms on the edge of the table and pushed himself to his feet. He moved behind the men on the bench as if he was heading for the door.

"I ain't likin' ta be eatin' with no dirty redskin bast—"

An arm, roped with muscles, whipped around Pete's neck, choking off wind and words. Sam jerked the man's head back, knocking his hat onto his plate. Pete arched his back and clawed at the arm that, with a simple twist, could break his neck.

"When talking to my friend, you call him *Mister* Two-Horses." Sam spoke softly, pronounced each word clearly. "Do you hear me, or are you deaf as a stone? And...I don't care to eat at a table with dirty slobs who stink like they've been rooting with the hogs. Get out until we've finished."

As Sam loosened his arm, he fastened his other hand round the other man's wrist.

"Touch that knife and I'll break your arm and his neck," he said quietly. "Now get out."

"We paid to eat—"

"So did I. But I didn't pay to eat with hogs. I'll say it for the last time—get out."

The men got to their feet. The one Sam had nearly choked picked his hat out of the stew, glanced at it and shoved it on his head.

"Ya ain't heard the last o' this," he mumbled threateningly.

"If you want to take it further, I'm ready," Sam said, steely-voiced and calm. "I'll take on both of you at once, if that's the way you want it."

"C'mon, Pete. Don't make sense ta get kilt over a Injun."

The men stomped out.

"Them fellers is bad medicine." Burley slipped his six-shooter into its holster. He had been holding it beneath the table, and Jim had palmed his knife.

Sam shrugged. "All they've got is whiskey courage."

"Guess me 'n' Jim'll be sleeping in the barn with the freight wagon," Burley growled, as if it was Sam's fault.

"Where did you expect to sleep, old man?" Sam retorted as he straddled the bench, sat and reached for his coffee. "On a feather bed?"

"Don't be givin' me no sass, Sammy boy. It might be a spell since I boxed yore ears, but I can still do it."

A loud string of profanity came from the barroom, followed by a crash.

"Here now! Here now! Hell, boys! Stop it!"

Burley chuckled. "'Ppears like Haggerty's got his hands full tonight."

"Buffalo gun'd speak louder," Jim muttered. He got to his feet and walked silently out the back door.

"What do you have in the freight wagon in the way of blankets and camp supplies, Burley?"

"The usual. Not thin's for a woman like Miss Cald-well."

"What do you suggest I do with her? I sure as hell can't leave her here. I've got a hunch that our Miss Cald-well has got more grit than we're giving her credit for and that she'll make out just fine. She was worn out tonight, but did she complain?"

"Not to me," Burley said staunchly. "She jist barely made her legs hold her when she got down outta the buggy, but she didn't squawk 'bout it none at all."

Sam got up and stretched. "I'll get more blankets, another lantern and some coal oil from Haggerty in the morning. Damn! I hope Jim is wrong about the snow."

"Don't count on it. Get a canvas or two from Haggerty. The only ones we got cover the freight. Ya don't reckon Haggerty's got a tent, do ya?"

"I doubt it. If he did, it would be a ragtag thing. We can throw up a brush shelter for Steve's woman. This'll be something she can tell at tea parties when she gets back to Saint Louis. She'll tell how she roughed it in the wilds of Montana Territory with an Indian, a crusty old mountain goat and a handsome lumberjack."

"Which one's the goat?"

Sam grinned. For all his ribbing of Burley, Sam thought almost as much of him as he did his pa.

"I'll bed down out there in the walkway." Sam dropped a hand on Burley's shoulder and gave it an affectionate clasp. "We don't want anybody busting in on our Miss Caldwell, now, do we?"

Sam threw some blankets on the floor beside the door to Elizabeth's room. He was tired, but he didn't go to sleep immediately. He thought of the treacherous down-hill trail they would take tomorrow. He thought of Jim's prediction of snow and of a green-eyed woman who belonged to his brother.

Chapter Six

The rap on Elizabeth's door a half hour before dawn awakened her, and she rolled onto her back. A small cry escaped her lips at the unexpected pain. She turned onto her side and pushed herself out of bed as the rap came again, heavier this time.

"Are ya awake, ma'am?" It was the gravelly voice of Burley Owens.

"Yes. I'm awake."

"We be leavin' soon."

"How soon?"

"Soon's ya can get ready."

"All right. I'll hurry."

Shivering with cold, Elizabeth lit the lamp and blinked at the light. She used the chamber pot, then carefully felt for the sore spot on her buttock. She couldn't tell if it was any larger, but the slightest touch was painful. She dreaded to think that it was a boil. A knot of fear caught in the back of her throat, and she almost panicked at the thought of sitting in the buggy all day. She backed up to the bed and eased herself down, winced, then shifted her weight to her left buttock. Cautiously she crossed her right leg over her left, testing to see if it would lift the pressure off the sore spot. It did.

But it was not proper for ladies to cross their legs except at the ankles. How many times had she heard that? *Proper,* be damned! Her main concern was just getting through this day.

She allowed herself a moment of self-pity, then washed her face in the cold water and dressed quickly. The night before she had laid out the clothes she would wear today. She had chosen a heavy black skirt, stockings and high-lace shoes, a white blouse and a light hiplength coat.

At the last minute she put her corset into the trunk, not because Sam Ferguson had suggested it, she told herself, but so she could bend sideways at the waist. He wouldn't know if she had worn it or not. The waistband on her skirt was a bit snug, but the loose coat would cover it. She pulled her hair to the top of her head and pinned it securely. Then she put a few things she would need during the day, including a long scarf, in her small travel bag and closed the trunk.

Sam was coming down the walkway when she opened the door. In the dim light she could see that he wore a sheepskin vest over a flannel shirt. Forcing herself to stand and face him, Elizabeth could feel the heat that rushed to her face at the thought of his parting words the night before. Sam, however, seemed not to be in the least embarrassed. Rather he was cheerful.

"Morning. Sleep well?"

"Yes, thank you."

"Go on out to the kitchen and eat. Burley is there. I'll load your things."

The kitchen, when she reached it, was warm compared to the room in which she had slept.

"Morning, Mr. Owens."

"Morning, ma'am. Sit 'n' have a bite." He set a bowl of mush and a pitcher of milk on the table. "Coffee's fresh made."

"I think I'll stand. I'll be sitting all day."

Elizabeth smiled at the old man and poured milk on the hot mush. Sam came through the kitchen carrying her trunk. She looked up, and their eyes caught. When he hesitated, Elizabeth quickly lowered her eyes to the heavy trunk he carried so easily. Then she slowly raised them again. His eyes had not left her. A sudden smile arced the corners of his mouth. She thought he was going to speak, but his eyes shifted to the doorway when the innkeeper called to him.

"Here's the blankets, Sam."

"Bring them out and total up what I owe you."

"Mr. Ferguson—" Elizabeth opened her travel bag "—I'll pay for my lodging."

The dark eyes that caught hers were no longer friendly. They held a hint of contempt and bit of anger.

"The Montana Fergusons are not rich like the Saint Louis branch of the family, but we're not dirt poor, either. I think we can manage to pay for temporary quarters for a guest coming to visit, especially one that will not be staying long." The sneer in his voice angered her.

"Very well. But I'm sure Stephen will reimburse you."

"Oh, yes. I'm sure he'll try." His faint smile was as cold as his eyes.

Sam carried the trunk into the crisp, cold morning and strapped it to the back of the buggy. Haggerty had piled blankets on the buggy seat. Sam spread them out to sit on, leaving one on the floor to lay over Elizabeth's lap, then returned to the inn for the rest of her luggage. He didn't as much as glance at her when he passed through the kitchen. He returned with the valise and hatbox.

Dawn was lighting the eastern sky when Elizabeth came out of the inn. The freight wagon, with Jim on the seat, was waiting on the road. Sam's horse was tied behind the buggy.

"Let me help ya, ma'am." Burley came to take Elizabeth's arm.

"It's all right, Mr. Owens. I can get in by myself. I want to tie my scarf over my head. My, it's cold."

"Shore is." Burley watched her loop the scarf over her head and wrap the ends around her neck.

"Are you going to ride with me this morning?"

"No, ma'am. I'll ride with Jim and work the brake."

"Oh." The sound that came from her was low, but not low enough.

"Disappointed?" Sam asked from behind her. "Well, it can't be helped. You'll have to make do with what's at hand." He walked past them and went to speak with Jim.

Elizabeth pulled herself into the buggy, sat carefully and looked at Burley.

"Pay him no mind, lass. He's got a burr under his tail for certain. It'll take a day or two ta work it out."

"Don't worry, Mr. Owens. I can stand most anything...for a few days."

Later in the morning she was not so sure. She sat tilted on one side, holding the bar that supported the buggy top. Sam had climbed into the buggy and without a word had unfolded a blanket and covered her. She welcomed the warmth and the concealment, which allowed her to cross her legs. Even at that, when she did let her weight press on her buttock, the pain was so bad that she almost cried out.

Moving slowly, they followed the freight wagon down a rocky tree-lined track. The sky was overcast with gray clouds, the wind sharp. They reached a level, smooth path that allowed Elizabeth to free one of her hands and pull the blanket up to her chin. Suddenly the wagon ahead moved faster. The trail plunged sharply down a steep incline.

"That's why Burley's riding the freight. He knows when to brake and when not to." Sam spoke as if they had been carrying on a congenial conversation for the past two hours, when, in fact, not one word had been said.

"And you don't?" As soon as the words left her mouth, Elizabeth regretted saying them. It had not been her intention to belittle his ability, and she was relieved when he did not appear to be offended.

"I can, but Jim and Burley each know what the other will do in any given situation. They've been together a long time. This is a dangerous trail for a heavily loaded wagon, and I don't want to take any chances. Working together, they're the best drivers in the territory."

"Do they own a freight line?"

"They work for me and my father. In the summer they freight in supplies. In the winter they bring logs down to the mill on skids after the ground freezes."

"I suppose you've known them a long time."

"Burley was here in the territory when Pa first came. Jim showed up about fifteen years ago."

This was the most normal conversation she'd had with him, and Elizabeth wished to prolong it, but the only way was to ask questions. Because she didn't want him to think that she was prying, she remained quiet.

As the ground leveled off, the horse began to trot. Sam glanced over to see that Elizabeth, turned so her back was to him, was holding on with both hands. He immediately reined the horse to a slower gait.

"You needn't be afraid. She's not a runaway horse."

"I'm not afraid." She looked at him over her shoulder, her face white and strained.

"Then sit back and relax. Are you warm enough?"

"Yes, thank you." She turned her face away, but her gloved hands still clutched the rods that supported the buggy top.

Sam didn't know much about women, especially this kind of woman, but he knew enough to know that this one was miserable and doing her best not to let it show. He kept seeing her in his mind's eye as he had seen her last night with her hair around her shoulders. She'd looked young, alone and scared.

"Would you like a drink of water?" Sam reached for the canteen at his feet.

"No, thank you. I'm fine." Elizabeth turned to look at him and forced her lips to curl upward in a smile, but Sam was looking at her eyes. They were as bleak as a rainy sky.

Sam let the canteen fall to the floorboard. He felt an emotion he was afraid to acknowledge for fear it was admiration for the lady. She wasn't complaining, but she wasn't giving out any information about herself, either.

"Are you and Stephen going to wait until you get back to Saint Louis to be married?"

"I won't really know until I talk to him."

"Do you love him?"

The question came so unexpectedly that her head swiveled and her startled eyes met his.

"Of course. I've always loved Stephen. He's like a

bro—'' She cut off the word, not wanting this strange, wild man to know the feelings she had for his brother.

But Sam wouldn't let it go. ''Are you saying that you love him like a brother?''

''I'm saying I love Stephen Ferguson.''

''Are you *in* love with him? Wildly, passionately in love with him?''

''I'm saying I love him. And it's no business of yours how much or what kind,'' she said in a frigid tone.

''You're right about that. Are you looking forward to going to bed with him?''

''You are the most insensitive boor I have ever met! I don't see how you can possibly be Stephen's brother.''

Sam shrugged. ''How long have you been engaged?''

''Before my father died, he spoke to Stephen. That was a few years ago.''

''Why didn't you get married then? Lord! You're old enough to wed. Most women have three or four babies by the time they're your age.''

For endless seconds their eyes held. Hers had a green, glacial light, his were unperturbed. The reference to her age hurt. In Saint Louis she'd had to endure Netta's constant harping on the fact that at twenty-five she was still unmarried.

''You are unbelievably bad-mannered! I'm under no obligation to answer your rude question. However, I will. Stephen has been in the East. He returned only a few months ago, and we set our wedding date.''

''And you decided that you couldn't wait for him? Or were you afraid he'd not come back?''

''My reason for coming is between Stephen and me.''

''Why didn't you marry him and come with him in the first place? That would make more sense to me.''

"It is only proper that we should wait a reasonable time after his mother's passing."

"Ah...yes, dear Eleanor. Even after she's dead she's arranging people's lives." His voice was heavy with sarcasm, and Elizabeth's already strained temper flared hotly. Green eyes clashed with brown.

"Don't you dare speak of her in that tone of voice. She was like a mother to me."

"To you maybe," Sam sneered, "but not to me."

"You don't know how she grieved. My father told me—"

"Poor, grieving Eleanor. She left a brokenhearted husband and a child who couldn't understand what he had done to make his mother hate him so much that she'd go off and leave him. Years went by without a word from this poor grieving soul who chose a soft, easy life rather than honor her marriage vows. My heart bleeds for her."

"We never talked about it, but I know she didn't want to leave you—"

"Bullshit!" Sam yelled.

"Just...shut up!" Elizabeth shouted in a voice she hadn't used since she was a child. "You're a mean, vulgar man without an ounce of sensitivity. And...I don't even want to talk to you." She stared out the side of the buggy, surprised how good it had felt to yell at him even though tears of frustration blurred the trees they were passing.

"So Miss Prissy can get her little prissy tail over the line after all. It's nice to know you're human, Liz, and not one of those plaster dolls they dress up and stick in a dressmaker's window."

"Don't call me that!" Elizabeth turned and glared at him. "You don't know anything about me, and you have no right to judge me or my reason for coming here. I didn't ask to be your *guest*, and I will no longer endure your insults.''

Her face was filled with vulnerability, and tears made her eyes silver-green pools. Her mouth trembled, yet her voice was strong. Sam felt as if someone had kicked him in the stomach. Gutsy. He'd be damned, the woman was gutsy!

"No, I don't have the right to judge you. And I was rude and crude. I apologize...for everything.''

Elizabeth had turned her back to him. All he could see was the side of her face. A lone tear came from the corner of her eye and slowly slid down her cheek. That lone teardrop pierced Sam's heart like nothing had done in a long, long time. Suddenly he wanted her to understand what had been eating at him for so long.

"My problem is that I've had all this resentment bottled up inside me since I was ten years old. I thought I had learned to live with it. But the sight of you, the kind of woman you are, brought out a flood of unwanted memories," he said, speaking to her, to himself. He took a deep breath and slowly exhaled. "You...remind me too much of *her*. I resented her intrusion my life, in my thoughts, and took my resentment out on you. I'm...sorry." It was a blanket apology, covering everything, and as much of an apology as Sam had ever made in his entire life.

"I...accept your apology." Her soft voice trailed off to a whisper.

Sam's words tore at Elizabeth's heart. This big, angry man had offered her a glimpse of his soul, and she didn't know what to say to offer him comfort. Words and phrases came to mind. She discarded them in favor of silence. It was better to say nothing at all than to say the wrong thing and break this fragile thread of civility strung so suddenly between them.

Sam followed the freight wagon into a clearing beside the narrow track and stopped. While he was busy setting the brake and looping the reins over the brake handle, Elizabeth dabbed at her eyes with the end of her scarf.

"Jim must have seen something up ahead and pulled over to let it pass," Sam said quietly. "I'll be right back."

He climbed down and checked his horse, which was still tied behind the buggy. He walked to the wagon, checked the ropes holding the canvas over the bed, then made his way to the front. Elizabeth watched as his steps took him out of sight. She felt she understood him a little better now. She thought of him as he must have been as a small boy, feeling hurt and rejected, grieving over a beloved mother who was still alive. Had she died, he could have put his grief behind him. Instead, he had protected himself the only way he knew how: by denying his love for her.

Elizabeth carefully uncrossed her legs, threw off the blanket and backed out of the buggy. Her legs were wobbly, and she held tightly to the buggy. It seemed to her that the soreness was not localized in one spot, but that the whole side of her bottom throbbed. She wanted to cry. Her only hope was that wherever they stayed tonight there would be a woman she could confide in, one who would help her with hot packs or a poultice that would bring the wretched thing to a head.

A big wagon pulled by three teams of mules had stopped up ahead. Sam was talking to the driver, bracing his tall frame on spread legs, his hands in the back pockets of his britches. The gun that lay against his thigh was like a part of his clothing. Elizabeth had never met a more masculine man than Sam Ferguson. It was men like Sam who had settled this vast country beyond the Mississippi.

The horse tied behind the wagon whinnied, bringing Elizabeth's head around. Two riders were approaching, both rough-looking men. She looked toward Sam. He and the driver of the other wagon had moved out of sight.

The riders came to within a few feet of her before they stopped their horses. Elizabeth had never seen two more unsavory characters in her life. The one closest to her was a grossly fat man, wearing dirty, shapeless clothing and a greasy leather hat. A crooked nose that shone red at the end sat askew on his unshaven face.

"Ain't that the fancy buggy we saw back at Haggerty's?"

The other man had a black patch over one eye. The other eye was bloodshot. He spat brown tobacco juice from thick, slobbering lips that wore a lustful leer as he eyed Elizabeth up and down.

"Can't be more'n one like that'n in the whole world." The fat man's voice was hoarse. "The old nag pullin' it ain't much, but that'n tied on behind is a horse 'n' a half. That yore horse, honey?"

Elizabeth could have answered, but she said nothing. Her throat was too dry to talk, and she was too busy trying to hide her fear behind a bland expression. She had the feeling that if she turned her back on them to look for Sam they would pounce on her.

"Cat's got her tongue, Vernon. I'm thinkin' she don't take ta ya. Maybe she'd take ta me." The one-eyed man grinned a snaggletoothed grin, and tobacco juice dribbled from the corner of his mouth. "You travelin' with that freighter, purty woman?"

Elizabeth lifted her chin and met his gaze silently.

"Mighty fine buggy. Be my pleasure ta ride in it with ya, ma'am." The fat man was eyeing her trunk and the boxes ties to the back of the buggy with a greedy glint in his eye.

"Do ya reckon she's with the Injun that was sleepin' in the buggy at Haggerty's?"

The fat man didn't answer. His eyes were on the tall man in the sheepskin vest running toward them.

"She's with me." Sam's voice came from somewhere behind Elizabeth. Seconds later she felt his hand on her shoulder and leaned into it gratefully.

For a moment the good eye of the one-eyed man shifted to his companion, as if waiting for a signal. The fat man settled back in the saddle, took off his hat and scratched his head.

"Jist offerin' help ta the lady," he said in a pious tone.

"The lady doesn't need or want your help," Sam replied in a cold, no-nonsense tone. "Move on."

The fat man slapped his hat on his head and nodded to Elizabeth. He moved past, his eyes never leaving her face. The one-eyed man followed. They rode around the two freight wagons and were out of sight.

"Where did they come from?" Sam asked.

"I don't know. I turned around, and there they were."

"They probably came down through the woods from that upper trail. Get in the buggy. I've a few things to say to Jim and Burley."

Elizabeth pulled herself into the buggy as soon as he left her. She quickly rolled the end of one blanket into a a cushion of sorts, and moving slowly, carefully, until she found the position that gave her the least discomfort, she sat. The mountain wind was bitingly cold. She shivered as she covered herself with another blanket, pulling it up to her shoulders.

The men on the freight wagon heading in the opposite direction tipped their hats as they passed. She acknowledged their greeting with a nod, then watched Sam lope toward the buggy. Burley's wagon had moved onto the trail by the time Sam released the brake and slapped the reins against the horse's back.

The buggy jarred across the ruts and onto the track. Elizabeth's hand pressed down on the seat between her and Sam to brace herself. Even at that, the pain was severe. She gritted her teeth and tried desperately to keep her mind off her misery.

It was autumn in the mountains, and the leaves were turning. The gusty wind blew golden yellow, dark crimson and mottled orange leaves at them. At any other time Elizabeth would have been excited about traveling through this wild, beautiful land and would have loved every mile. Now, she was sick with pain and worry. She scarcely heard Sam when he spoke to her.

"Another bridge is out up ahead."

"What does it mean...to us?" Elizabeth forced herself to speak.

"It means we'll have to take the long way around. Someone's making it impossible for the Northwest Stage Company to maintain a schedule. That's between the two of them, but when they tear up the bridges it hurts everyone in the territory."

"Why would anyone want to do that?"

"Any number of reasons. Wells Fargo, Overland Express or some other line may want this route. The easiest way to get it is to run Northwest out of business."

"That's underhanded."

"That's business. I've got to get that saw blade to

Nora Springs within the next seven days or Ferguson Lumber will not be able to honor a contract, and we may be in deep trouble.''

''And I'm holding you back.''

''No. Didn't Burley tell you? We're starting at dawn and stopping wherever we are when it's too dark to travel. Have you ever camped out?''

Elizabeth's heart stopped dead before it galloped so fast it made her breathless. She knew he was looking at her. She turned to meet his eyes and slowly shook her head.

''You'll not be able to say that this time tomorrow,'' he said with a chuckle. ''But don't worry. You'll be snug and warm. We'll throw up a shelter of sorts.''

A shelter of sorts? Elizabeth turned her face away in case disappointment and dread were mirrored there.

Chapter Seven

The day proved to be far worse than Elizabeth imagined it could be. By midafternoon they had crossed a deep gulley and the narrow trail slanted upward. She was in such misery she no longer cared if Sam thought her rude and unsociable. She turned on the side of her hip with her back to him, murmuring that she was tired, and pulled the blanket up to her chin. Tears filled her eyes, but she blinked them away in case they should bring sobs she could not hide. At times she wiped cold sweat from her forehead; at other times she was too warm, but the pain was continuous.

Late afternoon brought a cold wind. Sam had not spoken since she turned her back to him, and she was grateful. She tried not to indulge in self-pity, knowing it was a useless pastime. But occasionally a few if-only thoughts crowded her mind. If only Stephen had come for her she could have told him about this embarrassing predicament. If only his brother had been a kinder, gentler person. If only Sam didn't resent her, or rather resent the type of woman he thought she was.

Huddled beneath the blanket, Elizabeth gritted her teeth stubbornly and vowed that Sam Ferguson would not be delayed one hour, one minute, because of her. Surely somewhere in these mountains there was a woman who would help her apply hot packs and poultices. There was no doubt in her mind now that what she had was a severe boil, or even a carbuncle, which was a cluster of boils. She remembered the doctor ordering hot packs for the boil she had beneath her arm when she was a child. Later it had been lanced with a sharp knife.

She prayed they would come to a homestead soon. If a woman was there, Elizabeth would offer to pay for her help and for lodging until Stephen could come for her. Holding on to this small ray of hope, Elizabeth surrendered to her misery and tried to endure the constant jolting of the buggy. She had a blurred impression of going up one long slope, descending another and splashing over the bed of a creek.

Sam was uneasy. For the hundredth time he glanced at the woman huddled on the seat. She had said she was tired. He didn't doubt that, but instinctively he knew it was something more that had put the bleak, strained look on her face. At noon she had nibbled on the cold fried pie they had brought from Haggerty's, standing up all the while. She had refused the coffee Burley offered, excused herself and gone to the buggy. While they prepared to move out again, she had leaned against the buggy, looking in the direction they had come.

Sam wondered if she was homesick already, or afraid of going to this faraway, unknown place even if Stephen was waiting for her. But if she was afraid, she had a funny way of showing it. In fact, she had stood up well to the two scavengers who had so unexpectedly showed up beside the buggy.

Sam had known what they were the minute he saw them. They were hangovers from the old-time mountain men who had lived off the land fifty years ago. He had seen the fat man before. He was mean, but low-caliber. Sam didn't expect any trouble from the pair. They weren't the type to go up against three armed men. Nevertheless, he had told Jim and Burley what he knew about the fat man. He didn't usually range this far south. He was supposed to have a woman somewhere in the Salish Mountains.

The seldom-used trail they were on led northwestward, skirting Flathead Mountain where the pines grew thick and tall. Sam had been this way several years ago on horseback, but Burley and Jim had been over this trail with a wagon. He left it up to them to choose a campsite for the night.

In the deepening dusk the freight wagon left the narrow track and pulled into the woods. Sam followed, watching the careful way Jim maneuvered the wagon so the branches of the trees merely brushed the canvas covering the load. They stopped in a small clearing well back from the trail. Elizabeth had not stirred, and Sam decided she was asleep. He would not disturb her until a shelter had been built for her.

Elizabeth was so steeped in misery that she was scarcely aware when they turned off the main trail. She was grateful when Sam left her on the buggy seat without a word and began unhitching the horse. She eased herself down to lie on the seat and rested her head on her folded arm. The soft seat pressed pleasantly against her aching body. She drifted into drowsiness, then into a light sleep. Awakened by Sam's hand on her shoulder, she looked at the shadow that was his face.

"Elizabeth?"

"I had to come, Stephen. Netta wanted me to—" The daze of fatigue and pain slowly cleared. This man wasn't Stephen. It was his brother, Sam.

"Are you all right?"

"Oh, yes. I'm sorry. I was...dreaming—"

"Supper is ready."

"All right."

"Which one of your bags do you need?"

"Ah...my nightdress is in my trunk."

"I'll get it. Do you want me to help you down?"

"No, thank you. I'm fine." The words came out into the cold night air automatically, as if someone else was speaking them.

Sam looked at her for a long moment before he went around to the luggage platform. Elizabeth backed out of the buggy quickly but carefully, not wanting him to see her fumbling effort. With her feet on solid ground and her body shivering in the cold night air, she reached for the blanket and wrapped it around herself. Across from the buggy she could see the outline of the wagon, and in between the glow of a camp fire with shadowy figures moving around it. She was cold and terribly thirsty, but she needed to relieve herself before she could seek the warmth of the campfire.

"Behind the buggy and to your right is a good place... to be alone for a while."

Elizabeth swallowed hard as she looked into Sam's brown eyes. His gaze was as direct and intent as if her look was new to him. He scrutinized her every feature with the practiced care of an artist who was painting a portrait. The chilled wind had whisked a froth of hair across his forehead, softening the lines of his face. For a reason she couldn't begin to fathom, this big, rough man's reference to something as personal as bodily functions seemed perfectly normal.

"I looked around to make sure it was safe," he said with a gentleness that made her feel she had known him for as long as she had known Stephen.

"Thank you."

She watched him carry her trunk toward the camp fire, then made her way into the darkness behind the buggy. Slowly and painfully she did what was necessary. Then she returned to the buggy, wishing she did not have to join the men at the camp fire but knowing she must.

A lantern sat on a shelf let down from the side of the wagon. When she approached the circle of light, she could see Burley beside the fire spooning something from a black pot onto plates. A short distance away, Jim was piling pine boughs beneath a canvas that had been stretched between two saplings. Her trunk sat on the ground beside it.

"Come 'n' get it," Burley called.

Sam came out of the darkness with an arm full of ferny pine boughs and tossed them beneath the canvas. While Jim spread them out, Sam dug into the back of the freight wagon and pulled out a stack of blankets.

"Here ya be, ma'am." Burley picked up one of the plates he had filled. "'Tis the last of Haggerty's stew."

"Thank you." Elizabeth dropped the blanket onto her trunk and took the plate.

"Ya can sit right over here by the fire," Burley invited.

"I'll stand." She softened her words with a smile.

"Suit yoreself."

The last thing Elizabeth wanted to do was eat, but she didn't want to draw attention by not eating, so she ate.

Sam and Jim picked up their plates, moved to the edge of the circle of light and squatted on their heels.

Sam was somehow different in the mountains. She looked down on his dark head and wide shoulders, not seeing the cocky, devil-may-care scalawag, but an older, unpolished, but very capable version of Stephen.

She looked at the open-ended shelter Sam and the Indian had built for her. It crossed her mind that under different circumstances she might enjoy an adventure such as this. She had never been in the wilderness, never slept without a roof over her head. Her eyes passed slowly over Sam's face, then the Indian's stoic features and finally to the gray-bearded old man. It was strange, but she felt as safe here with Sam and his friends as if she was in her home in Saint Louis.

On the heels of that thought, the lonely howl of a wolf echoed from a distant mountain. Elizabeth's eyes went to Sam's. The spoon had stopped on its way to his mouth as he waited for her reaction. An answering howl came from farther away. She lowered her eyes to her plate and continued eating.

When she finished the stew, Elizabeth held her empty plate, not knowing what was expected of her. As he passed her, Sam reached for it.

"Feel better?"

"Yes, thank you."

Elizabeth went to the buggy for her small travel bag. While she was there, she drank from the canteen, then carried it with her to the camp fire. Sam was hanging a canvas over the open end of the shelter they had prepared for her.

"Would you like the lantern inside?" he asked.

"I won't need it. I'm awfully tired. If you'll excuse me—"

"You should be warm, but if not, yell and we'll dig out a buffalo robe." He moved her trunk into the shelter and held the canvas for her to enter.

"I'm sure I'll be fine. Good night. Good night, Mr. Owens, Mr. Two-Horses."

She heard the polite murmurs that came from behind her as she stooped to enter her makeshift bedroom. The boughs made a surprisingly soft bed, and the blankets were soft and new. On her knees she removed her coat and scarf, sank face down in the soft nest and pulled the warm blankets over her. *Alone at last.* How was she going to get through the night? She couldn't undress without turning over and sitting up. She couldn't even reach her feet to unlace her shoes.

Tears came. This time it was impossible to hold them back. The deluge wet the blanket beneath her cheek, but not a sound came from her trembling lips.

While Burley cleaned up after the meal, Sam checked on the horses and mules and filled the water barrel, carrying the water from a spring that trickled out of the rocky cliff. Jim disappeared as soon as he had finished eating. The Indian always found himself a place to rest away from the camp but close enough so that he could sleep with one eye closed and keep the other on the wagon. The three men had spent many nights together on the trail, and each knew what was expected of him.

When Sam finished his chores, he poured coffee into his cup and motioned to Burley. The old man followed him into the darkness beyond the buggy.

"Burley, I swear something's wrong with Miss Caldwell, but I can't put my finger on what it is."

"She et supper 'n' she's still thankin' ya all the time fer ever'thin'."

"That thank-you business has been drilled into her

since she was knee-high to a grasshopper. She'd do that even if she was dying.''

''She 'ppears a mite peaked. Did ya treat her nice today?''

''Yes, I treated her nice,'' Sam growled.

''I heard ya yellin'.''

''She yelled at me, too.''

''Stephen ain't goin' ta like it none at all when he hears how ya treated her back in Missoula.''

''Forget about that!''

''*She* ain't goin' to forget it.''

''Oh, go to bed. I should have known better than to mention it to you. You don't know any more about women than I do.''

''True.'' Burley spoke in a tone that said a *but* was coming. ''But I know 'bout Jessie. She'd not stand for ya pukin' around her.''

''Yeah.'' Sam grinned. ''She'd have taken a buggy whip to me.''

''After ya get this woman to Stephen, you better give Jess another look see. Jess is yore sort.''

''What do you mean, my sort?''

''Yore kind. Jess's life is here, same as yores.''

''Are you matchmaking again? Why don't you tend to your own business, old man?''

''Dang bust it! You 'n' Jess *is* my business. I ain't wantin' to see her heart busted in two. Miss Prissy-tail Caldwell ain't yore kind.''

''Why're you calling her that?''

''Why not? You've been doin' it.''

''Well, what's she got to do with it anyway?''

''Nothin'. I'm goin' to bed.''

''No, you're not! Not until you explain. Do you think I'd try to take my brother's woman?''

"No. I ain't saying that. I'm sayin' Jess's got her heart set on ya. It's the only dumb thin' she ever done. I'm goin' ta bed."

Sam let him go. Sometimes Burley got off on the wildest notions. Hell, Jessie was just a kid. He reckoned he loved her, but like a little sister. He had cleaned more than one man's clock for taking liberties with her. He supposed that in three or four years, if she hadn't found a man she wanted to marry, they might get together. By then she would have grown out of her tomboy ways and be ready to settle down, raise kids and take care of a man. By then the thought of going to bed with Jessie might not seem as...indecent as it did now.

Jessie was a child compared to Elizabeth. Although last night, with her hair down, Elizabeth had looked no older than Jessie. Sam cringed when he thought of the cruel words he had said to her about her age. A woman was touchy about her age, especially an unmarried woman. Hell, she was seven years younger than he was—and one of the spunkiest women he'd ever met, and that included Jessie.

Sam's mind flashed to when she had walked into the restaurant, and to her standing on the porch of the hotel, looking down her elegant nose at him while he was acting the fool. Something had happened to her since that time. Something that had partially taken the starch out of her but had not dimmed her pride, something she was determined to keep to herself.

Sam flopped over on his side. Hellfire! Why did he have to keep remembering her green eyes bright with wetness and that lone tear that had slid down her cheek?

The night finally ended. Elizabeth knew this because the birds were chirping in the trees overhead. She watched the light from the camp fire flicker on the canvas and heard the clang of the skillet and coffeepot being set on the fire grate. She had been warm in the nest of blankets, but it had been the longest, most painful night of her life. The pain in her buttock now extended down the back of her thigh and throbbed with every beat of her heart. She dreaded getting up, but more than that she dreaded the day ahead.

On her knees she tried to tidy her hair, but failing to do that, she draped the scarf over her head and wrapped the ends around her neck. With her warm breath fogging the cold, sharp air, she managed to get into her coat. Knowing she must, she lifted the corner of the canvas and stepped out into the still, dark morning.

"Mornin'." Burley was placing sliced meat in the skillet. "Cold, ain't it?"

"Yes, it is."

"Snowin' higher up, or goin' to."

When Elizabeth stooped to pull a blanket out so she could fold it, she let out a small grunt of pain. She caught her lower lip firmly between her teeth and began to fold the blanket just as Sam came out of the darkness.

"I'll put those on the buggy seat." He reached for the blanket. "On second thought, you'd better keep this one."

Sam flipped open the blanket and draped it around her. With the edges in his hands he held her captive while he looked into her face. The ravages of a sleepless night were evident in the dark smudges beneath her eyes, the hollow cheeks, the way she pressed her lips together to still the trembling. But most of all her misery was reflected in dull green eyes that looked into his and then away.

He scooped up the rest of the blankets and carried

them to the buggy. He returned and, with a quick jerk on the ropes, freed the canvases, rolled them, stored them in the back of the wagon and came back for her trunk.

Elizabeth watched, helpless to stop the events that would soon force her into the buggy. How was she going to sit in it all day? How was she going to sit at all? As soon as Sam and Jim came to the fire to eat, she went to the place behind the buggy where she had gone the night before. She blessed the split drawers that allowed her to relieve her aching bladder without squatting too low. At that, her legs trembled with the effort it took to support her, and she clenched her teeth to keep from crying out.

When she straightened, she cautiously cupped her hand over the painful lump and felt heat even through the material of her drawers and petticoat. The size of the boil frightened her. Now fears of fever and blood poisoning entered her thoughts, and she did her best to push them aside. She had to have help. Blinking her eyes rapidly to rid them of tears, she went to the camp fire and accepted the fried meat and biscuit Burley offered.

The mules were hitched to the heavy wagon, the horse to the buggy and Sam's horse was tied behind. Elizabeth waited until Sam was deep in conversation with Jim and Burley before she went to the buggy. She climbed up to the seat, carefully eased herself onto her left hip and braced her shoulder against the side of the buggy. After several grunts of pain, she managed to get into a position that would, at least, be bearable, and covered herself with the blanket. Her back would be to Sam, but it couldn't be helped. She searched her mind for a plausible reason, but none came to mind before she saw the wagon pulling out and him striding toward the buggy.

He appeared to be immune to the cold. He wore the flannel shirt with the sleeves rolled to expose his muscular forearms, the well-worn vest and a round-brimmed, flat-topped hat. Elizabeth admitted that he was the most masculine man she had ever known. An aura of power surrounded him, as if he was not afraid of anything or anybody. He was dangerously handsome. Her acquaintances in Saint Louis would be in a tizzy to meet such a man. To her, his masculinity and attractiveness were the barriers that made it impossible to confide in him. Those and his resentment of her because she reminded him of his mother.

If Sam wondered why she sat with her back to him, he kept his thoughts to himself. He flapped the reins against the horse, and they slowly left the clearing. Once they were out from beneath the trees, Elizabeth could see the sky. It was going to be another cloudy, windy day.

"Mr. Ferguson," Elizabeth said, and glanced at him over her shoulder. "Are there any people living along this road?"

"There was a family here a few years ago. But people come and go out here. I don't know if they are still there."

Elizabeth closed her eyes. *Oh, please, God, let them still be there.* She kept her eyes open, searching each side of the trail for signs of habitation.

They jarred across a rocky creek bed and went up a steep incline that passed through timber so thick she could see no more than twenty feet back from the trail. The light from the sky was shut off, making the trail dark and gloomy. The roadbed was so cushioned with pine needles that they couldn't hear the horse's hooves.

The quiet was awesome in the dark forest. There was not even a bird song to break the stillness.

Elizabeth welcomed the light when they came out onto a shelf that wound around and down a steep slope into a valley where the bushes grew thick. As the trail straightened, Elizabeth loosened her grip on the side of the buggy to pull the blanket closer around her. It had been hours since a word had passed between her and Sam. She was past caring if he thought her rude. The hip she was sitting on felt as if the bone was pushing through the flesh; the other hip felt as if it was on fire.

Sam was more puzzled than ever by Elizabeth's behavior. Once he had cleared his throat and had spoken her name. When she didn't answer, he had leaned over to see if she was sleeping. Her eyes were open and staring.

He was disturbed by Elizabeth's remoteness. The hardest part of the journey was still ahead. Was she losing her mind? The shout that broke into Sam's thoughts went right along with his thinking.

"Stop! Stop! Oh, please…stop!"

Sam pulled up on the reins. "Whoa, whoa!"

"Thank God!" Elizabeth threw off the blanket. "I see a house…and a wash pot and a clothesline."

Sam put his fingers to his lips and let out a shrill whistle. The freight wagon stopped. While he was winding the reins around the brake handle, Elizabeth climbed out of the buggy and hurried up the overgrown path to the house. Sam called for her to wait, but his call went unheeded.

Chapter Eight

Squatting low on the ground, the cabin was sturdily built of split logs and cobblestones. Weather and years had treated it cruelly, but recent repairs had been made—a new glass window had been installed, and the solid door was hung with black iron hinges, and a hinged iron hasp with a padlock was fastened to it. Smooth stones were laid flush with the ground before the door and a large one for a step.

Elizabeth knocked hard. "Hello! Hello!"

"Miss Caldwell! Good Lord! What in the world's gotten into you?" Sam said behind her.

"Hello!" She hit the door with her fist, making hardly any sound at all. "Lady, please...come to the door!"

"Why are you doing this?" Sam placed his hand on her shoulder in an attempt to turn her around. She resisted and slapped the door with the palms of her hands.

"Please, let her be here!"

"*Her!* What the hell?"

Elizabeth turned. Tears filled her eyes and streamed down her cheeks.

"I saw a...wash pot in the yard, and a...clothesline. A woman is here."

"There isn't anyone here. The door is locked." Sam's voice was low and patient, his eyes clouded with worry. *Had she lost her mind?* "Look at what's written here." He turned her to face the slab of white bark nailed to the wall beside the door. "It says, 'Gone to Helena. Back before snow I hope.' The people who live here have gone away."

"The woman didn't go," Elizabeth insisted, shaking her head. "She wouldn't have left the wash pot—"

"It's turned upside down so it won't fill with water, freeze and break."

"Nobody here." A whisper.

Sam had never heard two words uttered with more despair. Her face crumbled, her lips quivered, and her eyes, full of misery and defeat, looked into his. Suddenly the dam of her resistance broke; she buried her face in the crook of her arm, leaned against the door and burst into a storm of weeping. Fueled by disappointment and the misery of the past few days, the sobs gushed forth with a force impossible to hold back.

Sam was stunned. He couldn't equate this sobbing woman with the self-possessed one he had met in Missoula. He wanted to comfort her, but he didn't know what to do. He placed his hand on her heaving shoulder. She shrugged it off.

"Tell me what's wrong. I'll fix it if I can."

"You...can't—"

"I'd like to try." His hands were insistent on her shoulders.

She allowed him to turn her around, then came willingly into his arms. With her face against his flannel shirt, she continued to cry. He held her, stroking her back. The scarf had dropped from her head, and unruly black curls teased his chin. Over her head Sam saw Burley and Jim coming up the path to the house, puzzled looks on their faces. He waved them away and lowered his head to speak softly to the sobbing woman.

"You'll get cold standing here in the wind. Let's go back to the buggy."

"No. I...can't..."

Sam's mind spun crazily to his thought that perhaps she had lost her mind. "What do you mean, Elizabeth?"

"I can't r-ride...anymore."

"Why not? Are you sick?"

"I need a woman...to h-help me." The muffled words came from against his chest.

"There's no woman here. There isn't anyone here. Let's go back to the buggy."

"You don't understand. I can't...s-sit down!"

"Can't sit down?" Sam echoed stupidly, not really believing what he had heard.

"I've got a boil on...on m-my d-derriere." The dreaded words were out. Elizabeth turned her cheek to his chest and covered her face with her hands. Tears seeped between her fingers.

"Derriere? What is that?"

"M-my...b-bottom."

"Your sit-down place? Good Lord, woman! Why didn't you say something?"

She didn't answer, couldn't answer for the trembling that shook her. It started in her knees and worked upward. She would have collapsed if not for the arms holding her.

"Oh... I'm going to be s-sick—"

Sam turned her away from him just as she bent over. The contents of her stomach came gushing out. With his hands at her waist, he moved behind her to hold her. His thigh brushed against her.

"Oh... Please! Don't touch me—"

"I'm sorry! God, I'm sorry! Burley!" Sam shouted over his shoulder. "Bring a crowbar."

Elizabeth heaved and gagged. The spectacle she was making of herself made her sick to her soul, but there was nothing she could do but hang limply from Sam's arms.

"Ya ain't breakin' into this place?" Burley came up the path with Jim close behind him.

"That's exactly what we're doing. She's got to have a place to lie down."

"We can camp—"

"Pull the nails from the hasp. We'll put them back when we leave."

"Her pukin' serves ya right," Burley grumbled as he pulled the big nails from the door in such a way as not to bend them.

"Get the blankets, Jim. It'll be cold in there."

Elizabeth was shaking violently. Sam opened his vest and held her against him, trying to give her the warmth from his body. "You can lie down in a minute. Burley has just about got the door open." She was soft and trusting in his arms. An overwhelming feeling of tenderness filled Sam as he held her.

Elizabeth started to protest about delaying them, but Sam began to move with her, guiding her through the door and into the cabin.

"Lie down here on the bed." He spoke as if to a child. "The bed looks clean. Its even got a patchwork quilt on it. I'll cover you with the blankets while we get a fire going."

"I'm so ashamed! I'm...holding you back—"

"Don't worry about that. I'd help you get on the bed, but I'm afraid I'd hurt you."

"I can do it."

Elizabeth crawled onto the bed and lay face down, clenching her teeth to keep from moaning with pain. There was not a joint or a muscle in her body that didn't ache. The soft bed offered some relief for the aches, but none for the throbbing pain in her bottom. Not since she was a child had she been so helpless or forced into such a humiliating situation. The humiliation was almost as hard to endure as the pain.

Sam covered her with several layers of blankets and left her. Burley and Jim followed him outside.

"She can't sit down. She's got a boil on her bottom." Sam spoke almost as soon as he closed the door.

"Jehoshaphat!" Burley exclaimed. "No wonder she et standin' up. How bad is it?"

"She's feverish and sick. She thought there was a woman here when she saw the wash pot and the clothesline. She was too proud to tell us."

Burley scratched his head. "What are ya goin' ta do?"

"Me? Don't you mean what are *we* going to do?"

"No. I don't mean *we*," Burley said gruffly. "Ya know more 'bout women's bottoms than me or Jim. Yore the hell-raisin' Ferguson, ain't ya?"

"Damn you, Burley. This is no time for you to go stubborn on me."

"What ya goin' ta do?"

"The only thing I can do. Put a poultice on it and let it run its course. Hell! What else can I do?"

"Snow comin'." Jim's matter-of-fact statement was thrown in casually.

"We got ta get that blade ta Joe," Burley retorted with terse impatience.

"You don't have to tell me that," Sam said irritably.

"We'll have to know how bad the boil is before we decide if she can go on. If she can't, I'll have to stay with her and try to catch up. Take a look around and see what the homesteader left."

Sam opened the door and stepped into the cabin. Elizabeth had turned on her side. The green eyes came reluctantly to his, flickered with pain then with embarrassment.

"I th-thought you'd gone—"

Sam came to the side of the bed and knelt so she didn't have to look up. His face was only a few inches from hers when she looked into his eyes. They were a deeper brown than Stephen's, quick and brazen and tender all at once. He had just the suggestion of dark whiskers on his cheeks that, rather than making him look unkempt, emphasized his masculinity.

"You don't know the hell-raising side of the family very well if you think Sam Ferguson would go off and leave a pretty woman here all by herself." His teasing words were accompanied by a smile that dented his cheeks.

Elizabeth's large green eyes looked directly into his, stirring him in the most disturbing way. They transmitted a quietly confident knowledge that she knew his innermost thoughts and was aware that he was playing the fool again to cover his anxiety.

"I knew you'd not leave me by myself. I thought that you'd go on and Mr. Owens would stay with me."

"We've not decided yet what to do," he told her frankly. "If the boil is small and has already come to a head, we may be able to rig up a way for you to lie down in the buggy seat, and I'll lead the horse. We won't know until I see it." Her eyes were so raw with hurt and humiliation that he had to look away from them.

"This is embarrassing for both of us, but it's got to be done and there's no one else to do it. Will you be able to arrange your clothing so that I can see the boil?"

After a moment of silence, she whispered, "I'll try."

His hand closed, warm and reassuring, over her arm. "Trust me, Elizabeth. You needn't be afraid of me. I just want to deliver you safely to Stephen."

"I'm not afraid of you. I know that you don't like me much, and I'm holding you back—"

"As for not liking you—I think I'm just beginning to know you. And I don't blame you for not liking or trusting me. I wasn't putting my best foot forward back there in Missoula."

"I'm sorry to be such a bother."

"Out here in the West people help each other. If someone is sick, the neighbors come in to help. No one considers it a bother because it may be their turn next to need help." He got to his feet and backed away. "I'll start a fire in the cook stove and in the fireplace. It's cold in here. When it warms up a bit, I'll be back."

Elizabeth watched him fill the cook stove with kindling from the wood box and light a sheet of paper torn from a catalog with a match he took from his pocket. He hadn't sneered at her or been angry, as she had feared he would be.

He knelt to kindle a fire in the fireplace, and Elizabeth noted the spinning wheel at the end of the fireplace and the wool carders on the mantel alongside a ball of yarn with several sizes of wooden knitting needles stuck through it.

This one-room cabin was someone's home, Elizabeth thought, although it was scarcely larger than her bedroom in Saint Louis. It was neat and arranged to take advantage of the heat from the fireplace and the cook stove, one being on each side of the room. A single bunk was attached to the wall opposite the cook stove. The small square table was covered with a cloth, and a lamp sat in the middle of it. A long work counter, covered in front with a cloth curtain, stretched from the back door to the wood box beside the cook stove. Two hide chairs, a bench and a bureau were the only other furnishings in the cabin besides the double bed Elizabeth lay on.

"Do you need me to help you get out of your coat?" Sam stood at the end of the bedstead.

"No, thank you."

"I'll be back in a little while."

Elizabeth watched him walk across the room and let himself out the door, closing it behind him. She wondered how she was going to endure the humiliation of exposing herself to Sam Ferguson. Tears of self-pity flooded her eyes. She had no choice in the matter, she told herself sternly. The problem was how to do it and hold on to as much dignity as possible.

Slowly and painfully she removed her coat and pulled up her skirt and petticoat so that she could unfasten the waistband on her drawers. Never had she imagined having to do what she was doing—taking off her drawers to show a strange man her bottom. It was so unreal that she felt as if she was in another place and another time. With tears streaming down her cheeks, she tucked up her petticoat to bare the painfully swollen boil. She pulled the blanket over her legs and arranged her skirt so that only the inflamed area was exposed. Having done what she could, she tugged the corner of another blanket over her throbbing flesh, buried her face in her arms and waited.

"Feller cut a good bit of wood fer winter." Burley commented after he spit out a stream of tobacco juice.

"Got dry grass piled in the rafters of his shed."

Jim was carrying water to the team from the stream that ran along the edge of the woods. Sam noticed the homesteader had planned well. The lot where he kept his animals drained downhill, away from his water supply.

"That stream will freeze up soon. I wonder where he gets water then?"

"Hot springs is all over these parts. In the winter time ya can see them steamin'. Sam, I'm feelin' mighty bad about Miss Caldwell, but I'm thinkin' bout snow in Bitterroot 'n' Joe countin' on gettin' that blade in time ta stave off that hungry banker."

"I know it. I'm hoping that what she's got isn't as bad as she thinks it is, and we can rig up a way for her to travel. But if we can't, you and Jim will have to go on. She's been hurting something awful, or she'd never have broken down and told me."

"Womenfolk! Why in tarnation didn't she stay in town or at Haggerty's?"

"You know damn good and well she couldn't have stayed at Haggerty's without his wife being there. Maybe it wasn't bothering her much when we left Missoula."

"And maybe she was jist stubborn."

"I thought you liked her."

"She be all right as far as womenfolk go, I guess," Burley admitted grudgingly. "If'n ya ask me, they're all a parcel o' trouble."

"All but Jessie," Sam growled sarcastically. He turned and stomped away.

Somehow it didn't set easy with Sam to hear Burley criticize Elizabeth. Dammit! It wasn't her fault. She had held out as long as she could and hadn't let out a peep of a complaint. He remembered when Burley had a boil on his back. He had moaned and groaned and lapped up the attention Jessie and Amanda had so freely given him. He had lain about for a couple of weeks until Amanda caught on to his put-on and demanded that he take a bath. That had been the end of Burley's loafing around. Suddenly he was well enough to go back to work.

Sam rapped on the door before opening it slowly. "Is it all right if I come in?"

"Yes. Come in."

Sam hung his hat on the peg beside the door. The cabin had warmed up considerably. He shrugged out of his vest and hung it beside the hat. Knowing how embarrassing this was for her, and for him, he delayed going to the bed as long as possible. She lay on her stomach with her head in her arms. Sam didn't know what to do, so he knelt beside her and touched her arm.

"Elizabeth?"

She brought one of her arms down and pulled back a corner of blanket. Sam stood, bent over the bed and looked closely at the exposed flesh.

"God almighty!" he murmured.

The reddish-purple mound was the size of an egg, with red streaks fanning out on the soft white flesh of her buttock. As far as he could tell the boil was a solid lump without a sign that it was coming to a head. How she had endured riding in the buggy he would never know. He reached for the corner of the blanket, pulled it over her and knelt beside the bed again.

"You'll have no relief until it's brought to a head and lanced." Sam's voice was low, reflecting the tension gripping his body. He pushed her hair from her cheek with gentle fingers. "Did you hear me, Elizabeth?"

Drawing a deep breath, she whispered, "Yes." Slowly her hand moved toward his, then her fingers circled his thumb and held it tightly.

Sam realized with a jolt that he could barely breathe. She had reached out to him with a silent cry for help. A spasm of longing flicked across his face—a bittersweet yearning to fill the emptiness of his life, to have someone of his very own to love, to care for, to depend upon him for happiness and contentment just as he would depend on that sweet someone.

"We'll stay here," he said, rushing his speech in order to bring his thoughts into focus. "Burley and Jim will go on to Nora Springs. In case of a big snow up on Bitterroot, they'd have a time getting through with that heavy wagon. My father needs that saw blade or he stands a chance of losing the mill."

"I'm sorry. Truly, I am. I didn't intend to cause trouble for you."

"Don't say anything more about being sorry. I know you didn't want it to happen. But it did, and we've got to make the best of it. I'll go talk to Burley and Jim." Sam stood, then knelt again. "Elizabeth, you'll be safe here with me. You can bet that Burley wouldn't leave if he thought otherwise. He's straight as a string about womenfolk."

"I'm grateful to you, Sam. It never entered my mind to be afraid of you. Eleanor's son would never harm me."

At that his gut twisted, and he rose and headed out of the cabin.

An hour later Sam stood in front of the homestead and watched the freight wagon pull away. The buggy was in the lean-to beside the shed; the horses were in the pole corral. Elizabeth's trunk and boxes, Sam's saddlebags, a small valise, a lantern and extra blankets were just inside the door. Burley had sorted out foodstuff from the supplies on the wagon, also making sure Sam had ammunition for his rifle and handgun. While Burley was doing this, Jim vanished into the forest. When he returned, he put a lump of pine resin in Sam's hand.

"Melt with a little bit o' lard. Put on boil. Cut when white shows." Without another word, the Indian had climbed upon the wagon seat and sent the whip over the backs of the mules.

Sam looked at the resin. He had planned to put a raw-potato poultice on the boil. Burley had insisted that he use tobacco and had begrudgingly left a plug. Instinct told Sam the Indian knew best.

A cold wind whistled around the corner of the house, causing Sam to peer at the sky, dark and heavy with an impending storm. It depended on the temperature whether it would be rain or snow by night. In case of a heavy snow, he wondered how a citified woman would fare on a mountain trail. Don't borrow trouble, he told himself. At least they had a roof over their heads and plenty of food and wood to burn to keep them from freezing. He blessed the homesteader who had left his ax leaning against the wall behind the cook stove.

It was gloomy inside the cabin with light coming only from the small glass window. Sam put extra wood on the fire for warmth and also for light, wanting to conserve the fuel in the lamp. He filled the reservoir beside the stove and put the teakettle on to heat. He emptied a can of peaches into a bowl, washed out the can, added a small lump of lard and the resin and set it on the stove to melt. Every so often he glanced at Elizabeth. Believing she was sleeping, he moved quietly, storing the foodstuff on the counter and putting his extra ammunition on the bureau well away from the fire.

When he had done all he could until the resin melted, he stood at the end of the bed and looked at the woman lying there. What if he couldn't bring the boil to a head? What if she got blood poisoning? If it was a man lying there, he wouldn't have a doubt in his mind about what to do. But with a woman like Elizabeth who was new to the hardships of this country, who would have gone to a doctor in Saint Louis, who now had only him to take care of her...

The toes of her shoes were sticking out from beneath the blanket. Sam carefully folded back the cover and began to unlace the soft black leather shoes with the slender heels that flared at the bottom. He pulled off one shoe and held her slim foot in his hand for a moment before he unlaced the other one, pulled it off and covered her feet.

"Thank you," she murmured.

"I thought you were asleep."

"I dozed for a minute. Are they gone?"

"About a half hour ago. It's past noon. Are you hungry?"

"No. No, thank you."

"All right, we can eat later."

"Sam. Is is bad?"

"I won't lie to you. It's big and has to be brought to a head so I can lance it."

"How long do you think it will take?" She turned her head to look at him with anxious eyes.

"I don't know. I've got pine resin melting on the stove to use as a poultice." She looked scared, so damn scared, and she was trying not to show it. "I'm going out to chop some wood. I don't want to use up the homesteader's supply."

"Will you be gone a long time?"

"I'll be where I can keep my eye on the door, and I'll rap on it before I come in. Do you want me to bring your trunk over here and open it?"

"Yes, please."

Sam pulled the trunk close to the bed and lifted the lid. A scent of flowers wafted up to him. The scent was hauntingly familiar and brought back painful memories of his mother, young and pretty and sweet-smelling. Then, as though he was looking at a painting, his mother's face appeared in his head—the mother who had kissed him good night, the mother who'd rocked him...the mother who'd left him.

Without a word, Sam put on his sheepskin vest, picked up the ax and went out the door.

Chapter Nine

Elizabeth got off the bed as soon as the door closed behind Sam, glad for the chance to get out of the clothes she had worn for a day and a half. Surprised and a little frightened because of her weakness, she held on to the head of the bed until her dizziness passed. Then she shed her clothes as quickly as her aching limbs would allow.

The flannel gown felt wonderfully warm and comfortable, especially after she covered it with the thick, soft robe. She folded her clothes and underwear and put them in the trunk. She yearned for warm water to wash her face and hands and for a drink of water to rinse her mouth, but she had more pressing needs. It had been hours since she had relieved herself. She felt beneath the bed for the chamber pot, pulled it out and used it, not knowing when she would get the chance to empty it.

How her life had changed in just a few short weeks. Until two nights ago, the only man who had ever seen her in her nightclothes was her father, and that had been years ago. It seemed incredible that she was in an isolated cabin, totally dependent on a man she had known for less than a week.

Sam rapped on the door, cutting off her thoughts. She

had taken the pins out of her hair and was holding them in her mouth while she tied the heavy tresses at her nape with a ribbon.

"Come in."

She felt the cold draft on her bare feet when he opened the door. He went directly to the wall beside the cookstove and stacked the wood. The room seemed so much smaller with both of them standing.

"Before you get back into the bed, I'll spread one of our blankets on it. We have plenty." He spoke as if it was the most natural thing in the world to see her in her nightclothes with her hair hanging down her back.

"Mr. Ferguson? Is there a way I could clean my teeth and rinse my mouth?" She spoke to his back as he removed his vest and hung it on a peg beside the door.

"*Mr.* Ferguson." He turned and met her gaze with a chiding grin, although the tightness encasing his chest was destroying his breathing. "Are you going to call me that after you and Stephen are married?"

"I guess not."

"Come over here to the wash bench. Do you have something for your feet? There are splinters in this floor."

She stuck her feet in the slippers beside the bed and moved around to the heavy end posts that supported the frame. It seemed a mile to the wash bench. She turned her head, but Sam had seen the anguish in the green depths of her eyes.

"Are you all right?"

"Oh, yes," she said with forced lightness. "I'm just weak, and I forgot to get my toothbrush."

"Where is it?"

"You needn't bother."

"Where is it?"

"In a small ivory box in the tapestry valise."

Sam snapped open the valise, took out the box, then took her arm and held her firmly to his side. He was swamped by the most intense desire to take care of her. His response to her need of him was overpowering. He didn't try to analyze it or rationalize it. Instead he fought to stifle it. Feeling dangerously exposed, he left her at the bench and turned away, his hands curled into tight fists.

He spread one of the new blankets on the bed, then lit the lamp so he could see into the can of lard and resin.

"Do you have a clean cloth we could use to apply the poultice?" he asked.

"Yes, and towels, too."

"We'll need them."

"Why am I so weak all of a sudden?"

"You haven't eaten much for the past three days, and fever will make you weak."

"I don't know how to thank you for helping me, Sam."

"Then don't," he said curtly.

Sam's abrupt words washed over her like a bucket of cold water. With her head lowered so that she could watch each step she took, she went to the bed, determined not to ask any more of him than was absolutely necessary. Holding on to the bed with one hand, she rummaged in the trunk with the other and brought out a soft white tiered petticoat and several towels.

Sam watched her out of the corner of his eye as he stirred the resin. He wished he hadn't barked at her. But hell! He didn't want her thanks. He just wanted to understand why she aroused this fierce protectiveness in him. He should feel nothing but anger and contempt for her and her kind, but the feelings he was experiencing were far from that. His calm, rational mind told him that he was just feeling sorry for her. But Sam knew himself well enough to know that it was more than that. With that lone tear rolling down her cheek she had started getting under his skin. She struck a spark in him that had never before been touched.

Abruptly realizing that his thoughts were leading him toward treacherous ground, he attempted to eject her from his mind. He could not, no matter how strong the feeling he had for her, lose sight of two very important facts. She was a woman who was used to living in splendor, and she belonged to his brother.

Dammit to hell! Burley was right. She wasn't for him even if she didn't belong to Stephen. She'd not last out here any longer than Eleanor had. They were two of a kind!

"How large a cloth do you need?" She looked at Sam, her eyes tormented, her voice low.

"Not very big, but I'll need several."

"I have more if this isn't enough."

"It'll do."

He heard the creaking of the bed ropes when she crawled onto the bed. After a minute or so, he glanced at her to see that she was lying facedown and had covered herself with a blanket. Her face was buried in her arms. The swatch of thick dark curls lay on her back. He thought of how she had looked when she walked into the restaurant in Missoula, and he thought of how she looked now—pale, anxious and scared. There was a world of difference between that woman and this one.

Sam felt a pang of remorse for his sharp words and once again experienced feelings he dared not acknowledge. He swore silently, berating himself for being an unreasonable bastard. Hell! She'd had to swallow her pride, bare her bottom and accept help from a man she considered little more than a savage. This situation had to be a hell of a lot harder on her than it was on him. He picked up the white garment she had laid on the foot of the bed. It was soft and white and smelled like roses. He crushed it in his two hands, then took out his knife, made a slit in it and ripped off the bottom tier. Damn! The woman had punched a hole in his resistance, and it was becoming harder and harder to remain detached.

Elizabeth heard Sam ripping the petticoat and knew it wouldn't be long until he would be wanting to apply the poultice. The pain in her buttock was constant, unrelenting, but it would pass. The mortification of baring her bottom to this hostile man would be with her forever. While she arranged her gown and the blankets to cover every inch of her flesh except what he had to see, she wondered what she had done to deserve this humiliation, and what had caused the change in his attitude toward her.

"Here's the poultice. Do you want to see it?"

"No."

The muffled word was spoken as she hid her face in the bedding. She reached blindly behind her and moved the blanket as she had done earlier. The lump was larger than Sam remembered. A muscle twitched in his jaw as he saw it rearing up out of her white flesh. As gently as he could, he placed the resin-coated cloth over it, saw her flinch and cursed silently.

"Now we've got to put a hot, wet cloth over it, and a dry one to hold the heat in." His tone was low, and there was an impersonal quality to it. He was forced to move aside some of the covering, but he replaced it with the warm wet cloth and the towel. "That should take care of it for a while." He covered her with the blanket.

She had not moved or made a sound. Sam experienced a sudden flash of insight. This was an emotionally shattering experience for her as well as a painful one, even more than he had thought. He knelt beside her. This time she didn't reach out to him. She kept her face turned toward the wall.

"Did I hurt you?"

"You had to."

Sam could feel her withdrawing into herself, and suddenly it was important to him that she didn't shut him out. He stroked the hair from the side of her face with gentle fingertips. Willing her to look at him, he leaned forward and spoke in a low, urgent voice.

"Look at me, Elizabeth." He hadn't really expected her to, but she did. She turned her face toward him. Her green eyes were dry, but the soul-destroying look of utter despair he saw there caught him by surprise. "You're going to be all right."

"I know."

He tried to ignore the disturbing sensation her barely audible answer evoked in him.

"You need to eat something. How about a handful of raisins?" Not waiting for her to reply, he left her to return with a small bag. He pulled open the drawstring top and placed it on the bed. "Fresh from the store in Missoula. Raisins are a favorite of mine. Raisins and dried peaches and peanuts. We don't get many peanuts up here, but we have a lot of walnuts."

The only indication that she was listening to him was that her eyes clung to him almost desperately. Sam didn't think he could stand the tortured look in them any longer.

"Why don't you sleep for a while? I'll put some meat on to cook."

Moving around the cabin as quietly as possible, Sam found an iron pot turned upside down on a lower shelf. It was clean and had been greased to prevent rust. He blessed the homesteader's wife. This humble home was as neat and as clean as Amanda's rooming house in Nora Springs. He cut the meat in small pieces and put it on to cook, then filled the coffeepot and set it on to boil.

Elizabeth lay as before, except her hand was on the bag of raisins. Sam went to the bed to tell her that he was going out to see about the horses. Her eyes were closed. He moved quietly away and blew out the lamp.

Sam led the horses to the stream to drink, then to the shed, where he gave each a scoop of the oats from the bag Burley had left. He wasn't as restless as he'd thought he would be. It was almost pleasant knowing that meat was cooking on the stove and that a quiet evening with nothing to do but tend Elizabeth awaited him.

As he emerged from the shed, Sam's eyes fell on the small garden plot on the downhill side of the cabin. A row of ferny growth told him that there were still carrots in the ground. Telling himself that he would make it right with the homesteader, he pulled six long orange carrots and shook them free of clinging soil. A spattering of large, plump raindrops fell, causing him to look at a sky that had become increasingly dark. A bank of iron-gray clouds hovered on the northern horizon. Sam hurriedly stacked the rest of the wood he had cut beside the cabin door, took an armload and went inside just as the rain, driven by a gusty wind, pelted down.

Sam lit the lamp, then scraped the carrots and put them in the pot with the meat. He had learned to cook the first year he and his father were alone. At first neighbors had helped him prepare meals for himself and Joe. Later, when he had gone to school in Missoula, he had a room in the home of a spinster schoolteacher. Miss Margery Theiss had been a big influence in his life. She not only helped him with his studies so that he finished school in record time, but she also taught him to cook, wash his clothes, develop personal grooming habits, and most of all she had taught him cleanliness. Five years ago she had retired and had written to Sam that she was going East to be with her sister. Sam had made the trip to Missoula to see her off on the train.

An hour passed during which Sam drank two cups of coffee and cleaned his gun. He sat at the table. The cabin was tight; not a drop of the rain pounding on the roof came inside. Knowing that he must, Sam took a warm, wet cloth to the bed. Elizabeth's face was turned to the wall. He lifted the blanket and quickly exchanged the cool cloth for the warm one and covered her again.

"You don't make much noise." She turned her face toward him, lifted her hand and brushed the dark curls from her face.

He knelt so she didn't have to look at his knees. "I took off my boots. I was bringing in a ton of dirt, and I didn't want to have to clean it up."

"Makes sense."

"You'd better be hungry. I've got a pot of meat on the stove, and if you don't help me eat it, I'll be eating it for days."

"It smells delicious."

"Well, that's a relief." He smiled, and it spread charm all over his face. "Did you sleep?"

"A little."

"Did the rain awaken you?"

"I suppose it was the rain. You were certainly quiet. Will Mr. Owens and Mr. Two-Horses be all right?"

"Those two old mountain rats are used to all kinds of weather and are prepared for it. This little sprinkle will not bother them at all."

"I bet they're relieved to be rid of me."

"Their loss is my gain." He smiled into her eyes and suddenly, sincerely meant what he'd said. He wanted to keep her talking. He wanted to move his hand to cover hers, but he didn't dare.

A quick smile tilted her lips and brought a light to her eyes. "You're full of nonsense, Samuel Ferguson."

"Better that than whiskey," he said, then groaned, not wanting to remind her of what had happened in Missoula.

But it did remind her, and her smile spread so wide that it creased the corners of her eyes. "That's true."

His hand moved without his being aware of it and covered hers. He gripped it tightly.

"Elizabeth, I've never done such a rotten thing before in my life. I want you to know that I'm sorry. Pa raised me to be respectful of women."

"Even prissy-tail, citified women?" she asked, still smiling.

"Even prissy-tail, citified women." His smile answered hers until hers faded and a serious expression appeared in her eyes.

"I'd like to be your friend, Sam. I didn't come out here to disrupt your life or bring painful memories."

"I know that. You came to marry Stephen." Something like a chill settled around Sam's heart. His hand left hers, and he stood. Changing the subject abruptly, he said, "You're going to have a time trying to eat lying on your face."

"I'd turn on my side, but the poultice will fall."

"Not if I banked something against your...whatever it was you called it."

"My derriere? It's French."

"I'm not much good at fancy words. Let's just call it your sit-down place, shall we?"

"All right. I feel like an intruder using the things in this home without the owners' permission."

"They won't mind. It's done out here all the time. They'll appreciate the cash I'll leave. Cash money is hard for a homesteader to come by."

"They have so little, yet they've made this small cabin into a home," she said wistfully. Holding the poultice in place, Elizabeth turned slowly onto her side. Sam reached behind her and placed a pillow against her backside. "Is that better?"

"Yes, thank you."

"We'll change the poultice after supper and again in the night."

Elizabeth watched him as he went silently across the floor to the cookstove, lifted the lid on an iron pot and poked the meat with a long fork. She had never known a man who cooked until she saw Burley cooking over the camp fire. Sam seemed to be doing it as if it was something he was used to doing. His gray-stockinged feet were large like the rest of him. Tight britches, slung low on his narrow hips, showed sinewy strength in his hips and thighs and left no doubt as to his male endowment.

Sam Ferguson was a ruggedly handsome man. Her eyes fastened on the bulge at the joining of his muscular thighs. Her cheeks grew hot. Mercy! Had she lost her mind, staring at him *there*? She looked away quickly, but her wayward eyes returned to him again and again.

His face and neck were bronzed by the sun and weather. Thick brown hair grew low on the nape of his neck. Shoulders that had seemed broad in the buggy were even broader in the close confines of the cabin and were suited to his wide chest and slim waist, which carried not an extra ounce of surplus flesh.

Sam was nothing but a virile male, yet he was doing feminine things, cooking and tending her as if it came naturally to him. He was all muscle and masculine strength, gentle at times, hard at other times such as when he'd dealt with the fat man and his friend. He was a man well suited to this rough land.

The sight of him standing shirtless in the doorway of the room in Missoula flashed through Elizabeth's mind. The soft hair on his chest had been only slightly darker than the hair on his head, but not as dark as the hair on his upper lip. Was there a streak of vanity in him that caused him to keep the mustache so neatly trimmed? Or did he do it because the woman, Jessie, liked it? Another thought crowded unbidden into her mind. *What would it feel like to be kissed by a man like Sam?*

Elizabeth moistened lips that had gone suddenly dry. She felt like a schoolgirl who had become aware of the opposite sex for the first time. Surprised by her thoughts, she blamed them on curiosity. She had never been kissed on the lips the way it was done in some of the novels she had read. Stephen always gave her a peck on the cheek. One time it landed on the corner of her mouth. He had looked apologetic and hurried away.

Outside the rain continued to fall, but inside the cabin was warm and cozy. Elizabeth wondered about the two men and the freight wagon. She couldn't imagine, even without the painful boil, sleeping outside in such weather. When Sam brought a plate of food to her, she voiced her concern.

"Mr. Owens can't even build a fire in this weather. What will they do?"

"As soon as they were sure it was going to rain, they picked up wood and put it under the tarp. They'll have a fire and a hot meal tonight." Sam was surprised that she was concerned about them.

"Where will they sleep?"

"Under the wagon. They'll hang a canvas on the wind side, put an oilskin on the wet ground and their blankets on top of that."

"Is that sleet hitting the window?"

"It sounds like it. Temperature must have dropped. Would you like a cup of coffee?"

"No, thank you. I'd like a glass of water."

"Are you hot?"

"A little."

"That robe you're wearing looks as if it would keep you warm in a blizzard."

"It's made of angora wool."

"Hmm—goat or rabbit?"

"I don't know." She thought to tell him that her father had bought it for her in Scotland, but she didn't for fear he would think she was flaunting her wealth.

Sam ate at the table. He sat on the side facing her, and every so often Elizabeth looked up and found him watching her. She ate without appetite, forcing herself, knowing that she needed the strength and that it would be impolite not to eat the meal he had brought to her.

"It was very good," she said when he came to take her empty plate.

"Now *you're* full of nonsense, Miss Caldwell," he teased. "It was eatable, and that's all." He dumped the plates into a pan, sat and pulled on his boots. "I think I'll go out to see about the horses. If you should get up while I'm gone, leave off the poultice. I'll make another one when I come in." He put on his vest and pulled a poncho slicker out of his saddlebag. Without looking at her, he slipped it on over his head, put on his hat and went out the door.

Elizabeth knew Sam was making time for her to use the chamber pot, and she was grateful. Not stopping to think of the intimacy they shared, she threw back the covers and removed the poultice. Slowly, painfully she got off the bed, clenching her teeth against the searing pain. It was far worse when she was standing. She took off the heavy robe and tossed it on the trunk. She was hot and shaky and terribly tired of the steady, intense pain. Slowly and carefully she pulled the chamber pot from beneath the bed, used it and slid it out of sight.

Feeling as if her legs would no longer hold her, Elizabeth crawled onto the bed and lay facedown. Not until the pounding of her heart eased did she reach down and pull the blanket over her. She hurt all over—her buttocks, her thighs, her back. She closed her eyes tightly to hold back the tears of helplessness.

Chapter Ten

Sam sat in the hide-covered chair, his long legs stretched in front of him. He rested his head against the back of the chair, his eyes going from the toes of his stockinged feet to the dim form of the woman on the bed. This was the second night they had spent in the cabin. When morning came, Sam was sure he would have to lance the boil, and he wasn't looking forward to it. The resin poultices and the hot towels he had applied were finally bringing it to a head.

Elizabeth had lain with her eyes closed most of the day. He knew she was hurting badly, as she no longer reached to cover her exposed thighs when the blanket slipped down. The pain had robbed her of some of her modesty. Yet she had not complained. Since noon she had seemed to barely notice when he changed the hot, wet cloth.

Hearing a small sound, Sam listened intently. The wind had come up toward evening and was blowing hard. Burley and Jim should be in the Bitterroot Mountains by now and in a few more days should be in Nora Springs. He wondered what Stephen would think about his fiancée spending this time alone with him. Would he be outraged? Would he fear for his future bride's virtue?

Elizabeth was beautiful, gutsy, proud, intelligent: all the things Stephen had said she was. Sam's respect for her had doubled and redoubled since the morning they left Missoula. She was a woman of principles, not afraid to speak out for what she believed in. He thought about her riding in the buggy for two and a half days with the boil, enduring pain that would make some men weep.

Something had happened in Saint Louis that had frightened her into making this trip. He had never known a woman who had such rigid control, who kept all her emotions bottled up inside her. He wondered what she would be like if she ever let herself go and did what came naturally to her.

Sam heard the sound again, stood and walked silently to the side of the bed. All he could see in the light of the flickering fire was her shape beneath the blankets. A faint, muffled sound that could only be a sob reached him. He bent over her, touching her lightly on the back.

"Elizabeth? Are you all right?"

"Y-yes." The word came from deep in the soft pillow.

"But you're...crying."

When she didn't answer, he knelt beside the bed and stroked the hair from the side of her face. As she turned her face toward him, he felt the wetness of tears on her cheeks. Suddenly the need to comfort her was so great that he had to swallow the huge lump that clogged his throat.

"Ah...honey, don't! Don't cry...." Sam wasn't aware of the endearment. It was gut-wrenching to know that she was so miserable and that he couldn't do a thing to help her. Her hand found his and wiggled into it. Her fingers curled around his thumb. "Is it the pain that's making you cry?"

"Y-yes, and I'm so...l-lonely—"

"You're not alone, honey. I'm here. You need only to call me if you want something."

"I know, but—" Her voice broke on a sob.

"But what?" he murmured, his fingers slipping beneath her heavy dark hair to rub the nape of her neck.

"But...you don't want to be h-here," she choked.

"Have I said that?"

"N-no."

"Elizabeth, I want to be here. I want to help you any way I can."

"You've got...obligations, and I'm keeping you from them."

"Nothing that can't wait."

"But...I've been pushed off on you." She took a gulping breath, and when she spoke again, her voice was a tortured whisper. "Netta wanted to get rid of me, and now Stephen's stuck with me." She turned her face into the pillow, and sobs shook her shoulders. "He's too much of a gentleman...to...to go back on his word even if he doesn't want me."

"Ah...honey, Steve wants you. He was very concerned about you." Sam grasped her shoulders and pulled her into his arms. "A man would be crazy *not* to want you." He held her to him, stroking her soothingly, his cheek against her wet one. "Ssh...don't cry."

"Sam, hold me, p-please."

Her hand crept up to his shoulder, and her arm circled his neck. She clung to him almost frantically, her wet lashes, her wet cheeks and her soft, wet lips against his throat. Her trusting acceptance, coming into his arms

The Hell Raiser

with only the nightdress between them, was the most pleasurable thing that had happened to him.

Tightening his arms, he hauled in a ragged, shallow breath. An incredibly strong feeling flooded through him. He wanted nothing more than to hold her and relieve her despair. He couldn't move; he couldn't think. All he could do was savor the sensation of holding her, feeling the softness of her breasts against his chest. The palm of his hand moved searchingly over her back, feeling her ribs, her spine, her shoulder blades through the material of her gown. He wanted to touch every inch of this body that had suddenly become precious to him.

"Ssh...it's all right, love," he crooned. "You're not alone. This will be over soon, and we'll be on our way again."

Sam closed his eyes and brushed his lips across her brow. A tremor shook his powerful body as her face moved against his neck. It wasn't passion he was feeling; it was something deeper, stronger, something that filled that empty place in his heart. *I don't want to fall in love with you, Elizabeth Caldwell.* He nuzzled the line of her hair, his lips moving over her brow to sip the tears in her eyes. Her breath stopped. He waited for her to pull away, but she didn't.

"Have you k-kissed a lot of women?" He felt her lips move as the barely audible words were whispered against his neck.

"Not a lot, but a few."

"I'm j-just what you said. I'm a prissy old m-maid."

"No, you're not!" He moved his lips across her brow, wondering how he could have been so cruel to say that to her.

"It's true."

"I'm sorry I said that, honey."

"No one's ever kissed me or held me like this. No one's ever called me honey but my father, and that was a long time ago. I'm almost twenty-six years old, Sam, and no man has ever called me honey."

Drained and completely vulnerable, Elizabeth knew she was saying things to him in the dark that she could never say to him in the light of day, but once she started, she couldn't seem to stop. The words just tumbled out.

"Not even Stephen?"

"No. I don't think he ever wanted to kiss me like a lover. He always kissed me like a brother kisses a little sister."

"That isn't the way I want to kiss you! I want to kiss you like a man kisses a beautiful, desirable woman. I want it so much I can hardly stand it. But I won't... unless you want me to." Sam's heart sang and beat in a rhythm that barely allowed him to breathe.

"If we kiss like that, will you think that I'm...vulgar and loose?"

"How could I think that when you're the sweetest, bravest woman I've ever known?" he whispered brokenly.

"Then, kiss me, please."

Elizabeth tilted her face to his, refusing to question this irrational need for the kiss of this strange, tough, exciting man who was so intensely alive. His arms were a safe haven where nothing could harm her, where she would never be afraid or lonely. He felt so good, so strong. Even his breath on her face was strong, warm and sweet. Tears for all that she had missed in her life rolled from the corners of her eyes.

"'Lizabeth, honey, don't cry. It tears me up!"

He lightly brushed his lips across hers. That's all it was, a simple, light caress, but she felt a trembling in his strong arms. His lips remained on the corner of her mouth, his nose pressed to the soft, wet flesh of her cheek. He waited, wanting more but refusing to seize the sweetness of her mouth again until it was offered. Then his lips moved across hers in another fleeting kiss, as if they couldn't keep away.

"Don't tease...me—" she whispered pleadingly.

"I'm not! Oh, I'm not! I'm afraid I'll scare you if I kiss you the way I want to."

"I want...I want—"

His lips closed over hers, and his arms tightened. For long moments he simply savored the feel of her mouth—soft, wet, warm, sweet and so...innocent. It melted against his. In spite of his hunger, he didn't demand greater intimacy.

"Honey, you're...so sweet," he murmured, then carefully fitted his mouth over hers again.

For a time their lips clung and there was only their mingled breathing. Then he raised his lips, only to lower them again, rocking his mouth from side to side over hers. She sighed, and her hand moved to the back of his head to increase the pressure of the kiss. Her lips parted just a little, and the tip of his tongue moved slowly between them. When it was over, Sam moved his lips and buried them in the softness beneath her ear. His breath came in and out deeply.

"Thank you."

For what? he thought. He couldn't believe she had thanked him for kissing her.

"Did you like it?"

"Very much. Your mustache is so...soft." She cupped her palm against his cheek. "May I touch it?" He lifted his head, covered her hand with his and moved it to his mouth. Holding her fingers to his lips, he kissed them before he released them. Her fingertips moved lightly over the silky hair above his lip, then over his cheekbone to his brows, then to the mustache. "Do you wear it all the time?"

"I have for a long time. Usually in the winter, during the cutting season, I grow a beard to protect my face from the cold. By spring I look like a grizzly bear."

"I'll knit a face stocking for you."

"I'll hold you to that."

"Does Jessie like it?"

"The mustache? I've never asked her."

"Are you going to marry her?"

"Did Burley talk to you about Jessie?"

"A little. He said you were suited to each other, or words to that effect."

"I suppose he's right, just like you and Stephen are suited to one another."

"Mr. Owens is fond of her. He thinks she's pretty."

"Yes, Jessie is pretty. Her hair is like a flaming sunset, and her eyes are bright blue. She laughs easily. I think every man in Nora Springs is half in love with her."

"How old is she?"

"I don't know. She must be eighteen or nineteen by now. Her father worked for us. He was killed one winter during the cutting season. Since then my pa and I have looked after her and her mother."

"Do you...love her?"

"I suppose I do. I've known her since she was just a little squirt."

"Like I've known Stephen."

"Yes, like you've known Stephen."

"Have you kissed her like this?"

"I've never kissed anyone like *this*."

"My life is half over, Sam," she said sadly, and pulled away so she could look at his face.

"What makes you say that?"

"Most women have a husband and children by the time they're my age."

"You will...soon." Then feeling a desperate need to change the subject, he said, "I should change the poultice. I have a fresh one ready." He eased her down on the bed, feeling a chill where her warm body had lain against his chest.

"I hope you won't have to light the lamp."

"I'll put a few sticks of kindling on the fire. That will give me enough light."

He worked quickly. After applying the resin poultice, he poured hot water from the teakettle over a towel and tested it against his face to be sure it wasn't too hot. Then he put it in place and covered her. She lay with her face buried in the pillow, her arms in a circle around her head.

"Are you going to bed?"

"I might as well if there's nothing more I can do for you. Do you want a drink of water?"

"No, thank you. The night is so long. I wondered if...if you'd lie down here by me so I can hold your hand. No one will know. It isn't as if we'd be doing anything wrong."

Once over the initial shock of her request, Sam said in a matter-of-fact tone, "Sure, I'll get my blanket."

He lay on the far edge of the bed and pulled his blanket over him. He turned on his side to face her and took her hand in his when she reached out to him. Holding her hand tightly in his, he lay staring at the shape of her in the darkness. Although there were more than two feet between them, he feared she could hear the pounding of his heart.

"Tell me about your life out here. Where did you go to school?" Her voice was a soft, intimate whisper.

"When I was twelve, Pa took me to Missoula to go to school and found a room for me in the home of a teacher. I was there five years. I thought a lot of Miss Theiss, and I think she was fond of me."

"Didn't you go home?"

"For a month in the summer, but I wanted to finish my schooling so I could get back up north and work with Pa. Miss Theiss was willing to give me extra lessons, and she saw to it that I worked hard. Pa and I started the lumber business my first year out of school. I handle the logging end. I like the quiet of the forest. Since Pa likes working with machinery, he runs the sawmill."

Sam talked on, telling her about the logging camp and how the town of Nora Springs grew around the mill. He was careful to leave out any reference to his mother and the sadness he and his father felt after she left them. He stopped talking when he realized she had fallen asleep.

After a while the fire died down, and only glowing coals remained. Sam lay listening to the regular breathing of the woman beside him. He had to be sure she was sleeping soundly before he could take care of a chore he must do in the dark because it would be too humiliating to her if she should see him doing it.

Sam gradually loosened his thumb from the grip of her fingers and eased himself off the bed. He slipped on his boots, then went quietly to the side of the bed and pulled out the chamber pot. He carried it to the door and let himself out into the dark, crisp night.

A short time later he returned, slipped the chamber

pot under the bed and banked the fire. For a long while he stood staring at the glowing coals. He felt exhilarated, frustrated and aroused when he thought of holding Elizabeth in his arms. Thinking about her soft breasts against his chest and her lips on his neck caused his stomach to knot with savage want.

His logic told him that he should be putting up barriers between him and this woman, instead of tearing them down. She was a city woman like the one who had broken his father's heart, *and* she was his brother's future wife.

Sam muttered a curse. It was too late. She had seeped into his soul. She had woven a spell, so gracefully, so innocently, and there was no escape. He started for the bunk on the opposite wall, then paused and looked toward the bed. *The night is so long. No one will know.* Her whispered words came back to haunt him. He pulled off his boots and shirt, and closed his mind to the pain he was inviting.

As quietly as possible, he lay on the bed beside her. When he reached for her hand, hers met it halfway and her fingers curled tightly around his thumb.

Elizabeth's eyes felt as if they were full of gravel when she opened them and looked around the room. It was day, according to the light coming through the small window and through the doorway. The door had been left partly open. She had lain in the same position for so long that the upper part of her body was protesting. The lower part was terribly aware of the pain that tormented her flesh.

Several times during the night she had awakened, aware that Sam was beside her on the bed. One time she thought she was alone and had reached blindly for him.

He was there. In the light of day, what had happened between them seemed like a dream. Had it been a dream? No. She felt her lips. She had been kissed. She had asked him to kiss her.

"I'm not going to be embarrassed about it!" she muttered. "I'm not!" She had wanted the kiss, craved it, and she was entitled to it. At the time it had seemed a right thing to do. It hadn't hurt anyone. And now she had a memory to carry with her into a future that was likely to be loveless.

Sam pushed the door open farther and came in. He had the ax in his hands and was carefully wiping the blade on a cloth. Their eyes caught and held. He smiled.

"So you're awake. I thought you were going to sleep all day." He set the ax behind the stove and came to the bed. "We're going to lance that thing this morning, then you'll feel a lot better," he said confidently.

"When will you do it?"

"In a little while. I removed the poultice while you were sleeping. Do you want me to help you get up before I go outside?" He spoke so gently and with such a caring look in his dark eyes that she wanted to cry.

"No, thank you. I can manage."

"Take your time, but stay next to the bed. I don't want you trying to make it to the washstand and keeling over." His mouth smiled, his eyes teased. "I'd have to mop you up off the floor."

"I've got to wash. I can hardly stand myself."

"Later. After we finish with that thing on your sit-down place, I'll bring you a pan of warm water and you can wash and change your gown if you want to."

From the doorway Sam looked at her. Her hair was a black cloud of ringlets, her face almost as pale as the white pillow she lay on. She looked so slim, so fragile, but her eyes, staring into his through thick black lashes, were a startling emerald green, and they showed not a trace of regret or shame for what had happened between them. He dragged his gaze away from her, releasing them from the spell that bound them together, and went out the door.

After it closed behind him, he stood on the step and breathed deeply. He had expected her to be embarrassed, unable to look at him, maybe offering excuses for her "irrational behavior." But she wasn't at all ashamed of what had happened between them. He felt as if a tremendous burden had fallen from his shoulders.

Sam went to the shed and stooped to look once again at the footprint he had discovered that morning. It had been made by a down-at-the-heel boot sometime during the night. The rain the day before had left the ground soft but not muddy. Whoever it was had let the bar gate down and failed to put it back. Had someone intended to steal the horses or just let them out to draw Sam away from the cabin? It was an old trick. Sam's horse had been too smart to leave a place where he was given a measure of oats each day, and the mare had stayed with him.

Irritated with himself because he had been careless, Sam went to the front of the cabin and looked down the narrow, seldom-used track. Two freight wagons had passed the cabin yesterday. Sam had talked to both drivers. One had met Burley and Jim on the upper trail and had told them the bridge at Bitterroot would be fixed by the time they got there. The other freighter was heading north. He had said the bridge above Haggerty's was being repaired and that the freighters waiting to cross had pitched in to help.

It worried Sam that someone was sneaking around

near the cabin. If the man was on the up-and-up, he would have come to the cabin and asked for a meal or permission to sleep in the shed. Sam didn't want to leave Elizabeth alone, or he would have saddled up and scouted the area for more signs. The best thing to do, he decided, was to get back on the main road. He decided that they would go tomorrow or the next day. Elizabeth could lie on the buggy seat. He would ride his horse and lead the mare pulling the buggy. Once they reached the stage road, they could stay at the stage stations and wait with the freighters for the bridges to be repaired.

He sat on the step, took a small whetstone from his pocket, spit on it and began sliding the blade of his knife over it. The thought of cutting into Elizabeth's flesh was so repulsive to him that he refused to think about it.

After Sam went out, Elizabeth threw back the blanket and moved backward off the bed. She stood for a moment before she reached under the bed for the chamber pot, moving it carefully. When she removed the lid, she was surprised to see that it was empty. She straightened and covered her face with her hands. *Sam had emptied it while she slept.* Merciful heaven! She had shared an intimacy with this man during the past few days that she hadn't shared with anyone before. *Sam. Samuel.* Just thinking his name caused crazy things to happen to her heartbeat.

Her hair brushed and tied with a ribbon, Elizabeth lay on her side watching the door. When Sam rapped, she called out and he opened the door. He didn't look at her immediately, but went to rummage in their supplies. Then he looked at her, really looked at her, and she at him.

A part of her wanted him to cross the few feet that separated them and lift her in his arms. Then logic prevailed. It would be insanity to fall in love with Sam Ferguson. They had nothing in common. She had a lot in common with Stephen. They were used to the same life, and they were fond of each other. Then, she asked herself, why couldn't she see Stephen's face clearly in her mind when all she had to do was close her eyes and she could see Sam's? Maybe it was because he was such a raw, sexual, masculine man, and she was attracted to the forbidden. Or maybe it was because she was totally dependent on him. The thought was immediately rejected.

Gratitude had nothing to do with the feelings she had for him. There was more, much more, to Sam than his raw good looks. He was as much Eleanor's son as Stephen was. His exterior was rougher. He had been terribly hurt when the mother he adored left him, and he used his hell-raising image to cover the deep and lasting hurt.

"I'm not going to drink it—" Sam was speaking and holding up a bottle of whiskey "—but maybe you should. If you're drunk enough you'll not feel the pain."

Chapter Eleven

Elizabeth wondered at Sam's silence as he tore strips of cloth from her petticoat and sterilized his knife in the pan of water boiling on the cook stove. She had no dread of what he was going to do. The pain had been with her for days, and this was the means of getting rid of it. She turned on her stomach and arranged her gown and the blankets to preserve as much modesty as possible.

When Sam came to her, his mouth was stretched in a smile, but there was little humor in the expression.

"Ready for the big operation?"

His words were light, but she could see the agony in his eyes, could feel it as if it were her own. She wanted to put her arms around him and tell him that it was all right, that she understood his reluctance to perform the distasteful task. She reached out her hand, and his fingers tightened over hers.

"I'm ready. And, Sam, don't worry about hurting me."

He released her fingers to loop a dark curl over her ear before he bent and placed a light kiss on her cheek.

"I'll be as quick as I can," he promised, his voice huskier than usual.

"I know."

Elizabeth circled her head with her arms and buried her face in the pillow. When Sam folded back the blanket, she felt the cool air on her hot flesh. She gathered herself for the pain. It came suddenly and sooner than she expected. It was so sharp that she gasped and bit into the pillow, bracing herself for more pain. Sam's fingers touched her, squeezed gently, moved and touched again. Then he was swabbing with a whiskey-soaked cloth. She turned to see the side of his face. His jaw was clenched, and the vein in his temple was throbbing.

"It's over, honey! It's over! Now all I have to do is clean up. It'll not hurt so much now."

He splashed more whiskey on the cloth and continued to dab. She could feel the sharp bite of the whiskey, but the sting was nothing compared to what she had suffered. He made a quick trip to the fireplace and tossed the cloth he had used into the fire. The relief was evident on his face and in his eyes when he looked at her.

"That wasn't so bad, was it?"

"It happened so fast, I didn't have time to dread it."

"I'm a damn good surgeon! I just might give up logging and practice medicine. Is there something else you want cut, Miss Caldwell? I'm at your service."

"You've let your success go to your head, Doctor."

"That I have." His relieved smile showed white teeth against the bronze of his face.

"What now?"

"I'm wondering how in the hell we're going to keep a bandage on that part of you. You should get up and move around a little. We've got to get all the matter cleaned out before that cut I made heals over."

"Where did you practice medicine, Doctor?"

"Ferguson logging camp, five miles north of Nora Springs, in Montana Territory, ma'am."

"Then you haven't heard about the new glue tape they use for holding bandages in place?"

"No! Do you have some?"

"No." Laughter danced in her eyes when he lifted his to the ceiling in a gesture of exaggerated frustration. "But leave the bandage to me. I'll rig up something if I'm given a little privacy."

"We can arrange that." He showed her the stack of cloths he had folded into pads. "Dampen one of these with the whiskey. The whiskey will help keep down infection."

"Oh, my! You do know a lot about medicine."

"Of course, I know about medicine. And I'll have none of your sass, woman. Treat me with a little more respect or I'll not fix your breakfast when I come back."

After he left, Elizabeth lay for a long time with a smile on her lips. Never in her life had she indulged in such nonsensical banter with a man. Sam was charmingly witty when he wanted to be, and she had responded with whatever came to mind without a thought of decorum.

She got off the bed and stood for a moment, surprised that most of the pain was gone. Plenty was left, but it wasn't the agonizing pain of before. When her head stopped feeling fuzzy, she pawed in her trunk and found a pair of tight-fitting knit drawers that she wore in the wintertime. She searched in her valise until she found a small box that contained safety pins and selected two. Then, holding the pad in place with one hand she pulled the drawers over her hips with the other.

By the time Elizabeth had pinned the pad in place she was worn out. Hanging on to the side of the bed, she waited until her breathing slowed, then reached for her robe. She was not going to spend the day in bed even if she had to stand up all day. She wanted to wash, dress and make herself tidy. She refused to admit that she wanted to look nice for Sam.

Elizabeth was brushing her hair, her arm feeling as if the brush weighed fifty pounds, when Sam knocked on the door.

"Come in," she called, and turned her back, conscious of her appearance now that she was on her feet. No one except her maid had ever seen her in such disarray.

"How are you feeling?"

Elizabeth heard him cross to the stove and open the door to the firebox.

"Much better, thank you. But I'm weak from lying in bed."

"And you haven't eaten enough to keep a bird alive." He came up behind her and reached for the hairbrush. "Hold on to the bedpost. I'll do that."

"I can do it."

"I'm the doctor. Remember?" He started at her forehead and brushed all the way down to the end of her hair, which hung several inches below her waist. She held the bedpost with both hands and tilted her head back. After several long swipes with the brush, she sighed with pure pleasure. "Feel good?" His voice was like a caress, low and intimate.

"Oh, yes. It feels heavenly."

"You have beautiful hair."

"It's too thick, too curly—"

"I don't think so."

"I hated it while I was growing up," she rushed to say. "One of my mother's friends had a little girl with beautiful blond hair. When she got mad at me she'd tell me my hair looked like a horse's tail with cockleburs in it. I wanted to scratch her eyes out.''

"Why didn't you?'' His laughter was husky and deep.

Elizabeth glanced at him over her shoulder. He had lifted a handful of her hair and was staring at it with the hungry look of a small boy looking into a jar of peppermint sticks. She dragged her eyes to her hands and stared at them while she pondered his expression.

After what seemed to Elizabeth a very long time, he began to brush again. She loved the scrape of the bristles against her temple. When he placed his hand on her shoulder to steady her, her fluttering heart felt as if it would jump right out of her breast.

"You're very good at brushing a lady's hair," she said when she felt she could keep her voice light. "You must have had a lot of practice.''

"I've never brushed a lady's hair except my...'' His words faded as memories of standing behind his mother's chair, brushing her lustrous, honey-colored hair, flashed into his mind. *Ah, Sammy, that feels so good! That's my boy. Come sit on Mama's lap....*

The brushing stopped. She turned to look at him. His expression told her a battle was raging inside him. His brows had drawn together, and he was looking at her as if she was his enemy.

Abruptly, he tossed the hairbrush on the bed. "That's all I have time for. I've things to do.'' Quick strides took him to the door.

Once outside, Sam went toward the shed and the pole corral. He leaned his arms on the top rail and looked toward the mountains, where the clouds hovered threateningly. The wind that struck his face had a bite to it, but he didn't notice. He swore, using words he had not thought of for a long while. When he exhausted that vocabulary, he hit the rail with his clenched fist.

He loved her! He had lost his heart, suddenly and irrevocably!

The realization had been there all the time, but he had to acknowledge it. He was totally, recklessly in love with his brother's intended bride—a woman who was as much like Eleanor as two peas in a pod.

The awful part of it was that it was not the kind of love he'd known once or twice when he was younger, the randy kind of love centered in his groin and disappearing once he got the woman into bed. This love had crept up on him and sunk deeply into his heart and mind. It was the cherishing kind of love that made him want to be with her every minute of the day and night, both mentally and physically. He wanted to hold her in his arms, plant his children in her warm, fertile body, keep her by his side forever.

He swore again. He should have known it was happening. He had not been able to think of anything else since he had met her.

Closing his eyes, he could see her as vividly as if she were standing in front of him. Her eyes were a bright, clear, emerald green when she was smiling, stormy green when she was angry, glassy green when filled with tears… Shifting uneasily, he tried to shut out the images, but they refused to go from his mind.

He knew that a woman like Elizabeth had no place in his life. They were as different as night and day, rain and sunshine, silk and steel. When they reached Nora Springs, they would say goodbye. Stephen would take her to Saint Louis, where they would pick up the threads of their lives. Sam would stay in Montana, logging in the winter, working at the mill in the summer. Would he forget her when she was gone? Would she be only a pleasant memory?

On his way to the cabin he realized it would not be any easier for him to forget Elizabeth than it had been for his father to forget Eleanor. He had not understood the extent of his father's grief at the time, but he did now. He didn't want to feel the pain, but it was inevitable.

Elizabeth washed her body the best she could without stripping completely. It was wonderful to be clean again and rid of the throbbing ache and accompanying worry that had plagued her. The soreness that lingered was irritating, but not painful.

After dusting herself with powder, she put on fresh underclothes and an ash-gray cotton dress with a white V neck collar. The sleeves were long, the bodice fit the curves of her breasts perfectly, and the skirt was full. The comfort of being without a corset was spoiling her. She dismissed the thought with a shrug, a puckered frown, then a sigh. When she reached Nora Springs, she would once again be forced into the mold of propriety. Stephen would expect it.

She searched in her trunk for something warm and pulled out a frothy three-cornered shawl the color of her eyes. Flinging it across her shoulders, she tied the ends in a knot just below the neckline of her dress.

Moving around seemed to strengthen her. She paced the small room, then rested on the bed when she began to feel shaky. Her empty stomach drew attention to itself. A handful of raisins staved off the hunger pangs for a while. She pondered whether or not she should attempt to prepare a meal and decided to wait for Sam.

It seemed to her he had stayed away for an unusually long time.

When he rapped on the door, her heart picked up a beat. She smoothed her skirt with the palms of her hands and adjusted the shawl to frame the collar of her dress. He entered, hung his hat on the peg and added a few sticks of wood to the coals on the grate. He seemed totally unaware of her. As her eyes traveled over the lean, powerful length of him, he suddenly turned to face her. He was scowling. His eyes were hard, his mouth firm. He looked at her as if seeing her for the first time. She swallowed, trying to think of something to say.

"With your hair pinned back like that you look like an old maid—or a peeled onion."

The attack was so sudden that she blinked at the shock of it. She could feel the color draining from her face and caught herself just in time to prevent her teeth from biting into her lower lip. An invisible protective shield slid suddenly into place, a shield developed to deal with Netta. She couldn't give him the satisfaction of seeing how much his cruel words had hurt.

"I'm sorry if my looks displease you." Her voice was calm, even. She hardly recognized it.

"Take it down and throw away those damn hairpins. While you're with me you'll look like a woman should—soft, pleasant to look at, and not like a skinned rabbit. When you're with Stephen you can fix yourself any damn way you please."

He strode to the stove, banged a big spider skillet on the iron top and began slicing strips from a slab of bacon.

Elizabeth turned to the window and blinked rapidly to stave off the tears she felt stealing into her eyes. Why had he turned on her so suddenly? What had she done to earn such contempt? She lifted her hands to remove the pins, wondering why she was obeying him, why she wanted to please him. With her hair hanging down her back, she massaged her temples with her fingertips for a moment before she went to her trunk, put the brass hairpins in a small box and pulled out a length of white ribbon. She slid it beneath her hair at the nape of her neck and tied it loosely. When she turned, her features were carefully arranged to show no expression. She didn't speak until she was sure there would be no quiver in her voice.

"May I help?"

"No, you may not. You don't know the first thing about how to cook on a stove like this."

"I may surprise you."

"It would surprise me if you didn't burn yourself."

"I'm not helpless—"

"Stop jawing, Elizabeth, and sit down."

Her tongue stuck to the roof of her mouth for a moment before she could answer. "Y-you know I can't."

She went to the window to look out, seeing nothing but watery trees and gray sky. Couldn't their unspoken truce have lasted just a little longer? Regret and humiliation fought for control of her thoughts. For a terrible moment she could do no more than stand and stare through the small glass pane.

Sam came up behind her. She didn't know he was there until he cupped her shoulders with his hands.

"I'm sorry, 'Lizabeth. I didn't mean to hurt you. I'm just a bear at times." He made a disgusted sound.

"It's all right." A lie. "You didn't hurt me." Another lie.

Her words and the forced lightness of her voice cut

him deeply. "Then look at me." He tried to turn her to face him, and she resisted the pressure.

"Please don't. Even an old m-maid has her pride."

"Oh, Lord!" He lowered his face to her shoulder and rested it there against her neck. His hands moved up and down her forearms, lightly stroking. When he tried to turn her again, her body was unresisting. He tilted her face to his. He had dreaded seeing tears, but what he saw hurt him even more. Her eyes were wide and... empty. "Don't look at me like that," he whispered urgently. She shivered, and he realized how tightly she was holding on to her emotions.

"I'm sorry."

"And don't ever say you're sorry to me again!" The words exploded from him; his hands clasped her shoulders in a tight, unrelenting grip. "Hear me?"

"Yes. I'm not deaf."

He stared into her calm face, his eyes caressing every feature before looking into hers.

"'Lizabeth! Oh, God! What am I going to do?" His voice cracked and his features twisted in agonized despair. Breath hissed from between clenched teeth as he stared into her face.

The hands on her arms slid slowly over her back and crossed. He pulled her against him, locking her to him with gentle strength. Elizabeth closed her eyes against the impact of her body against his. This was insanity. She should move away while there was still time. Then, quite unexpectedly, there was no more time. The palms of her hands were against his chest, feeling the strong beat of his heart. She could feel his breath stirring the curls at her temple. She could smell the masculine odor of his body. She was tired. Tired of being strong, tired of being alone. It felt so good to be able to rest against him—just for a moment. She struggled to keep from blurting that she never wanted to leave this safe haven.

He bent his head. His lips moved lightly across her temple and into her hair. They stood that way for a long time. When he finally spoke, it was in a whisper against her ear.

"You're a beautiful woman, Elizabeth. Beautiful and sweet and proud and spirited. You're all the things a man wants in the woman he plans to spend his life with."

"Sam—"

"Don't say anything, honey. Let me say these things while I can. I'll never be rich. I'll never be anything but what I am—a woodsman. I spend a good part of the year in the forest among men, cussing and fighting and getting drunk on Sunday. I love this country and wouldn't trade places with Stephen for all the money in the world. I'm what you said, a hell raiser. What you need is a gentleman." He moved his hand under her hair and curved it around her neck. His hard fingers stroked behind her ear.

"Yes," she agreed in a dreary, low voice. "I need someone, but no one needs me."

"That's where you're wrong, honey," he said, then went on determinedly. "I'll never forget this time with you." He clasped her head tightly in his two hands, burying his fingers in her hair. He tilted her face and looked into green pools, wet and shiny. His heart thumped with the pain of lost dreams. "We've got to leave just as soon as you can travel. I've got to get you to Nora Springs— to Stephen."

"You're anxious to get back to Jessie?"

"Yes," he said slowly, his eyes moving hungrily over her face then away. "I'm anxious to get back to Jessie."

The climate inside the cabin was as bleak as the weather outside. The sky had darkened to a smoky gray that had the look of late evening instead of midday. The noon meal was eaten in almost total silence. Afterward, Sam insisted that she lie down and rest. He went out and cut wood until he had more than replenished the homesteaders' supply. Then, taking a pair of buckskin breeches from his pack, he went to the shed.

Time crawled for Elizabeth. When she could stand the inside of the cabin no longer, she put on her coat, covered her head with a shawl and went out. It was the first time she had been outside the cabin since they arrived. She walked toward the almost overgrown track, turned and scrutinized the squat and comfortable-looking cabin. A plume of smoke came from the chimney, drifted upward and was lost. With all her heart she envied the woman who lived there, envied her preparing the meals for her man, washing his clothes in the black pot, sitting with him beside the fire in the evenings, sharing with him what had occurred during the day.

When she and Stephen were married, they would live in New York at least part of the time. She would entertain the wives of his business associates—women like her stepmother, who scratched and clawed for social recognition. At the top of their list of priorities was the need to be seen with someone more socially prominent than they. The highlights of their lives were invitations to gatherings of the rich.

Those people did not even know what life was about. *This* was life—carving something out of a new land for the generations that followed. What in the world had caused Eleanor to give up all this for the shallow life of ease in Saint Louis?

Elizabeth began to fantasize about morning glories

planted beside the door, a rope swing hanging from the limb of an oak tree for the children, a garden that included tomatoes and green beans that she would can in glass jars for winter meals, Sam coming home after a day's work to grab her up in his arms, whirl her around and tell her he'd missed her.

Why was she thinking these foolish thoughts, dreaming these foolish dreams? They were not for her. Sam would do these things with Jessie by his side. Tomorrow they would leave this cabin in the mountains. She looked at it for a long time, imprinting it in her memory for future dreams.

Elizabeth went into the cabin, her mood as dreary as the day. She changed the bandage on the boil, hurrying before Sam returned. In light of what had passed between them, she wondered how she could have bared her backside to him. She washed, then prowled through the supplies. There were flour, lard and dried apricots. Unable to stand another idle minute, she rolled up the sleeves of her dress, tied the remainder of one of her petticoats around her waist and went to work.

An hour later, when Sam came in the door carrying something over his arm, he stopped in open-mouthed astonishment.

"What in the hell are you doing?"

Elizabeth, flushed from the heat of the stove, glanced at him briefly then looked at the skillet. "Making pies," she said matter-of-factly as she lifted one out of the pan and onto a dish, adding it to the ones lying on a cloth on the table. "I'm making enough to last for several days. They keep well if cooled first and wrapped in a cloth."

"I didn't know society women knew how to cook."

She ignored the slight disdain in his voice, added another pie to the hot grease and moved it around with a fork to make room for another.

"This one does. I was taught at boarding school so I could supervise a cook when I had a home of my own. Later, I was taught by our cook, Mary Lincoln—"

"Mary Lincoln?"

"Yes, Mary Lincoln. Her mother loved people who were involved in the war. She named one of her boys Abraham Lincoln and another Ulysses S. Grant and insisted he be called by his full name. Anyway, Mary Lincoln taught me to make pies. I spent a lot of time in her kitchen." Elizabeth didn't add that it was a good place to avoid her stepmother, who seldom went to the kitchen. The butler conveyed Netta's orders to Mary Lincoln.

"You do surprise me, Miss Caldwell. What else do you cook?"

"Curried rice, lobster bisque, chocolate mousse, marble cake with cherry frosting—"

"I shouldn't have asked," he said dryly.

"—fried chicken, cream gravy, buttermilk biscuits, pot roast with onions and cabbage rolls, apple cobbler—"

"Well, I'll be damned!"

She glanced at him, smiled at the pleased look on his face and flipped the pies over without as much as a single splash.

"What's that? What have you done to your britches?"

"I'm trying to make something for you to sit on. I've stuffed the legs with straw. I'll tie the top and the bottom—"

"You're making a ring! That's a wonderful idea. How did you ever think of it?"

Her praise washed over him like a cool breeze on a

hot summer day. He hid his feelings behind mock arrogance.

"I'm no dummy! Miss Theiss told me so—once."

"Only once? I think I'd like your Miss Theiss. She didn't want you getting a swelled head."

"I figured you'd want to sit down sometime during the next few days."

"You figured right. Now, as soon as I finish these pies, I'm going to mash the beans you cooked yesterday, make them into patties and fry them in the skillet. I already have a pan of corn bread in the oven."

Chapter Twelve

Whether she liked it or not, she was in love with Samuel Ferguson.

The thought was not a sudden discovery, but rather a quiet inevitability, seeming to be something she had known all along. She was in love for the first time, and there was no possibility of a future for her and this man who had been propelled into her life and had turned it upside down. Their lives lay on different paths. Those paths had only converged briefly.

Sam cleaned up after the meal. He insisted. She eyed him as he swiftly and efficiently washed and greased the iron skillet and set it on the back of the stove. With the lamplight casting shadows over his lean features, she saw the strength of his jaw, the curves of his cheekbones, the flash of white teeth when he smiled at her, as he was doing now.

"Don't wrap up all those pies. I get another one for cleaning up."

"You had two already." Her eyes shone at him.

"I could have eaten them all."

"That's why I'm getting them out of your sight."

Why had she not noticed the velvet warmth in his

voice? It eased down her spine and spread warmth all the way to her toes. Her heart threatened to stop, as if the sudden rush of happiness was more than she could bear. His nearness caused the tension that had lurked in her stomach all evening to tighten. A flush came to her cheeks. She bowed her head, grateful for the loose curls that covered her face.

She wanted to touch him, slide her hands over his shoulders and feel his strength. She wanted the magic of being held in the haven of his arms as he had held her the night before. She wanted to relive that time, return to that heaven she'd had for only a moment.

"You're awfully quiet. Are you all right?"

His hand on her shoulder and his words brought her to the present with a jarring thud. What a fool she was, sitting here daydreaming. She prayed that he didn't know that his touch caused her heart to race in undignified delight, or that it awakened anew her wild hopes and dreams. The warmth of his touch lingered after he took his hand away.

"I'm fine, thank you. Just a little tired."

"You did a lot today. How's your...sit-down place?"

"Better." Watching him, she had almost forgotten it.

"Good. We'll leave in the morning. It'll take us a full day to get back onto the main road and to Underwood's Station. Are you up to it?"

"Yes. I can drive the buggy."

"Not the first day. I'll ride my horse and lead the gray. That way you can lie on the seat and rest."

"We'll have pie to eat on the way."

At first all she had wanted to do was to get to Nora Springs and Stephen. Now she wished the journey would last forever. Leaving here would be heartbreaking. This was the last evening she would spend alone with him.

Her eyes skimmed over the room—his hat on the peg, his rifle in the corner, her trunk beside the bed—imprinting the scene firmly on her mind. It had to last forever.

"I'd like to clean the cabin—leave it as we found it," Elizabeth said.

"We will."

"And leave payment for using it."

"It isn't expected."

"But I want to."

"I'll take care of it." He lifted his gun belt from the peg, strapped it around his waist and settled the gun against his thigh. "I'd better see about the horses." He put on his vest. "I want to see the pad you take off the boil."

"Why?"

"So I can tell if it's draining."

"I mean why wear the gun to go see about the horses?"

"Habit. A man gets used to wearing a gun in this country. He puts it on before he puts on his hat."

Elizabeth nodded, accepting the explanation. His eyes caught hers and held them for a timeless moment with a strange intensity. She wasn't sure what she saw in their velvet depths before he slipped out the door, but it wasn't happiness.

Elizabeth shook the thought from her mind and slipped off her dress. The boil was not nearly as sore as before. She blindly probed the area with her fingertips, then washed it with a whiskey-soaked cloth and pinned a clean pad in her knit drawers. In her nightdress and robe, she packed her clothes, leaving out the heavy shirt, blouse and coat she'd been wearing when they came to the cabin. How long had they been here? How could a person's life change so drastically in such a short time?

Standing beside her trunk filled with clothes far more valuable than this cabin and the land surrounding it, she looked at the stark walls, the sparse furnishings, and took a deep, shuddering breath. Happiness was not possessions. Happiness was living rabbit poor if there were no other way, with someone she loved and who loved her.

Deep in her heart Elizabeth knew that what she felt for Sam was real and that it would be with her forever. It was more than sexual infatuation, although it was that, too. She liked the way he had accepted the responsibility for her even though he didn't want to. She liked his sense of fairness when he told her that he was a woodsman, would always be a woodsman, and that she would not fit into his life. She liked his sense of humor and his innate kindness. What she didn't like was the resentment or hatred he felt toward his mother. Knowing how sweet and loving Eleanor had been, Elizabeth couldn't believe that Eleanor had left Sam without good cause. She remembered Eleanor telling her that true love was when a person loved someone despite their faults, not because they had none. Eleanor had loved Joe Ferguson until her dying day, Elizabeth was sure of it.

Elizabeth suddenly wanted to leave a gift for the woman whose home would always hold such cherished memories, memories of Sam holding her, kissing her, calling her honey. She wanted the gift to be something pretty and frivolous. She untied her hat box and took out the gray felt hat with the pink silk rose dangling on the brim. Her gift should be something she liked herself, and this hat had always been her favorite.

She was removing the long hat pin, thinking to replace it with a different pin, when the door opened.

"Sam, I'm going—" Aghast, she stood stark still.

"Howdy."

She was in such a state of shock that she didn't realize who the man was at first. Then it dawned on her that it was the fat man who had talked to her a few days ago. On horseback he had seemed taller. On the ground he looked like a fat toad. His short arms made parentheses around the curved sides of his body. His eyes, made smaller by his fat cheeks, darted around as he waddled into the room, leaving the door ajar.

"Get out! You've no right to come in here."

"Button yore lip, sister." He held up his rifle. "This gives me all the leave I be needin'."

Fear knifed through her. Her stomach rolled, and bile rose in her throat.

"Sam..." It was a whimpering sound. Then, "Sam!" Her scream filled the room and echoed into the night. She darted for the doorway. The fat man's bulk filled it before she could reach it.

"Back off, missy!"

"What have you done to him?" Her voice was shrill with near hysteria.

"Nothin' yet. Ya behave yoreself or he'll get his head blowed off. Hear?" His eyes darted around the room and rested on the trunk. He wet his thin lips. "Yore a city woman, ain't ya?"

She could do no more than nod.

"Where'd ya come from, anyways?"

"Saint L-Louis."

"Where's that?"

"In Missouri."

The fat man lifted his head and sniffed. "Ya been cookin' up a batch o' grub. Fix me a bit."

Elizabeth stood as if she was nailed to the floor. "Where's Sam?"

"I'm thinkin' ya ain't hearin' me, sister. I'm wantin' ta eat some fixin's."

Elizabeth tossed the hat on the bed and slipped the hat pin in the pocket of her robe. The fat man reached out and grabbed her arm as she was trying to go around him.

"Get your filthy hands off me!" She tried to jerk her arm away and struck out at him with her other hand. He growled menacingly but let her go. She hurried to the other side of the table to put distance between them.

"I'm thinkin' ya don't know who's got the upper hand here, sister. I'll do more'n put my hands on ya 'fore we're done." He made an obscene movement with his hips that left no doubt about his intentions.

Elizabeth's face flamed then turned white. Her heart pounded as if it was trying to escape her body. Something had happened to Sam or he would be here. The door had been left open, so the fat man must be confident that Sam wouldn't come rushing in. Her stomach churned. She felt herself go cold. The next second she was burning hot. In a daze of fear, her hands trembling, she unwrapped the fried pies and set them on the table.

"Pie! Hell! It's a spell since I had me some pie." A dirty hand snatched one off the table and crammed it in his mouth. He chewed with his mouth open. It was sickening to see the food in his open mouth and the gluttonous look on his face. While he was eating, he watched her like a snake might watch a small frog.

"Take the pie and go!"

"I'm takin' ya with me when I go. I'm thinkin' ta make ya my woman."

"No!" she croaked. A fresh flush of fear raced through her body. She screamed, "Sam! S-Sam!"

At that instant Sam was shoved into the room. His

holster was empty, and his hands were clasped behind his head. His eyes sought Elizabeth then moved quickly to the fat man, who was still shoving pie in his mouth. The man with the leather patch over his eye prodded Sam in the back with the barrel of his gun, urging him farther into the room.

"What's she hollerin' fer, Vernon? Ya ain't done nothin', have ya?"

Elizabeth dashed around the table toward Sam. The fat man dropped the pie and grabbed her arm with a greasy hand.

"No, ya don't."

"Let go of her!" Sam's angry shout filled the room. "Hurt her and I'll hunt you down like a mad dog and kill you!"

"Talks big, don't he?" The one-eyed man jabbed Sam with the gun barrel. "He's thinkin' he's gettin' off free 'n' clear, Vernon. Want me ta shoot him now?"

"Ya don't shoot till I tell ya. Hear? We got thinkin' ta do." Vernon's fat jowls quivered. "Stay back!" he commanded, and turned his rifle on Elizabeth when Sam took a step toward her. "Stay back or I shoot her purty face off."

Sam obediently froze. "Take what you want and get out!"

"Why, thanky." The one-eyed man leered at Elizabeth. "Ain't that good o' him, Vernon? I'll jist take this woman, seein' as how he's givin' thin's away. She be the sweetest-smellin' woman I ever smelt. 'Sides, I ain't never had me a highfalutin woman. Is they different from a regular woman, Vernon?"

Vernon ignored his companion, puckered his lips and spit toward the fireplace. His beady eyes danced over the room but returned to Sam.

"What ya doin' here, anyways?"

"Maybe we live here." Sam's eyes darted to Elizabeth and back.

"Hog waller! I know who lives here, and they ain't got no fancy buggy. This ain't a place a tony woman like her'd settle for."

"You don't know diddly squat," Sam said contemptuously. "You don't have the brains of a pissant or you'd know that every law man in the country will be on your tail if you harm her."

"Why's that, Mister Know-it-all? Why'd they know it was us what done it?" Vernon spat again.

"Because if we don't show up tomorrow my men will come looking for a fat bastard and a one-eyed son of a bitch. We took your measure when we met you on the trail. You're nothing but a couple of no-good scavengers."

"He's lying, Vernon. Want me ta shoot him in the leg?"

Elizabeth's heart dropped like a rock, and fear had a cold hand at her throat.

"Not yet." The fat man edged toward the trunk. "What ya got in there, sister?"

"C-clothes." Elizabeth's voice shook. Her eyes sought Sam's and found fleeting comfort in the calmness she saw there. His eyes held hers. He was trying to tell her not to get rattled, to stay calm, to wait.

"That ain't all ya got. Open it." The fat man wiped his mouth on his sleeve.

"We can take the whole kit and caboodle, can't we, Vernon? We can load it in the buggy." The one-eyed man's good eye was like a bottomless pit of evil.

"We ain't takin' that buggy, ya dunderhead! Everybody what's seen it knows it's her'n. It'd be like puttin' our head in a noose. I swear, Ollie, ya ain't got no sense at all.''

"I ain't likin' ya talkin' to me like that, Vernon. I do too have sense. Plenty a sense. You 'n' me is partners in this. Ya said we was.''

"I ain't sayin' no different. I'm sayin' we got to use our heads. Open the trunk, sister.'' Vernon pushed Elizabeth toward the trunk with the end of his rifle. Her terror-filled eyes sought Sam.

"Open it, honey,'' he said calmly. "Give the scums what they want so they'll get out. They're smelling up the place.''

"Ya sure talk big fer a man on the down side of a gun. I jist might shoot that thin' off 'tween yore legs afore I go, *then* shoot ya in the head.'' Ollie emphasized the words with pokes of the gun in Sam's ribs.

The words seeped into Elizabeth's mind as dread spread over her like a chill. Then sweat broke out on her forehead, gushed cold and clammy in her armpits. Dizzily, she reached out and steadied herself against the bedpost.

"Open the trunk.''

Elizabeth heard the order as if it was directed to someone else. *They were going to kill Sam!* What were their plans for her? If they killed Sam it wouldn't matter. The smelly, low-life bastards! This was too much! She'd not stand for it. They were not going to hurt him. He was worth a million of their kind. She was sure he'd not give up without a fight even if the odds were against him. He was staying calm, waiting his chance. If she could only give him one—

"Girly, I ain't askin' ya again.''

"What? What?'' Elizabeth looked dazed. She put her hand to her head as if she was going to faint.

"I ast ya to open that fancy trunk. A tony woman like ya is ain't travelin' stone broke."

"You want my money? Oh, for goodness sake! All this over money."

Beady eyes flicked with interest. "Have ya got money, sister?"

"A little."

"How much?"

"Not much," she said in a small, scared voice.

"Gol darn it! Don't ya be stallin' or I'll give Ollie the go-ahead to shoot yore man. How much?" Vernon's voice was shrill with impatience.

"Only about six or seven hundred. It's in a secret place." Her voice dropped to a weak whisper. "You won't find it unless I show you."

"D-dollars?" Vernon almost choked on the word.

"What's that? What's that she said, Vernon?" Ollie moved around Sam until the gun barrel was pressed beneath Sam's upraised arm. The face with the patch over the eye swiveled from Sam to the fat man. "Move," he snarled at Sam. "Move closer, so I can see. What'd she say?" he demanded again.

"Said she had money in a secret place," Vernon yelled angrily. "Now hush yore mouth!"

"Tell her to get it, or…or I'll blow his head off!"

"Oh…"

"Shut up, Ollie. Yore scarin' her. Get the money, missy. We ain't goin' to hurt ya none. We just be takin' it 'n' leavin' ya 'n' yore man be." Vernon spoke in an oily, placating tone.

"You'll not hurt…h-him if I sh-show you?" Elizabeth asked in a thin little-girl voice.

"I'd promise on a Bible if'n I had one. I ain't ne'er

killed nobody in all my born days. Ollie gets to runnin' off at the mouth, but he don't mean no harm."

Elizabeth let out what she hoped would pass as a sob of relief. She lifted the lid of the trunk, removed the tray, set it on her hatbox, looked straight into Sam's eyes and blinked rapidly.

The fat man grabbed her arm. "Get the money, gal."

"It's...down there." She put one hand to her head as if she was going to faint; she put the other hand in her pocket.

"Where?"

"In the corner under the...c-corsets is a little panel. Just slide it back." She moved to the side of the trunk.

A smile splitting his fat face, his eyes bright with greed, Vernon bent over the trunk and grabbed a fistful of clothing and threw it out. He held the rifle in one hand as he searched the bottom of the trunk with the other.

Elizabeth waited, the head of the hat pin snug against her palm. When the fat man chortled on finding the panel, she drove the pin into his bottom with all her strength. He screeched and reared into Sam, shoving Sam back a second before Ollie's gun discharged. The roar was thunderous. It reverberated through the room. The fat man fell screaming to the floor. Sam's arm sent Ollie flying across the room where he crashed against the solid plank door.

Elizabeth's fear turned to relief when she saw Sam on his feet. Within seconds it turned into anger and blossomed into full-grown rage. She grabbed the rifle Vernon had dropped and swung it at his head as he lay writhing on the floor. He screamed and tried to cover his head with his arms.

"You nasty, vile, stinking piece of horse dung! How

dare you do this?'' She whacked him sharply on the head with the rifle barrel. ''Stupid, ignorant lout! I'd horsewhip you if I could.'' She hit him on the back with the rifle stock.

''Honey! Stop! It's over.'' Sam took the rifle from her hands and pulled her to him.

''Dirty swine! Fat pig! I'll k-kill him,'' she gasped.

''You've done enough to him.''

''No! I want to shoot him!''

''You've given him something to remember. He'll not sit down for a while, and old One-eye here shot him in the leg when he stumbled against me. Besides that, he's going to have a hell of a headache from the pounding you gave him. Are you all right?''

''I'm all right. Just mad. Did they hurt you?'' She moved her hands over his upper arms to his cheeks.

''No. I'm all right, thanks to you. Good Lord, sweetheart, you're a regular buzz saw once you get going.''

She looked around him. Ollie, out cold, was slumped against the door, his nose spouting blood.

''They're m-mean, rotten! They were going to shoot you, weren't they? I was so scared!'' Her arms tightened around him. She pressed her face into the curve of his neck.

''I was scared for you, sweetheart. That bastard said the fat man would cut you if I didn't give up my gun. Lord! I'd have given him my head to keep you safe.'' They were both trembling, each scared for the other.

A loud wail came from the fat man on the floor. Sam glanced at him, then held Elizabeth away so he could look into her face.

''Are you sure you're all right? Really all right?'' He gazed at her upturned face with a loving look in his eyes that went all the way to her soul.

"Yes." She shivered as what had occurred began to sink into her senses. Sam could have been killed! She could have lost him. Just to know he was not on earth, even if not with her, was more than she could bear. Gooseflesh rose on her arms. Her mouth was suddenly dry. She pressed the tip of her tongue to her lips to moisten them.

Sam bent his head and kissed her forehead as if she was as fragile as a dandelion puff. Then he walked her backward until she was against the wall beside the bed. She made no protest. He stroked her cheek with his fingertips and gave her a soft, sweet peck on the lips.

"Stay out of the way, honey, while I get this trash out of here."

She nodded and watched him with bright, anxious eyes. The bond between them had been made stronger. She knew it. He knew it. They had faced death together, fought together. His smile made her heart race with happiness, his voice melted away her fears, his arms were her haven. Whatever she needed, he seemed to supply it magically.

Sam tossed the rifle and the handgun on the bed. He jerked his own gun from the belt of the man slumped against the door and shoved it into his holster. The fat man was moaning and trying to reach his buttock, where about an inch of the hat pin was visible. Sam put his foot in the small of the man's back and jerked the pin out.

Vernon bellowed with pain.

"You drove this thing to the bone, 'Lizabeth." He held up the five-inch pin and tossed a glance at her white face. Her eyes were as large and as green as new oak leaves in the spring. Sam was astounded at what she had done. A strong surge of pride was reflected in his brown eyes.

The toad of man groaned again. Sam poked him in the ribs with the toe of his boot.

"You're lucky this hat pin didn't break. I think you should keep it as a reminder not to bother *tony* women." The grin he threw at Elizabeth was beautiful. Sam slipped the knife from the fat man's scabbard, slit his britches up the side and looked at the gunshot wound. "You're not hurt much. The shot went through the fleshy part of your thigh. Hell! You've got so much blubber on you it spattered fat all over the floor. I'll tie a rag around it. That's all the help you'll get here."

"I'm hurt! I'm bleedin'," Vernon moaned as Sam tied the cloth.

"I hope so. I hope you bleed all the way to Missoula. Now, get on your feet."

"I can't—"

"You will or I'll roll you out the door."

"Oh, God! Oh, Holy Mother! I'm hurt bad—"

"You'll hurt worse if I shoot you in the other leg."

The fat man grasped the end of the bed and pulled himself up. He stood, swaying. "Oh...my head," he whimpered.

Sam watched cold-eyed. "You're alive, but you won't be for long if you don't get the hell out. It goes against the grain to let you walk out of here, but if I ever see you again, if you even look at anything that's mine, I swear to God, I'll kill you." Sam was seething. "You'd better tell that to that one-eyed bastard friend of yours, too."

Ollie was on his hands and knees, shaking his head. Sam reached him in two strides, lifted him by the scruff of the neck with one hand, opened the door with the other and flung him outside. Then he was beside the fat man, shoving him toward the door.

"Our guns—"

"Hell! What guns? You don't have any guns, you filthy bush-bottomed clabberhead."

"We got ta have guns!" Vernon's voice rose hysterically. "There's bears 'n' cats—"

"You'd make a good meal for a cat. Now get the hell out of here before I change my mind." An expression of fury was on Sam's face. He put the sole of his foot against the fat man's rear and shoved him out the doorway.

"Oh...Oh, sweet Jesus, help me—"

"Hush your blubbering. Bar the door, honey," he said over his shoulder.

Elizabeth could hear Sam cursing and the two men begging. Sam was using words she'd never heard even from the dockworkers along the river. She moved around the bloody spots on the floor and hurried to the door.

"Sam," she called. "Where are you going?"

"I'll see these two on their way, honey. Bar the door and don't open it for anyone but me."

Elizabeth didn't want to leave Sam out there in the dark with those two vile men. But she closed the door, leaned her forehead against it and pondered for a second about taking the rifle and going out to help him. No. She knew him well enough to know that he would resent that. He had told her to stay inside. She would stay. Her "man," as the fat man had called him, knew better how to cope with those two bastards than she did.

Chapter Thirteen

The voices outside the cabin faded away. Elizabeth stood with her back to the door, her arms wrapped around herself, and listened to the silence. She locked her knees in an attempt to strengthen legs that were weak and trembling. The minutes passed without sound until a low rumble of thunder broke the stillness. Centuries seemed to pass before she was able to draw an easy breath. When she did, she looked around the cabin as if seeing it for the first time. It seemed a strange and unfamiliar place with the ugly spots of blood on the floor.

She would not tolerate them here in this sacred place! She ladled water into the wash pan, poured it onto the soiled floor and began to sweep the mess away with a straw broom she found behind the wood box. Most of the water went into the cracks between the boards; the rest she swept out the door, which she opened a fraction. When she was finished, she built up the fire in the cook stove and set the coffeepot on to boil.

The wind came up and moaned over the rooftop while she tidied the cabin. Gusts came down the chimney and set sparks dancing in the fireplace. Rumbles of thunder came nearer. She went to the window to peer into the darkness. Flashes of lightning lit the sky with eye-searing brilliance. Thunder roared in its wake. In the brief silence that followed she heard a sharp crack that could have been a shot from a gun. Fear grabbed at her throat with icy hands. She closed her eyes tightly and prayed.

"Oh, God! Bring him back! Please bring him back! I'll never ask for another thing."

To stave off her feverish imaginings, she reminded herself of how perfectly adapted Sam was to this wild country. She forced herself to believe that he knew how to take care of himself. He had acted quickly and put two armed men out of commission. Didn't that prove his ability? Oh, Lord! He had to be all right. He had to come back with that hell-raising grin on his face or...

Outside, the wind slammed against the side of the cabin. Inside, Elizabeth huddled beside the window and tried to think of absolutely nothing. She didn't want to think about Sam, out there in the gathering storm with men who would kill him if they could. She didn't want to think of anything at all. She just wanted to hang on to her control.

The coffee boiled up and out the spout, and sizzling drops landed on the hot stove. She grasped the handle of the pot with a cloth and pulled it to a cooler spot. The pounding on the door startled her, and she almost burned herself. The pounding came again before she could let go of the pot.

"Hey! Open up. It's me."

Her heart leaped. She sped to the door and lifted the bar. Sam came in with a gust of wind that flattened her robe against her legs. He pushed the door shut and dropped the bar.

"Storm coming," he said calmly as if they had not

faced death an hour ago. His eyes skimmed over the room quickly before they settled on her face.

She looked into his eyes and the world danced, then faded away, leaving only the two of them. She held her hands to keep them from reaching for him, while her eyes could find nothing else to do but stare into his. Even her feet moved her closer to him.

"I heard a s-shot." Her tongue felt thick and awkward.

"Just a little send-off. I didn't think about it scaring you."

"They're gone?"

"Yeah, they're gone. Lord, Lizabeth, I'm sorry I let it happen. I thought the one-eyed man was by himself until he told me Vernon was in here with you. Then there was nothing to do but play it by ear. I knew you were up to something when you put on that helpless act."

"Are you all right?"

"Yes. You?"

The intense silence that followed seemed to press the breath out of her and drain all coherent thought from her mind as love for him flared in her heart. She felt his need, his desire pulling her. She felt the hunger in her heart echoing the hunger in his. Silently she went into his arms without a single doubt that he wanted her there, without a single doubt that that was where she belonged.

His arms welcomed her, drawing her closer. He pressed his cold face against the side of hers. Her breath left her in a half sob. All that mattered was that he was safe, holding her as she was holding him. They stood with their arms wrapped around each other for a long while.

Then sparks as alive as those in the fireplace flew through her veins, igniting an intense longing in her heart to know that every inch of him was all right. Her hands crept over him—his upper arms, his shoulders broad enough to shield her from any storm. Her hands moved over his chest to his back and up to his face, touching, touching. When assured, she turned her head to seek his lips with her own.

With a savage sound, Sam pressed her so close to him that their hearts seemed to be beating as one. Her mouth was soft, giving welcome to his, trying in every way to let him know how very precious he was to her. Elizabeth's heart was pounding so hard that it frightened her. She spoke his name with such an imploring inflection that he raised his head to look at her.

"Sam! Oh, Sam!"

"Ah...sweet—"

His open mouth moved to hers as if it would be too painful to stay away. Gently, he barely touched her lips. They exchanged breaths until he felt her yearning body strain against him and her parted lips reach for his. They kissed as if they were starved for each other. He was her universe, her protector, her comfort, her love.

"Liz...sweetheart. I died a thousand times thinking what would happen to you if they killed me."

"Ssh...it's over. Let's don't think about it." She dropped kisses around the curving lines of his mouth, loving the feel of his mustache against her face. His breath quickened; his arms tightened.

"Honey, sweetheart, we shouldn't be doing this."

"I know. But—"

The word ended with an indrawn breath as Sam's tongue delved into the corner of her mouth. She shivered, enjoying the gentle, exciting caress.

"You know I want you." His voice trembled with

raw emotion that sent a shiver down her spine. He spoke with his lips pressed against hers. "Don't you?"

"Yes."

She couldn't deny the rigid evidence swelling fiercely between his legs, for it was pressed tightly to her belly. Her unschooled body moved against it and met its masculine, urgent thrust with one of her own. Mindless of what she was doing to him, she stood on her tiptoes in an attempt to cuddle him between her thighs. He moaned against her mouth.

Suddenly it wasn't enough just to hold her. He needed to feel more of her, needed to let his hands and his heart and that most vulnerable part of his body feast upon her tenderness. He loosened her robe, opened it. His hands moved over the sides of her breasts and spread wide over her back, pulled her so close that her breasts were flattened against his hammering heart. Her breath quickened and her mouth clung to his, opening so he could drink more fully of the passion burning between them.

The fire in him was building hotter and hotter, and with each moment it was harder to control.

Sam lifted his head and looked into the jeweled green eyes. She was as innocent as a child when it came to sex. The knowledge gave Sam a deep and unexpected pleasure. He smiled into her eyes and nuzzled her mouth, licking her tender, swollen lips.

"Do you like that, little sweetheart?" he asked in a soft whisper, feeling her answer in the quivering breath she drew. His fingers smoothed the hair from her ears. She looked as hungry for his love as he was for hers.

"Yes. Oh, yes." The words were a soft sigh against his mouth. "It's wonder—"

The word was cut off by the flick of his tongue caressing the soft inner surface of her lips.

"Oh, honey, I like it, too!" He covered her mouth with fierce, hungry kisses, random and violent, different from the gentle kisses he had given her before.

Clasped tightly to his chest, she could feel her heart hammering against his.

"I want you so much," he whispered against her lips.

"I want you, too...."

Breathing raggedly, his face flushed with passion, he pulled away from her, took her hands, drew them from his neck and brought them to her sides.

"If we don't stop now, I won't be able to." His voice was unsteady.

Coming out of her daze, she felt as if her heart as well as her body was exposed and quickly lowered her eyes. She wrapped her robe around her and tied the belt.

"You must think...that I'm—"

"Hush!" He picked up her hand and held it to his chest. She felt the thud of his strong heartbeat. "You do that to me."

His words sent a shower of joy through her. She closed her eyes for an instant and shivered with pleasure.

"I'm a normal man with normal urges, and you're a beautiful woman. We just got carried away." He dropped her hand and turned away.

Her heart reeled with an inexplicable disappointment. Dear God! She loved him so much, and that gave him this awesome power to hurt her. Keeping her voice carefully in check, she said, "I'm sorry."

Shaking his head, he said something, but thunder drowned out his words. He went to the stove for coffee. She put the straw ring on the chair and sat, because she didn't know if her legs would hold her another minute.

"Coffee?"

"No, thank you. I made it for you."

Sam brought his cup to the table and sat. It took all her courage to face him as if her love wasn't tearing her apart.

It was a physical effort for Sam to look into those luminous green eyes and keep his hands from reaching for her.

"Tell me about Stephen."

It was the last thing she had expected him to say. Stephen. Her mind refused to accept thoughts of Stephen. It was as if he was a stranger intruding in her dreamworld. A long shudder shook her, and a chill passed over her skin. Embarrassment rosied her pale face.

Sam flinched at the pain he saw in her eyes. His hand reached out and covered hers. "What we did was no more your fault than mine."

Always sensible and straightforward, she nodded in agreement, even though pain jabbed at her heart. She squeezed his hand, wishing she could ease the pain of guilt that must surely lie in his heart, too.

The light from the lamp on the table began to flicker. It drew their attention, and their hands pulled apart.

"We're about out of oil. I can get the lantern out of the buggy."

"Don't bother on my account. I think I'll go to bed."

"It was a gutsy thing you did tonight." He smiled, spreading that irresistible charm across his face. "You were great. No woman I know could have done better."

"Not even Jessie?"

"Not even Jessie."

"That's gratifying to know." Her eyes met his briefly. Then she got to her feet and went to the bed.

The smile faded from his face as he became aware of

the hopelessness he had seen in her eyes and heard in her voice.

"I'll put on my slicker and go out for a while."

"There's no need for that. Do you think they'll come back?"

"No. We've got their guns. They'll find a place to hole up and nurse their wounds. They're low-caliber crooks."

"Well, thank you for what you did."

The words hung in the air between them. He watched her take off her robe and get into the bed. She turned her face to the wall and pulled the blankets up to her ears.

Sam sat at the table with his hands around the coffee cup and pondered her words. *Thank you for what you did.* So cold, so formal. There'd been a huskiness in her voice when she'd said them. Dear Lord! He didn't want it to be this way, but what else could he do?

The lamp flickered and went out. Sam sat and listened to the rain on the roof. Through the shadowy darkness he could see Elizabeth, curled up on the bed. He shut his eyes, willing the image of her face, her large sad eyes, out of his mind. God, how it had hurt to push her away. The knowledge that he could have carried her to the bed and made her his ate at him. She had been as eager for him as he was for her. But had he carried her to the bed and taken her, it would have been total commitment, and how could he have faced Stephen when they got to Nora Springs?

The wind died down and the rain settled into a light drizzle, then stopped. Sam let the fire go out. He told himself to go to bed and try to get some sleep. He thought of Vernon and the one-eyed man. The bastards! He didn't care if they died in the rain and the cold. He had given them their lives. It was more than they had planned for him and Elizabeth.

A small sound came from the bed, breaking the silence and sending a shard of pain through his heart. What dreams were haunting her? Was it Vernon and his friend, or was it guilt for what had happened between them? He was at her side even as the thoughts crossed his mind.

"Elizabeth," he whispered, and sat on the edge of the bed. "'Lizabeth, honey. Are you dreaming?" He touched her face with tender strokes and felt her tears. "You're crying! Is it your...sit-down place?"

"No. It's my...my heart."

"Your heart? Ah...honey..." It was a sigh, a prayer.

He rubbed her back, trying to ease her tension. It also satisfied his need to touch her.

"I'll get up, Sam. It wasn't fair of me not to tell you about Stephen."

"Don't get up. It's cold in here. You can tell me tomorrow."

She reached for his hand and, holding it in both of hers, brought it to her lips, then held it beneath her chin.

"I keep wondering what I've done that fate would play these cruel tricks on me." For her, the words just came out. It was like talking to herself.

"What cruel tricks?"

"Making me...wanton, lustful, forgetful of my promise to Stephen. I've been acting like a common wh-whore...wanting you to kiss me."

"How many whores have you known?"

"One."

"That's what I thought. Whores don't want kisses. They want money."

"Mary Lincoln's daughter, Becky, was one. She gave

her favors to every man she met, colored, that is. She wouldn't have anything to do with white men. But she'd make them sing to her before she'd do it—even if they couldn't sing very well.''

''Did she tell you that?'' Sam wanted to chuckle, but most of all he wanted to keep her talking.

''Becky and I played together when we were little. I learned a lot of things from Becky. She liked to tell me about the things she did because it shocked me.''

''It doesn't sound to me like Becky was a whore. A whore gets paid.''

''Mary Lincoln finally made her marry George Brown. Becky didn't care—he sang and played the banjo.''

''What's this got to do with you?''

''I remind myself of Becky. I wanted you to l-love me.'' Her voice cracked. ''I s-still do.''

Sam leaned over and buried his face in the curve of her neck. ''Lord, honey—''

''It's wrong even to want to, isn't it?''

''For us it is,'' he said regretfully. ''If we were free to love each other, it wouldn't be wrong or lustful or wanton. It would be natural and beautiful. I would...love you all night long.''

''I shouldn't have put the burden on you to call a halt to our madness.'' She lifted a hand to stroke his head, not even wondering how she could be saying these things to him. ''I'm sorry. Oh, Sam, Sam...'' She murmured his name as her lips glided over his straight brows, short, thick eyelashes, cheeks rough with stubble. The thought that this was as much as she would ever have of him was a stab of agony in her heart.

''Let me lie down here beside you.'' His urgent whisper came from lips pressed to her neck. "I won't do anything but hold you. I swear it."

Her answer was to move over, make room for him and fold back the blanket that covered her. He unbuckled his gun belt and let it slide to the floor, slipped off his boots and pulled his shirt off over his head. He lay down and drew the blankets over them. Then, turning on his side to face her, he reached for her and pulled her into his arms.

Their groans of pleasure mingled as her soft body came against his. She placed her palm against his chest and snuggled her face in the curve of his neck. The happiness she felt made her a little crazy. *I love you.* The words echoed in her heart and mind. She thought that surely he could hear them. She turned her lips to his skin, knowing that she shouldn't, but needing to, for later, when all she would have would be sweet memories. She felt him tremble violently.

"'Lizabeth—Oh, love, please don't. It's agony to be with you like this and not do more. I should never have lain down by you." He moved to take his arm from beneath her head.

"Don't go!" Her plea came whispering out of the darkness and echoed back to her like a lost wail. She clung tightly to him.

"You don't know what it does to me. It's agony not to kiss your sweet mouth, hold your breast in my hand, feel you surrounding me." As he spoke, he turned on his back and drew her head to his shoulder. Her breasts, pressed to the side of his chest, were like a hot brand.

"Sam?" Her fingertips raked across the soft fur on his chest. She had felt his throbbing hardness through his britches and her nightgown as she lay against him.

"If it hurts you so badly, I'll move away." She began to inch away.

His arm tightened, drawing her closer to his side. "It hurts like hell, but it would hurt more if you moved away. Just lie still, honey. Go to sleep."

"I couldn't."

"Try."

"What are you thinking?"

"I'm...pretending." The words were wrenched from him. The arm beneath her head moved slightly, and his fingers fondled the hair over her ear. He drew in a long, shaky breath and stroked the hair at her temples.

"Pretending what?"

"Don't ask me, beauty. Don't ask me," he said wearily.

"I don't want to cause you pain."

"Then talk to me. Tell me about Stephen."

"All right." She moved her hand on his chest and felt his heart thudding beneath it. The rest of him was still, with a peculiar, silent waiting. "We played together as children."

"Did Becky teach him the facts of life, too?"

"No! He had gone away to school by then. My grandfather and his grandfather were business partners, and had been since before the war. The families were close, and I think they wanted my widowed father and your mother to marry, but it didn't happen."

"Why didn't Eleanor divorce Pa and marry your father? She had the money."

"I don't think it even occurred to her."

"Bull!" The word was wreathed with contempt.

"Stephen went off to school when he was twelve," Elizabeth went on quickly, wanting to get off the explosive topic of Sam's mother. "Two years later I went away to school, and Stephen and I saw each other only during the summers. After he finished school, he worked in the New York office of the shipping company. He would come home for a month or two, then go back. We have always been friends.''

"It would seem to me that you should be more than *friends* if you're going to marry him," Sam said harshly, and grabbed the hand on his chest to hold it still.

Elizabeth was quiet for a while. She could feel the emotions roiling in him. Anger. Resentment. Frustration. Whatever they were, they were tearing him apart.

"Well...let's hear the rest of it," Sam said.

"Two years ago my father died. He was very ill for more than six months. When Stephen came home for the summer, they spent a lot of time together. Father was worried about what would happen to me when he was gone. He'd married Netta when I was fourteen, thinking to give me a mother. It was a mistake. He came to realize it a few years after they married. Netta had no intentions of mothering a girl my age."

"Why didn't he take off and leave her? That seems to be what *tony* people do when they make a mistake in marriage."

Elizabeth knew the bitter words referred to his mother, and she hurt for him, but she made no comment.

"Father asked Stephen to look out for me. We both knew that the family wanted us to marry, so Stephen asked me."

"Why didn't you marry him right away?"

"I couldn't leave Father. He died soon after, and we had a year of mourning. And then...Aunt Eleanor's health began to decline. I didn't want to leave her, either." His hand stopped stroking her hair when she mentioned his mother. "As soon as Father died, Netta began putting pressure on me to marry."

"Didn't Stephen want to?"

"She wanted me to break my promise to Stephen and marry Judge Thorpe. He's twice my age and has a daughter in her teens who is bedridden. He's very wealthy and influential. Netta craves social power, and being stepmother-in-law to the judge would put her in the top echelon of society."

"Why doesn't she marry him herself?"

"He doesn't want her. He wants…me. If she can't have him, it's the next best thing."

"I can't blame him for that," he murmured wearily.

"Stephen came home when his mother died. We decided we'd be married right away to keep Netta from scheming with Judge Thorpe. Mr. McClellan, Stephen's grandfather, thought it a good idea, too. He didn't want his relationship with the judge strained in any way, because they do business together."

"Greed rears its ugly head."

"That's one way to look at it. By then Stephen had found out you and his father were alive. He was so excited and could hardly wait to come to see you. I wanted him to come—it meant so much to him. I didn't think Netta would go as far as to start arranging a ball where I was expected to act as hostess for Judge Thorpe. I was being drawn into their net."

"So you packed up and ran. I'm surprised you didn't stay and fight." The condemnation in his voice cut her to the quick.

"I was tired, and I guess frightened I'd get caught in Netta's trap. After talking it over with Stephen's grandfather, I decided to come out to Stephen. Mr. McClellan is afraid Stephen won't come back."

"There's not much chance of that." There was a hardness in Sam's voice that softened when he added, "It's a different kind of life out here. I can see where it wouldn't suit him."

Elizabeth could feel the ache that lay deep in his heart. His resentment of a mother he had adored and who had abandoned him in childhood was eating at him. It would be there forever unless a way could be found to bring him peace. She was mystified as to why Eleanor had left Montana, mystified as to why Eleanor would tell Stephen his father and brother were dead. Eleanor had been one of the sweetest, kindest people Elizabeth had ever known. Eleanor had suffered, too. Sorrow had turned her hair gray and lined her face at an early age.

"Sam?" She hesitated after saying his name. "Sam, let me tell you about...your mother and what she was like."

"I know what she was like. She was a spoiled, pampered bitch!" The words were spit out harshly.

"She wasn't!"

"She fled to a life of ease, leaving the man who had worked his fingers to the bone for her, keeping from him the pleasure of seeing his son, his *seed*, grow into manhood." He drew a deep, ragged breath. "I'm glad I wasn't the one she took with her. Pa and I got along just fine without her. She and her kind don't have the guts for real living. At the first little hardship, they tuck in their tails and run."

"You're wrong about her—"

"What's it to you? I'll thank you not to meddle in matters that don't concern you." His voice vibrated with hurt and anger.

The harshness of his words cut her to the heart. They

brought a knot to her throat and incipient moisture to her eyelids. She had expected resentment, but not rage.

Physically they were still close, but there was a spiritual distance between them that was a mile wide. He had retreated from her, putting her firmly in the place of an outsider. She wanted to weep.

After he threw off the blanket and left the bed, she gave in to the urge.

Chapter Fourteen

It was a cold, damp morning.

Elizabeth had spent a restless, sleepless night and was awake when Sam placed his hand on her shoulder to awaken her. He immediately went to the shed to tend the animals. He hitched the mare to the buggy and saddled his horse, then brought them to the front of the cabin.

After a quick meal, Elizabeth sat at the table to write a note to the owners of the cabin, telling them of her appreciation. She placed the gray hat with the pink silk rose in the middle of the bed and the note beside it. She wanted to leave money, too, but feared she would step on Sam's masculine pride, because he had said he would take care of it.

Sam was a polite escort and nothing more. She was hurt and confused by the swift change in his attitude toward her. He treated her as if they had just met, as if he had never held her in his arms, called her honey and sweetheart and kissed her. It was as though what had happened between them had meant nothing to him at all. The only conversation he offered was what was necessary to their departure. The warm rapport they had shared was gone.

Sam poured water on the ashes in the stove and in the fireplace. Elizabeth swept the floor one last time and looked around to see that everything was in place. She didn't want to linger for fear that she would show some sentiment for this place that had already been filed away in her bank of things to remember. She put on her coat and scarf, picked up her travel bag and the package of food for their noon meal and went to the buggy. She didn't notice the gawdy top with the red fringe as she climbed in and settled herself on the straw ring.

Sam hammered the nails into the hasp Burley had removed the day they arrived. Elizabeth listened and said a silent goodbye to the little cabin that had sheltered her when she had needed shelter so desperately.

"Are you comfortable?" Sam placed the hammer on the floor of the buggy alongside the weapons he had taken from Vernon and his one-eyed companion. He had put on a heavy coat and turned the collar up to shield his neck from the wind.

"Yes, thank you. The ring helps a lot."

"It's going to be cold. You'd better cover yourself with one of the blankets."

"I will if I need it."

"It could be snowing in the mountains." He avoided eye contact with her and pulled on a pair of leather gloves.

"I can drive—"

"No need for that now. Maybe later." He mounted his horse and moved out ahead of the mare, who seemed content to follow on the lead Sam had attached to her halter.

Elizabeth glanced back. The cabin seemed so small,

forlorn, even terribly shabby. She could almost doubt her memory of what had taken place there. She turned away, her eyes seeking the man riding ahead. Could that polite but distant stranger be the same Sam Ferguson who had held her in his arms last night, who had trembled when she'd raked her fingers across his naked chest, who had been as hungry for her kisses as she had been for his? How long would it take her to forget him? With a growing dread she heard the voice of her heart answer insistently—until the end of eternity.

They were riding into the cold wind. Sam looked over his shoulder and saw Elizabeth pull the blanket over her lap and hug it to her chest. Curls that had escaped the shawl on her head framed her white face. Dark shadows outlined her brilliant green eyes. She was as weary from the sleepless night as he was. She had been through an experience that would have caused most women to go into hysterics. Although she'd been scared half to death, she had stood up as well or better than a woman who had lived with danger all her life.

Sam had no time to dwell on the thought. His horse's ears began to twitch, and Sam reached for his rifle. He let it drop in the scabbard when a deer darted from the brush ahead and raced for cover amid the thick growth of sumac that lined the opposite side of the trail. Sam was glad he'd brought Old Buck. He was spooky. His sire had been a wild mountain mustang, and self-preservation was bred in him. Old Buck could hear every sound and could see and hear better than a man. If there was a living thing nearby, the horse would know it.

Trusting the horse to pick his way, Sam searched every foot of the landscape with the eyes of an experienced woodsman. He would not be taken by surprise again. They came to the crest of a hill, and from where he sat, Sam could see over a broad stretch of country. Nothing moved as they followed the trail into a meadow that lay at the foot of the rugged mountains. He allowed himself another look at Elizabeth. His eyes collided with hers. At that distance he couldn't see the expression in them, but their impact was just as powerful as ever. She stared at him for a long, intense moment before she looked away.

Of all the women in the world, why did he have to fall in love with her? Just looking at her made his pulse quicken! She was like a china figurine he'd seen dancing on top of a music box, but there was nothing hard and rigid about her. She used her cool reserve to hide the fact that she was a frightened, lonely woman. There had never been a woman so beautiful, feminine and soft. She was sensual and exciting, loving and giving. When they were wrapped in each other's arms, he knew that she was as eager for their mating as he was. Yet he had never known a woman who was so totally wrong for him. Born to wealth and luxury, she would come to hate this country and him for keeping her here.

Elizabeth! What was she thinking? How could she know the effort it took not to make love to her? Had it happened, she would not have married Stephen—she'd have been Sam's forever. A woman like Elizabeth would not give her maidenhead to one man and marry another. But what would Sam have? He would have a brother who despised him and a woman who despised his kind of life—and later him. It would be history repeating itself. Hell! He would put her out of his mind, his heart, his life. When they reached Nora Springs, he would turn her over to Stephen and head for the logging camp.

They stopped at midmorning to let the horses rest and drink from a stream that came out of the mountains.

Elizabeth got stiffly out of the buggy, taking the blanket with her to wrap around her. Her cheeks were red from the cold; her warm breath steamed.

"Is it this cold in Nora Springs?" she asked.

"Not this time of year. Nora Springs is in a valley. It's cold in the mountains even in the summertime." Sam pulled his horse away from the icy stream. "That's enough, boy. That water is cold."

Hugging the blanket around her, Elizabeth walked back and forth to get the blood circulating in her legs. Her bottom was healing. It was still sore but not as painful as before.

"Do you think you could drive for a short while? I'd like to ride ahead and look around."

"Of course."

"I'll not be far away." He waited beside the buggy while she climbed in and arranged the blanket over her lap. He reached out and tucked it more snugly around her legs. "She's lazy," he said gruffly. "You'll have to slap her back with the reins every so often to keep her going."

Sam mounted Old Buck and rode beside her for a moment before he moved ahead. Soon he was around a bend in the trail and out of sight. It surprised Elizabeth that she wasn't afraid. The guns lay at her feet. She was sure she'd be able to use them if she had to. How fast one could adapt to one's surroundings, she mused.

Her reverie turned to Sam and the way he had looked at her last night when he returned to the cabin after taking the men away. His gaze had told of a longing in him perhaps secret even from himself. He was lonely and hurting. Oh, Eleanor, how could you have hurt him so?

Nothing in Elizabeth's life had prepared her for loving a man, especially a one-of-a-kind man like Sam Fergu-

son. During her lifetime she had seen little of love between a man and a woman. Her stepmother had certainly
not been in love with her father. And she couldn't remember that any of her friends spoke of undying love
for the men in their lives. They spoke of the man's assets
and his standing in the community. Most of them married to escape from the control of parents and have a
home of their own.

She was alone in this vast country without another
human in sight, and it was pleasant to daydream of a
life with a man like Sam to love, to build a home around,
to bear his children. *His wife would be a queen.* But it
wasn't for her. All she would have of him were her
memories.

She gazed at the trail ahead, but what she saw was a
vision clear and powerful—Sam's intense brown eyes
and the strong lines of his face. She recalled his mouth
when he smiled and the way it rocked across hers in a
seeking caress. The taste of his lips was in her mouth,
and the feel of his silky mustache caressed her cheek.
His hands, the only male hands to touch her breasts,
cupped and caressed them.

Elizabeth shuddered helplessly. It was too late for her.
Sam would never forgive her for being like the mother
he despised. He wanted a woman like his Jessie, who
was waiting for him in Nora Springs. In her mind she
groped for a solution and found only one. It was not too
late for Stephen. She would not let him toss away his
chance for love and happiness because of her. She loved
his brother, and she could not possibly marry him now.
When they reached Nora Springs, she would talk to him,
make him understand, without involving Sam in any
way, that she loved another. She would free Stephen to
seek love with a woman who would truly love him. Then

what would she do? Why in the world was love so gut-wrenchingly painful?

She was jarred from her reverie when she saw Sam coming toward her in a gallop. As he motioned for her to stop, she pulled up on the reins.

"A party of Indians are riding this way," he announced casually. "I want to make sure the guns are covered." He flipped a blanket over the weapons on the buggy floor and tucked it snuggly around them. "Just keep going." He stepped back into the saddle.

"Are they...wild?"

"Not any wilder than Vernon and Ollie," he said dryly, but she thought she caught a glimpse of laughter in his dark eyes before he turned them away. He reached over and slapped the mare on the rump to get her started again and rode along beside her. His calm, steady manner was all that kept Elizabeth's terror at bay.

As they topped a crest, she saw five Indians riding single file on spotted ponies coming toward them. These were the first Indians she had seen beside the ones who loitered around the train stations of the towns she'd passed through on her way west. Stories of Indian atrocities sprang into her mind. She ran her tongue over dry lips at thoughts of scalps and burnings and flaming arrows.

"Crow," Sam said in a low voice as the Indians moved to the side of the trail. "Stop and stay here." Sam lifted his hand in greeting and rode ahead.

Elizabeth couldn't hear what was being said. The Indians sat their ponies stone still and stared at her and the buggy. They wore unadorned doeskin britches, tunic type shirts and seemed to be immune to the cold. Glistening black hair hung straight to their shoulders, framing stoical bronze features.

One of them said something to Sam. He answered with a gesture of his hand toward the buggy. What did they want to know about her? Then to Elizabeth's utter astonishment the Indians began to laugh. They laughed uproariously, pointed at her and nodded their heads in approval. She felt hurt and angry that Sam would permit them to ridicule her. She was even more angry when Sam turned his horse and came toward her with a huge smile on his face. The Indians yipped and raced their ponies around the buggy. The mare became excited, and it was all Elizabeth could do to hold her. One of the Indians rode up close to the buggy, bent his head so he could see beneath the top, and gazed at her.

"Why are they laughing at me?" she demanded angrily.

"Smile," Sam said. "They just want to look at you."

"Why?"

"I'll tell you later. Keep the blanket tucked around you."

Sam took his knife and slashed a length of the fringe from the buggy top. He gave it to one of the Indians. The brave whooped, and holding one end high over his head raced his pony so that the length flowed out behind. The others gathered around Sam, jabbering excitedly while he stripped the fringe from the buggy, giving each a share. They ran their ponies up and down the trail, yipping and yelling and stirring up a dust cloud.

"They're showing off for you," Sam said.

"They needn't bother." Elizabeth took a deep breath and wished that her lips would not quiver so noticeably. "Can we go on?"

"Not yet. Keep smiling."

Elizabeth kept her smile in place, letting no trace of

the anxiety that had settled in her heart affect her smile or her voice when she asked, "What will they do?"

"They'll not hurt you."

As suddenly as if it had been rehearsed, the Indians came to line up in front of the buggy. The first one tied the strip with the fringe attached around his forehead; the others followed. Elizabeth smiled, thinking how ridiculous they looked with the red balls dangling over their eyebrows. The Indians took her smiles as approval and smiled back at her. A puzzled expression replaced Elizabeth's smile when one of the Indians took a blue feather from inside his tunic and placed it on the seat beside her.

"Smile and thank him," Sam said softly from the other side of the buggy.

"Thank you very much. It's a beautiful...feather."

The next brave rode up and handed her three brass buttons strung on a leather string.

"Thank you. I'm delighted to have...the ah... buttons."

She was then presented with a string of colored beads. "They are lovely," Elizabeth exclaimed. "Thank you."

A quirt made of three thin strips of leather bound with hide was placed on the seat, and the rider sped away before she could thank him. Then to Elizabeth's openmouthed amazement, the last man took off his moccasins and handed them to her.

"Oh, but...I can't...take—"

"Yes, you can. Take them and thank him," Sam murmured quickly.

"His feet are...bare."

"Take them! Exclaim over them. He's trying to outdo his friends."

Elizabeth reached for the moccasins and hugged them

close to her breast. She smiled broadly into the face of the pleased young brave.

"Thank you very much. It's sweet of you to give me your...shoes. I shall treasure them always. Thank you."

The young man raised his hand in farewell, gigged his pony with his bare heels and raced away. The others followed. Elizabeth sat still for a moment, then stuck her head out the side to see if it was safe to drop the gift. She saw nothing but a cloud of dust. She let out a long sigh of relief.

"Move over. I'll drive for a while." Sam tied his horse behind the buggy and climbed in beside her.

"What will I do with those...shoes?"

"Moccasins. One thing you'll not do is throw them away where that brave or any of the other Crow will find them." Sam put the mare into motion and they moved on up the track.

"Why did he give them to me?"

"You'll notice that the value of the gifts kept increasing. Each brave tried to out-do the other. First it was a feather; then the buttons, the beads and the quirt. The Crow use the quirt in combat. It's a valuable possession. If the young brave wanted to outdo the one who gave you the quirt, he had to give his shirt, his britches or his moccasins. He chose to give you the moccasins."

"Thank God he didn't choose to give me his britches!" Elizabeth looked at Sam and burst out laughing. He grinned back at her, his eyes drinking in the sight of her smiling mouth, her bright, laughing eyes.

"You came through fine, Liz. Just fine."

His praise was like a warm healing balm.

"Why did you give them the ball fringe, and why in the world would they want it?"

"They thought the buggy the most beautiful thing they had ever seen. They gazed at it in awe."

"So did I when I first saw it." This brought forth another burst of giggles.

"You thought I'd picked out this rig to embarrass you, didn't you?"

"Of course. What prissy-tail woman from Saint Louis wants to ride in a circus buggy?" she asked teasingly.

"I didn't choose it. I was as surprised to see it as you were. I told Jim Two-Horses to get a buggy with good springs and a top. This was all he could find on short notice." Sam looked at her and grinned. "It's awful, isn't it?" The warm light in his eyes was so beautiful that she couldn't look away.

"Awful is a mild word for it. It's atrocious! But you enjoyed it, didn't you?" She tilted her chin, and her eyes gleamed at him. "Sam Ferguson, you were a genuine horse's patoot that morning."

"Uh-huh. And I had a hell of a headache."

"That's no excuse. You'll get no sympathy from me after what you did." She was looking at him again in that alluring way, a smile curving her lips, laughter in her eyes.

"Lord, honey! I've apologized!" The endearment slipped out without his realizing it. "I'm trying to forget it, but I'm afraid that if I live to be a million, I'll not forget *that*!"

"I'm glad! Terribly glad, because I'll not forget it either," she stated flatly, and looked straight ahead, thinking that she would never forget for a different reason. "You still haven't told me what you told the Indians."

"Oh, that! Well...I told them I had given you the buggy as a special gift, that you were a special woman."

"That was sweet of you, Sam, but there's more. What did you tell them that made such an impression on them that they would give me gifts?"

"I told them that you were...pregnant."

"You...told them that I was...?" She shot him a look that questioned his sanity.

"...going to have my son any time and I was trying to get you to Nora Springs so my son would be born in my lodge."

She bristled instantly. "Sam! You liar!"

"They were really impressed when I said you were so big we were sure there would be two sons." His dark eyes sparkled with laughter. "Then I worried that you'd drop the blanket and stand up." The look he gave her was the old devilish look, both sweet and mischievous.

She couldn't resist asking, "Why would you tell a story like that?"

"The Crow are especially protective of their women, and they love their children very much. We're in their territory. You can never tell when we might need their help."

"Sam Ferguson! If you aren't the limit. Do you think they would have hurt us otherwise?"

"They might have tried to steal something."

Time passed swiftly. He told her the Crow Indians were an enemy of the Sioux, and if Custer had taken the advice of his Crow scouts, he would not have been wiped out at the Little Bighorn. Elizabeth listened with rapt attention. She was unaware that they had reached a summit and stopped until Sam said, "Hungry?"

"I hadn't even thought about it."

Sam tied the mare's lead rope to a branch. Elizabeth climbed down from the buggy and turned her back to the cold wind.

"You can go off if you want to. There's no one around."

"How do you know?" She desperately wanted to hold on to the friendly companionship that had existed between them during the past hours.

"Look at Old Buck's ears."

"Old Buck?"

"My horse. His ears will twitch if there's a rabbit within five hundred yards."

"Heavens! I'm not scared of rabbits! How does he feel about a man, a bear or a wildcat?"

"Don't worry, Liz. Take your hatpin and you'll be safe." He threw the teasing words over his shoulder.

Elizabeth went behind the bushes, her head spinning with dizzy waves of happiness.

When she returned, it was to see Sam coming from across the trail with a bucket of water for the mare. He held the canteen out to her. She took off the top and drank deeply of the sweet, cold water and gave the canteen back to him. Sam drank, his gaze locked with hers.

When he went to get a bucket of water for his horse, she opened up the food pack and laid out the fried pies, the bean patties and squares of last night's cornbread. They ate standing up at the side of the buggy away from the wind, and Sam told her about the trail ahead.

"We're about five miles from the main road. There's a particularly hard stretch between here and there. It's rocky and goes almost straight up. It may be that we'll walk up that incline. I wouldn't want you to be in the buggy if the mare should slip and it rolled backward."

"Will we reach the stage station tonight?"

"We'll get there if we can make it up that incline without breaking a wheel. When we reach the station, you may not have a room to yourself. The women usually stay in one room and the men in another."

"That's all right. I'll be fine."

The expression in his eyes as they roamed her face was softer somehow. "You won't be put out?"

"Put out? Heavens, Sam. I can adapt to my surroundings. It isn't as if I'll be sleeping in a communal room forever."

Sam was silent and thoughtful while he devoured two pies.

"I'm glad you poked Vernon with the hatpin. If nothing more than for eating my pie."

"I'll make you some more...." Instant regret for making a promise she would never keep caused her to turn away from him and wrap the beancakes and cornbread in the cloth should the misery be reflected in her face. "We have enough food for tomorrow noon if you'll be satisfied with two beancakes, two squares of cornbread and one pie."

"We'd better be going. Are you sure you don't mind driving?"

"No, I don't mind at all." She loosened her shawl to retie the ribbon at the nape of her neck. The wind blew strands of her hair against her cheeks. She turned, facing the wind. The cloud of dark curls fanned out behind her.

"Let me help." Sam took the ribbon from her hand, gathered the mass at her nape and tied it. "There. That should keep your neck warm."

For an instant before he lifted the shawl to her head she thought she felt his warm breath on her neck, his nose in her hair. Surely she was mistaken, she thought, when he came to tuck the blanket over her lap and about her legs without as much as glancing at her face.

Chapter Fifteen

"We have two choices. We can cut up a steep incline to the main road and make the stage station by night, or we can continue on this lower, longer trail to by-pass the bridge and camp out."

"You mean camp out every night until we reach Nora Springs?"

"Every night. There isn't another way to get on the upper road that I know of."

They had stopped behind a thick stand of cedars that shielded them from the north wind. The sky was gray directly overhead but slightly blue in the north. It had become increasingly colder as the day wore on.

"I thought you had already decided we would go up the incline to the upper road."

"I had, but I've been thinking that I'd better take a look at it first. There may have been a landslide since I saw it last. It may be impossible to get the buggy up there. Will you be afraid if I leave you here for a while?"

"I'll be all right."

"That isn't what I asked you. Will you be afraid?"

"Maybe a little," she said honestly. "But I have a gun if something jumps out at me from the bushes."

"Can you shoot it?"

"Of course, I can…if I have to." She dug into her travel bag and brought out a small derringer.

"Good Lord! That thing wouldn't stop a jackrabbit."

"I hadn't planned on shooting a jackrabbit."

"Put it away." Sam stepped from the saddle and uncovered the pistol he'd taken from the one-eyed man. He checked the load and placed it on the seat beside her. "If you need me, fire the gun and I'll come."

"Do you think I'll need you?"

"No. I wouldn't leave you here alone if I did." He handed her the canteen and watched her while she drank. "This will give the mare a chance to rest—she'll need it if she has to pull the buggy up that slope."

Elizabeth held out the canteen, wiped her mouth on the back of her hand and let her thirsty eyes drink of him.

"I'll be here. Waiting." *I'd wait for you forever in this cold, lonely place if I thought there was a chance you'd come to me.*

His coffee-brown eyes were watching her so intently that a tingling started in her stomach and spread upward. Had she said aloud what had been in her mind? The skin on her face and neck felt as if it were being pierced by a thousand tiny needles. He pulled off his glove and touched her cheek lightly with the back of his hand. Unknowingly, she leaned into it to increase the pressure.

They stared at each other.

Her cheeks were rosy from the cold wind but warm to his touch. Small white teeth nibbled the inside of her lower lip. Her eyes… Good Lord, her eyes were driving him out of his mind! Gazing at him through the thick brush of sooty lashes, they were the wistful eyes of a child that yearned for some unobtainable something. Sam's throat was suddenly tight.

"I'll be back as soon as I can."

"How long will you be gone?"

"A half hour or so."

Elizabeth watched him step into the saddle. Their eyes caught and held for an instant, then he was riding up a narrow path and out of sight. She heard the sound of his horse's hooves striking rock, and then they faded. She was alone. Her eyes stayed on the empty path for a long time. Silence. Not even a bird song broke the stillness.

She wound the reins around the handle of the brake, threw off the warm blankets and climbed down out of the buggy. On the upward side of the trail was a stand of cedars. On the downward side a landscape of scattered pines, some cedar, and shrubs of which she knew nothing spread out before her. She had not realized that they were up so high. Not a thing stirred in all the vast area except for the gray clouds rolling overhead.

As she squatted beside the buggy to relieve her aching bladder, the wind struck her warm bottom with icy fingers. When she finished and adjusted her clothing, she walked briskly up and down alongside the buggy to limber her legs. It was then that she noticed the smell of pines and cedars.

This was Sam's country, his land. It was a strong, beautiful, challenging land. Elizabeth inhaled deeply. There was something about the mountain air, fresh, clear, like cold water in a dry throat, that made one want to inhale deeply.

Samuel...Sam. It was strange how the solid name fit the exciting man. She thought of all the great men she had read about who were named Samuel. Samuel Johnson, the English author. Samuel Adams, a hero of the War for Independence. Samuel Morse, inventor of the electric telegraph. *Her* Sam was just as great in his own way. He and his father had helped build this new land for future generations. Life had not been kind to *her* Sam during his younger years and perhaps that accounted for the hell-raiser side of him. If only she could tell him that she had enough love in her heart to make up for what he had missed.

Back in the buggy she snuggled in the nest of warm blankets and waited, wishing she had the small pocket watch she sometimes wore on a chain around her neck. Sam had said a half hour or so. Surely that much time had passed. Her mind wandered. She was strangely comfortable with her decision not to marry Stephen. She didn't know what she would do beyond that point, but she was sure of one thing; she would never return to Saint Louis. Stephen would understand and help her find a place to live.

It seemed to her that Sam had been gone for hours when she saw him coming back down the path on foot carrying his rifle. His long legs quickly covered the distance between them. He had turned down the collar on his coat and pushed his hat back. Breathing easily, he came up to the buggy before he spoke.

"I left my horse at the top," he said, but his eyes were asking if she was all right.

She saw the concern there and nodded. The bonding between them was becoming tighter and tighter. "What do you want me to do?"

"You'll have to walk. But before we start, I want to distribute the load in the buggy. I'll put your trunk up here on the floor, that is if it will fit on its side, and the other things on the seat."

"I'll help you."

She threw aside the blanket. Before she could turn to get out of the buggy, his hands had gripped her waist and he was lifting her down. Her heartbeat doubled its rhythm. She steadied herself with her hands on his shoulders and looked into his face. Time for her stood still. *Hold me,* she begged silently. He did. For a perfect moment that was over all too quickly he held her against him before his arms dropped and he turned away.

They worked together. He instructed; she obeyed without question. When the load was arranged to his satisfaction, he attached the lead rope to the mare's halter.

"It will be rough going, but if we take it slowly, we'll make it. Ready?"

"Ready." She smiled at him. "Lead on."

"No. You go ahead. I don't want you behind the buggy in case it should break away."

Elizabeth stepped out quickly, walking up the path that narrowed and became rocky as they left the stand of trees. She looked ahead at the steep incline and for a second doubted Sam's wisdom in attempting to take the buggy up over it. On either side of the upward path huge boulders jutted out. Only clumps of bushes dotted the hillside. As she progressed upward, small stones beneath her feet rolled and cascaded down the slope with each step.

"Slow down," Sam called. "You'll wear yourself out before you get halfway up."

She paused and looked back. The path she had come up was steeper than she'd realized. Sam was holding on to the mare's halter, calming her. The horse didn't like the stones rolling beneath her hooves and was putting each foot down carefully. The buggy rocked precari-

ously as one wheel climbed over a large stone. The
higher they climbed, the larger the stones seemed to be.

Conscious of the man behind her, Elizabeth was determined not to show any weakness. She moved steadily.
Once she attempted to look back while still moving. Her
foot slipped, and she went down hard on her knees. The
sharp stones cut into her flesh, but even so she quickly
got to her feet.

"Are you all right?" Sam called anxiously.

"I'm fine. It didn't hurt at all," she answered, watching now where she put each foot. Tears stung her eyes.
It did hurt. "Damn!" she muttered aloud. Dear Lord!
What was happening to her? She never used to even
think swear words and here she was saying them.

They continued to climb, every step an effort for Elizabeth. Sam was taking it slowly, letting the buggy
wheels ease over the large stones.

"There's a flat place just beyond that red boulder up
there. We'll stop and rest a minute."

Elizabeth didn't answer. She was laboring to breathe
and concentrating on putting one foot ahead of the other.
Every so often she grasped a boulder with her gloved
hand to help her along. Behind her she could hear Sam
talking to the mare, urging her on up the grade. By the
time Elizabeth reached the red rock jutting out from the
hillside, her chest hurt and a moist film covered her face.
She moved around to where Sam couldn't see her and
leaned against the cold stone, breathing heavily, hoping
to get back her wind before he reached her.

The mare's sides were heaving when she pulled the
buggy up over the rim to the flat area. Sam patted the
side of her face and talked to her.

"You did good, girl. We'll rest here awhile before we
ask more of you." He dropped the lead rope to the

ground and placed a couple of stones behind the buggy wheels. He checked the wheels over for cracks and inspected the shaft and harness before he took out the canteen and came to Elizabeth.

"Everything's all right so far."

"I didn't realize it would be so hard on the horse."

"She's doing all right. How're you doing?"

"Fine."

"Did you hurt yourself back there?"

"Not much. I just wasn't looking where I was putting my feet. You don't seem to be winded at all."

"Well, I am, a little." He held out the canteen.

"Did you ride up the first time?" She drank while waiting for him to answer.

"Part of the way." While he drank, his eyes stayed on her face. "It'll be cold on top. Do you have something I could use to wipe sweat off the mare? I'd use a blanket, but we may have to use them later, and I doubt you'd want to wrap up in dirty blanket."

"I'll have something in my trunk."

Sam capped the canteen, tossed it in the buggy and came to stand beside her. He leaned one shoulder against the boulder and looked intently at her profile. The hair at her temples was wet, and her face was flushed.

"Pretty hard going for a city woman, huh?"

She turned to look at him. He flashed her a smile, and she knew he was laughing at her. She was so tired that she was almost light-headed. She was hot but didn't dare take off her shawl and let the cold wind hit her damp head. Her knees felt as if holes had been bored into them straight through the bone. She looked into his grinning face and mocking brown eyes. Her temper flared out of control.

"You're hateful to say that! I'm not a mountain goat," she spit out.

"I'll agree to that." His low laugh only increased her anger.

"I've not done so badly—for a *city* woman! I've gotten this far without any help from you. You've not had to prod me or push me, have you? You haven't heard me complaining, have you? I'll even push the damn buggy if need be."

He gave a low whistle. "Hey... I didn't mean—"

Elizabeth's temper was so out of control that he could have been singing Yankee Doodle or reciting the Lord's Prayer and she would not have known the difference.

"You've been putting me down, Mr. Hell-Raiser Ferguson, since the morning we left Missoula, and I'm tired of it! I'm here to tell you that *this* prissy-tailed *city* woman has as much *guts* and stamina as your *sainted* Jessie has and is a whole lot smarter, because I see you as the cad that you are."

She turned her back to him, refusing to allow him the satisfaction of seeing her eyes tear and her lips tremble. Despite her inner turmoil, she was terribly conscious of him. She had tried her best. Evidently it was not enough. His ridicule hurt, angered and humiliated her.

"Honey, I didn't mean—" His hand on her shoulder tried to turn her. The action only angered her more.

"And don't call me something you don't mean! It's...it's deceitful, condescending and...demeaning! I'm immune to your flattery, Mr. Ferguson."

"How do you know I don't mean it?" His voice was low and rumbled close to her ear.

"Because...you say it as if you can't even remember my name."

"Hmm...by the way, what is your name?"

She whirled. "Samuel Ferguson, you make me so damn mad I could spit nails!"

He lifted his brows. "We might as well go if you're not going to at least try to be pleasant company."

"It will be my pleasure to put as much distance between us as possible."

"Then get going, Miss Prissy-tail city woman. If I come to within a yard of you, I'm going to poke you in your beautiful behind."

"If you so much as touch me, you'll be sorry. You and your damn buggy can roll back down the hill straight into hell as far as I'm concerned. You think you're so damn smart, but you're damn dumb! *Dumb as a stump*," she shouted over her shoulder.

"Now, now, now, Lizzy honey!"

"Don't Lizzy honey me, you...damn hell raiser, you!"

"Shame on you. Nice tony ladies shouldn't swear."

"Bull," she yelled defiantly. Then, "Damn it to hell! Damn it to hell! Damn it to hell!"

"Stop that!" he shouted. "I'll wash your mouth out with soap."

"You'll have to catch me first."

With angry tears blurring her vision, Elizabeth tackled the incline with a purpose—and that was to reach the top and watch him struggle with the mare and buggy. She climbed with fierce determination, concentrating on one step at a time and oftentimes leaning over to go on all fours, unmindful that her skirt was hiked, showing him an expanse of her legs and thighs. What difference did it make? He'd already seen more of her than anyone else except for old Aunt Marthy, her childhood nurse.

Watching her, Sam chuckled. He hadn't intended to make her angry, but as long as she was, he hoped she'd stay that way until she reached the top. It was giving her the extra energy she needed. Lord, what a wonderful, crazy, exciting woman! She would drive a man wild, but having her would be worth it. When they reached the top, he was going to bury his hands in her hair and kiss her sweet mouth until she was breathless.

He turned his attention to the mare, coaxed her up and over a high ledge. She stood quivering while he went behind the buggy and lifted its wheels over a large stone.

When he looked ahead again, Elizabeth was climbing over the rocks on all fours. Her skirt was hiked so high that he could see her drawers. What a sight! Miss Prissytail Caldwell scrambling over the rocks like a billygoat. The laughter he suppressed almost choked him.

Elizabeth reached the top. For a minute the cold wind felt good on her face. She drew great gulps of air into her tortured lungs. While her heartbeat slowed, she looked down the slope and felt satisfaction at what she had done. Now, just let Sam accuse her of being a weakling and she would laugh in his face.

She watched him and the mare labor to get the buggy up the last dozen yards. Dark shale shifted beneath the mare's hooves and Sam's boots. The buggy wheels jarred up and over stones as they made their way up the craggy hillside. Elizabeth forgot how weary she was and how angry she had been. She sent silent messages of encouragement to the horse and the man. Just a little farther. Come on, come on...

The last few yards were tortuous. Then the mare dragged the buggy onto the road and stood with her head down, her sides heaving, her coat covered with sweat. Elizabeth reached into the buggy for her valise and pulled out a long flannel nightgown and the only other thing she could find, a small towel.

"It'll be ruined. It might not come clean again," Sam said when she handed him the gown.

"That's all right. She's earned it."

Elizabeth wiped the mare's face and neck with the towel. Sam worked on the rest of her.

"It was mean of us to ask that of you," Elizabeth crooned. The mare's ears flopped as if in agreement. "You're a good girl and you deserve an extra treat tonight."

"It's a good thing Jim didn't get a pretty, dainty mare, or we'd never have made it."

"Pay no attention to him, pretty girl," she said to the mare. "He's insinuating that you're not pretty, and you are. He only sees what's on the outside."

When Sam finished wiping the horse, he tied the trunk and valises on the platform behind the buggy to make room for Elizabeth.

"If she stands there much longer, she'll stiffen up. Let's go. But first—"

He spun Elizabeth around, cupped her face with his hands, then moved his spread fingers beneath the shawl to comb through her hair. With his thumbs locked beneath her jaw, he tilted her head and put his mouth to the sweet, soft one that was driving him crazy. His lips pressed recklessly hard, giving hers no choice but to part. She clutched at his coat as she felt his tongue flick the corner of her mouth, slide between her lips and move across her teeth.

Lord, help me! She's so sweet, and it's been so long since I kissed her.

The pressure of his kiss forced Elizabeth's head back even though he cradled it between his hands. His lips moved hungrily, furiously over hers before he broke away and looked into her face. Their eyes locked; green eyes looked into brown unwaveringly. Ragged breaths hissed through wet, throbbing lips.

"Why…did you do that?" she gasped.

"That was for…swearing."

"That was punishment?" The question tumbled out of her heart through her lips.

"No," he muttered huskily. "That was wonderful." He lifted her into the buggy and wrapped her in the blankets.

Sam mounted his horse and picked up the lead rope. They moved down the road. Elizabeth sat in a daze, looking at the broad back of the man riding ahead. What had inspired the intimate kiss? Her heart thumped at the question that played over and over in her mind. Punishment for swearing was a feeble excuse. He had kissed her because he wanted to kiss her, and she had kissed him for the same reason.

Elizabeth ran the tip of her tongue over her kiss-bruised lips, searching for a taste of his. He was so blatantly male that when he touched her, she lost her anger and her need overcame her common sense. It wasn't fair. It wasn't fair that a man have such power over a woman that she would sell her soul for a few glorious hours in his arms.

As light faded from the sky, the air became increasingly colder. Sam kept doggedly on. The road was rutted in places but smoother than the trail they had been using. Elizabeth found herself dozing, then sat up straight, refusing to be overcome by weariness. She would not be caught sleeping. It would be a sure sign that she was not as strong or as durable as his infallible Jessie.

It was twilight when they approached Underwood's Station. Elizabeth saw a two-story ranch house. The lower part was stone, the upper hewn logs. It was a sturdy-looking structure with outbuildings and a network of pole corrals surrounding it. Light shone from glass windows in the front. A half a dozen heavy freight wagons were parked to block the wind, and several men loafed around a small fire.

When they passed the first wagon, Elizabeth realized how fragile the buggy appeared in comparison to the wagon. The huge wheels on the freight wagon were almost as high as the top of the buggy, and the covered load rose above the wagon's six-foot sideboards. Their arrival was an event. The men at the fire stood and gawked. Sam answered their greetings but ignored their remarks about the buggy. He didn't stop until he reached the station door.

Elizabeth threw off the blankets, climbed out of the buggy and waited for him to tie the horses to the hitching rail. Without a word he took her arm and escorted her inside. The large square common room was well lighted and filled with cigarette smoke, and it smelled of whiskey and beer. Three of the four tables in the room were occupied by men playing cards. Conversation stopped when Elizabeth and Sam walked in, and she pulled the shawl off her head. A man with bushy black hair on his face but none on his head came from behind the counter. He wiped his hands on the white apron tied around his middle.

"Howdy, Sam. Where'd you come from? Travelers has been scarce as hen's teeth since the bridges were knocked out."

"Hello, Roy. Have you heard who's behind it?"

"There ain't no doubt it's that new outfit, the Utah Stage Company, trying to keep Northwest from filling the contract. They've hired some good-for-nothin' drifters to do their dirty work. It's been hard on everyone who uses this road. The teamsters will string them up if they catch them.''

While the man was talking to Sam, his eyes were darting between Sam and Elizabeth. He was plainly curious.

"How about the bridge up ahead?"

"Workin' on it. Shoring it up. Not strong enough yet for freight wagons.''

"How about a buggy?"

"I heard they took a wagon across. How's Joe doin'? And Jessie? She was here a few weeks back, visitin' the woman.''

"They're fine, far as I know. I've been away for a while. Do you have a room for the lady, Roy?"

"We're full up with freighters, but we'll find something. Come on back and we'll talk to the woman."

Mrs. Underwood was plump and pretty and considerably younger than her husband. Delighted to see Sam, she asked immediately about Jessie. After Sam gave her the same answer he had given her husband, she launched into details of the fine time they'd had when Jessie came to visit. She was polite but reserved when Sam introduced her to Elizabeth without any explanation as to why they were traveling together. Elizabeth was sure Mrs. Underwood was making comparisons between her and Jessie, whom everyone seemed to hold in such high esteem. Her dislike for the unknown woman built rapidly.

Mrs. Underwood took Elizabeth to a room not much larger than a closet. It had a narrow, neatly made bed and a stand for a pitcher and bowl and that was all. Several dresses for a small girl hung on pegs on the wall.

"I'll fix something for you to eat," Mrs. Underwood said, and left her.

After washing, Elizabeth returned to the kitchen and

ate alone at the end of a long table. The eggs, potatoes and hot bread she was served were delicious. Again the innkeeper's wife was polite but offered no conversation. Elizabeth caught the woman glancing at her from time to time but was too tired to make the effort to be friendly.

Within ten minutes after she returned to her room, she was in the bed and asleep.

Sam lingered in the barroom, talking with Roy Underwood and watching the men play cards. Two men at the far table looked familiar, and he finally realized they were the two who had tried to pick a fight with Jim Two-Horses at Haggerty's. Tonight they were sober. They'd had only one drink each in the hour Sam had been observing them.

"What do you know about the two in the corner nursing their drinks, Roy?"

"Not much. They've been here a few days. Pay their way, so I can't kick on it."

"Know their names?"

"They say their names are Pete Matson and Fred Davis. The one with the red kerchief is Pete. He's the mouthy one."

"Are they freighting?"

"Naw. They came in with only a couple saddle horses and a bedroll. Said something about goin' on up to Canada."

"They'll never make it hanging around here." Sam finished his drink. "I'll turn in. I want to get an early start. Is there a crew up by the bridge?"

"They've got a camp up there. One of the men said they're out cutting timber to use for shoring up. The freighters are gettin' heated up over this."

"Burley and Jim took the lower road. They should be in Nora Springs by now."

"The wagons out front got caught between here and Haggerty's. There ain't no way they could get on the lower trail. It'll snow any time now, and they're worrying about it up on Bitterroot."

"So am I. That's why I'm crossing that bridge in the morning. If it'll hold a wagon, it'll hold a buggy."

"In a hurry to get home, huh?"

"Yeah. I could be logging now."

"Sam, who...ah...is the lady?"

"Elizabeth Caldwell from Saint Louis. I'm escorting her to Nora Springs. Well, good night."

Sam was sure Roy was going to ask more about Elizabeth but thought better of it. Sam didn't see any reason to satisfy his curiosity.

Sam's departure did not go unnoticed. The two men in the corner had been watching him as closely as he had been watching them.

"That son of a bitch almost broke my neck at Haggerty's. I knowed him soon as he rode in with that woman in the buggy. Ain't no mistakin' that buggy," Pete said.

"They took out from Haggerty's with that Injun and old man. Where do ya reckon they went?"

"How in hell do I know?" Pete glared at his friend. "They was takin' the lower trail, Haggerty said. There ain't no way up from that lower trail with a buggy less'n ya got wings on it. How'n hell did he get here?"

"Stay clear of him."

"Don't be tellin' me what to do. I'm takin' him down a notch for what he done."

"He ain't a man to be messin' with."

"No? I reckon he's got to cross that bridge less'n he's stayin' here."

"You dunderhead! Mess this up tryin' to get even with that feller and I'll shoot you so full of holes you'll look like a screen door."

"I ain't messin' nothin' up. The crew is off cuttin' lodgepole, ain't they? They is wantin' ta make that bridge strong enough to hold the stage, ain't they?"

"Yeah."

"Underwood told that son of a bitch a wagon crossed. He'll be takin' that buggy 'cross in the mornin'."

"Pete! I swear I'll—"

"Wait. Hold yore horses and listen—"

"We ain't gettin' paid ta settle yore grudges."

"If'n ya'll jist listen, I'll tell ya how we can do both and nobody'll be the wiser. They'll think the bridge warn't strong enough ta hold em."

"I told ya that Ferguson ain't to be messed with."

"He bleeds like any other feller."

"What do you have in mind?"

"It'll be as easy as fallin' off a log."

Pete put his head close to his friend's and began to talk earnestly.

Chapter Sixteen

"Elizabeth."

Her name was a soft whisper wooing her from the depths of sleep. She awakened with Sam's hand on her shoulder. She knew instantly that it was his voice, his hand, and reached to cover it with hers.

"Are you awake?" he whispered.

"Yes."

"Dress and come out to the kitchen. You can eat while I load the buggy."

"It was an awfully short night."

"It's cold, so put on your warmest clothes." He struck a match, lit the lamp looked at her. Unruly dark curls framed her face. Her soft pink lips parted as she squinted her eyes against the light. "Open your eyes so I'll know you're awake."

"Mmm. I'm awake." Sleepy green eyes looked at him. A grin split her lips.

"Hurry up so we can get going," he said almost gruffly. Then he went out the door.

Shivering with cold, she used the chamber pot, then dressed, and packed her night things in her valise. Hoping for warm water to wash with, she hurried to the kitchen.

Mrs. Underwood, her forearms covered with flour, was kneading bread at one end of the table. She glanced up, her eyes rudely assessing Elizabeth's blue pinstripe wool skirt and the matching jacket she wore over a white high-necked blouse.

"Good morning. It's cold this morning." Elizabeth hung her coat with the Hudson Bay seal collar on a peg and went to the washstand.

The murmur that came from the woman was scarcely more than a grunt. So much for trying to be friendly, Elizabeth thought, and ladled water into a washdish. She carried the teakettle from the stove and poured in enough hot water to take off the chill. She washed her face and hands, then dried them on the towel that hung at the end of the wash bench.

"Help yourself to meat and mush." The woman spoke almost grudgingly, and Elizabeth's hackles rose.

"Thank you, I will."

Elizabeth served herself mush from the kettle on the stove and sweetened it with honey from the crock on the table. She poured coffee into a heavy cup and weakened it with milk. Then she seated herself at the far end of the table and silently began to spoon the mush into her mouth. It was hot and surprisingly good.

"Do you have relatives in Nora Springs?" the woman asked suddenly.

The question caught Elizabeth by surprise. She wondered why Sam hadn't explained who she was and why she was traveling with him. She didn't see any reason to satisfy the woman's curiosity, so she said, "No."

"Are you going to stay long?"

"I haven't decided for sure, but if I like it, I may stay there permanently."

"What will you do? The only work for a single woman in Nora Springs is in the laundry or keeping house for a widower with kids."

"Is that right? Well, don't worry about me, Mrs. Underwood. I plan to buy the bank."

She looked up to see the woman's mouth fall open and a blank look settle over her face. Elizabeth smiled around the spoon in her mouth.

"I've known Jessie for a long time," Mrs. Underwood said then. Elizabeth waited and wondered what that had to do with what she was going to do when she reached Nora Springs. When Elizabeth made no comment, Mrs. Underwood went determinedly on as if there had been no pause. "She and Sam stop here when they go to Missoula."

"Really? How nice." *Do they share a room?* She wished she had the nerve to ask, just to see the woman's jaw drop again.

"It gets awfully cold up there in the winter. The church women have quilting bees, and the church has a box social once in a while. Other than that there isn't much to do. They're snowed in up there for weeks at a time."

"That sounds delightful to me," Elizabeth exclaimed happily. "I'd get a chance to catch up on my reading." She smiled although she would have dearly loved to throw the bowl, mush and all, into Mrs. Underwood's bread dough.

"We'll go as soon as you've finished," Sam said from the doorway.

"I'm ready now."

"Sam, be sure to tell Jessie I said hello and to hurry

back for another visit. You and Jessie stop for a few days when you go to Missoula in the spring. We always have such a good time while you're here.'' The short, plump woman pounded the dough as if she was trying to kill it.

''I'll tell her.''

Elizabeth tied a scarf over her head and put on her coat. She smiled sweetly at the other woman.

''Thank you so much for the warm hospitality, Mrs. Underwood. Goodbye.''

''Goodbye.''

Elizabeth followed Sam through the darkened barroom and into the cold gray morning. He helped her into the buggy and wrapped the blankets around her.

''I don't think Hazel caught the sarcasm in your voice, but I did. What was that about?''

''She was about as warm as a frozen pond. She treated me as if I was a bear about to grab a choice morsel from her dear friend Jessie.''

''She and Jessie have been friends for a long time.''

''I'm terribly happy for both of them.''

''What does she think you're trying to take from Jessie?''

''You.''

''Me?''

''You. She and Mr. Owens both took pains to let me know that you are Jessie's property. Somehow everyone has the stupid idea that I'm a threat to their precious Jessie.''

''Listen, lady. I'm nobody's *property*.''

''Well, don't tell me about it. I'm not interested.''

''Yes you are.'' His face wore a grin that she didn't trust. ''You damn well are interested or my name's not

Sam Ferguson.'' His grin broadened so that she could see the flash of his white teeth.

"Then, hello, *George Smith*,'' she snapped waspishly.

Still grinning, he mounted his horse.

They left the station, moved past the freight wagons and went onto the road. There was no sound except for the thud of the horses' hooves and the whistle of the wind as it whipped the tops of the evergreens. Warm breath fogged the crisp morning air.

Sam looked back. All he could see was the white blur of Elizabeth's face framed in the fur collar of her coat. *She was jealous of Jessie!* That had to mean she had special feelings for *him*. She had responded to his kisses, but that could have been because she was love-starved. This was different. She resented Hazel pairing him with Jessie. The warm glow of that discovery lasted until Sam was forced to turn his mind to other matters.

He wished he'd made sure that Pete Matson and Fred Davis were still in their blankets in the room where the men slept. Something about the two men bothered him. Saddle tramps usually didn't hang around stage stations paying for bed and board. If they had money, they would rather spend it on whiskey than a place to sleep. There had to be a reason these two were being cautious.

Daylight brought the promise of another cloudy day. Sam heard a stream of honkers heading south. He peered up, and could barely see the V formation of a hundred or more birds. Their long necks were stretched in flight as they followed their leader to a feeding ground.

"You can't be fooled, can you?'' he asked aloud. "You know when it's time to get out before the snow.''

Sam loved the sights and the sounds made by the beautiful Canadian honkers. He loved the changing seasons—spring with the deer and antelope roaming the mountain meadows; summer with its clear flowing streams; fall with a panorama of color; winter with the country white and still. The sound of an ax biting into the trunk of a pine could be heard for half a mile.

As much as he loved the woman riding behind, Sam knew his life was here. He would never forget her, just as his father could not forget his mother, but time healed, and in the distant future Sam might find a woman who would give him some measure of contentment.

They came to the bridge an hour after daylight. Sam had not remembered it being that close to Underwood's Station. He stopped, tied his horse and the mare to a downfall beside the road and came back to the buggy.

"I'm going to walk out on the bridge."

"Can I come with you?"

"I guess so, but only as far as the edge."

The span, some fifty feet across and twenty feet above a cut made by a fast-moving mountain stream, was shored up with lodgepole pine. The sideless roadway, made of thick, rough plank, sagged in places, giving it a wavy look. The fierce wind rippled the loose boards, causing a rumbling sound. It also ripped at Sam and Elizabeth as they stood at the edge of the bridge, jarring them with sudden gusts that caused Sam to put his arm around Elizabeth, to hold her at his side.

"There isn't much water down there," Elizabeth said from the shelter of his arm, her voice almost lost in the wind.

"In the spring, when the snow thaws, it'll be bank to bank." He held her. "I'm going to walk across. You'd better go back to the buggy."

"Be...careful." She clutched his arm with her gloved hand before he pulled away from her. He anchored his hat firmly on his head and turned his collar up to shield his face from the wind.

Elizabeth didn't take her eyes off him or draw a deep breath as he crossed the bridge. The wind buffeted him so that he had to plant his feet wide apart to keep his balance. It seemed to take forever for him to reach the other side, but when he did, he paused, looked at her and waved his hand. He came back across the bridge holding the brim of his hat with one hand, the collar of his coat with the other.

"It seems to be pretty solid, but that damn wind is awful. I'll take my horse across and come back for the buggy. We'll have to take off the top or the wind will get under it and lift it right off the bridge, taking the mare with it."

"What do you want me to do?"

"Stay here. I'll take my horse over, then the buggy, then I'll come back for you. I figure if the bridge will hold the buggy and the mare, it should hold you." He grinned his devilish grin and bumped her chin with his gloved fist.

Elizabeth looked up to meet his smiling gaze. She had seen those eyes in so many moods; they had laughed, teased, grown fierce with anger. Now they were filled with warmth as the smile she adored claimed his face.

"Oh...you—"

Sam had to coax Old Buck to leave solid ground and take the first few steps on the bridge. The sound of his hooves on the planking scared him, and he balked. Finally, tossing his head and rolling his eyes, he allowed Sam to lead him onto the windswept span. Elizabeth watched with her heart in her throat until they reached the other side. Sam tied the horse securely to a tree branch and made the trip back. He went to the buggy and began removing the bolts that held the top in place.

"We could have given the whole top to the Indians if we'd known about this," Elizabeth said.

"I was wishing we had as we were coming up that slope. It would have made it easier on the mare."

As Sam unscrewed the last bolt, the wind helped him lift the top to the side of the road. He turned the top upside down and left it.

"The buggy doesn't look so bad now." Elizabeth stood back, tilted her head and laughed. "I'm almost fond of it. It's become a second home."

Sam checked the load, making sure the blankets in the seat were weighted down so they wouldn't blow out.

"You came up that slope, girl," he said to the mare. "The bridge shouldn't give you any trouble at all."

"Sam—"

"Don't worry. I'll be back for you." He motioned to the side of the road. "Why don't you stay down there in the gully out of the wind."

The mare was even more frightened than Old Buck had been. When she had all four feet on the bridge plank, she tried to rear. Only Sam's weight on the halter, holding her head down, prevented it. He talked to her, coaxed her, and finally she calmed enough to follow him.

It was torture for Elizabeth to watch Sam cross the bridge. She moved into the gully as he had told her to. Unable to help herself, she cast quick glances up, keeping track of his progress. She couldn't bear to watch, yet she had to know what was happening.

To keep her mind occupied, she glanced up and down the gorge. Among the rocks and trees a flash of color caught her eye. She squatted so that she could see beneath the bridge. What she saw was incredible, unbelievable. Two men, one with a red kerchief tied around his neck, were working furiously with a two-man saw, cutting through the timbers that supported the far end of the bridge. As she watched, they sawed through one pole and hurried to another!

"Sam! Sam!" she screamed as she scrambled out of the gully. Without a thought of danger to herself, she ran onto the bridge. "Sam!" Her wail was lost in the wind that pushed her perilously close to the edge, threatening to sweep her off the platform. Elizabeth stiffened her body, throwing her weight forward, and staggered on. "Hurry!" she sobbed. "Please, please hurry!"

It took all Elizabeth's strength just to stay on the bridge, and she made little progress forward. The wind billowed her skirt and swept the scarf from her head. Her hair flowed out behind her. She was halfway across the span when she felt the bridge shudder beneath her feet and saw the back of the buggy tilt. One side of the bridge sank, causing the plank behind her to pop loose and slide into the river. Crazed with fear, she got down on her hands and knees, hiked her skirt up around her waist and began to crawl across the tilted span.

It seemed an eternity before she heard a shout. She was too frightened to look up for fear Sam and the buggy had plunged to the rocks below. Sobbing his name, she crawled as fast as she could. Then he was there, pulling her to her feet, forcing her to run with him over the slanting planks, stumbling over those that had come loose and were flopping in the wind. They reached the end. A gap of several feet separated them from the bank, but Sam didn't slow the pace or hesitate.

"Jump!" he shouted.

She did. They landed on solid ground and took several staggering steps before they could stop. Elizabeth turned and flung her arms around his neck. Sam crushed her to him, lifting her off her feet and swinging her around. He held her in a vise-like grip, buried his face in her neck. Low moaning sounds came from his throat.

"Oh, sweetheart! Oh, my precious love!" The words broke from him in a sob when he was finally able to speak. "You silly, wonderful, precious woman! I love you! I love you so much!" Then he was kissing her eyes, her nose, her lips. "Oh, Lord, I died a million times! Are you all right?" He didn't wait for her to answer. "I thought I'd lost you. Oh, sweetheart! I thought I'd lost you!"

She clutched him with fierce desperation. "I thought…I thought…you'd not make it across in time."

"Dear God! My heart stopped when I saw you out there!"

"I had to come…to tell you to h-hurry."

"I felt the bridge go." His lips moved over her cheek. "I looked back and saw you. My heart almost stopped…I had to get to you…I ran…Somehow the mare got the buggy to the bank. Oh, love…" Words tumbled from his mouth in snatches, words whispered against her ear.

"The men were sawing the posts…so you'd fall—"

"Sweetheart! Thank God, you're safe! I didn't realize you were so precious to me." Hungrily his eyes slid over her face. He kissed her hard on the mouth. Then he raised his face and looked into her eyes. "What did you say?"

"Two men were under the bridge. They had a saw, one on each end. They were sawing through the posts. I wanted you to hurry—I was scared you'd not make it across in time!"

"They were cutting the shoring on this side? Where it sank?"

"I could see them from the other side. They sawed through one post and ran to another."

He swore viciously and put her from him. "Lead the mare away from here and stay with her. Can you do that?"

"Yes. What will you do?"

"Do as I say, sweetheart." He ran to his horse and grabbed his rifle from the scabbard. "Stay away from the bridge," he cautioned, and went into the bushes that grew along the roadway.

Sam dug his heels into the hillside and slid to a ledge above the water. He moved, hunched over, until he reached a pile of partly burned and split poles left by the building crew. He crouched. He could see where the support posts had been cut. One side of the bridge angled almost straight down. The boards creaked as the bridge swayed in the wind. The end of the bridge would break loose at any time, pulling the rest of the bridge with it. Thankfully he was on the windward side.

For what seemed a long while Sam saw nothing. Then he caught a movement on the bank upriver. As he watched, he saw it again. A moment later two men emerged leading horses. One had something red tied around his neck. Without hesitating, Sam got to his feet, lifted the rifle to his shoulder and took careful aim. The bullet struck one man in the leg, right where Sam wanted it to go. Before the echo of the shot died, Sam pumped another shell in the chamber and fired again. The bullet struck the other man high up on the thigh. Both men fell to the ground. The frightened horses took off, splashing across the river.

"Don't touch those guns, or I'll blow your heads

off," Sam shouted as one of the men clawed at the holster on his thigh.

Minutes ticked by. When the men didn't move, Sam went toward them, edging his way along the rocks. He had needed those minutes to control the fury that raged within him. The bastards had come within an inch of killing Elizabeth. Had they finished their mission a minute sooner, she would have fallen into that rocky gorge. As he approached, one of the men was thoroughly cursing the other.

"Damn you for a stupid son of a bitch. You boneheaded idiot! I should never have hitched up with a brainless fool! We're through!"

"You sure as hell are," Sam snarled. "I should belly shoot both of you for what you've done. Toss your guns in the river and be damn quick and damn careful doing it. I'd just as soon save the marshal the trouble of taking you to jail, that is if you live that long."

"Don't...shoot," Pete begged.

Both men, keeping their eyes on Sam, tossed their weapons into the stream.

"You're the ones that's caused the trouble for the stage line. The bridge crew and the teamsters will give you a welcome when you get back to Underwood's. Get going up that bank unless you think getting shot is better than what's waiting for you."

"We can't! I...can't walk..." Pete whined.

"Then crawl. I don't give a damn how you do it. I'll give you to the count of three to get started or I shoot you in the other leg. One—"

Fred staggered to his feet. "Get up or lay there and get shot, damn you! I'm not carin'. Ya had to get your own back and ya ruined everythin'!"

"Two—"

Moaning with pain, Pete got to his feet. Both men climbed slowly up the bank, leaving a trail of blood on the rocks and boulders. They had almost reached the top when three men came from the road.

"We heard the shots. The lady told us what happened."

"You're the bridge crew?"

"Part of it. The rest is bringin' in the poles we cut this mornin'."

"You'll need plenty, thanks to these bastards, who sawed through your shoring and almost dumped us in the gorge."

"We didn't do nothin'. It was two other fellers. We was chasin' 'em," Pete blabbered.

Sam ignored him. "You'll find a two-man saw around here someplace," he said. "Get on up to the road." He poked Pete in the back with his rifle. "The lady will know if you're the ones she saw cutting through the piling while I was on the bridge."

"We ort to string 'em up," a bearded crewman growled.

"I suspect they're being paid to keep the bridges out of commission. How's the one up north?"

"All right, far as I know."

Elizabeth was waiting at the edge of the road when they reached it. Her worried eyes sought Sam's. She hurried to him and slipped her hand into the crook of his arm.

"I heard the shots!"

"These two felt the bullets. I should have aimed higher and they'd have felt nothing at all." Sam looked into her anxious face. "Are you all right?"

"Uh-huh. You?"

"Yeah. Honey, are these the two you saw cutting the timbers under the bridge?"

Elizabeth faced the men. Neither of them could look her in the eye.

"They're the ones. That red neckerchief is what I saw first. Then I bent down and saw what they were doing." She placed both hands on Sam's arm as if to reassure herself he was all right. "They were hurrying to cut the posts so that you and the buggy would fall in the river. You are despicable creatures," she fumed at the men with her pert chin high in the air. "You are the dregs of humanity, unfit to live among decent people, and you should be locked up."

"And you should be—"

"Don't say it," Sam said softly.

"They are the ones who were trying to kill Sam," Elizabeth said to the men of the bridge crew. "I will go to court and identify them if that is what it takes to convict them."

Suppressing a grin, Sam looked each crewman in the eye. "Is that enough for you?"

"More'n enough," one answered.

"Then they're yours." Sam walked to his horse and shoved his rifle in the scabbard.

"We'll hold them for the marshal. That is if we don't decide to turn them over to the teamsters at Underwood's for a hangin'." The big black-bearded crewman winked at Sam.

"If they give you any trouble, tie them together and throw them in the river."

"Now, wait a—" Pete sputtered.

"Shut up!" the black-bearded man snarled, then motioned to one of the crewmen. "Tie them up. If they give you any lip, bust them in the mouth.'' When it was done, he turned to Sam. ''What's your name, mister?''

''Sam Ferguson.''

''The Sam Ferguson from up around Nora Springs?''

''The same.''

''Well, what do you know! I thought your face was familiar. Reckon when I saw it you'd let it grow over with whiskers. It'd be a pleasure to shake the hand of the best all-round lumberjack in the Territory.''

''Grossly exaggerated.'' Sam extended his hand.

''Ain't no such. One time I saw you shimmy up a lodgepole pine and top it before a man could gather a mouthful o' spit.''

Sam grinned. ''That was when I was young. I'm getting too old for such shenanigans.''

''I might come up to Nora Springs someday and hit you up for a job.''

''Do that.'' Sam turned to Elizabeth and led her to the buggy. ''We'll be on our way.''

''The stage company will be obliged to you for catchin' these two. They've given us a heap of trouble.''

''They've given all of us a heap of trouble, especially those freighters back at Underwood's. I wouldn't want to be in their boots when you take them back there.''

''We'll see to it they're turned over to the law.''

Sam tied his horse to the back of the buggy, climbed in beside Elizabeth and tucked the blankets around her. He lifted his hand to the crew and flicked the horse on the back with the reins.

Chapter Seventeen

Rested, the mare stepped out briskly without much encouragement.

Elizabeth buried her chin in the fur collar of her coat to shield her face from the wind. *They had almost been killed.* The horror of it was still with her, but it was too new for her to think about.

"The mare seems eager to go," Elizabeth said after a silence of several miles.

"She doesn't have to work as hard without the buggy top to hold the wind."

"I hadn't thought of that."

After letting the mare trot for a while, Sam slowed her to a fast walk.

"This buggy will make a good sleigh. I'll remove the wheels and fit it with runners when I get home."

"Do you have a house in Nora Springs?"

"Not a house. I have land, a barn and sheds. The house burned a few years ago. It was just a shack anyway. I was going to tear it down. I've some good lumber aging to build a house when I get around to it."

She wanted to ask if the house was for Jessie. Instead she said, "I've never ridden in a sleigh."

"No? Don't you have snow in Saint Louis?"

"Yes, but seldom so much that a buggy wouldn't do."

"Didn't you have a sled when you were a kid?"

"Young ladies didn't slide down the hill on their bellies and roll in the snow." She laughed nervously. "I used to watch out the window with envy at Becky playing with the stable boy and think it would be fun not to worry about getting wet and dirty and not care what the neighbors would think."

Sam made no comment, and they rode in silence. It seemed strange to Elizabeth to be riding in the buggy without the top. Strange, but nice. She felt more attuned to her surroundings—she smelled the tall pines that lined the road, heard the crisp leaves drifting with the wind, watched the gray clouds rolling overhead. She was acutely aware of the man beside her, and she knew he had mentally distanced himself from her since they left the bridge. She glanced at him. He appeared to be deep in thought.

Perhaps she had imagined that he had said he loved her. And if he had, he was likely sorry about it now and was probably wondering if she had taken his words seriously.

Elizabeth was so engrossed in her thoughts that she did not notice that a few snowflakes had begun to fall. She wished she could move closer to Sam, tuck her shoulder behind his and snuggle against his side.

"How many stations between here and Nora Springs?" It was suddenly very important for her to know how much time she had with him.

"One station, but there are several homesteads where the stage stops for fresh horses."

"Then we'll be in Nora Springs two days from now."

"If all goes well. Are you tired of traveling?"

"I'd be lying if I said I wasn't. I'd like a bath and a chance to wash some clothes. But—"

"But?"

"I'm not anxious to get there," she said in a rush.

Emptiness flowed through her at the thought of not being with him, of seeing him with Jessie, of knowing she and Stephen would be leaving, never to see him again.

Sam's head swiveled slowly. She was looking straight ahead. He couldn't see her face, but he knew she would never make the statement she had just made without giving it serious thought.

"Aren't you eager to see Stephen?"

"Oh, yes. I'm eager to see Stephen. He's a wonderful man."

"I wouldn't know about that. I don't know him very well."

"I do. I know him very well, and he'll understand when I tell him that I want to break our engagement."

"You…want to…what? You're not going to…to marry him?" Sam had never stuttered in his life, but the words just refused to come out.

"No. It wouldn't be fair to him. He's a good, sweet person, and he deserves a wife who would love him to distraction. If I free him, he'll meet her someday and be grateful to me."

"And you…don't love him…like that?"

"I love him like the dear brother I never had. He's been my best friend, my protector, the buffer that stood between me and my stepmother. Now I realize that isn't enough. My heart doesn't pound at the thought of kissing Stephen or spending the rest of my life with him.

I'm sure he feels the same about me. Stephen is honorbound to marry me, and I mean to release him."

"How come you didn't realize all this before you left Saint Louis?" Sam demanded almost gruffly.

"Somewhere along the way I forgot the talk I had with your…a dear friend who told me about love between a man and a woman. My friends were getting married. I was reaching the age of spinsterhood and feeling depressed, thinking that I'd never find a man to love me for myself alone."

"Are you saying that no one came to call? I can't believe that."

"No. I had plenty of callers. Most of them saw me as a connection to one of Saint Louis's most respected families, and my inheritance was an added incentive."

"Didn't any of them appeal to you?"

"Not a one."

After a long and profound silence, Sam asked, "What were these words of wisdom you've suddenly remembered that have caused you to change your mind about marrying Stephen?"

"My friend told me that love is the strongest emotion in the world. She said that the love between a man and a woman can be even stronger than the love a mother has for her child, that I would know it when I met the right man, and that I should never settle for less. She believed that there was a certain man for every woman, and when she found him, she would give him her heart and soul regardless of any differences between them."

Sam thought about what she said. He knew for certain that he was in love with this woman—completely, utterly, ridiculously in love for the first time in his life. It was as if God had taken his rib and made this woman just for him. Looking at her made his heart stop, then race wildly as it did when she explained her feelings for his brother.

A chill wind caused him to hunch his shoulders and grit his teeth. Even if by some miracle Elizabeth loved him and married him, he would live each day with the fear that she would leave him without warning, just as Eleanor had left his father. To live with that fear each day would be worse than not having her at all.

Large flakes of snow were falling. The mare had slowed to a fast walk. Sam sat hunched over, his forearms resting on his thighs. Elizabeth felt strangely relieved now that she had made her intentions known.

"I'm sorry for the trouble I've been, Sam. I firmly intended to marry Stephen when I left Saint Louis."

"What will you do?" Sam asked without turning his head.

"I don't know. Stephen will help me. Money is not a problem."

"I didn't think it was," he said dryly, making her wish she hadn't mentioned it.

"I don't regret the trip," she said quickly. "I've lived more in the weeks since I left Saint Louis than I have in all my twenty-five years. I've seen the country, the towns, the people. You know, Sam, some people in Saint Louis think all people west of Missouri are savages or uncouth misfits. They're not. They are open and friendly and caring and strong. Good, solid people settled this land."

"Some are also mean, cruel and shiftless, as I'm sure I don't have to remind you. Those two men we just left were harassing Jim Two-Horses at Haggerty's, and I stepped in. To them it was reason enough to kill me— and you, too. This country breeds hard men. The winters are long and cold, and the summers are short and hot."

He talked as if doing all he could to disillusion her. "Some people can't stand the isolation. I love it. I don't want someone breathing down my neck all the time."

"We've been through a lot together, haven't we, Sam?"

"To you it may seem a lot, but to us out here it's nothing out of the ordinary. Well...maybe a little." As he looked at her, the devilish grin spread over his face. "I've not had to lance a boil on a tony lady's sit-down place before."

"Then I'll have a special place in your memory?" Her eyes caught and held his. She watched the grin fade from his face.

"You bet," he said fervently.

It was growing colder. Large flakes were drifting from the gray sky, faster and thicker. Sam saw a snowflake settle on a curl on Elizabeth's forehead and stay there. Her nose was red, her cheeks rosy. The blanket over her lap began to whiten.

"Are you cold?"

"No."

"You're the stubbornest woman I've ever met," he growled. "If you were freezing to death you'd not say so." He reached across her lap to tuck the blanket more firmly around her.

Elizabeth had no idea if it was noon or afternoon when Sam stopped the buggy to allow the horses to drink at a spring coming from a rock formation beside the road. The sky was full of snowflakes. The wind whipped the white fluff across the road, making it impossible to see very far. Since she had expected Sam to ride his horse, she was pleasantly surprised when he got back in the buggy. He sat closer to her. And as if he expected her to do it, she lifted the blankets, covered his legs and snuggled against his side.

He started the horse, prodding her until she settled into a trot. They were alone in a wonderland of drifting snowflakes. Elizabeth's thigh was snug against Sam's. His big shoulder pressed hers against the seat. There was no world outside, just the two of them alone in the vast whiteness. She was so happy that she was surprised when Sam tilted his head to look at her and ask, "Scared?"

"Scared? Why would I be scared?"

"We're a good ten miles from shelter, and if I'm not mistaken, we're in for a ripsnorting blizzard."

"Is this the Bitterroot you were talking about?"

"This is it. It's about thirty miles across and the meanest place in the world for a snowstorm. It kills two or more travelers every year. They get lost up here in the snow and freeze to death."

"I'm not worried, Sam. I'm hungry."

He grinned, and before she realized it, she was holding his arm with both hands, and she was sure that he hugged her hand to his side.

"So am I. I'd like to have one of those apricot pies you made."

"Sam Ferguson, you've got a sweet tooth. Did you know that someone has discovered sugar can rot your teeth?"

"There's nothing wrong with my teeth." He snapped them at her.

"What else do you like?" She loved it when they could talk like this.

"Dumplings. Amanda cooks big, soft dumplings in the broth of rabbit or prairie hen or pheasant—"

"Who is Amanda?"

"Jessie's mother. She had a boardinghouse, and I eat there a lot."

Elizabeth was quiet for a while. She didn't want to talk about Jessie or think about Jessie. She didn't want Jessie intruding on the time she spent with Sam on this mountain road with snowflakes all around them.

A soft sigh escaped her lips. "It's pretty, isn't it? And quiet—"

"You wouldn't think so after four or five months of it."

"It's so peaceful."

"It would be boring after a while."

"Is it for you?"

"Lord, no. I have so much to do, I hardly have time to think."

"I wouldn't be bored. I'd—"

He cut her off with sharp words. "Yes, you would. Believe me, you would."

Silence. He had withdrawn from her again, not physically, but mentally. She was still snuggled to his side and she could turn her face into the shelter of his arm, but it was different now. Glancing at him, Elizabeth saw that he was peering ahead intently, trying to see through the driving snow. He was so sure that she would be bored and unhappy because his mother had been. She prayed for a way to convince him that being with him would be all she would ever want out of life.

The storm intensified steadily until they could see no more than a few feet ahead of the mare's ears. Even then, Elizabeth didn't worry. It didn't occur to her that she and Sam could become lost and fail to find shelter.

It had, however, occurred to Sam. As the minutes turned into an hour, he began to wonder if he had missed the small homestead where old Slufoot lived and tended the horses for the stage company. Sam had never heard the old man called anything but Slufoot. One leg dragged when he walked, and his tracks in the snow were unmistakable. Someone had pinned the name on him, and it had stuck.

Sam could see tree trunks on the left. There would be a break in the trees when they reached Slufoot's place. If they didn't come to it soon, he'd have to start thinking about what to do. A shelter of pine boughs in the thick woods would be the alternative. Even this early in the year the temperature could dip to below zero here on Bitterroot, and a howling blizzard could last for days. Sam cursed himself for not staying at Underwood's, for risking Elizabeth's life on the bridge and in this blizzard.

Then, there it was, the break in the trees. Lord! He had thought for sure he had missed it. Sam pulled on the reins, and the tired mare stopped.

"I think this is it," he said, getting out of the buggy. "Sit tight."

He walked, leading the mare, his head tilted against the wind. Straining his eyes to see through the curtain of snow, he found the path to the house. Finally the log house loomed before him. He rapped on the door.

"Slufoot," he yelled.

All was white and still. He rapped harder. Only then did he see the square of paper stuck in the crack of the door. Turning his back to the wind and holding the paper close to his eyes, he read:

Gone to Petersons till the stage runs. Eat if you've a mind to but clean up the mess. No whiskey. If'n I had some I'd stay. No money. I took it to buy whiskey.

Randolph Higgenbothem

Sam chuckled. *Randolph Higgenbothem.* Who would have thought old Slufoot would have such a fancy name? He lifted the latch and the door swung open. He closed it and went back to the buggy.

"The owner is gone, but he left a note." He reached for Elizabeth and lifted her down.

"Do all homesteaders leave notes on the door when they leave?"

"Most people leave a message of some sort. You may find it hard to believe, considering some of the people we've run into on this trip, but most folk in this country respect another man's property."

Elizabeth was glad to get out of the wind even if the cabin was dark and cold. Sam unloaded the buggy, and she stayed at the door to help. He carried things as far as the door. She took them and set them in the room out of the way. After he brought in her trunk, he went to unsaddle his horse and bring the saddle and saddlebags inside.

Sam struck a match, found a candle and lit it. The room was small and sparsely furnished, but there was fuel in the wood box and a fire was laid in the hearth. He adjusted the damper so the smoke would go up the chimney, then held the candle to the tinder and fanned it with his hat until the blaze caught.

After Sam went out to put the horses in the shed, Elizabeth looked around at the crude furnishings. Two bunks were built into the wall opposite the fireplace. There was a table, two chairs, a wash bench, a cabinet of sorts and a cook stove. And it was clean.

Elizabeth hung her coat on a peg beside the door and, shivering with the cold, set about starting a fire in the stove. Sam would need something hot. The water bucket was empty, so she poured the water from their canteen into the coffeepot that sat on the back of the stove. Then she lifted a round lid on the stovetop and set the pot directly over the flame. She couldn't be unhappy about being in this place. For the short time they were here, she would make it a home for Sam.

Sam came in and stamped the snow from his boots.

"It's getting bad. By night you'll not be able to see your hand in front of your face. I ran a line from the shed to the house just in case it's this bad tomorrow."

"Will the horses be all right?"

"Yeah. They've got shelter. I see you've got the cook stove going. I didn't know you knew how."

"I didn't learn to cook on a cold stove." Her eyes twinkled merrily. "I used the water we had in the canteen—"

"Give me the bucket, I'll get some."

They ate cornmeal mush. Elizabeth dropped in the last of the raisins while she was cooking it and found a jug of sorghum for sweetener. They sat at the table with the candle between them.

"Will that hold you for a while?" she asked after Sam had finished the second bowl.

"For now. I'd rather have had pie."

"Oh, you! We don't have anything to make pie. Too bad Mr. Slufoot doesn't have chickens. I'd make you some dumplings."

"How about rabbit?"

"We don't have a rabbit."

"We will by morning. I'll set a couple of snares."

"Oh, Sam. Don't go out again in this weather."

"Don't worry. This is my country. I've been through as many blizzards as you have garden parties." His grin was back, and she basked in it.

"There wasn't much danger of my getting lost and

freezing to death at a garden party, but I did almost choke at some of the maneuvering that went on. Sam, you wouldn't believe the things a mother with a fat, bucktoothed daughter approaching the age of twenty will do to get her-married off.''

Sam's grin widened as he watched her eyes light up.

''I thought a garden party was when women got together and planted potatoes and onions.''

''Far from it! They dress in their best and go to see and be seen. I'll have to tell you about the time Netta had a dress sent all the way from New York for a certain party, and old Mrs. Bloomington, who weighs over two hundred pounds, showed up in a dress identical to the one Netta wore. Netta almost had apoplexy. She was cross as a bear for days.''

Laughter bubbled as she looked at him. Sam thought she was delectable enough to grab a man's heart right out of him.

''It was that important to her?''

''Oh, yes. It was very important.''

Sam's eyes were on her frequently, softly dark and intent, but Elizabeth, unsure of why he should gaze at her so, stared back questioningly. He didn't look away, but rather studied her openly.

''What would we have done if we hadn't found this place?'' she asked, not wanting to think about her life in Saint Louis.

''I would have built us a shelter in the woods out of pine boughs, covered it with the canvas and built a fire. We would have snuggled in the blankets and survived, although we'd have been hungry as hell.''

''You are so capable, Sam, and so self-reliant. It would be nice to be a man and not have to depend on anyone,'' she said wistfully.

She turned away then and, anxious to be busy, tidied up after the meal. While she worked, she thought carefully about Sam, about their kisses…their needs. He was certainly keeping his distance, still afraid of being hurt. If only she could tell him that all she wanted in the world was to be with him, that she would never leave him.

Sam went to the shed to check on the horses, and Elizabeth quickly changed into a flannel gown and heavy robe. She was sitting in a fireside chair, brushing her hair, when he came in carrying an armload of firewood. He closed the door quickly against the rush of cold air and put the wood in the box beside the fireplace.

"Snow's piling up," he said. He hung his coat and added another stick of wood to the fire, squatted on his heels and held his hands out to the flames.

Elizabeth filled her eyes with him, the broad shoulders, the narrow waist, the lean hips. *I'll always love him*, she thought. *How could I possibly love another man after knowing him?* She continued brushing her hair in order to have something to do with her hands. This could be her last night alone with him. The thought tortured her.

He sat in the chair opposite her and stretched out his long legs. Because he was so still, she thought he was looking into the fire, and dared to look at him. His brown eyes were staring at her. She held his gaze for a moment, then dropped her eyes, the color coming into her cheeks as she remembered the night in the other cabin when he had brushed her hair.

"It's cold in here. Are you warm enough in that thing?"

She recalled what he had said in the buggy about her freezing and being too stubborn to admit it.

"All except my feet. They feel like two clumps of ice."

He moved his chair over beside her, lifted her feet to his thighs and began unlacing her shoes.

"Hmm. It seems I've seen these shoes somewhere before." His smile was beautiful. Elizabeth couldn't take her eyes from his face.

With his big hands he held her stockinged feet and rubbed them until they tingled.

"Ah... That feels good." She leaned her head against the back of the chair.

Abruptly he set her feet on the floor, got up and went to the bunks where she had spread the blankets. He took a blanket from one bunk and spread it on the other, tucking it in at the foot.

"Go to bed, 'Lizabeth."

Elizabeth looked at him dazedly, her trembling fingers working on the end of her braid, tying it with the ribbon she took from her pocket. With bowed head and shaky legs, she stood.

"You'll only have one blanket."

"It's enough. I'll keep the fire going." He went to the mantel and stood with his back to her, kicking at a log that had rolled off the grate.

Elizabeth was on the point of tears. Why was he being so abrupt? If the storm let up, this would be their last night together. An ache settled in the pit of her stomach and a pain in her heart. She was desperate for him to love her. She yearned to give him all her woman's sweetness and to know the joy of being one with him. She knew with a certainty that he would not make an overture toward her. She would have to do it.

Eleanor had said that someday a man would come into her life who would fill it with his presence. She would love him, he would cherish her, she would give him children. When the time came, he would be an extension of her. Elizabeth wasn't sure if Sam loved her, but she needed sweet memories to take with her into a loveless future. She had to reach out if she would have those memories.

Tension held her very still. Then her decision was made.

Sam turned to her as she dropped her robe onto the chair. His dark, questioning eyes traveled her up and down.

"Sam?" Fear of rejection kept her from saying more.

"Go...to bed," he said huskily, barely moving his lips.

"Sam..." she started again bravely. "Stay with me. Sleep with...me." Holding her chin steady with an effort, she went to him, leaned against him and lifted her hands to his face, feeling the drag of new beard. As her palms held his cheeks, her thumbs stroked the soft hair of his mustache. She trembled with unbelievable tension. "I want to be with you...tonight. I'll not hold on to you. You'll be under no obligation afterward."

"Do...you know what you're saying?" he rasped out hoarsely.

"Yes! Yes, I do. I'm almost twenty-six years old— no longer a girl. I want to know...you."

"'Lizabeth...I can't!" The words were torn from him. It was hard for him to take a deep breath. He could see that she was desperate and uncertain and near tears.

"I love you." She pressed her face to his shoulder. "You don't have to love me back."

"Ah...sweet woman..." His hands on her shoulders pushed her away from him.

Green eyes flooded with tears looked into his. "You don't want me...like that?"

"Dear God! I want you so bad it's tearing my heart right out of me, but there's no future for us, 'Lizabeth. No future at all! You should save yourself for the man you'll share your life with."

"There will not be another man. Never," she whispered. "Give me tonight...please." Her voice vibrated with emotion. Her barriers were down, and her pride was gone.

"But...Stephen loves you!"

"Stephen loves me like a sister! Please believe me!"

"Sweetheart, I want to. It's been hell being with you, knowing you were his."

"I'm yours...all yours, if you want me."

"I want you! Oh, Lord, how I want you—"

He wrapped her in his arms, lifted her off her feet and buried his face in the curve of her neck.

She trembled with unbelievable happiness.

Chapter Eighteen

"God help me—but I can't resist you! Sweet woman, I'll despise myself tomorrow."

"Oh, no! Please don't. I love you so much," she whispered into his ear between kisses. "Are you afraid I'll try to hold you? I won't! I promise, I won't!"

"Wanting you is...killing me!"

"I don't want you to hurt!"

His mouth moved over hers, soft then hard. She felt the tremor that shook him when her lips opened to him. His hand moved to her hips, and he pressed her against the rock-hard part of his body that had sprung to life.

"Love me, Sam," she gasped. She tore her lips from his and looked earnestly into his face. "For a few hours let me be your lover."

The emotional plea came from the depths of her heart, bringing a mistiness to her eyes and a tightness to her throat. Her arms closed around him with desperation, and her innermost thoughts leaped to her lips.

"I love you. You fill my eyes with beauty, my heart with joy."

"Oh, love...oh, my sweet love..." His answer was a groan that came from deep inside him.

Her mouth was trembling and eager against his as he lifted her and carried her to the bunk. He sat her on the edge and knelt. She stroked his head while he rolled her stockings down and pulled them off. The bed was cold when he laid her in it and covered her, but she scarcely noticed. Sam went to the fireplace and set a small log on the grate. Then he blew out the candle.

Scarcely breathing, she watched him in the flickering firelight as if she was in another world and this was happening to someone else. He took off his boots, his shirt and pants and came to stand beside the bunk in a suit of long underwear. He undid the buttons to below the waist, then pulled the garment off his shoulders and over his lean hips. Seconds later he slipped beneath the blankets and gathered her to him.

He was warm flesh, hard muscle. She was warm flesh and sweet-smelling softness.

"My...sweet, beautiful woman, you're too elegant for a rough man like me. But, God help me, I can't help myself...." He buried his face in her hair and quietly held her as if he was holding something far more precious than life. After what seemed like an enchanted eternity, he tilted her face to his and kissed her lips softly, tenderly, again and again.

Sam had no experience with *good* women. The women he'd known had been eager and willing and far more experienced than he. He had placed money on the table beside the bed when he left them and within hours could not recall their faces or names. *Go slowly,* he cautioned himself. Her body was tender and sweet and virginal. He would go where no other had ever been.

Then her soft hands were on his flesh, soft breasts against his chest, long, strong thighs between his, and her mouth...dear God—she was driving him crazy. His body flamed and hardened and began to quake.

"I don't want to frighten you," he muttered thickly.

"Nothing you could do would frighten me." She cupped his cheek with her hand and turned his lips to hers. "I love you," she whispered into his mouth.

Sam's heart was drumming so hard that his breath came jerkily. He was too stunned with happiness and joy of her to utter a word. His hand moved slowly under her gown to stroke her thigh, her hips, and then his hand was at her breast. She moved slightly away to give him access. The need to feel her soft flesh against his caused him to pull at the gown until it was above her breasts.

She slipped the gown over her head and wound her arms around him, pressing every inch of herself to him—her breasts to his hard chest, her soft belly to the taut muscles of his, the soft, furry mound covering her femininity against the maleness that stood hard and firm, a monument of his desire for her.

"Ah..." A sound of pure pleasure escaped her.

She burrowed into the haven made by his arms, tasting the clean moisture that dewed the skin of his throat, stroking the crisp hairs of his chest and running her hand over his hard, muscled back.

"You feel so good, my darling. Sam...oh, Sam, you are my darling tonight and forever. This...this is the most wonderful night of my life."

Her hands fluttered over his smooth, muscled shoulders and down along his rib cage to his narrow flanks with a freedom that was new and wonderful. A half-choked cry came from him as her fingers touched his quivering flesh. He had not expected this sweet willingness, the astounding passion that lay slumbering beneath her innocence. She was more, far more than he had ever dreamed a woman could be.

"This is the mysterious part of a man I've heard about. Oh, my," she said with wonderment in her voice. Her fingers moved over his aching hardness.

He moaned and murmured, "Ah...love—"

"Does it hurt you like it did—the other time?" she asked against his mouth. "Tell me what to do...."

Her mouth trembled against his as his hand cupped her hips and moved them so that the silky down between her thighs teased his hardened flesh. In a frenzy his heated blood raced, swelling him even more. An inarticulate sound escaped from him.

"Oh, sweet, sweet, you tie me in knots."

"Do you love me...just a little?"

"Dear God! How can you ask?"

"I love you. I love you." The words were wrung from her, accompanied by fevered kisses on his mouth.

His murmured reply was lost in her kiss. He kissed her hungrily and murmured endearments during the brief intervals when he was not taking the lips she offered so eagerly. "Sweet, sweet, darlin' girl..."

His hands moved over her, touching her from breast to thigh. She tangled her fingers in his hair as he made small nibbles across her shoulder and down her neck to her breast. The drag of his rough cheeks and the brush of his mustache sent a powerful tug of desire pulsing between her thighs, where his fingers seemed compelled to go.

He rolled her onto her back and raised himself on quivering arms to hover over her. He kissed her lips, feasted on her lips, then with his hand beneath her breast, holding it up, he buried his mouth in its softness.

Unable to restrain himself, he slid his muscular body

over hers. He positioned himself between her thighs with firm but gentle insistence. With new, sweet freedom, she opened her legs to welcome him when she felt the first firm, velvet touch of his probing flesh at the moist opening in her body. The gentle nudging started a fire that surged through the seat of her femininity, causing involuntary shudders of delight. Wholly caught up with the sensations trembling from that secret place, she spoke to him in snatches of almost inaudible words.

"My love...my wonderful man..."

"Ssh...darlin'. Be still and let me love you."

Holding her buttocks in his hands, he slowly slid into her until he felt what he had never felt before, the membrane guarding her virginity. It was a once-in-a-lifetime moment for both of them, one that both of them would hold in their memories like a secret treasure for as long as they lived. He held himself there for endless seconds while little spasms of exquisite pleasure rippled through her.

"Liz, honey..." Her name was a caress on his lips.

"Sam?" There was uncertainty in her voice, and she began to kiss his face frantically and thrust upward. "What's wrong?"

"Nothing's wrong, love. It's all so perfect, so damn perfect!"

A low, growling sound came from deep in his throat as she rose to meet the driving shaft of pleasure. Then suddenly, unexpectedly, there was a pain so intense that she cried out his name. Then she was floating on a mighty wave, seeking more and more of the delicious pleasure of being filled where before there had been emptiness. An unending moan rose in her throat with every surge of his magnificent, probing flesh. Her arousal intensified to so great a pitch that fire ran along her nerves and her eyes flew open. She had the strange sensation of not knowing where his body ended and hers began.

"Oh...oh, my—"

When gratification came, it split her body into fragments, each alive with vibrant sensations. The explosion sent her rising, gasping upward, spinning her into the warm, misty darkness. The only thing holding her was the glorious spear that pierced her very soul.

Sam's bursting body writhed in the sweetness he had entered. He felt himself enveloped in a sheet of flame that ignited his every nerve. He was enclosed in sweet softness, pillowed in a warm and silken place where an irreversible tempo built to a consuming release. Then his mind and his body separated, and he was floating, flying and drowning all at once. He felt his soul reeling somewhere above his body, which erupted and filled her with his life-giving fluids.

Reason returned. He turned with her in his arms. They lay, their arms wrapped around each other, breathing deeply. When he finally stirred, it was to pull the blankets more snugly around them. Still cradled in the loving folds of her body, her belly tight against his, he solemnly kissed her forehead, her eyelids one after the other, and smoothed the tangles of hair from her face with gentle fingers.

"What happened?" she whispered in a low, husky rasp. "It was as if I left my body and went to this beautiful place." Tears trickled from her eyes and rolled down her cheeks and onto his shoulder.

"Did I hurt you?" he asked anxiously.

"Oh, no! I didn't want it to end. It was so beautiful."

"It was for me, too."

"You've...done this before. You knew what to expect."

"No, love, I've not done *this* before." His voice was a shivering whisper. His hand stroked her hair gently, as though she was fragile and infinitely precious. "Not like this," he repeated with a world of meaning in his voice.

"Are you warm?" she asked, feeling along his back to see if it was covered.

"Uh-huh."

The completeness of their lovemaking had left her exhausted. She fell asleep almost immediately. Sometime later she was drowsily aware of a hard body pressed to her own, of the hand that cupped and fondled her breast. With tender eagerness she turned her face to his and accepted his hungry kisses, gently shifting her hips to welcome him to her most private self. The feel of him was exquisitely pleasurable. His heart thundered against hers, and she moved her hand down to his taut, driving buttocks.

"Sweetheart!" he whispered helplessly, and with a long breath he thrust with frenzied urgency.

She held him tightly to her when his body jerked repeatedly, filling her with a healing warmth. From some far-off place she heard a soft, triumphant, "Dear God!"

"I love you," she whispered.

Feeling wonderfully loved and relaxed, she cuddled in his arms and was almost instantly asleep.

Sam sat in the fireside chair, his hands clasped over his stomach, his booted feet stretched out to the fire. The storm had intensified. Snow, driven by a gale-force wind, had sifted in under the door and onto the windowsills. He looked across to the bunk where Elizabeth lay sleeping. He had covered her with all the blankets and his heavy sheepskin coat.

He stared into the fire, assembling and sorting out his thoughts. He had not meant for the intimate, soul-stirring, gut-stomping experience he'd shared with Elizabeth to happen. His intentions had been to take her to Stephen, then head for the logging camp where he hoped to get her out of his mind, if not his heart. He admitted that every night since he'd met her he had fantasized about holding her, warm and naked, in his arms. What man in his right mind *wouldn't* want to hold her? He was a man with the same desires for a woman as any other, and hunger for her had torn at his groin.

She had said she loved him. Did she? He wondered if she had been only carried away by thoughts of a romantic interlude. Yet she had given herself openly, completely, and had been more loving than any woman of his dreams. He recalled hearing that physical love was distasteful to the so-called *refined* women. This glorious creature had taken uninhibited pleasure in their mating, and the thought of parting from her brought on acute despair.

Sam reached the conclusion that this was a woman he could give his heart to, but with whom he could not share his life. A man needed a woman who would share the hardship as well as the joy. Living with her would be like living with a keg of powder that could erupt at any moment. She would vanish, leaving his life shattered.

In the quiet of the night, with only the sound of the wind lashing the cabin, he reflected on his future. He would build his house amid the tall pines. In a few years he would find a steady, quiet, undemanding woman who would give him children. He in turn would give her a home and security. Elizabeth would find a man to love her as she deserved to be loved.

Sam was so lost in his thoughts that he didn't know Elizabeth had gotten out of bed until she was beside him. She stood there in her long white gown, her bare feet on the cold plank floor.

"'Lizabeth!" He drew up his legs. "Go back to bed. It's cold in here."

"Why did you get up?"

"I...had to tend the fire."

She took his hand. "Come back to bed with me."

"No. I'll sit here a while."

She turned and sat on his lap, then wrapped her arms around his neck and snuggled against him, bending her knees to place her feet on his legs.

"Let me stay with you." She turned her face into his shoulder and nuzzled the warm flesh of his neck.

"'Lizabeth..."

She raised her head to look at him. He was so close she could see every detail of his face: the dark half-closed eyes, the strong nose, the sensual curve of his mouth, the darkened cheeks, the silky hair on his upper lip, the sweep of his brows. *Oh, please, God, don't let that be regret in his eyes!*

He drew her close against him, her breast against his chest, her head on his shoulder. She curled her arm around his neck. He pulled her feet up and covered them with with her gown. She felt his fingers in the mass of hair that had come loose from the braid. He stroked it for a long while. The sigh of the wind and the crackle of the fire were the only sounds she heard above the beating of his heart.

"You're sorry, aren't you, Sam?" She gnawed on her

lower lip, refusing to acknowledge the tears that gathered behind her eyelids.

"It would be better for both of us if it hadn't happened. But what's done is done."

"Why do you say that?" He was silent for so long that she brought her hand up to his face. "Tell me."

"We both know why, 'Lizabeth. We have no future together. We would make each other miserable."

"I'm not trying to tie you to me, Sam." Swallowing the lump that clogged her throat, she tried to speak naturally.

"Someday when you're back among your own kind, you'll be glad."

"Thank you for giving me a wonderful memory." Thank God her voice didn't reflect the misery that covered her like a black shroud.

"You've given me a cherished memory, too." He murmured the words in her hair.

She held her lips tightly between her teeth. Tempestuous feelings were threatening to overpower her. She was at life's crossroads; one road would lead her to heaven, the other to hell. Only her strength of character kept the inner misery hidden.

Later, when Sam carried her to the bunk and covered her with the blankets, she lay there and cried silently. Then the weight of her wretchedness hit her, sending her into the black pit of despair that not even tears could reach.

Elizabeth was awakened by the sound of the door closing. Drugged with sleep, she raised her head to see Sam lowering an armload of wood into the box. When he straightened, he glanced at her, and their eyes met briefly.

"Storm hasn't let up one bit."

Elizabeth wanted to say she was glad. Instead she said, "I smell something cooking."

"I caught two rabbits in my snares. One is in the pot." He went to the door. "I'll bring in more wood."

"You don't have to leave so I can get dressed. Just turn around." She laughed nervously.

He went to the wash bench and poured water in the washdish from the teakettle and carried it to the bed. His eyes caught hers as he set it down on the floor.

"Thank you."

"I'll be out for a while," he said, and went out the door.

Elizabeth used the chamber pot and washed herself in the warm water Sam had so thoughtfully provided, then dressed hurriedly. In the light of day it was hard for her to believe that she had lain in the narrow bunk wrapped in Sam's arms and that they had done the dreadful *thing* she had heard discussed by her friends. There had been nothing dreadful about it. It had been wonderful, glorious, and she would not let herself think that it would never happen again.

Sam loved her. Otherwise how could he have been so sweet, so gentle, so loving? He had admitted his love at the bridge. Now he was afraid to commit himself. She had to find a way to convince him that, although she and Eleanor came from the same background, she was not Eleanor.

A rush of cold air swept across the floor when Sam came in. His mustache was frosty, his face red with the cold. His eyes caught hers the instant he came in the door.

"It's below zero."

"How can you tell?"

"By the way the twigs snap and the snow crunches under my feet."

He hung up his coat. She poured coffee for him and set it on the table. With a rag she lifted the lid on the iron kettle where the rabbit was simmering and poured in more water from the teakettle. These were the things she would be doing, she thought, if they were married and living in a home of their own. She would see to her husband's comfort, pour his coffee, cook his meals. At night he would hold her in his arms and they would whisper intimate things for only each other to hear. In the morning, over breakfast, they would talk about everyday things like the weather.

"I wonder if it's blizzarding in Nora Springs," she said while refilling the teakettle from the water bucket.

"Could be. These quick blizzards hit the mountain ranges, and usually they move on down into the valleys before they play out."

Elizabeth poured coffee for herself and sat across from him. She looked into his face, but he looked everywhere but at her.

"Do you work outside all winter?"

"Sure. It's sheltered up in the woods. It gets colder than hell, but as a rule there's not much wind."

After that Elizabeth couldn't think of anything to say. The silence in the cabin was deep. They were like two polite strangers. Elizabeth squirmed inwardly. She felt a desperate desire to plunge into the subject uppermost in her mind.

"Sam, will you listen to what I want to say?"

Although he finally looked at her, he waited so long to speak that she was not sure he was going to.

"Say what you're determined to say." His dark eyes

raked her face searchingly while remaining inscrutable themselves.

"Please let me tell you about your mother. Don't you want to know what kind of person she was? How she lived? What she did?"

"I figured that was what was on your mind." His unreadable scrutiny sent an icy chill through her body. "You forget that I *know* what kind of a person she was."

"But—"

"And I don't give a damn about how she lived or what she did, just as she didn't give a damn about how I lived or what I did. She is dead to me and has been for the past twenty-two years."

"Sam...please. What harm will it do if I tell you about her?"

One brow lifted, and his dark eyes glinted with anger.

"Leave it be, Elizabeth. You're meddling in a family matter that is none of your concern."

For a heart-stopping moment she sat there, her face slowly turning scarlet. Her green eyes misted. This couldn't be happening—not after all that had transpired between them. She looked into his face and realized things could not possibly get any worse between them. It was too late to turn back. She took a deep breath and plunged in.

"You're a lonely, bitter man. Your mother didn't die for you twenty-two years ago. Deny it if you will, but she's been in your heart all this time—"

"Enough!" Sam slammed his hand on the table.

Elizabeth refused to be intimidated by his loud voice. It was now or never, she thought.

"You loved her so much. Eleanor had a way of making people love her."

"Oh, yes," he sneered. "She was a sweet, delicate little thing with the soul of a viper!"

"What she did to you and your father was wrong," Elizabeth went on determinedly, "but I knew her. I know that she loved you, Sam."

"Did she tell you that, Miss Prissy-tail Caldwell?"

"No, but—"

"Did she mention me at all?"

"No, but—"

Sam got up so fast his chair tipped over. He bent over the table and glared into her face. His eyes were cold, his words clipped when he spoke.

"I don't want to hear another word! Not another damn word about that bitch!"

Elizabeth stood. "You love her still."

He jerked his coat off the peg and slammed his hat on his head. "I despise her!" he shouted, and pulled on his coat.

"You love her. She was your mother. She gave you life—"

"I'll show you how much she means to me." He went to his saddlebags and pulled out a packet of letters. "Stephen brought these letters from my *dear mama*. I've not read them. I will *never* read them." He flung them into the fireplace and stomped out, slamming the door behind him.

"No! Oh, no!"

Elizabeth grabbed the poker, raked the packet from the fire and stamped out the flames that burned along the edges. The four envelopes were tied together with a blue ribbon. She recognized the handwriting and the stationery. Eleanor had written to Elizabeth regularly while Elizabeth was away at school. Elizabeth held the letters in her hands and read the name on the envelope through a blur of tears: "Samuel Ferguson."

Oh, Eleanor. How could you? You not only have made your son a bitter man, you have ruined my life!

Elizabeth took the letters to the table and sat. She looked at them for a long time. As far as Sam was concerned, the letters had been destroyed. What harm would it do if she read them? Knowing she shouldn't but compelled to do so, she opened the first letter and began to read.

After she read all four letters, she folded her arms on the table, buried her face in them and cried. She cried for Eleanor, for Stephen and for Joe Ferguson. But most of all she cried for Sam.

Chapter Nineteen

The storm of weeping passed.

While Elizabeth washed her face and tidied her hair, she mulled over every word that had been said between her and Sam up until he slammed out the door. She had seen him angry before, but never this angry. He was a man of changing moods: fierce and cruel when he was angry, sweet and gentle when he was pleased. He was also honest and straightforward. The anger that flared so suddenly was the result of deep and lasting hurt. Last night he had said that they had no future together. He sincerely believed that to be true. She had understood his feelings perfectly and had asked, even begged him to take her to bed.

Sam didn't want a future with her even though he cared for her. A man like Sam wouldn't blurt out his love as he had done at the bridge without meaning it. That he chose to ignore his feelings was his way of shielding himself from hurt.

She would not, could not make another overture as she had done the night before. Where had all that courage come from? She had read someplace that love had no pride. She was beginning to believe it.

Sam was going to know what was in the letters regardless of how angry he became. She would do that much for him, and then it would be up to him. He could live with his bitterness or he could put it behind him.

Elizabeth straightened the bunks and swept up the snow Sam had tracked in; the plank floors were so cold the snow had not melted. She searched their supplies and those in the cabin and found what she needed to make dumplings, all except for sage, which she decided she could do without. Grateful for something to do, she stirred up the batter. When the rabbit was tender enough to fall from the bone, she dropped large spoonfuls of soft dough in the boiling broth and covered the pot with a tight lid.

Time went by, and Sam hadn't come back. Elizabeth moved the kettle to the back of the stove. She went to the window to look out. It was still snowing, but the wind had died down. The world outside the cabin was a white wonderland. The ground, covered with a foot of the fluffy white snow, was a sharp contrast to the deep green of the evergreen trees that surrounded the cabin. Elizabeth watched tiny brown sparrows flit from the trees in search of food. Nothing else stirred.

Sam had been gone for a long time. It hurt her to know that he would rather be out in the cold than inside with her where it was warm. Worry for his safety set in. She began to pace the length of the small room. She was so nervous that when a burning log fell from the grate, she jumped and her hands flew to her throat in fright.

Something could have happened to him. His rifle was in the corner, but his gun belt was missing. At least he was armed...but he had been armed the night the one-eyed man slipped up on him. Had the one-eyed man and the fat man come looking for Sam? Fear knifed through her, and she decided to take the rifle and go looking for him.

She was reaching for her coat when the door opened and he came in. She was relieved yet angry at him for the worry he had caused. He hung up his coat and hat before he looked at her.

"Your dinner is ready," she said quietly, but was unable to keep the chill out of her voice.

Without waiting for him to say anything, she dished up a generous helping of meat and soft, fluffy dumplings. She set the plate on the freshly scoured table, poured coffee in a cup and set it beside the plate.

"Are you going to eat?" he asked when she made no move to fill a plate for herself.

"No. Not now."

"Why not? You didn't have breakfast."

"I'm not hungry. I'll eat something later." She found herself looking directly into his eyes and watched his gaze fall away and become fixed on the plate before him.

"Suit yourself." He shrugged his shoulders and sat down.

Elizabeth went around the table to the fireside chair. The emotional strain had taken its toll on her strength and knotted her stomach, making it impossible to eat. As her fingers clutched the letters in her pocket, she wondered where in the world she would find the courage to bring up the letters. But bring them up, she would.

When Sam finished eating, he came to the fireplace and added several large split logs to the those burning in the grate.

"The dumplings were good."

"Thank you."

"You should eat something."

Elizabeth washed the plate Sam had put in the pan

and covered with water from the teakettle. He was a man used to doing for himself. He didn't need a woman to do for him. She forced herself to look directly at him as she dried the dish and wiped the crumbs from the plank table.

He was watching her. She refused to be moved by the shadow of hurt she saw in his eyes. She was hurting, too, and unless she acted, she would go on hurting for the rest of her life. When she finished the meager chores, she hung the wet cloth on the oven door handle to dry and sat at the table.

Sam sat in the fireside chair, his forearms resting on his spread thighs, his clasped hands dangling between his knees.

She felt both pity and irritation. Pity for the small boy who had been hurt, and irritation at the man who had refused to try to understand his mother.

For a long time Elizabeth stared at his broad back and bowed head. The silence that enveloped them was utterly complete. Taking a deep, trembling breath, Elizabeth pulled the letters from her pocket, opened them, took out one and placed it on top of the others on the table before her. She closed her eyes tightly and said a silent prayer that when she began to read he would not explode into a rage.

Then, into that continuing stillness, she began to speak in a not quite steady voice.

My Dearest Sammy,
Today is your fifteenth birthday. Are you as tall as your father? You were well on the way when I saw you last. I can still see you strutting proudly into the woods with your little ax on your shoulder, do-

ing your best to be like him. Joe was so proud of
you, our firstborn.

Elizabeth dared a glance at Sam's back, surprised that
he hadn't jumped to his feet and snatched the letters
from her. Encouraged, she read on, slowly now, pro-
nouncing each word distinctly.

I have written to you on each of your birthdays,
knowing that you may never read my words, but
taking comfort in writing because it made me feel
a little closer to you. I don't suppose a young man
wants to read that his mother loves him, but, oh, I
do love you, Sammy. If only I could turn back the
clock. But if I could I don't know if I would do
anything differently, feeling as I did at the time. I
was so frightened that summer five years ago, so
frightened that I feared for my sanity. You see, my
dearest Sammy, I thought by leaving you, I was
doing what was best for you and for my precious
Joe, whom I loved with all my heart.

I am taking pen in hand on this fifteenth anni-
versary of your birth to tell you why I left you, not
to offer any excuses for myself.

When I was growing up, my mother's sister,
Clara, lived with us. She was a sweet, gentle person. At age twenty she suffered from a sickness
unknown to the doctors. She lost the use of her
hands, then her legs. Her muscles seemed to dis-
solve. In a year's time she was completely helpless,
unable to move except to swallow the food put into
her mouth. She had to have constant care during
the three years she lived. Thankfully my parents
were able to afford that care. All that the doctors

could tell us was that they believed it a weakness in the females of our family.

Can you imagine my fright that summer when at times I became so weak that I sank into a chair because my legs wouldn't hold me and I was unable to raise my arms above my head? There was not a doubt in my mind that I had Aunt Clara's sickness and that soon my husband and my boys would be burdened with a helpless woman. To me it was unbearable to think of my Joe having to take care of me. How could he work and support a family with a helpless wife on his hands? I had to come home to my parents.

Dearest Sammy, I couldn't take both of Joe's boys from him. You shared his love for the woods. Stephen was so young. I was selfish enough to want one of my sons with me during what I considered my last days. So I sneaked away like a coward. Your little tear-stained face has haunted me every night for the past five years, and I'm sure it will haunt me until the day I die.

At the time I comforted myself with the thought that I had saved you and Joe the agony of seeing me die a useless pile of flesh and bone, bedridden and helpless.

The irony of it, sweet Sammy, is that I didn't die. When I arrived home, I took to my bed, a total wreck of a woman who believed her life was over. After a few months I was stronger. The doctor said I had suffered from exhaustion. I didn't believe him at first. Finally I had to, but it was too late. I knew in my heart that you and Joe despised me. I had told Stephen his brother and father were dead because the poor little boy grieved so for you both.

How could I tell him otherwise? He is happy here, while I am locked into a nightmare.

There you have it, my dearest boy. I hope someday to have the courage to mail this to you. Never, never think that I left you because I didn't love you. Happy birthday, darling. You are in my heart now and always.

Mother

Her voice cracking, Elizabeth finished reading the letter. With tears in her eyes she looked at Sam. He sat hunched over, his head bowed. There was no way for her to tell if he had heard the words she had read to him. She looked at the next letter. It was written on his twentieth birthday, and the next one when he was twenty-five years old. The last letter had been written two years ago, when he was thirty. In the last letter there were also four yellowed pages that recorded a line or two written on each of Sam's birthdays. All the pages had smears from what surely must be Eleanor's tears.

Sam sat as still as a stone. Elizabeth sighed deeply. She had done what she could to bring him peace. The rest was up to him. She placed the letters in their envelopes and got up from the table. She went to his side and held the letters out to him, fully expecting him to snatch them from her hand and to throw them in the fire.

He didn't move.

Elizabeth waited. Then her eyes moved to the clasped hands hanging between his knees. *They were wet!* She bent to see his face and saw tears falling from his eyes like drops of rain. *He was crying!* Not a muscle moved, but he was crying. Her shock held her immobile for a dozen heartbeats before she slipped the letters into her pocket and dropped to her knees between his spread legs. She put her arms around him and pulled his tear-wet face to her shoulder.

"Oh, Sam! Oh, please try to understand and forgive her."

In a quick movement he grabbed her to him as if she were a lifeline in a storm-tossed sea. He crushed her in an embrace and buried his face in the curve between her neck and her shoulder. His large frame shook with great, silent sobs. Elizabeth held him and stroked his back.

"My dearest, my love, your mother suffered a living death knowing you and your father were lost to her forever."

With tears rolling down her cheeks, she offered him what comfort she could.

"Eleanor didn't leave because she hated this country or the hardships. She told me many times how beautiful the trees were and how clear the mountain streams. She said the sky was bluer than blue here in Montana. The reason she never mentioned you or your father was that it was so painful. She kept you all to herself, locked in her heart. She didn't want to share you with anyone. Not even Stephen."

Finally his arms loosened, and he raised his head. He looked into her face unashamedly. His thick lashes were spiked, his brown eyes glistening with tears. Elizabeth lifted the end of her apron and wiped his face, then cupped his cheeks with her palms and kissed his eyes, then his lips.

"I'm so glad you can cry, Sam. My father told me that only strong men feel deeply enough to cry."

He pulled her off the floor and onto his lap. She snuggled in his arms. He nestled his warm mouth against her forehead with a gentle reverence that turned her heart over.

"Thank you for fishing the letters out of the fire," he whispered huskily.

"You were hurting, hurting so badly." She lifted a trembling hand and stroked his cheek.

"I've lived with it for a long, long time," he murmured.

"The other letters will tell you more about her. The one I read explained her leaving."

"I'll read them...later."

"The Eleanor I knew was sweet and gentle, and her eyes were always so sad. I don't think I ever heard her laugh."

"I thought for a long time that I had done something to make her leave us." His voice was strained, husky. "Later I convinced myself that she just wanted to go, that she liked the easy life and didn't love us enough to stay and make a home for us."

"She must have been desperate. I remember my father talking about Clara and how someone had to be with her day and night. She couldn't talk or turn her head. Eleanor didn't want the ones she loved to see her like that."

"Pa loved her so much. It tore the heart right out of him when she left."

"Poor lonely man," she whispered, and moved her face so she could place kisses along the line of his jaw. "Will he let me tell him about her?"

"He never said a word against her. He loves her still."

"Your mother wrote to you on each of your birthdays."

He started to speak and failed. They were silent for a long while. He slowly stroked her back in silent communication. Finally he lifted her face with a firm finger beneath her chin.

"What about us, Elizabeth?" His eyes met hers and held them steadily.

"You know how I feel. I love you. I want to spend the rest of my life with you, be your wife, your lover, have your babies. You said we didn't have a future together. I know you were afraid to depend on me for your happiness. Let's depend on each other and build our future together."

In an instant his face changed as if an inner light had been turned on. He turned the full impact of a coaxing smile on her upturned face.

"You're willing to spend the rest of your life with a hell raiser?"

"Well—" she pretended to be in deep thought "—I guess I can live with a hell raiser if you can live with a tony prissy-tail." Her eyes, made all the greener by the dark smudges beneath them, sparkled happily into his.

He lifted his hand to push a strand of hair behind her ear; there his fingers lingered, their tips against her earlobe. He watched her face in fascination as her eyes changed from sparkling with devilry to being soft with love.

"I'm in love with you, pretty little prissy-tail." His voice shook with emotion. "I want to spend every day of my life with you. When I come home from a day's work, I want you there waiting for me. At night I want you in my bed loving me." His hand moved up and down her arm. She didn't know she was crying until his fingers brushed the tears from her cheeks. "Darlin'! Don't cry!"

"I'm crying b-because I'm so h-happy, you...big p-pea-brained—"

"Then hush up your bawlin' and kiss me." His last words were a mere whisper against her lips.

Her arm slid around his neck as she surrendered her mouth to his. His kiss was sweet, gentle, one of deep dedication.

"Liz...Liz, you're sweet...so sweet," he whispered, his lips moving to her eyes. "You were sweet before...but now that you're mine..." His voice was no more than a sigh. His mouth returned to hers, and his tongue gently stroked her lips, the moist, velvet caress sending spasms of delight down her spine.

She gently stroked the soft hair above his lip.

"Do you like it, love? I'll grow a beard if you like." The words were said between nibbles on her fingers.

"No beard. I love this." She angled her head so that their noses were side by side and rubbed her face against his mouth. A soft sound came from his throat, and she felt the trembling in his body when she wiggled against hardness that was suddenly pressing against her hip.

"Keep that up and I'll carry you over to the bunk and have my way with you," he threatened.

She leaned back to look at him. "Do decent people do *that* in the daytime?" Her fingers combed the hair at his temples.

He chuckled softly, his eyes moving lovingly over her face. "Some do."

"Will we do it after we're married?"

"Why not...before?"

"Ah... Samuel Ferguson, you are an extremely smart man." Her voice was soft and beautiful, and her eyes were achingly anxious. "Come to bed and love me. I can't think of a nicer way to spend a cold, blizzardy afternoon."

"Oh...sweetheart, I don't deserve you." He buried his face in the side of her neck.

"Hmm. That sounds familiar. I think you said that when you met me in Missoula."

He groaned. "I was as dumb as a stump!"

"You're a fast learner," she teased between pecking kisses.

"Get in the bed," he whispered anxiously. "I'll stoke up the fire and drop the bar across the door."

Elizabeth shed her clothes and climbed between the cold blankets on the bunk, shivering in anticipation more than from the cold. Her eyes feasted on each part of Sam's body that was revealed to her as he undressed. He stood before her on muscular legs, and where they joined she saw the thatch of dark brown curls that enclosed the root of his maleness. For the first time she saw the male body ready for love. His member stood firm and hard. She stared at him with the fixed expression of the hypnotized before her lips parted and the air escaped from her lungs with a pleasurable sigh.

He lay beside her. She pressed her body's full length to his. He felt her satiny breasts crush against his chest, felt the down covering her mound brush his hardening body and the warm writhing skin of her slender thighs interlace with his. He gathered her close to his long, muscular body with a sigh.

"I love you, my pretty little prissy-tail," he muttered thickly between kisses, and stroked the thick, dark curls from her face.

Her arms held him closer, her body strained against his. He covered her face with kisses, releasing his pent-up desire with each touch of his lips. He stroked her breasts, bent to look at them and caressed them with his eyes, then his mouth. His hand moved between her thighs, stroking her soft inner skin, moving upward. She gave a muffled, instinctive cry as his fingers found her wetness and probed gently inside.

After a prolonged, delicious discovery of each other, they were interlocked and breathlessly surrendering to a voracious hunger that found her as impatiently eager to receive him as he was to insert himself into her yielding warmth. And then they were one fierce flesh, seeking the peaks that could not be found alone. He was deep inside her, and she gloried in the delicious invasion. Soon they were swept beyond the limits of return, into a private, mindless tilting world. When it righted again, she was holding him tightly.

"I love you, love you…" She held his head pillowed against her breasts until his breathing audibly calmed.

"I love you, darlin'."

"Is it getting easier for you to say?"

"Much easier. I'm going to tell you every day of our lives."

"I'll never leave you—"

"It…would kill me if you did."

"Oh, love…"

He placed a kiss on her breast and laid his cheek on it with a long, gusty sigh. "I could stay here forever."

"You're tired. Rest, darling."

"Am I too heavy for you?"

"No! Heavens, no!"

He lay quietly. She stroked his head. Love for him filled her heart. Now that she knew of this pleasure she could give him, and he her, she would banish that lonely, love-starved look from his eyes and fill his life with love. She needed him. He needed her. Oh, it was so wonderful to belong to him. She would take care of him always.

She reached to secure the covers over him, delighting

in the sensation of his warm body against hers. They were in their own little private world. Never had she felt so safe, so loved, so complete. And never had she been more determined that nothing, and no one, would take this happiness away from them.

Chapter Twenty

The sun shone brightly on a countryside cloaked with white. The world was glistening snow, green trees and a wide expanse of blue sky. Elizabeth's laughter rang out in the still morning air as she pelted Sam with a ball of snow when he came from the shed, leading his horse.

"I'll get you for that," he shouted, and hurried to tie his horse behind the waiting buggy.

She let fly another missile that missed him completely and struck Old Buck, causing him to dance sideways. She hurriedly formed another ball as Sam came toward her. She rushed her throw, missed him again and began to run, her laughter trailing behind her.

Sam caught her easily, whirled her around and received the fistful of snow she had secreted in her hand.

"You little devil! I'll wash your face..."

She broke away while he was wiping the snow from his face. "Sam, Sam, catch me if you can!" she chanted.

He caught her after a dozen yards, as she knew he would. An expression of warmth and laughter shining on his face, he wrapped her in his arms just as his feet slipped out from under him. They fell into the snow with her on top of him. He lay there, holding her, staring in fascination at her sparkling green eyes, rosy cheeks and pink, parted lips. She lay between his spread thighs and laughed at him. Then she propped her elbows on his chest.

"Shouldn't you be looking down at me?" she asked seriously, then laughter rang out as she grabbed another handful of snow.

"Not always and...no, you don't," he said, and grabbed her wrist.

"Kiss me and I'll let you up," she murmured sweetly.

Sam was still chuckling as she lowered her head and tantalizingly caressed his lips with her tongue while he pressed her tightly to his groin. She ended the kiss and lifted her nose with prim confidence.

"That will teach you not to get smart with me."

Laughing, Sam stood and brushed the snow from her coat and skirt. With their arms around each other they went to the buggy. Sam settled her on the seat and tucked the blankets around her before he climbed in beside her.

"I read the note you left for Slufoot," he said as he put the mare in motion. "'Your cabin is beautiful,'" he quoted, and snorted.

"It *is* beautiful. I'll remember it forever," she said defensively, and tucked her hand under his arm.

When they reached the road, it was a sea of unbroken white. Sam put the mare into an easy trot as they rolled silently over the snow.

"When we get home, I'll put runners on the buggy and take you for a sleigh ride."

"With sleigh bells?"

"Sure. I've got several strings."

"I love you."

He looked at her and saw that the laughter had gone from her face.

"What brought that on?"

"I'm scared. I'm afraid your father and your friends will disapprove of me. I know Mr. Owens will."

"I don't care if anyone approves of you or not, sweetheart. Why is it important to you?"

"Mr. Owens said everyone expected you to marry Jessie. He said Jessie loves you and that the two of you are suited to each other."

"Burley talks too much."

"Mrs. Underwood said—"

"She talks too much, too."

"But would you have married her?"

"Maybe someday. You would have married Stephen."

"What will you say to Jessie?"

"About us? Nothing. I've known Jess and looked out for her since she was knee-high to a grasshopper. I've never given her any reason to think I was going to marry her."

"She'll hate me if she's in love with you."

"If she is, she'll get over it. I hope the two of you can be friends." He chuckled and shook his head as if what he was hoping was impossible. "You're as different as night and day."

"Oh…" Elizabeth didn't know whether to be hurt or not.

"You'll be good for Jess. I've not see her in a dress for a good ten years. She needs someone to take her in hand and show her how to act like a lady. I'm afraid that she'll end up an old maid unless she settles for some man like Frank Grissom, a logger who works at the mill."

"You don't like him?"

"He's a good worker, but—"

"Not good enough for Jessie."

"No. Jessie needs a man with a firm but gentle hand."

Elizabeth felt a surge of pity for the unknown girl. If she was in love with Sam, she was in for a letdown.

"Where will I stay when we get to Nora Springs?"

"I've been thinking about that. I'll take you to Amanda's until we're married." A worried frown puckered his brow. "Stephen is the one I'm worried about. He didn't want you to ride the stage because you'd come in contact with toughs. He said you had been sheltered and would be unable to cope. What's he going to think about you marrying me and living here?"

"I guess Stephen didn't know me very well if he thought I was so helpless," she said slowly. "But he is a gentleman," she said quickly. "He'll release me from the engagement when I tell him I've fallen in love with you."

"I would rather he approve, but if he doesn't, it's not going to make any difference," Sam said firmly.

"Glad to hear it, Mr. Ferguson," she said pertly.

They reached Peterson's Station in the late afternoon. The wind had blown the snow off the road in places, and they had made good time. Sam introduced Elizabeth as his fiancée. Everyone was friendly and congratulated them. Sam told the story about Vernon and the one-eyed man and how Elizabeth had buried a hat pin in the fat man's rear end. Then he told about the two drifters trying to kill them at the bridge, and much to her surprise, Elizabeth was looked upon as a heroine. She basked in the warmth of Sam's proud smiles.

The next morning they left the station with invitations to hurry back ringing in their ears. Mrs. Peterson had been especially friendly to Elizabeth after Elizabeth had offered to help her with the evening meal and had stayed to clean up after the others had left the long table. They had talked of many things, and Jessie was not mentioned, much to Elizabeth's relief.

"I missed you last night," Elizabeth said the minute they were alone. "How long until we can be married?"

"I missed you, too. One more night, sweetheart. We'll be married tomorrow. I'd like Pa to be there, and Stephen, if he wants to come."

"He'll want to come. I expect he and Charles are eager to get back to Saint Louis. Will you invite Jessie and her mother?"

"Would you mind? They're like family."

"Of course, I don't mind. Oh, sweetheart, I'd love to make this same trip again someday—without the... complications, of course." They both laughed heartily.

"...and Vernon and the men at the bridge," Sam added, and his face turned serious. "It scares the hell out of me when I think of what could have happened."

"But it didn't. We handled things together, didn't we?" Her green eyes begged him to smile again.

"Remind me, honey, to hide your hat pins."

"I'll do no such thing," she replied sassily. "I never know when I may need one."

"Lordy! I've got a little fighting cat on my hands!"

"Do you know, Sam, I've not worn my corset since that day you told me that no one out here cared if my waist was an inch smaller? I think I'll wear it only on Sunday from now on."

"I'm going to get rid of those damn corsets," he growled, then added firmly, "and you'll not have to remind me."

Elizabeth began to giggle uncontrollably. "What would people think if they knew you had seen my bottom before you even thought about kissing me?"

"Honey, give me due credit as a hell raiser. I had thought about it." His eyes, brilliant with laughter and love, held hers. "Did I ever tell you that you've got the prettiest little bottom I've ever seen?"

"How many little bottoms have you seen, Mr. Ferguson?" she demanded sternly.

"Whoa." He laughed. "I shouldn't have mentioned it."

"You bet your life you shouldn't. Just for that I'm going to tell Stephen you practically puked on me. He'll probably challenge you to a duel."

"Oh, sweetheart, don't mention *that*, ever!" He tilted his head so he could look into her eyes. His face was wreathed in smiles, and his eyes shone with happiness.

She laughed, hugged his arm and rested her cheek against it. His heart swelled with pride and pleasure. Knowing they would reach Nora Springs that day, she had worn her maroon suit under her heavy coat and had pinned her hair back before she carefully covered it with the shawl.

"Sam…" They had started toward the valley.

"Yes, love."

"When will we get there?"

"In an hour or so. It isn't far from Peterson's Station."

"Did I understand you to say the afternoon we spent in the bed that you were going to keep me in that position for a week after we are wed?" Under the blanket that covered their legs, she moved a caressing hand to the inside of his thigh and stroked upward.

"I said I'd like to. Ah...honey, don't!" He took a deep breath.

"You said you were going to. Promise." Her fingers inched up and spread out.

"You little...devil! Stop that, or I'll—"

"Are you threatening me with bodily harm, sir?" she exclaimed in a horrified tone, and squeezed, then burrowed her fingers beneath his thigh.

"I'll do more than threaten if you don't behave." He bent and kissed her lips, then slapped the reins against the mare's back to hurry her along.

In the middle of the afternoon they came onto a shelf that overlooked the town. Sam stopped the buggy.

"This is it, honey. That's the mill at the far end of town. The church with the white cross is where we'll be married tomorrow. See that piece of land on the other side of the mill pond? That's where we'll build our home. The spring is there. Nora Springs, Pa named the town. He always called my mother Nora."

"Eleanor would be so happy to know that. I wish she could see it."

"I wish she could, too," Sam said wistfully. "I wonder if Stephen told Pa why she left us."

"I don't think Stephen knows."

From within the circle of Sam's arms Elizabeth gazed at the town that would be her home.

"I'll be a good wife to you, Sam. It will take time for me to learn everything I'll need to know about living in this country, and no doubt I'll make you angry at times."

"I know a good way of making up," he whispered, kissing her on the nose.

"We won't have to wait for a blizzard, will we?" she asked with hope, her eyes shining.

"Sweetheart, we won't even have to wait till dark."

Sam stung the mare on the rump with the end of the reins, and the buggy moved down the slope toward town.

* * * * *

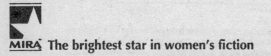

Take 4 bestselling love stories FREE

Plus get a FREE surprise gift!

Special Limited-time Offer

Mail to Harlequin Reader Service®

P.O. Box 609
Fort Erie, Ontario
L2A 5X3

YES! Please send me 4 free Harlequin Historicals™ novels and my free surprise gift. Then send me 4 brand-new novels every month, which I will receive before they appear in bookstores. Bill me at the low price of $3.94 each plus 25¢ delivery and GST*. That's the complete price and a savings of over 10% off the cover prices—quite a bargain! I understand that accepting the books and gift places me under no obligation ever to buy any books. I can always return a shipment and cancel at any time. Even if I never buy another book from Harlequin, the 4 free books and the surprise gift are mine to keep forever.

347 BPA A3UJ

Name _____ (PLEASE PRINT)

Address _____ Apt. No. _____

City _____ Province _____ Postal Code _____

This offer is limited to one order per household and not valid to present Harlequin Historical™ subscribers. *Terms and prices are subject to change without notice. Canadian residents will be charged applicable provincial taxes and GST.

CHIS-696 ©1990 Harlequin Enterprises Limited

Harlequin® Historical

From rugged lawmen and
valiant knights to defiant heiresses
and spirited frontierswomen,
Harlequin Historicals will
capture your imagination with
their dramatic scope, passion
and adventure.

Harlequin Historicals...
they're too good to miss!